THE SWORDSMEN CHRONICLES

CURSE OF
THE SLEEPING SICKNESS

BY

ROBERT W CELY

ATHANATOS
PUBLISHING GROUP

THE SWORDSMEN CHRONICLES

CURSE OF THE SLEEPING SICKNESS

ROBERT W CELY

Published by

ATHANATOS
PUBLISHING GROUP

The Swordsmen Chronicles
  Curse of the Sleeping Sickness

By Robert W Cely

ISBN: 978-1-64594-230-6

Published by Athanatos Publishing Group | www.athanatos.net

CONTENTS

In memory of Rick Hiers, a true swordsman in every way.

Prologue - Sid Alone

Sid Bickley sat in his car feeling more desperate than he ever remembered. Despite all the desperate and trying times he had gone through, this felt worse to him than all those others combined.

Outside, the rain continued to pour down in the dark and forbidding night. A deluge of water battered his windshield and joined in rivers pouring over the glass surface, obscuring the lights outside into indistinct blurs. He could hardly read the sign that read, "Reedland Memorial" on the outside of the hospital, or the bright red "Emergency Room."

Sid hardly noticed these things, consumed with an inner sense of dread that seemed to take over every thought in his mind. The old man sighed and looked down at his hand and wondered where the strong limbs had gone, the ones that had fought and defeated immortal enemies and touched the face of divinely beautiful women. Now, that same hand was thin and mottled, draped in crepe-like skin. It was the hand of an old man.

To look at Sid Bickley would be to see a man in the last stages of life. His hair, though still thick and full had long turned a pristine white. Tonight, it was disheveled through the many times his hands had nervously run through it. His aquiline nose, high cheekbones and icy blue eyes gave him an aristocratic look, a remnant of an old world and high-born man, maybe even a touch of haughtiness. It was the kind of man the world didn't make anymore.

As he sat in his car with rain pouring outside, those handsome features were drowned in a despair that took over his face. The ice-blue eyes were drooping and sad. The deep wrinkles on his face hung lower and heavier. The disheveled white hair gave him a wild, almost maniacal look. Altogether, he looked like an old man hanging on his last string of sanity.

If someone had passed by they would likely take him for a new widower, one who had just been told his wife had died. Or maybe he was newly discharged after being diagnosed with a fatal disease. Whatever assumptions a passerby would make about Sid Bickley, sitting alone in his black 1952 Packard 300, the old car almost swallowing him up, they would certainly never guess that he was a man who had saved the world a dozen times over.

Maybe it is because I am all alone now, Sid thought to himself. He tried to analyze his feelings, but got no further than this. He was never much of an introspective type. Things were what they were. This time he didn't need to get far. His feelings had an obvious source. Of all the other dangers he had faced in life, he had faced them with others. Now, they were all gone.

Faces passed before his memory. They rose up from happier, stronger days. Well, maybe not happier, but definitely stronger. Barkley with his kind and wise ways, Harrod who always seemed to know what to do, Graves, a man of unstoppable courage; he missed and mourned them all. Even that fool Rip who had ended up betraying them, Sid would have given anything to have them back at his side again.

Sid sighed and let his head drop down. There was no else but him. There hadn't been anyone else for a long time. Sid was all that was left, the last of the Keepers of the Flame.

Long ago Sid had resigned himself that his fighting days were done. There was no one left. Despite their brave battles and stunning victories, they had lost in the end. The enemy they fought against had been relentless, and had fought a battle they never anticipated. He had failed, and his days had nothing left in them except the sweet relief that death would bring.

This had become his new reality and he had long ago resigned himself to this. Then, one day, out of nowhere, Sid awoke with a new energy. A surge awakened in his bones, a strength he hadn't felt in a long time. He felt renewed, full of purpose and passion again.

He also knew there was a reason for the new strength. His strength never really was his own. There was work for him to do again. The one who had called him first was calling him again. And if there was one thing Sid had learned in his many years of life, it was that you never ignored that call. It was the reason he uncovered the Packard and drove it out into the pouring rain at night.

Sid leaned over and turned on the radio. A woman's voice crackled out over the old speakers, carrying a grim report out into the night.

"The mysterious illness that has been striking children across the country, dubbed the Sleeping Sickness, has claimed another victim in the Tricities area. Seven-year-old Jeremiah Thomas was pronounced dead this afternoon at Reedland Memorial Hospital. His death marks the fourth victim in the Tricities. All across the country there have been forty-three children who have died, including a Boston toddler who succumbed earlier this morning. Doctors and disease experts still have no answers as to how this disease is spreading, or what it even is. Symptoms entail a general lethargy and exhaustion, combined with unresponsiveness. Victims slip into a coma days after the onset of symptoms. So far, none of the victims have exhibited fever or any other signs of infection. There have been no reported survivors or recovery.

"Speculation remains rampant about the origin and cause of this disease, even among the medical community. Some are even proposing a new variant of dementia that strikes the young, or perhaps a new prion infection that is commonly called Mad Cow. The Director of the CDC urges no one to believe these unfounded rumors and for everyone to remain calm and have patience as they continue to investigate this horrific disease. The President also addressed these concerns, assuring the public that the government is doing everything. . ."

Leaning forward Sid flipped off the radio. There was nothing the news could tell him that would help. He already knew more about the disease than anyone else, including who was behind it. Unfortunately, he was old and alone, and also the only one who could do anything about it.

With a shake of his head Sid decided the time for self-pity had come to an end. He knew this was the reason for his new surge of energy. The Spirit had awakened in him again, probably for the last time, because of the dying children. It wasn't up to Sid Bickley to question or doubt these things. His job was to obey. And if he could nothing else, he could do that.

Resolve and strength overcame his despair as Sid opened his door into the pouring rain and stepped out. As soon as he had risen to his full height, standing just over six feet, something of his native confidence returned to him again. Something of the old aristocrat could be seen again as he stepped into the hospital. His dark suit was immaculate and cut to perfection. His walk belied something of a man used to wielding authority. Even the rain that poured over him allowed him to slick his hair back and assume a more dignified appearance.

Gaining his confidence back with every step Sid posed a dignified figure in the hospital corridors. Everyone who passed him by nodded, assuming he was a person of great authority. Even the restricted areas of the hospital opened up to him. He approached every locked door at the same time as someone with card access. They never questioned him, but stepped out of the way, or even held the door open for him.

Sid continued through the hospital, following the hallways unto he reached an office with the sign, "Hospital Administrator" on the outside. A young girl, no more than thirty-five years in Sid's estimation, sat behind a desk and typed on a laptop. She didn't even notice when Sid stepped inside. A plaque on the desk told him her name was Tina Jeffers.

"Mrs. Jeffers," Sid began, taking a seat just as the Administrator noticed him. Her eyes went from confused to surprised.

"My name is Sid Bickley and I was sent here by the Department of Health. I was hoping you could help me."

Tina looked over at Sid with a skeptical glance.

"You got some ID?" she asked.

Sid nodded and picked up one of the business cards sitting on Tina's desk. It was a generic hospital business card with her name and the office number printed on it. The logo of Reedland Memorial was emblazoned on the top center.

"Here you are," he said, handing the woman her own business card. "It says that I am an important, high-ranking figure in the Health Department and it is in your best interest to comply with anything I ask of you."

A glassy look fell over Tina's eyes. She stared at the card in her hand, but her eyes were focused somewhere far away. A slackness came into her face as her mouth relaxed and her head bobbed forward. It jerked back up and the light returned to her eyes.

"Of course, Dr. Bickley" she answered, her own mind inventing the title. "Whatever we can do to help."

Moments later Sid was pocketing a flash drive that held the medical records of every child that had come through Reedland with the Sleeping Sickness. Sid thanked the administrator.

"There is no need to remember any of this," he told Tina as he got up to leave. "You have done an excellent job today, but no one came into your office tonight."

The glazed look returned to Tina's face as she nodded. Before realization came back to her Sid quietly stepped out of her office. As he moved into the hallway, he almost bumped into a figure waiting for him.

Sid was taken aback, but only for a moment. Though the doctor was glaring at him, Sid immediately recognized the handsome man in the white coat.

"Did you think you could come into my hospital and I not know about it?" the doctor asked.

Sid smiled and shrugged his shoulders. "I was just about to come and see you, Dr. Canta."

He placed a strange inflection on the word, "doctor" as if he were making fun of him.

"Let's talk," the doctor said, and turned for Sid to follow.

The two men made a notable pair as they walked through the hospital. Sid, with his aged and dignified bearing of authority. Beside him strode Dr. Canta, a man of striking good looks; blond hair, olive complexion over a perfectly shaped face, and a muscular build beneath his clothes. His good looks were otherworldly, almost untouchable.

The two men took distant seats in the mostly empty cafeteria. A pair of nurses sat on the far side, eating a late dinner and complaining to each other about their shift. Dr. Canta put a cup of coffee in front of Sid and sat opposite him with a cup of his own.

"You want to tell me what this is all about?" the doctor asked after looking around.

Sid smiled and took a sip of his coffee. "Need I tell you what this is all about?"

The doctor shook his head, a tight smile on his face.

"This has nothing to do with you, Sid," he said through gritted teeth. "This is an unfortunate disease striking young children. That's all."

"A disease with no known origin or pathology?" Sid returned. "Do you expect me to believe this is natural in origin?"

"So what if it isn't?" he asked. "What are you planning on doing about it? For crying out loud Sid, we thought you were all but dead. You haven't stepped foot outside the mansion in, what? Ten years?"

"Regardless," Sid told him. "This is something that involves the Keepers and you know it. I want you to tell me what's going on."

"Keeper, Sid," Canta the corrected. "Keeper. Just one. You're the only one left. And even if you were in your prime there's nothing you could do about this, okay. This is . . . this one is serious to them. This goes deep. This is something the Family has been working on for a very long time. They'll do anything to see this happens. I mean anything."

"Even risk exposure?" Sid asked.

Canta shrugged his shoulders as he sipped again at his coffee. "Well, maybe not that. At least not yet. But they'll do anything to anyone else. And that includes you."

Sid waved away the threat. "That's the least of my concerns."

Canta looked around the cafeteria, making sure no one was listening. He leaned in close to Sid.

"What do you think you can do?" he asked. "Seriously, Sid, what are you going to do? I mean, I can tell you got a new lease on life and everything and I'm happy for you, but seriously. Even if you were in your prime and had all the Keepers with you and this was like the old days you would still be in for the fight of your life. Alone, you can nothing. And I mean that. Nothing."

"What do you know?" Sid asked, unperturbed.

"I'm not doing this," Canta protested.

Sid leaned forward and put all of his power and authority into his words.

"Tell me what you know," he commanded.

"I don't know anything," the doctor protested.

"You made an oath," Sid reminded. "You have to help me."

"Times are different now."

"I know your real name," Sid threatened. "Don't make me use it."

Canta stood up, unmoved by the threat. He spread his arms wide.

"Go ahead. Use it then," he said.

Sid opened his mouth, ready to speak the words. To his horror, he realized he couldn't remember. It was a name he was sworn to keep, one that stood as the keystone of the oath that bound Canta and his people to the Keepers. But he had lost it.

"You can't speak it, can you?" Canta said. "Like I told you, Sid. There's nothing you can do about this. Not you, not me. I'm just a doctor."

"But I will tell you this," he said, his voice dropping to a whisper. "Whatever it is that is making these kids sick is completely beyond my power. Think about that, Sid. I can't touch it at all. This is something deep and powerful and I don't even want to know whose really behind all this. I can't afford to get involved, Sid. Not this time. Those days are over."

"But Canta," Sid said, reaching out and grabbing hold of the doctor's sleeve. "After all these years, after all we've been through, you won't help me again?"

"Look at the great Sid Bickley," the doctor said in disgust. "Begging me, of all people, for help. Sid begging. I never thought I'd see the day.

Goodbye Sid."

The doctor tore his arm away and turned to leave. He stopped and lifted a finger in warning.

"And I don't want to see you in my hospital again," he said before leaving Sid alone in the cafeteria.

All at once that great surge of energy that was fueling him dissipated into a helpless despair. Canta couldn't help. Canta wouldn't help. And whatever powers Sid once had to compel him were gone. How had he forgotten the name?

His new surge of power, his new chance at life - it was for nothing. Sid had fooled himself into thinking that he was, just for a moment, the old Sid Bickley. The unstoppable and irresistible Sid Bickley was no more.

Now he was just the old and powerless Sid Bickley. He was the washed up, the has been, the dried-out husk of the legendary man he once was.

Shaking his head part in disbelief, part in despair, he stood up and made his way out of the hospital. As if to drive home the fact of his fallen estate, he was stopped by a security guard.

"You can't be in this part of the hospital," the guard told him.

Sid nodded and apologized. The guard insisted on escorting him out.

"You got some family that can come and get you?" the guard asked as Sid stepped out into the downpour. "Maybe a grandkid or something?"

Sid ignored the comment and let his feet take him mechanically across the parking lot to his car. He gave no regard for the rain that was quickly soaking through his suit. It simply didn't matter anymore. He had been fooling himself anyway. Who did he think he was besides an old man with dreams of old glory?

Just as he got to his car Sid could feel a pair of eyes on him. He looked up and across the lot and saw a menacing figure with his gaze fixed on him. The figure was tall and broad shouldered, handsome as Canta was, but in a darker way. His face was hard, and the eyes that stared at him were both dangerously intelligent and cruel. He wore a black suit and stood barefoot on the asphalt parking lot, oblivious to the rain that fell over him.

Sid felt a pulse of fear shoot through him as he recognized the man staring at him. Sautorus.

Canta was right. If Sautorus was involved then the Family was certainly throwing all they had at this.

Sautorus laughed and pointed at Sid. He touched his temple as if to say, do you remember. It was a challenge as well as a reminder. They may have had their battles in the past, but Sid had gotten older and Sautorus had not.

The wicked and deep-set eyes turned serious after the taunt. Sautorus shook his head, a clear warning to him not to get involved.

Sid fumbled with the keys and hastily got into the car. As soon as he turned the ignition the radio came to life. The music of Charles Trenet singing "La Mer" played over the sounds of the rain. He stared at the radio in disbelief as his mind flashed back to a Chicago hotel almost sixty years earlier. The smell of fire and the sting of betrayal flooded into him at once. He could almost hear the sounds outside of a riot raging while tear gas filled the air.

Sid punched the radio off and threw the Packard into gear. Headlights cast the shadow of Sautorus large and ominous as he tore out of the parking lot. A cold sweat broke out over him, bringing with it all the fears he had allowed to rule over him since that disastrous night so long ago. All the guilt and failure, the loneliness and despair, crashed into him at once.

By the time he got home Sid was trembling in cold and fear. He stumbled into the house, greeted by a butler who stood waiting with a towel.

"Master Sid," the butler remarked as he wrapped him up. "Whatever has happened to you?"

Sid explained everything as Gerard listened patiently. The butler helped him out of his wet clothes and into something dry and warm. He set up Sid's chair in front of the television and prepared a hot soak for his feet. By the time he handed Sid a glass of brandy his trembling and sweating had ceased.

"Fret not, Master Sid," Gerard said. "We know the Lord works in mysterious ways. There is a reason for all of this yet. Remember, as long as I breathe . . ."

"I hope," Sid finished for him. At the moment he wasn't feeling so hopeful.

He took a few warming sips of the brandy and allowed it to soak into him. Back in his house and with the comforting presence of his servant and friend made him feel better. True, tonight had not been an overwhelming success, but maybe it had been partly his fault, charging into the hospital like he was a young man still. It had worked in the old days, but these weren't the old days. The Spirit had woken him up again, that was certain. That didn't mean he could do things the same way as before. Maybe this time he would have to do something different.

As soon as he started to feel better the image of Sautorus' face crept back into his mind. The evil smile, the promise of retribution was almost enough to dampen even the modest feelings he was experiencing. It seemed hopeless to even think about.

Sid shook his head and tried not to think about everything all at once. One step at a time, he told himself. He turned his attention to the television, hoping it would help him forget for a little while. A news story was on about the funeral of a famous preacher, Bob Garen. Dead at ninety-five his funeral procession was passing through the town of Black Mountain where he had lived most of his life.

Only absently paying attention Sid sipped at his brandy while the news showed the crowds lining the street as the procession passed by. The story turned to interviews, asking people on the street about the famed preacher and what he meant to them. One interview featured a man in his mid-forties. He wore a long-sleeved white t-shirt. Men stood behind him dressed in identical shirts. Something about the interview piqued Sid's interest.

"So, what does the legacy of Bob Garen mean to you and your group?" the interviewer asked.

"Pastor Garen was huge in encouraging a strong men's movement in the church. We're here at a retreat this weekend and much of what we do is part of his legacy. What he reminded us of is that manliness is a gift of God, not something that needs to be repressed or discouraged. It should be embraced. And when we embrace it, we can use it for God's glory. He came at a time when masculinity was being looked down upon, and even the church looked down upon it. But Pastor Garen reminded us that masculinity wasn't bad and it wasn't toxic. It was how God made us. It should be celebrated, but also trained up in the right way. And that's what our group is all about."

Sid leaned forward, paying close attention now. He noticed a sigil on the man's shirt, a sign that made him feel like pieces of a puzzle were falling into place. It was a sword, printed on the shirt in red dye.

"So, what's the name of your group?" the interviewer asked.

As soon as he answered Sid knew what he had to do. There was a way, he saw, but it wouldn't be the same as before. God did, indeed, work in mysterious ways.

The man looked right into the camera as he answered. Sid felt he was talking right to him.

"We call ourselves the Swordsmen."

PART I: THE BIBLE STUDY

Chapter 1 - Not Against Flesh

Malachi Green pulled into the parking lot of Westfield Presbyterian Church. The car idled as he looked over the last bits of his lesson, tucking notes into his Bible. With a last look at the immaculately clean car to make sure he wasn't forgetting anything, Malachi stepped out and made his way across the lot.

Danny Taylor was already waiting by the front doors by the time Malachi made his way over. He held four pizza boxes in his hand as he waited, a sheepish grin on his face.

"I know I said I was going to make something tonight," he explained. "But the day just got away from me and I decided to grab some pizzas. Next time, though, I promise I will make some of my world-famous manicotti. No bailing on the cheap stuff."

Malachi nodded as he fished the church keys out of his pocket. He couldn't help but grin at what Danny said. He'd been promising that world famous manicotti for years now, but every time it was his turn to provide the meal for Bible study, he always ended up bringing pizza. "The day got away from me," he always said. It had actually become a Swordsmen tradition, and a running joke. Malachi wasn't sure what he would do if Danny actually showed up with manicotti.

Not that Malachi begrudged Danny at all for his choice. The man was perpetually stressed out. He had been running an IT department at a bank for years now, and the stress ate at him continually. His pale features, made paler by the raven black hair and the long hours spent inside, wore a perpetually worried look. His brows were always furrowed together and his lips pinched as he seemed lost in perpetual thought. It was a stress that Malachi wouldn't wish on anyone.

"Oh, I don't think anyone has ever complained about pizza," Malachi assured him as he slipped his key into the steel and glass doors.

Malachi held the door open and the two men stepped into what was called "the new building." Never mind the annex was over thirty years old, but compared to the rest of the church that had been built in 1930, it would always be the new building.

Cool air hit Malachi as the two made their way to a nearby classroom. A long table filled up the little room, surrounded by bookshelves sporting theological heavyweights such as Calvin, Luther and Augustine. In between these venerable titles were more recent works like *Purpose*

Driven Life, Twelve Ordinary Men, and *Wild at Heart.*

Half an hour later the pizza boxes stood empty and stacked on each other. Night had fallen outside and the church was dark and quiet except for the classroom. Eight men sat around the table, their paper plates empty except for bundled up napkins and the uneaten pieces of crust.

Malachi looked around the table before he began. What he saw always gave him a swell of pride. Surrounding that table was a group of Christ lovers from all ages, races, professions and backgrounds. Without trying they had achieved a kind of diversity that others attempted, but only achieved artificially. With the Swordsmen, it was natural, and being natural, their differences didn't matter near as much as what brought them together.

"Alright, gentlemen," Malachi began. "Let's bring this meeting officially to order."

"The Lord is my light and my salvation," Malachi intoned.

"Whom shall I fear?" the men responded in unison.

"The Lord is the stronghold of my life."

"Of whom shall I be afraid?"

"Excellent, thank you men," Malachi continued. "Before we begin tonight, I would like to extend a special welcome. We have a guest with us today as you have all no doubt noticed. Mr. Sid Bickley, I would like to welcome you to the group tonight."

The older man, sitting opposite Malachi nodded and thanked the men for welcoming in that evening. Malachi nodded in return and tried to seem as open and friendly as he could, but at the same time couldn't shake his suspicion about the visitor. When he had first arrived, Sid told them all he had seen the interview at Bob Garen's funeral and was intrigued about the group. It was a likely enough story. Still, something about the old man bothered Malachi.

For one, there was an aura of arrogance about him that was almost automatic. Despite his age the old man was handsome and carried himself with what Malachi would call a superior bearing. He looked like someone who thought he was better than everyone else. His formal dress didn't help matters. Sid was decked out in a dark dinner jacket with wide lapels and a red ascot tucked into the neck. Or maybe it was a cravat, Malachi thought. He never could distinguish the two.

Even worse was the way he looked at everyone at the table. Sid's ice blue eyes looked around the table and seemed to be assessing or measuring each one of the men. They blazed with intelligence and insight. All through dinner Sid quietly appraised each of the men, looking at each intently as a smile crept across his face. It unnerved Malachi, and he didn't like the older man being there at all.

The voice of Malachi's grandmother echoed in his head, "Can't judge a book by its cover, Malachi." If he had any vice at all, Malachi was quick to put people into categories. He knew it and worked hard to keep it at bay. Still, it crept up from time to time.

"Let me introduce everyone here to you," Malachi spoke up as he pushed aside that skeptical and too judgmental voice in his head.

"These here are our two firemen," he said as he pointed to his right. "Victor Dodds and Gary Walsh."

"Just call me Vic," Victor said by way of introduction.

Vic was ex-military, and he had the moustache to prove it. At least that is what he always said. He also had a sense of humor that never seemed to quit, even times when it should.

"We usually call him Vicky," the man beside him elbowed him and said.

Gary was thirty-seven and easily the biggest guy a person would run into on any given day. Standing close to six-four, he was also broad-shouldered with thick arms and hands almost as big as catchers' mitts. Despite his size, he was easily the gentlest soul of the group.

"For obvious reasons, we call him Big G," Malachi tagged on.

"Next to him is Giovanni Santos, or Gio for short."

The forty-year-old Hispanic man nodded when introduced. Gio was a music teacher at a local high school. He was usually quiet, sometimes so quiet you would forget he was there. Then, he would speak up and say something wise and insightful and you knew immediately that his silence was the result of a mind ruminating on a subject to its full depth.

"Over here you have Zachary Metts," Malachi pointed to the man seated to Sid's right.

"Just call me Zach," he said, waving a calloused and oil-stained hand.

Zach was the youngest member there at only twenty-seven years old. He worked as a mechanic at a dealership, and always showed up in his blue shirt with his name printed on the pocket and grease stains all over.

"Next to him you have Tresmond Bettis, our local celebrity," Malachi smiled as he introduced him.

Tresmond was a thirty-two-year-old black man who worked as a personal trainer. His workouts were streamed three times a week and garnered thousands of views. He wasn't famous by any real stretch, but

3

they still couldn't help but introduce him as a celebrity.

"We all call him Tres," Malachi mentioned before pointing to the man to his left.

"And this is Danny Taylor," he finished.

"We call him Tayse," Vic said with a stifled laugh.

Danny shook his head as the men all joined in, unable to resist the joke. Malachi found himself laughing too, although he knew bringing up Danny's nickname always irritated his friend.

"Interesting nickname," Sid observed.

"Story for another time," Danny waved dismissively. This only brought more laughter from the group.

"And we've already been introduced, but I'm Malachi Green," Malachi finished up the introductions.

"Malachi," Sid repeated. "Like the prophet."

Malachi nodded, thinking back to his grandmother, devout and formidable, the matriarch of his family. He had grown up a bi-racial child in the deep south, and though there was no Jim Crowe or official segregation in his childhood, there was still the remnants of the darker side of American history. The white side of his family had nothing to do with him, so even though he grew up thinking of himself as truly half of each race, the culture around him assumed he was black, and eventually that was the assumption he made about himself. If he thought about it, strange questions about how we think of race cropped up in his mind. Even stranger questions would follow, especially about how easily we, as a culture, accepted such assumptions even when they made little sense.

"And what do you do, Mr. Green?" the old man asked.

"Just call me Malachi," he answered. "We're not that formal here as you can probably tell. But I manage the Heart Center at Reedland Memorial. Been there for about thirty years."

"Ah, a natural leader," Sid responded.

A smile crossed the older man's lips that made Malachi uneasy. There was something decidedly unsettling about the man, and for the second time that night he had to check the judgement that came rising so effortlessly to the surface of his mind.

"We're continuing our study of Ephesians tonight," Malachi began, opening his Bible and forcing himself not to think about the uneasy feeling he got from Sid Bickley. "We're looking at Chapter six, verses ten to twenty."

4

Malachi paused and let the men get their Bibles opened and turned to the appropriate place. Sid, he noticed, did not open a Bible. He just stared at Malachi with that arrogant smile plastered on his face.

"Finally, be strong in the Lord and in the strength of his might. Put on the whole armor of God that you may be able to withstand the schemes of the Devil. For we do not fight against flesh and blood, but against the rulers, against the authorities, against the cosmic powers over this present darkness, against the spiritual forces of evil in the heavenly places. Therefore, take up the whole armor of God, that you may be able to withstand in the evil day, and having done all, to stand firm."

"Spiritual warfare," Victor said, rubbing his hands together in anticipation. "Time to go down the rabbit hole."

And down the hole they went.

An hour later, with no signs of the discussion dying down, Malachi was forced to bring them to a conclusion. As Victor had predicted, the topic was one that had them peel off in many different directions. It was one of those topics that seemed to breed no end of discussion.

"So, in conclusion," Malachi said, signaling it was time to shut it down. "What can we say about Ephesians six?"

"We're involved in spiritual warfare," Gary started. "And there's nothing we can do about it. We're all involved, whether we like it or not."

"Fight isn't against other people," Tres chimed in. "It's against the evil that tries to consume other people."

"The fight is actually for other people," Danny echoed.

"It's not a physical fight at all," Victor added. "It's a fight that takes place within. It's a battle of ideas, of . . . I don't know, spirits. Whatever kind of fight that is. An invisible fight. Like, you can't see it, but I'm spiritually fighting Big G right now and I'm whipping his puny little spirit all over the place."

"You better enjoy it," Gary answered with a smile. "Cause it's the only way you're ever whipping me."

The table chuckled appreciatively and Malachi quickly brought them back around before they got started on another side topic.

"Well, Sid," Malachi said, looking across the table at the older gentleman. "Usually, the new guy gets the last word in and you haven't said anything all night. Any thoughts?"

Sid leaned back and thought for a moment. Looking over at Victor he pointed.

"I actually have to disagree with Mr. Dodds there," he said. "When you said this fight, this spiritual warfare wasn't physical. The text doesn't say that. It only says the fight isn't against flesh and blood."

Victor looked confused. He shook his head.

"But a fight against flesh and blood is a physical fight," he argued.

"Yes, a fight against flesh and blood is a physical fight," Sid agreed. "But a fight that is physical is not necessarily one against flesh and blood."

Silence fell over the table as the men tried to grapple with what the older man had just said. From their looks Malachi could tell they were thoroughly confused. Some had that look that was beginning to wonder if the old man wasn't going soft in the head. Malachi felt alarm. He couldn't say why, but he was certain they were about to be pulled into something dangerous.

"How do you have a physical fight with a spiritual being?" Danny asked, cutting right to the point.

"You're assuming this spiritual being is not physical," Sid answered.

Danny shook his head, waving his hands at the same time. "No . . . what? That doesn't make any sense. Spiritual beings are called spiritual exactly because they aren't physical. They may not even be beings in the sense that we are beings. This may be all metaphorical language. The fight against evil is not a physical fight at all. It's . . . well it's spiritual."

"Ah yes, the assumption that all things amazing in Scripture are metaphorical," Sid said. "That is the great comfort of the mundane world. What I am getting at does not make that same assumption. If somehow, the spiritual appeared to you in a physical way, spiritual evil manifest in the world of physical things, would our fight, then, be against those things?"

Still more confusion around the table. Zach was the first to seem to get it.

"Are you saying that if a demon appeared to us in reality, in a way we could see and touch, we should fight it then?" he asked.

"Precisely Mr. Metts," Sid answered. "If this spiritual evil we are to wage war against, like a demon, were to appear, should we fight against it?"

"Or does that qualify as a fight against flesh and blood?" Tresmond clarified.

"If it has a body then it has to be flesh and blood," Victor suggested.

"Flesh and blood are not the only kinds of bodies," Sid interjected.

"Trees are not considered flesh and blood but they have a body, of sorts. Rocks are physically present but also are not of flesh and blood."

"Yeah, but if a demon, or some spirit, is going to . . . you know, appear in a body in some way, what kind of body would that be?" Gary asked.

"Would it matter?" Sid asked back. "All I am asking is if our fight is against these forces of darkness in the heavenly places, if they were to somehow manifest here among us on earth, not in possession of another human body, but in one of their own, where they could walk our ground and move in our air, influence the world around us, even infiltrate our institutions; what then? Would it be necessary to take up that fight against them? And fight them in physical ways, body against body, sword against sword, steel against steel?"

"I guess if you put it that way," Victor said with a noncommittal shrug. "Then bring it on baby."

"Yeah, actually I would crap myself, then do my best to fight," Gary chimed in.

"Nothing more intimidating than losing control of your bowels to start a fight," Vic teased.

"Sure, you see a demon rise up out of the ground and see if your tighty-whiteys stay clean," Gary shot back.

"I don't see what the point of this is," Malachi said. His defensive hackles were fully raised now. As much as he wanted to say the older man was talking utter nonsense, he could sense there was danger in the words.

"It's only a question," Sid answered. "If such a spiritual power of evil were to somehow manifest itself in our physical world, would we be obliged, as Christians, to fight against it?"

"I agree with Vic and Big G," Danny chimed in. "But that is just an academic argument. Spiritual evil doesn't manifest into the physical world. You may be able to convince me of possessions, but a demon sprouting wings and flying into our world, I don't think so."

Sid fished into his jacket and produced a newspaper folded in half. He opened it up and spread it across the table. Printed at the top in large, bold letters was the headline, *Sleeping Sickness Claims Fourth Victim in the Tricities.*

"I'm sure you're all familiar with the recent scourge that has afflicted out nation's young," Sid began. "Children falling ill for no apparent reason, becoming unresponsive and falling into a coma. Days later they die despite the best interventions that medical science can offer. All the experts stumped as to what this may be or what is causing it."

Sympathetic heads bobbed around the table. Everyone had heard of the Sleeping Sickness. It was all anyone talked about. It was the fear that was keeping every mother up at night and every father wondering if their children might be next.

"Of course we have heard of it," Malachi said. His own hospital had been the site of three of those deaths. It caused an undertone of panic that could be felt throughout the whole institution.

"Our hearts and prayers go out to the victims and the families," he said. "But I don't know what else we can do. Or what this has to do with us."

"What if I told you that this mysterious disease is not a thing of flesh and blood?" Sid asked, sending a chill among the men at the table. "What if I told you that this thing, this Sleeping Sickness is from the principalities and powers of this present darkness?"

The question hung in the air like a cold mist.

Malachi opened his mouth to say something before realizing he didn't know what the right response would be. On the surface, what Sid had just said sounded more than a little crazy. That some dark conspiracy was behind the recent illnesses was already an idea that had taken hold on the stranger corners of social media.

Then again, looking across the table at the well-dressed stranger, though his clothes were a bit antiquated, he looked anything but crazy. His blue eyes were cool and sparkled with intelligence. His obvious mastery and self-control didn't speak at all of madness, but of a strong sanity.

"Yeah, we all know dark forces are at work in our world," Malachi finally said. "That's why we pray. It's all we can really do against those powers. Pray and believe."

"Is that really all you can do?" Sid asked, fixing Malachi with a stare that made him squirm.

"We live in a fallen world," Danny said, taking up the argument. "Of course we have dark forces operating around us. It's the reason for any sickness in the world. It's human sin that has destroyed the natural order of things and keeps bad things like the Sleeping Sickness cropping up again and again. But it's just every day, ordinary, run of the mill human sin. Nothing more."

"Quite right Mr. Taylor," the older man said. "You have described well the human condition. And that is a perfect explanation for your everyday evil, and for all the evil that happens involving these powers of darkness working behind the scenes, tempting and deceiving mankind.

"But there is a more present form of evil that infects the world. It is an evil that has manifest itself, not in spiritual ways, but in material ways. It is an evil that walks among us, disguised as one of us. It is an evil that takes advantage of man's helpless estate, and the many ways he has made himself more helpless over the years. It feeds off of us and threatens our very existence. It is not an evil of flesh and blood, but it is an evil that has awakened in the world around us."

Sid fell quiet and let his words hang in the air. Malachi looked around the table and saw the same conflict on the other faces that he felt within himself. On the one hand, what Sid was telling them sounded like utter nonsense. It sounded like a plot he had plucked out of the last fantasy novel he had read. Or maybe he just watched too many movies by himself. But on the other hand, he could feel something stirring among them, something that drew him to those cryptic words.

"And this is what you're saying is causing the Sleeping Sickness?" Giovanni asked, speaking up for the first time.

Sid nodded his head gravely. "Precisely."

"And what is it you want of us?" Gary asked.

Sid leaned forward and spread his hands out on the table.

"This is an unnatural form of evil," he said. "And it requires a special way to combat it. For many years I have been part of an organization that has hunted down and fought against this sort of evil. As of late, our members have dwindled. Alas, I am the last one left. I am old and can't do this alone. I need help."

The men at the table silently processed the strange request. Malachi could see that the more Sid talked, the less the men believed him. He was sounding more and more like an old man who had fallen headfirst into his delusions.

"So, you want us to help you?" Tres asked. "Help you fight this evil and end the sickness."

"That is correct," Sid answered. "I want you to help me face down this evil and stop the sickness."

"How do we do that?"

"There are certain powers that have been granted me," Sid answered. "It is a part of a gift we have been given in order to take up the fight. You will be given gifts as well. We find out who is behind this and what they are doing, and if need be, we get ourselves into an old-fashioned fight."

"Powers?" Tres asked. "What kind of powers?"

"Gifts of the Spirit. The capacity to do things normal human beings cannot do."

"That sounds pretty cool," Vic chimed. "I want super powers."

"Wait, are you talking about magic?" Zach asked, suspicion thick in his voice.

Malachi knew Zach to be an old-style Baptist. He detested and feared any hint of magic or the occult and was constantly on the lookout for their influences in the world. Every week it seemed like he had a new book or movie that had to be avoided due to its occult influences.

"You use the word magic for that which you cannot explain," Sid told them. "I never use the word myself. I only said that this evil was not natural and the gifts we use to fight this evil are not natural either. Call it whatever you want: supernatural, mystical, magical, I don't care. The circumstances require us to use a greater power."

"Whatever you call it, I don't want any part of it," Zach insisted. "Sounds like witchcraft to me."

"You won't be doing what I do," Sid told them. "You really couldn't if you tried. Your gifts will be of a different nature."

"Like what kind of gifts?" Tres asked.

"It has been common in my organization to employ soldiers to help our cause," Sid explained. "Your gifts will be along those lines. You will be the strength and the steel. I will . . . I will do what I do. Together we will find the exact cause of this scourge and extinguish it."

"You want us to serve in your infantry?" Vic asked. "You command us where to go and who to fight and when to fight?"

"In as sense, yes," Sid answered. "I am asking you to join my army."

Vic smiled and shook his head. "Then in a sense, my answer is no. I served my time in the infantry and I swore I would never go back. Thanks, but no thanks."

As soon as Vic has refused it opened up the door for the rest of the men to express their skepticism and reluctance.

"Would we have to leave our families and jobs?" Tres asked.

"For a time, yes," Sid admitted. "But I will make sure they are waiting for you when you get back. Or if I cannot I can assure you another equal position when we are done."

"Out of the question," Tres said, shaking his head. "I can't leave my family or my job. Impossible for me."

"It's going to be a no for me too," Giovanni added. "I've got too much going on at work."

Malachi put his head down and smirked. Giovanni worked as a teacher and was his summer break. When none of the men exposed him, Malachi could tell they were all letting him down gently. No one believed a word he said but none of them wanted to take up that fight.

"This sounds too occult to me," Zach added. "I don't want any part of it."

Danny leaned forward and gave a tight, toothy smile. It was a tell he had that meant he was about to say something that might offend.

"Frankly, this all sounds fantastic to me," he began. "No offense, but I don't believe a word you have said about all of this. Whatever the Sleeping Sickness is it has a natural cause and we will find a natural cure. So, it's a hard no for me."

All eyes turned to the seat next to Sid. Gary was the only one besides Malachi that hadn't given an answer.

"What about you, Big G?" Malachi asked the big man who had gone thoughtfully silent.

Gary shrugged his shoulders. "I don't know. Maybe we shouldn't dismiss this outright."

Vic barked out a laugh beside him. "So, we join his army of monster hunters?" he asked. "I think your wife has been making you watch too many episodes of Supernatural."

"I'm not saying that," Gary answered, sounding defensive.

"Then what are you saying?" Malachi asked.

"Look, we come here every week and study this book," Gary said, reaching down and picking up his Bible. "And every week we read stories about God doing amazing things and calling people to do amazing things. He brought plagues down on Egypt and split the Red Sea so his people could walk through it. He helped David defeat Goliath. He brought people back from the dead, performed great miracles and did wonders so people could see and believe. And at least once every time we meet someone asks why God doesn't do these incredible things anymore. Maybe you just got your answer. Here is a man who has come to us today saying something amazing. And what is our reaction to this? We say we don't believe. We say we're too busy. Maybe that's why we don't see God doing amazing things anymore like he did in the Bible."

"Yeah, but he's asking us to pick up and leave our families," Tres pointed out. "Families that depend on us. And some of us don't have jobs that we can just pick up and leave."

"Didn't Jesus make the disciples leave their families?" Gary argued.

"He's not Jesus," Zach pointed out.

"I know he's not Jesus, but you know what I mean. If this is God calling us and asking us to do something difficult, something incredible, I think we should listen. And maybe he is calling us away from our jobs and families for a time. But if this is really the call of God then we can't just ignore it and walk away."

"What do you want us to do?" Victor asked. "You want to pack up tonight and run off with this stranger because he said God wants us to?"

"No," Gary shook his head. "I'm not saying that at all. I'm just saying we should listen. And listen with an open mind. If this is a real call, we don't want to let it pass us by."

"Fine," Danny chimed in. "I'm willing to listen. But you're going to have to give me a lot more if you want me to go running off with anyone. If God is really calling us then he would make himself a little better known. You know, the whole burning bush thing."

"Ok, that's fair," Gary agreed. "This is all I'm talking about. Keep an open mind."

Turning to Sid he said, "I think this is reasonable. We'll listen, but we need something more to go on. Either some solid proof that what you say is real or some sign that we're supposed to go with you."

"That's certainly more than fair," Sid nodded and said.

With that the older man closed his eyes and leaned back in his chair. Drawing in a deep breath he let it out slowly. He seemed to be concentrating on something only he could see or hear.

For several moments Sid remained in this position, eyes closed and breath cycling slow and deliberate. The seconds ticked by as the men watched in silence. Anticipation gave way to impatience, and impatience quickly grew to awkwardness. Heads turned and stared at each other as they watched Sid meditating quietly. The quiet became deafening around the table.

"Did he fall asleep?" Zach asked in a low whisper.

"Maybe we need to call his nurse to come and get him," Vic suggested. The tension broke in the room as the other men snickered.

Sid smiled and opened his eyes. "No, Mr. Dodds, I don't need a nurse. But thank you for that gentle reminder of my age. I wasn't sleeping. I was listening."

"Listening for what?" Gary asked.

"For the voice of God," he answered.

12

The tension returned in the room with those words. All the men around the table felt the gravity of the situation before them. Whatever they thought about the old man, he was serious about what he said and demanded a serious answer.

"Did you find what you were looking for?" Malachi asked, suddenly unsure he wanted to know the answer.

The smile on the old man's face was sad as he nodded.

"You will all receive a sign," he told them. "By the end of this week. All of you will be invited by the Holy Spirit to take up the sword of God. Look, and you will see. Even the hardest skeptic among you will not be able to deny the call that has been placed upon your life."

Danny ducked his head, feeling this comment was directed at him. Sid let his gaze touch each of the men around the table. It stopped at Tresmond.

"I'm sorry," he said, locking his gaze on the young man. "But the sign you will receive will be the hardest one of them all."

Chapter 2 - Signs

Malachi woke up the next morning with thoughts of his wedding day. He found it strange, for the minute he opened his eyes it was already on his mind, as if he were finishing a dream about it. Turning over he looked at his wife, Clara. Dark hair spilled over her sleeping form that rose and fell with the steady breath of slumber. Once again, he wondered what he had done to deserve such good fortune in the woman he had made his wife.

Stepping out the bed quietly so as not to disturb her, Malachi got dressed in the darkness of the predawn morning. The house was still except for his movement. All their children had grown up and left to build their own lives, and Clara didn't get up for another hour, so these mornings belonged to him.

Wondering why he was thinking of his wedding day Malachi did a quick mental check to make sure he wasn't forgetting their anniversary. That was still two months away. It had to be a dream, he told himself.

Whatever the reason he could not shake the memories. All through breakfast and the drive to the hospital he found himself reliving the details of that day. He experienced again the excitement he felt upon waking, not able to believe he was about to marry the woman of his dreams. Details he had long forgotten came back to his mind: the way she smelled during their first dance, the taste of the mimosas at their post wedding day brunch, one of his groomsmen, Roger, talking about which bridesmaid he wanted to hook up with. All of these and more flooded his mind with an irresistible insistence.

The memories gave him a certain shield throughout the day. When he got to work tensions were running high as usual. Fears about the Sleeping Sickness had everyone on edge. Even at the Heart Hospital, where he managed the staff and doctors, a nascent fear hovered on the edges of their minds. Everyone from the hospital administrators to the cafeteria workers were plagued by thoughts of this strange disease.

That day Malachi felt none of this tension. An unusual optimism had taken hold of him, a sense that life was good. Memories of that happy day kept all the tension and fear at bay. All Malachi felt that day at work was the anticipation and excitement of starting his life with Clara. All life seemed in front of him once again.

The mood stayed strong with him throughout the day. The hours that could sometimes drag on flew by instead. He was even a little surprised to see that the clock read four-thirty as early as it did. Packing up a little early he headed across town to the nursing home where his grandmother had been housed for the last three years.

It was Malachi's day to visit - a responsibility that he shared with his mother, two other siblings, and four cousins. She had developed dementia just before they moved her out of her old house, and they found the regular visits helped her keep whatever sharpness still remained with her. She had good days and bad days.

As soon as Malachi pulled into the nursing home parking lot, that sense of joyful anticipation that had been with him all day suddenly took a dark turn. It felt like a cloud moved over the sun, darkening the sky with grey and ominous shadows. A cold dread seeped into his bones, and his mind went to Sid Bickley again. For the whole day he hadn't spared the old man a single thought. Now, his words drummed into his head: this week you will receive a sign.

Malachi tried to shake off that sense of dread as he crossed the parking lot and stepped into the nursing home. Try as he might, the feeling followed him down the linoleum halls, past the nurse's station, beneath all the white, florescent lights and down into the dementia unit. He knocked on the open door of his grandmother's room and stepped inside.

"Is that you, Leo?" his grandmother asked as he greeted her.

She was in her wheelchair by the window. Outside, the family had put up bird feeders so she could enjoy a past time she always loved. A pair of nuthatches picked at the sunflower seed as they hopped over the feeder.

Malachi bent down to kiss her head as he took the quilted blanket off her legs. His grandmother always ran hot and hated having blankets over her. The staff always insisted on wrapping her legs despite her protests, and the family telling them she hated it.

"No, it's me, Malachi," he reminded her, though he knew it would be pointless. Ever since the dementia had gotten bad his grandmother always thought he was his uncle, Leo.

"I'm glad you came today, Leo," she continued. "I think it's time for me to go home."

"Why do you want to go home?" Malachi sighed. It was the same conversation he had with her every time he visited.

"I'm done with my vacation," she said as Malachi mouthed the words in unison. "I'm sick of this resort, Leo. I need to get back to work. Mr.

Elman will fire me if I stay gone any longer. He fired that other girl, Tonya. She called out sick too much and Mr. Elman fired her. I'm glad he did, though. That girl was after your father. She needed to get fired."

"You're going home tomorrow," Malachi told her.

It was a lie, but a well-intentioned and agreed upon lie. After months of arguing with her about why she needed to stay in the nursing home they just decided to tell her she was going home tomorrow. It seemed to satisfy her and she never remembered anyway.

"Oh good," she said, once again content with the knowledge that she was going home soon. "Because I have to get back to work, otherwise Mr. Elman will fire me. You know he fired that girl, Tonya. She was after your daddy so I'm kind of glad."

For the next half hour Malachi had the same conversation he always had with his grandmother these days. She continued to call him Leo. Three more times he had to tell her she was going home tomorrow. At least five more times he had to hear about the plots of the scheming Tonya. In between these recurring thoughts she mentioned the farm, her father's bad back, the assassination of JFK, and made Malachi promise to stay away from the Devlin boys because their father was member of the Klan.

"Alright, Gramma, I have to go," Malachi said after checking his watch.

She opened her mouth to say something, then stopped and nodded. A vacant expression came over her face as she turned to look out the window. Malachi patted her hand and rose to leave.

"Malachi," she said as he reached the door.

A chill came over him at the sound. She never called him by his right name anymore.

"Malachi," she said again as he turned around slowly.

The look on her face was clear and lucid. It was the face Malachi remembered growing up. It was the face of steely determination and an unwillingness to quit. It was also the face of an unyielding faith and a quiet wisdom that made her the glue that held the family together.

"Don't forget, Malachi," she said, her voice full of command. "Don't forget that God is calling you. Take up the sword, Malachi. God wants you to take up the sword."

The morning after Malachi witnessed his grandmother's moment of lucidity, Danny Taylor stepped into work to find a storm waiting for him. The low, wide building that housed the central office of Southern Trust

Bank rose up in four stories of white brick just off the frontage road of the interstate. Danny walked across the parking lot while absorbing his last few minutes of the new podcast on colonial America. It was a ritual that got him though every day. All the alerts on his phone were cut off on the drive in, allowing his mind to focus on something else for just a few minutes. It was crucial for him, because he knew that as soon as he walked through the doors of the bank and showed his ID to security, he would be swept off by the storms that always seemed to be brewing inside.

Like he did most mornings, Danny wondered whether or not he really wanted to be in the IT business. He had majored in History, and all of his post-college plans were about teaching. But at that point in time no one wanted history teachers and everyone seemed to be needing IT help. It was early enough in the game and the demand was growing that one could get away with having a history major and working himself into the computer game. Danny was pretty good at it, after all, and unlike most of the IT professionals he knew how to deal with people. He could work and communicate in both languages. This made him perfect for running an IT department.

The downside was that it was a continual strain and Danny was not one of those people who thrived under stress. When there was a storm at work, he always found himself getting carried away by it. And the worries followed him home and plagued his sleep at night. He always felt that proverbial sword hanging over his head, and knew it would drop at any moment. While a part of himself dreaded that inevitability, another part of himself couldn't wait.

That morning, when Danny showed his ID to security, he still had his earbuds in. Inside his head he heard the narrator wrap up his talk about the founding of Charles Town Landing. The guard said something to him that he couldn't hear. Danny shook his head and took out one of the ear buds.

"What was that?" he asked.

"The place is going nuts looking for you," the guard said.

Dread washed over Danny as looked up at the glass doors leading into the interior of the building. He could feel the chaos spilling out from behind them. Electricity crackled on the air. The storm was waiting.

Before he could even reach the doors, they flew open and the slight, blond form of Candice flew at him.

"Boss, where the Hell have you been?!" she asked, all deference forgotten in her panic. "We've been trying to get you all morning. There's a shit storm in there."

Danny didn't bother to correct her as he usually would. Something had rattled her, and hard. Danny followed Candice through the doors and immediately heard it for himself.

The shock of what he saw stopped him in his tracks. Panicked sounds buzzed through the first-floor cubicles. People hurried from one place to the next, talking with desperate panic into their phones. It was a storm, alright, one of epic proportions.

"What's going on here, Candice?" Danny asked, afraid to hear the answer.

"It's down, boss," she said, leading him through the maze of cubicles towards the IT office in the back.

As he tried to wade through the crowd people screamed questions at him. One on top of the other they demanded his attention, begged him to stop and look at their computers. He couldn't make sense of any single one request, but only stared in disbelief at the chaos that had become of the home office of Southern Trust Bank.

"What do you mean, it's down?" he asked as they passed through the doors of the IT office.

The sounds of the chaos outside abruptly quieted as Candice closed the doors behind them. Four desperate faces looked up at him, the other techs in his department. He could see the strain easily visible on their faces. The only sound in the room was the hum of the servers and the muted chaos just beyond the doors.

"Everything is down," Candice answered. "We've lost every network and unit in the entire company."

Danny shook his head, unable to comprehend what his tech just told him.

"What do you mean, every unit?" he asked.

"Everything," Collins stepped up and answered. The short, thin man pulled at the khakis that were always slipping down his waist.

The tech gestured to the laptop he had just been working on. Danny leaned over and saw only a blank screen. The only indication of life at all was a blue cursor flashing at the top of the screen.

"What is this?" Danny asked, his mind still not fully comprehending.

"This is every computer at the bank," Candice answered. "In every branch. We've gone totally dark. No one can log in or access anything. It's like every computer has stopped working."

Danny forgot his panic for a moment as his mind struggled to grasp what Candice had just told him. His mind ran through the myriad of possibilities, each one worse than the one before it. The excecs would be freaking out right now and probably every one of their customers who had tried to log onto their accounts. This was worst case scenario for any bank.

"So, this is what everyone sees when they power up?" Danny asked, pushing his panic aside. He couldn't do anything about what fallout might be coming. But what he could do was work the problem.

"When they log on," another tech chimed in. "Everything is fine until they log onto the system. When they do, it just goes blank."

"It's a hack," Collins moaned.

"I think it's a virus," Candice suggested.

"What's the difference to us?" Collins asked.

"If it's a hack then we will get a ransom demand of some sort," Danny said, surprised at how calm his words came out. "Unless they already have our data, which I doubt."

"Of course, they already have our data," Collins whined. "Believe me, they have every bit of it. Shit, my savings is probably in the Cayman Islands as we speak."

Danny shook his head. "If they have our data then they probably wouldn't have shut down our network.," he pointed out. "In fact, if they had stolen anything they wouldn't want us to notice until it was too late to track them down."

Trying to quickly assess the situation Danny straightened up and looked up at his team. The fear he felt rattling his bones was clearly written on every face. He opened his mouth to speak when the door to the server room banged open. The harried face of Thompson, the executive assistant to the CEO looked in. The call they had all been waiting for had come.

"Mr. Briggs wants to see you," he barked. "All of you. In the boardroom. Now."

Five minutes later Danny and his team stood in the top floor board room. Nine angry faces of executives in suits stared back at them.

"You want to explain how every computer in our bank went down today?" Briggs asked, the CEO's hands folded on the table in front of him.

"We're still in the assessment phase," Danny tried to explain but was quickly interrupted.

"I need answers, and I need them ten minutes ago," the CEO growled. "Do you realize what's at stake here?"

"Sir, I understand completely . . ." he began before being cut off again.

"I don't think you do," Mr. Briggs continued. "We're a bank. The basic operation we carry out is to keep people's money safe. That's why they do business with us in the first place. They trust us to keep their money and investments safe. Right now, it looks like it's safer in a cookie jar in their kitchen than in our bank. Do you understand that? I need answers now or we will start bleeding customers. Not to mention the FDIC will start breathing down my neck in about fifteen minutes. Answers Danny. I want them now."

"We are getting it under control," Danny tried to assure the executives, hoping they couldn't see he didn't believe his own words.

"What the hell happened?" Briggs asked. "Have we been hacked? Is this a data breach?"

"I'm fairly certain this isn't data breach," Danny assured them. "If someone was stealing data, they would want to cover their tracks better than this. If this is deliberate then it's someone who wants us to know they're there. If it was a hack for ransom, we probably would have gotten demands by now. My guess is this is some kind of virus."

The board groaned at Danny's announcement.

"What the hell is all this security for?" one of the executives grumbled. "I thought all this software we were paying for was to keep shit like this from happening."

"They are," Danny agreed. "But no system is full proof. And nothing can prevent an attack that was brought in from the inside."

The room rumbled in concern. Danny had just suggested the one thing no one wanted to consider, that this was an inside job.

"Are you saying one of our own did this?" Briggs asked.

"Maybe not deliberately," Danny said. "Could have been an email attachment or an unauthorized flash drive that was already infected. All we know right now is the system went down this morning when users tried to first log in."

"Well, hell, I could have told you that," the CEO barked. "Where does that get us?"

"It means the automated systems were up and running just fine all night. The shut down was triggered when someone first logged in. That indicates someone wants us to know what they did. Some kind of activist group. And the servers could be just fine if this is affecting only the individual units."

"Here is the deal," Briggs said, spreading his hands out on the table. "Nightshade Pharmaceuticals has already been on the phone today. I've managed to buy us a little time with them, maybe an hour. If you can't find their money in an hour then we can kiss them goodbye. That's twelve years of good will gone, in a single morning. Do you understand that? Twelve years of impeccable service and even, dare I say, friendship, gone in a few hours. And I don't need to tell you what happens if we lose Nightshade, do I?"

Danny shook his head. "No sir, you don't"

"We lose Nightshade we all lose our jobs," Briggs answered anyway. "Starting with you and your whole department. Answers Taylor. I want answers."

"I understand," Danny said, feeling himself wither under the attacks. He felt fairly certain at that moment that whatever happened, he would be unemployed at the end of it all. Still, he felt the need to continue on. Some part of him that didn't want to accept defeat kept pushing him forward.

"We will figure this out," he assured the board again. "But right now all we know is that when someone tries to log on, they are immediately affected . . ."

Danny let the words trail off. He looked down at his feet, at the bag holding his own laptop. With all the chaos and confusion of the morning he had yet to log onto the system himself.

"Excuse me," he said to the executives, grabbing up his bag and hurrying out the door.

The confused and frightened IT staff followed Danny's quick retreat. Catching up to him at the elevators they managed to squeeze in before the doors closed behind them. Breathless figures looked up to him in anticipation.

"Boss, you want to tell me what's going on?" Candice asked.

Danny held up his computer bag in answer.

"I haven't logged on yet," he said. "I powered off last night when the storm started to roll in. I haven't cut it on since which means I'm not infected yet. I least I don't think I am."

The group hurried down to the server rooms and Danny and booted up in safe mode. He bypassed the automatic contact with the servers and held his breath as the computer whirred to life without any problems.

"No trojan horse," Collins said. "It's got to be something coming out of the servers."

Danny agreed and they hardwired his laptop into the servers. From there Danny booted up a diagnostic that began combing through the entire system. They all watched as the program examined every facet and piece of software.

Suddenly, the screen went blank. Without any warning at all it fell to a dark screen. Only a blue cursor blinked at the top.

"No, no, no," Danny said, typing helplessly at the keyboard. "This shouldn't happen. Why is this happening?"

As if to answer, words appeared on his screen. Big, blue letters in the old, angular font of the first computers typed themselves out.

"Decide Danny," it said.

All the techs turned and looked at him, their faces awash in confusion. Danny felt his blood grow cold. He thought of Sid Bickley and the promise that he would receive a sign. He knew without realizing how he knew, that this was the sign.

"Make your choice," the words flashed up on the screen. "Will you take up the sword?"

Yes No

Hump day, Zachary Metts reminded himself as he wiped his hands. It was only ten A.M. and already his third oil change of the day. He shook his head in disbelief as he chucked the shop towel away and headed to the service window. Who in their right mind would take their car to a dealer for an oil change?

Zach looked up to the window and saw his boss hold up a clipboard and shake it in his direction. He sighed and put his head down, heading over to the window, his hopes of a little break in the morning dashed. Instead, it was going to be one of those days.

"What you got for me?" Zach asked through the window.

"Mrs. Peterson is back," Todd said, smiling. There was a morbid pleasure in his voice that Zach dreaded to hear.

The groan that came from him this time was audible. Mrs. Peterson had already been in twice this month, and at least four times that year. And every time it was some minor or phantom problem with her car that she was convinced needed immediate attention. Only for Zach it was a major nuisance because lately she had been insisting on him.

"What is it this time?" Zach asked as Todd slid the window open and handed him the work order.

Todd didn't answer. Instead, he smiled as Zach read for himself.

"A loose screw," Zach said, waving the clipboard. "She brought the Impala in for a loose screw?"

"She says there's a rattle underneath the hood," Todd said with a shrug. "Convinced there's a loose screw somewhere. She's scared that one of the wheels might come off or her engine will drop if you don't look at it."

"She brought it in with a rattle two weeks ago," Zach complained. "There was nothing wrong with it then and there's nothing wrong with it now."

"What do you want me to say?" Todd asked defensively. "She said there's a screw loose so go search for a loose screw. Make some noise with the drill and tell her you tightened a mounting bolt."

"How much are you charging her for this?" Zach asked, not sure he wanted to know the answer.

"You let the big boys handle that," Todd said with a smile. In that one look he told Zach all he needed to know. "You just deal with the loose screws."

"There's a loose screw alright," he muttered as he headed over to the metallic silver, '02 Impala.

Opening the front door Zach switched on the radio. At least Mrs. Peterson always had a decent station on. Good, Christian music was always programmed on her radio instead of the Satanic trash that was coming out these days. Although Zach did indulge in some classic rock now and then if he could keep his mother's voice out his head long enough to enjoy it.

"Do you want to just hand your soul over to the dark one?" his mother would ask, sometimes with tears streaming down her face. "Oh, have I prayed and prayed, until my knees are bruised Zachary. Don't you know how I've prayed that you be spared from the same evil that took your father. Booze and the music of hell, that's what did him in. The Devil's drink and the Devil's song, and a good man was drawn into the fire of hell. Oh, Zachary, my only boy, don't make my prayers in vain."

That had been almost twenty years ago, but her voice still echoed in his head. It had gotten worse since she died, so bad that it amazed him how powerful that voice, and that guilt, could still be. All the while she probably never realized how deep and far reaching the damage she had done to him went. Some days he hated her for it. But even as he realized how much she lied to and manipulated him; he couldn't do anything to shake the feelings of guilt that she had instilled in him at an early age.

23

"Not today, mother," he said as he listened to pure and soulful sounds pour out of Mrs. Peterson's radio.

The car went up on the lift and Zach did a quick assessment of the Impala. Checking around he found exactly what he expected, nothing loose to cause a rattle. Still, he fired off the drill a few times hoping Mrs. Peterson could hear it from the waiting room.

On a whim, Zach let the car down and decided to look inside, wondering if maybe she had heard something shaking inside. He leaned into the back, checking under the seats as the music came to an end and the DJ from WTMZ began reading the weekly list of testimonials they had received. It was a regular segment called, "How God is Working Among US." Zach had always thought of sending one in himself but never had gotten up the courage to do it.

"We got a special testimonial today," the DJ announced in his crisp voice. "This one from a Mrs. Peterson with a rattling Impala."

Zach stopped, not sure of what he heard. He got out and slid into the driver's seat, wondering if Mrs. Peterson actually sent something in about her car. Maybe that screw was looser than he thought.

"That's right, a very special testimonial from a very special lady," the DJ continued. "And this one comes with an important message. It goes out to a Zachary Metts, trying to find a mysterious rattle. Zach, there's a tin box on the passenger seat floor with beads in it. The handle is shaking and if you put it in the seat the rattle will stop."

Still not believing what he was hearing Zach let his eyes wander over to the floor of the passenger seat. There, he could see clearly, a small, tin box. It looked like a mini lunch box, decorated with a twisting burst of flowers. He reached over and picked up the box and gave it a gentle shake. A metallic rattle sounded. He would have laughed if his blood had not gone ice cold.

Zach had forgotten about the strange man that had come to Bible. He had put him out of his mind along with his icy blue eyes and talk of magic that he didn't trust at all. Now, the image of Sid Bickley and all the dangerous things he represented came floating back into his mind. Most of all, he remembered the promise that he would receive a sign.

Somewhere in the back of his head he could hear his mother warning him of occult forces that would drag him to hell if he wasn't careful. But for once that voice was drowned out by a deeper, more primitive fear.

"The big question for Zachary," the DJ said. "Is will you take up the sword?"

About the same time Zach was hearing the impossible come out of Mrs. Peterson's radio, Giovanni Santos was wondering how a song got stuck in his head. This wasn't all that unusual for Giovanni, or Gio as he was known by friends closest to him. Being a music teacher he had songs stuck in his head all the time. It was kind of part of the job.

Except this song wasn't like every other song that had gotten stuck on the replay button inside his head. Usually, when he kept replaying a piece of music, he knew what it was and where it came from. This day, not only did he have no idea where the song came from, he didn't even know the name of the song. This was not only unusual, but for a music teacher a little bit embarrassing as well.

It was a simple melody, one that he could easily hum. At the same time there was a grandeur to it, a loftiness that reminded him of Beethoven's Ninth or Tchaikovsky's Piano Concerto #1. For his life, though, he couldn't figure out the name or where it was from. He went through in his head the catalogue of every composer he could think of, his vast collection of vinyl at home, the pieces he had played at school, and he still couldn't figure it out. He even whistled it to the band director to see if he had heard it before. Mr. Tunstill just shook his head and said it was a new one to him.

"Maybe it's a Santos original," the band director suggested.

Gio shook his head as he pondered the tune. He highly doubted he had come up with the song. Though he considered himself a highly competent musician and director, he was no composer.

The song continued to haunt him through the day. It got so bad, that as he was trying to conduct his fifth period through the 1812 Overture, he kept messing up his direction. The timing of the song in his head dominated him so much he could not keep the pace with the music in front of him. With a sense of defeat, he dismissed the class early and tried to get the song out of his head.

Pacing up the school halls his thoughts turned to Sid Bickley and their Bible study Sunday night. While everyone else had expressed skepticism, and Gio certainly had a share of his own, inwardly he was thrilled at the prospect. As soon as the old man had spoken up Giovanni had felt excitement course through him. Part of him even wanted to throw everything down in his life and follow the man whole-heartedly. But as was his habit, he let the other men take the lead and was content to follow where the others wanted to go.

As the week wore on his excitement grew with the upcoming

opportunity. In some way, he had to admit he had been waiting his whole life for this. Being raised in a devout Catholic family, first in El Paso as a first-generation citizen, then in the southeast, he had been steeped in stories of miracles done through the power of saints his whole life. As he heard them, he always wondered if something like that would happen to him. So far, it had not.

But then came Sid's promise that they would all receive a sign to take up the sword. It was just like a story out of the legends of the saints. Giovanni woke up giddy that Monday morning, looking all around him for the promised sign. He turned over every event, every conversation, wondering if it was hidden there somewhere.

Nothing had come yet. Part of him feared it would not happen at all, that Sid really was a delusional old man. He had to keep reminding himself to wait, that many of God's people had to wait and remain faithful. Hadn't the cripple by the Bethsaida pool had to wait twenty years for his miracle? Hadn't Zechariah waited his whole life to see the messiah? Certainly, Giovanni would wait until the end of the week for his miracle.

Lost in these thoughts Giovanni's steps took him back towards the music department. A student worked through his horn technique inside one of the practice rooms. The scaled played out faithfully, up then down, as they had all been taught.

Suddenly, the scaled turned to a melody. Giovanni stopped in his tracks - it was the same song he had been hearing all morning. It was unmistakable, the simplicity, almost pastoral tune, mixed with the soaring grandeur came out of the practice room.

Giovanni raced to the door and threw it open, the question already forming on his lips. He stopped short and looked around, the words half formed in his mouth.

The room was empty.

He stepped back into the hallway. The sound was gone. Giovanni darted up the hall, looking in rehearsal rooms, practice rooms, anywhere close by. All of them were either empty or giving class instruction. There was no horn player on the hall.

Thoroughly confused Giovanni continued to pace through the halls. His feet led him out of the arts hall and nearer the administrative wing. Just as he passed the teacher's lounge a familiar voice called out to him.

"Hey, Gio," Dr. Stuber said.

Giovanni stopped and redirected himself to the lounge. Principle

Stuber was eating a sandwich at one of the tables as he leaned over his phone.

"I was just thinking about you," he said. "I found a cool piece I thought the orchestra could perform."

Giovanni nodded his head and sat opposite the principal. He knew what was coming and was fully ready to humor the man. About once a month Dr. Stuber came up with ideas for the orchestra to perform. Most of them were impossibly complicated for a high school orchestra or intolerable to the kids. But he was the principal, so Giovanni always listened patiently and told him what a great idea it would be.

"You ever heard of the King Arthur Opera?" the principal asked.

Giovanni tilted his head. "Vaguely," he answered. "I believe it was an early attempt at English opera. Not very successful if I remember correctly."

"Yeah, something like that," Dr. Stuber said through a mouthful of sandwich. "But this new guy, Finibichi or something like that. Italian guy. He did some variation on it that turned out pretty good."

"From the King Arthur opera?" Giovanni asked, unable to keep the skepticism out of his voice.

Dr. Stuber didn't seem to notice as he was intent on scrolling through his phone.

"Yeah, and this piece is really good," he said as he held the phone out. "And simple too."

Sounds of a single violin came floating from the phone's speakers. A cello joined in, then an oboe. After a brief buildup then the violin took up the melody. Giovanni felt the earth heave beneath him as the simple yet grand composition echoed through the teacher's lounge.

It was the song that had been stuck in his head all day.

Here it was again, playing out of Dr. Stuber's as he absently chewed on a ham sandwich. Giovanni knew at once this was the sign he had been waiting for, knew down to the depths of his bones. Just like he knew more was coming.

"Pretty good, huh?" Dr. Stuber asked, misinterpreting Giovanni's stunned silence.

"What's the name of that piece?" Giovanni managed to ask.

Dr. Stuber turned the phone back to himself and touched the screen. He scrolled up, furrowing his brows as he searched. Giovanni had to keep himself from ripping the phone out of his hands and finding it himself.

"Here it is," the principal finally said, his head tilted back to read through his glasses. "I think it's from the first act. Yep, first act. It's called, *Will You Take up the Sword?*"

Later that night, as Giovanni was playing over in his mind the strange events of the day, Victor Dodds was having a more biblical experience of God. As had prophets and seers for thousands of years before him, Vic dreamt of the divine.

It seemed like as soon as he closed his eyes that night he was opening them again on the desert sand of Iraq. He knew he was dreaming, just as he knew exactly where he was. It was just like he remembered from the Second Gulf War. Hot sand swirled around his boots and across his desert fatigues. Robed women hurried through the alleys of brown, stucco buildings, pulling their veils tighter around them as they ran past the American GI. Spouts of flame surged hundreds of feet in the air, looking like the doorways of Hell had been ripped off and allowed its tortured heat to taste the earth.

The oilfields didn't burn in the Second Gulf War, Vic told himself. That was the first one. That was the Gulf War he had watched in middle school from the comfort of his home, the shock of seeing Saddam torch the Iraqi oilfields. Plumes of black smoke belched into the atmosphere just as it had on the TV all those years ago.

Or did they burn them in the Second War as well? Vic asked himself this as he wandered through the Iraqi village. He couldn't remember, but suddenly the answer didn't seem to matter anymore. There was something more important to do that day. In the strange logic only known in the dream world, Vic knew exactly what that was.

He knew without really knowing that there would be a church on the far end of the village. Wandering as he did on patrol, head on a swivel and finger close to the trigger of his rifle, Vic took hold of that sense of alertness he had honed in his time at war. He was ready for anything, even as something told him he wasn't in that kind of danger.

Daylight faded as Vic walked down the streets of the small village. Kids kicked a soccer ball down a distant street. Silence fell over him with the coming of night, a surreal and eerie silence.

Firelight from the burning oilfields lit up the whole eastern sky. The night raged with sinister, orange flames. There was a presence in that fire that made Vic afraid, much more afraid of any possible ambush from hostiles. He didn't want to look, but felt his eyes drawn to the angry spouts of flame.

Faces formed in the swirl of fire. Distorted creatures that barely resembled human faces groaned and screamed and opened their mouths in tortured agony. Except their screams came out like the rush of fire and he couldn't tell the difference between the two. A hatred burned out of that fire that made Vic shudder, knowing with that dream knowledge that he was the object of the blazing hatred.

Forcing himself to turn from the fire Vic saw the church up ahead. It didn't look out of place at all, built of the same brown mud as the other buildings in the village. The only feature that set it apart was the white dome topped with a gold cross. It looked like one from his memory, a church he had seen just like this during the war. Except the one he remembered had a bombed-out dome, and inside were the bodies of the priest and twenty-seven local Christians who had suffered the anger at the American invasion.

The memory made Vic pause at the door, his hand just inches from the long, brass handle. But he knew he had to go in. Whatever was inside, he had to face it again. Even if that meant coming face to face with his nightmares.

Gathering his courage Vic pushed open the door and stepped inside. Smells of incense greeted him as his eyes adjusted to the low light. Candles burned at the altar up front, providing the only light in the darkened sanctuary. Boot steps echoed off the stone floor as he tread slowly past the wooden pews. He looked up and saw the dome was blown away again, exposing the church to the clear, night air. An array of star shined down into the church and Vic couldn't help thinking that having your roof blown open had a strange upside to it.

A priest rose from the altar and turned to face Vic. He was dressed in traditional Iraqi garb but Vic knew it was the priest. It was the same priest from the war, the one whose blood ran across the church tiles in Iraq. He looked up at Vic with smiling eyes, though they also held the distant pain of life. Seated on the first row of pews were people with their backs to him. Vic didn't have to count them to know there were twenty-seven.

"We have been waiting, Victor," the priest said in a sad and tired voice.

Victor nodded and began to take off his rifle so he could set it down. He wanted so badly to set it down. The priest reached out and stopped him. He shook his head solemnly.

"It is not time to put down your weapon," he told him.

At these words Vic felt the tremendous weight of the rifle slung over his shoulder. It pulled him down, dragging at his back and shoulders. A deep ache radiated from his neck as his body begged him to get rid of the weight.

"There is another weapon you must take up," the priest said, leading him past the front altar and to the small, ornate gate at the top of the dais.

Vic allowed himself to be lead, all the while feeling the tremendous weight of the gun pulling him down. He followed the priest, almost dragging the gun that got heavier and heavier. He followed him around a screen, towards a dim candle glowing beyond it. Behind the screen another altar waited, this one hewn of stone and bearing the many scars of age.

Vic stared down at the altar. A naked sword rested on the top.

"Will you take up the sword?" the priest asked him.

The last thing on Gary Walsh's mind that night was the prophecy of the old man promising them a sign. Though he had thought it about a lot since that fateful night, and wondered to himself what the other guys were experiencing, at that moment he had no room in his mind for such things. The only thing that Gary could think about was the massive, three-alarm fire that was burning in front of him.

The call had come just half an hour ago. The old Greenshill apartments, known for their low income and crime, had caught fire. The nearly derelict buildings had gone up fast. And because the units were so close together the windy night had spread the flames almost too fast to contain.

Shouts were mingled with sounds of panic as commands were raised into the night. The angry, orange blaze spewed from the windows of the apartment and up into the sky. Orange and red hues mixed with clouds of black smoke. The incredible press of heat made the flames and smoke twist together, like some mad dance swirling into a tornado of destruction.

Gary adjusted his mask and tried to wipe the sweat that was pouring down his face. For just a moment his mind disconnected as he watched the angry dance of flame. For just a moment he could have sworn he saw a face in the fire; something malevolent and full of wrath, fueling the fire with a pent-up rage that had festered for a thousand years.

"Walsh!" a voice yelled out, shaking his from his stupor.

"Is that unit clear?" his captain asked as he pointed to one of the buildings that was beginning to catch fire.

"Aye, Captain," Gary answered. The captain nodded and moved on.

Gary was just about to move on himself when he heard a voice speak to him.

"It's not clear," he heard it say.

Gary lifted up his mask and turned around. No one was near him. Voices rose up in panicked shouts, and noises of rescue and flight mingled together. But there was no one near who could have just spoken to him. Yet he had heard the voice, as clear as the sounds of the burning fire around him.

"It is not clear," the voice said again, this time like thunder.

Gary looked over at unit three again, unsure of what to do. Smoke poured out the windows and he knew it would be thick inside. The eastern side of the building was covered in flames. They had already called it clear of inhabitants, everyone supposedly accounted for. End of story.

Except that voice told him something different. A deep certainty came over Gary. He knew someone else was in there.

Cursing to himself Gary pulled his face shield down and charged towards the smoking building. Voices cried out to him as he ran past, voices of warning and commands to stop, but he ran on. If he was wrong, there would be hell to pay. If he was right, there would be hell to pay. But something deeper and more powerful was driving Gary, and it was a force he could not deny.

Smoke enveloped his vision as he stepped over the threshold. The sound of his filtered breath rushed through his ears. Reaching out he felt the sides of the wall and guided himself by their touch. Nothing but thick smoke billowed before him. For now, he was flying blind.

Something hit his midsection and Gary doubled over. Reaching out he felt long, soft cushions - a couch. I'm in a living room, he told himself. Finding the wall again he continued forward, searching for the openings and doorways of the rooms.

The crackle of fire grew louder as Gary searched. The heat inside his suit stifled and made his head spin. Not much time left, he thought. He fumbled through two bedrooms, and a quick glance told him each was empty.

Gary stumbled back into the hallway, reaching out to find the walls again. Orange light filtered brighter through the swirl of smoke. The fire was getting closer. It was time to bail.

"It's not clear," the voice called out again.

"Damn it," Gary grunted to himself. "One more room."

Pushing open a swinging kitchen door Gary found himself face to face with the flames. Fire covered the back wall of a small kitchen. It swirled and pulsated, like a living thing. Tendrils of flame reached out, fingers searching for something, something to consume.

Gary watched in horror as a face formed in the flames. Two empty places opened in the fire to form eyes. Fire coalesced together, shaping a grimacing mouth. Words came out in rushing flames, as the figure stared at Gary in ancient and undimmed anger. He could feel the glare searching him, the rage radiating as the heat of fire. He felt a force push him back out of the room and he took an involuntary step back.

"God help me," he whispered into his mask, knowing he couldn't face whatever was in that fire alone.

As soon as he uttered his prayer a wind blew into the kitchen. It was a cold wind, impossibly cold. And despite the raging inferno Gary felt a chill pass through his suit and into him.

Smoke swirled on the cold wind. The face in the fire opened its mouth to scream. In a rush the flames snuffed out, as if a door had been closed on them. The fire died instantly, replaced by a thick billow of smoke.

Gary stepped back onto the kitchen, trying to see through the smoke. Up ahead he could see what looked like a square stone standing in the middle of the floor. He moved closer and as the clouds of smoke passed by, he could tell it was a stone block. Protruding from the stone was a sword, handle out.

As strange as the sight was it all felt completely normal to Gary in that moment. Sid Bickley's words came back to him, clear as the voice that had guided him into the building. They would all get a sign, he had told them, a sign to take up the sword.

Gary had no doubts in that moment. He knew exactly what he had to do. He even knew that his whole life had been building up to this one moment.

With a confident hand Gary reached out and took hold of the hilt of the sword. As soon as his fingers closed around the steel the hilt morphed into a human hand.

Gary started in confusion and tried to pull his hand away. Small, strong fingers held him fast. The hand lifted up and he saw it was connected to an old, thin arm. He pulled at the hand and the face of an elderly woman rose out of the smoke, gripping Gary's hand in a desperate bid to hold onto life.

"Will you take up the sword?" the old woman croaked.

Despite the shocking words Gary found himself moving by instinct.

32

Folding the woman up in his arms he lifted her off the floor. Her slight weight was almost unnoticeable as he rushed her out of the smoking building.

Minutes later he laid her gently on a stretcher as EMT's worked over her. A mask was fitted over her face through which she took deep and struggling breaths.

Three other firefighters gathered with Gary at the back of the ambulance. Like everyone else there they were stunned by the sudden disappearance of the flames from the third unit. All at once they had snuffed out, like an invisible hand had suffocated them.

"Never seen anything like that," one of the firemen shook his head and remarked. "I swear now, ten years fighting fire and never once have I seen something like that."

The other heads nodded their agreement, all stupefied by what they had just witnessed.

"It was like all the oxygen suddenly went out of the fire, and it just died. I mean, the whole thing. Just like that. It's impossible, right? If I hadn't seen it with my own eyes."

"What about you, Big G?" someone asked. "You ever see that happen before?"

Gary was scared to answer. He thought about the face he saw in the fire, the anger and wrath that emanated from it, the cold wind and the sword. What had just happened to him?

The old woman shook as another bout of coughs racked her frail body. She pulled the oxygen mask down and looked up at Gary. He tried to get her to put the mask back on her but she pushed his hands away, a determined and sincere look on her face.

"My hero," she croaked, reaching out a trembling hand to touch his face.

Gary groaned inside, knowing what was coming next. The paramedics loaded the woman into the ambulance as the other firefighters looked at Gary with restrained smiles on their faces. They all looked like they were about to burst.

"Alright, let's get it over with," Gary told them as soon as the ambulance door closed.

The other firefighters shared a glance, smiles breaking out across their faces. Together they cried out in falsettos.

"Oooh, Gary. My hero."

Chapter 3 - The Hardest Sign

Tresmond Bettis bounced from his car and made his way toward the gym. His bag felt light in his hand, the sun shined in a rich, blue sky, and life felt too good to be true. The characteristic energy that had guided him through life coursed through his veins. Cool air filled his lungs and gave him an even greater lift as he breathed deep in gratitude.

It was Friday morning and a great day to be alive.

Tresmond was one of those rare American gems, a man who truly loved his work. Every day as he made his way into the gym, he couldn't believe how lucky he was. While most people grinded away at jobs they couldn't stand, stuck in cubicles, staring at computer screens while they dreamt of a better life, Tresmond lived the life he always wanted.

"Morning, Dee," he chimed at the girl behind the greeting desk.

"Morning Tres," the young brunette smiled back at him, already catching his energy.

That energy radiated from him like a wave as Tres walked through the gym. Already starting to fill up with the morning crowd trying to get their reps in before work, he wove through businessmen and bankers sweating at the bench press next to stay at home moms perfecting their squats in the mirror. Everywhere he went Tres cried out greetings and encouragement. Everywhere he passed the weights got a bit lighter or someone found the strength for that one last rep. It was his gift, and he was always happy to share it.

"Dig Deep!" Tres yelled out as he stepped into the exercise room.

"Lift High!" came the response from the people already gathered there.

A smile came to his face that he couldn't resist. This is what it was all about. In a few moments he was going to start recording his daily workout show, watched live by thousands and replayed by thousands more every day. He wasn't a superstar yet, but he was getting there fast.

Once again Tres marveled at how blessed his life had become. His own unique brand of motivation had made him a media darling in the world of streaming workouts. He had always thought the problem with a lot of workout motivations was that people expected to feel good when working out. So many were unable to deal with the inevitable discomfort that they found themselves wearing down and giving up.

A few years back, when Tres was working as a personal trainer, he

34

wondered what it would be like if people not only expected, but started to look forward to the pain and discomfort of working out. Be honest, he thought. Don't just tell him it will hurt, but tell them that was what they wanted. Embrace the pain.

Dig Deep Lift High was born. Through Tresmond's infectious energy and open honesty he was able to work up a loyal following. The classes grew until the rooms couldn't fit anymore and interest had started to grow beyond the walls of the gym. Now, he had a professional crew filming him every day, dedicated assistants who helped him with the routines, and a waiting list a mile long to be a part of the live show. He was truly living the dream.

Music thumped on in the background, not loud yet but just enough to get people started. Tresmond stretched out and touched base with the crew and his trainers, making sure they were all on the same page. The energy in the room built up slowly, anticipation and enthusiasm taking over everybody. Tresmond took it all in, reveling in the raw power that was being generated, and always amazed to be a part of it.

"Everybody ready to dig deep?!" he yelled out when the time was right.

"Lift high!" they yelled back, taking their places.

The main lights went low as the crew began their adjustments. Tres jogged in place, unable to contain his energy. He fiddled with the earpiece and the mic he wore, never really comfortable with them, though soon they would be forgotten. The backlights, spots and underneath lights came on, giving that perfect mix of dark and light with a few colored bands to mix it up.

"Embrace!" Tres yelled out.

"The pain!" came the unison response.

"Embrace!"

"The pain!"

"Embrace!"

"The pain!"

Now they were ready. The music cranked up, thumping deep in Tresmond's chest as he felt it wash over him. Cheers went up as everyone there started to ride the wave of energy. It had to be strong in here, Tresmond knew, for the people online and watching it later to be able to feel it as well.

As suddenly as it started it all stopped. The music fell quiet and the lights came back on. A groan of disappointment went through the crowd as they all looked around, wondering what was happening.

Tres looked up, just as confused as everyone else. The back door opened and he saw Donald Rice hurry in, the manager of the gym. A worried look crossed over his features as he made a bee line over to Tres.

Dread washed over him as he watched Donald approach. Tres knew he was coming. And by the expression on his face, the tight lips and the wide eyes, he knew it wasn't good. For the first time that week Tres thought of the old man that had showed up at their Bible study, and the promise he had made them. They would all receive a sign, and Tresmond's would be the hardest of all.

Please, no, he thought as Donald stepped up to him. Some part of him knew exactly what the manager was going to say, and he didn't want to hear it.

"I'm sorry, Tres," he said, looking away.

"What's going on, Don?" Tres asked.

"Your wife called," he began, stopping again as he looked at the floor. "I'm sorry, it's . . . It's your son. He's at the hospital."

Two days later a somber group of men gathered for their weekly Bible study. The classroom was quiet. The buckets of fried chicken spread across the long table were largely untouched. No one had an appetite. A feeling of helplessness and rage swirled among the gathered men. There were seven this time. But all of their thoughts were focused on the eighth that wasn't there, and the older man sitting at the head of the table.

"What's the latest news?" Danny asked. The earnest concern in his voice was evident.

He had forgotten all about his troubles at work for the moment. Whatever bug had infected the computers at the bank had gone away as soon as he had clicked on the "yes" that had flashed across the screen. Like some runaway miracle all the systems booted up and began working normally. The brass was satisfied, but still they wanted answers.

All these concerns had faded into insignificance when he got the text Friday night.

"Brothers, we need your help in a mighty way. Please pray for our brother Tres. He has just gotten news that his son fell ill suddenly and is up at Reedland Memorial right now in the ICU."

"It's what they feared the most," Malachi answered.

"Sleeping Sickness?" Vic hung the question out there like a storm cloud.

Malachi nodded. "Mom found him just staring at the TV Friday morning. He wouldn't respond, blink, nothing. Apparently, he stayed that way for all of Friday and Saturday. This morning, he closed his eyes and went into a full out coma. Doctors are doing everything they can."

Grim nods bobbed around the table. Gary picked at his napkin. Thoughts of his own son and daughter, both of them teenagers now, swirled through his head. He couldn't imagine what Tresmond was going through. Having to face the sickness of a child, when rendered so helpless to do anything; there couldn't be a worse feeling in the world. He wished desperately there was something he could do for his friend. But what?

More than one set of his eyes stared angrily at the head of the table. Sid Bickley sat there, leaning back in his chair and absorbing the silent rage directed at him. To Malachi he looked more haughty than usual, his immaculate suit almost mocking, maybe even a bit smug. He felt there was an unspoken "I told you so," waiting in him.

Malachi was at a loss as to what to say. He had talked with the other men throughout the week, and they had all experienced some sort of cryptic sign, just as the old man had promised. Something was clearly going on, something his dad would call, "above my pay grade." All Malachi knew for certain was that Sid had something to do with this all and he didn't trust him one bit.

"Alright, I think we're all ready to listen," Malachi finally said. "You want to tell us what's going on here and what we can do about it?"

The old man looked up as if he were just realizing where he was. He stared at Malachi across the table, searching him, making him squirm beneath his scrutiny.

"I'm afraid I can't answer that right now," he answered calmly.

Malachi laughed and shook his head. "What kind of game are you playing with us?"

"I'm not playing any game."

Before Malachi could answer Vic butted in. "Didn't you tell us this sickness had something to do with dark forces that inhabit the world?"

"And you wanted us to help you," Giovanni added.

"Yeah, and I'm thinking you had something to do with this," Zach jumped in and said. "Something that has a bit of the dark itself."

"I assure you I had nothing to do with this sickness, or Mr. Bettis' son catching it," Sid answered.

"But you said he would receive the hardest sign," Vic accused, jabbing a finger at the old man. "You knew this would happen to Tres.

You knew! I think you need to start letting us in on what's going on here."

"Do I now?" Sid retorted. There was a threat that hung in his voice, something that made every man grow cold at the sound.

"Hold on, now," Danny spoke up. "You asked us for help. It's only fair that you let us know a little bit here."

"Starting with how you knew Tres' son would get sick," Gary added.

Sid breathed a big sigh and looked down at his hands. He seemed to be thinking carefully about his next words.

"It is true that I need your help," he began. "And that this sickness has a spiritual and supernatural origin to it. But beyond that I know very little about the character of it, where it came from, and more importantly, how we can stop it."

"What do you expect us to do then?" Malachi asked, his patience growing thin.

"I want you to help me find out these things," Sid said. "Once we find out more about it, confirm our suspicions, then we can strategize as to how we put it to an end."

"Confirm your suspicions," Danny stressed. "These aren't mine yet."

Sid nodded. "Fine. Confirm my suspicions. I know very little right now I am afraid."

"Then how can you even know that this disease has a supernatural origin?" Danny argued. His native skepticism was not willing to accept anything Sid was saying.

"I just do," Sid insisted. "I'm afraid you will just have to trust me for now. Soon, you will also see for yourselves."

Danny laughed and shook his head. Throwing up his hands he backed away from the table.

"Look, I admit, something very weird happened to me this week," he said. "I think we can all say the same thing."

Heads bobbed around the table in consent. Some murmured their continued disbelief.

"But this is something else you're asking of us," Danny continued. "You're asking us to just trust you blindly without you giving us anything, even a scrap, to prove what you're saying. Or at least tell us why you think you know this is all some supernatural evil."

"Sounds fair to me," Gary said.

"You are asking us to trust you pretty blindly," Malachi agreed. What he really wanted to say was to get the Hell out of the church and never show his face there again.

"I believe we were at this same point last week," Sid responded. "All of you asked for a sign and all of you received one."

"Damn it! We didn't mean that you put Tres' son in the hospital," Malachi spat, his anger finally boiling over. "That wasn't fair and you know it."

Sid let out another long sigh and dropped his head down. This time, he looked genuinely sympathetic. A heavy sadness descended on him that Malachi could feel. It was a weight that he knew he could never carry; one no human being should have to shoulder. He shuddered to think what could have happened to weigh the old man down like that. For the first time since he walked in the church door, Malachi felt something other than irritation or anger towards him.

"I'm sorry about your friend," the old man said. "I really am. I assure you I had nothing to do with that."

"But how did you know?" Danny asked, his voice pleading. "How did you know any of that was happening?"

"The same way the prophets of old ever knew anything," Sid answered. "By the Spirit of the living God."

"Are you saying God caused that little boy to get sick?" Vic huffed. "Cause I won't believe that for a second."

"Whether or not God caused that to happen I cannot say," Sid answered. "However, he knew it would happen. Furthermore, he allowed it to happen."

"How do you expect us to make sense of a God like that?" Danny asked.

"I wouldn't expect you to make sense of God at all," Sid replied. "If you could, he wouldn't be much of a God, now would he?"

"Okay, can I say something?" Giovanni leaned forward and asked. The normally thoughtful and taciturn man was ready to speak up.

"I think I can speak for all of us when I say we are ready to help Tres out in any way we can," Giovanni said. Heads nodded in agreement all around the table.

"But we need to know what it is we can do," he clarified. "You say you want us to help you, join your army or whatever. Well, we don't even know what that means, what that entails. Do we have to go away for some training? Leave our jobs and homes? What is it exactly we're fighting against? And how? There's just a lot of unanswered questions hanging out there and I think it's only fair that we get some answers."

Sid nodded and smiled at Giovanni. "That is quite correct," he said. "You not only deserve some answers, you need answers."

"Great," Giovanni said. "Let's hear it."

Sid shrugged. "It's not the time for those answers yet. Before we can proceed to that point there will be some things I need from you."

Malachi shook his head and stopped Sid from going any further. His patience had finally worn out.

"Look, Mr. Bickley," he began, the tension and anger clear in his voice. "We appreciate you joining us and considering us for your mission and all, but all we got from you so far is some bizarre signs and a cryptic promise to tell us things. I haven't heard anything so far saying we can trust you at all."

"You received the sign you were looking for, did you not?" Sid leveled a stare at Malachi and asked.

Malachi nodded, turning away from the penetrating gaze. "Yes, we all did. I'll admit that," he conceded. "But there was nothing in that sign that said we had to ditch all our responsibilities and run off after you."

"That's not what I am asking you to do," Sid insisted.

"What are you asking us to do?" Gary stepped in to ask. "I feel like we're talking in circles with you here. You wanted us to keep an open mind. We did. We all feel like we got some signs that this may be what we're supposed to do. But what now?"

Sid reached down and picked up the cane he carried with him. It was made if dark wood and tipped with a silver knob. Something was inscribed on the surface that Malachi couldn't quite make out. The old man held the cane as if he were about to get up and leave. Instead, he looked into the reflective surface of the silver knob, like he was probing it for answers.

"I will tell you all you need to know," he said. "I will tell you enough that you can make an informed decision about any level of involvement you may or may not want with me."

He paused and looked around the table, locking eyes with each of the men in turn.

"But there are two conditions that need to be met," he continued. "First, I need to see that all of you are ready to hear what I have to say. The things I will be telling you won't be easy to hear. Almost everything you've been raised to believe about our world, and about our history has been a lie. Some of it on accident, most of it deliberate. There is a terror and danger out there that is greater than you realize. You have been protected by your ignorance, and the fact that the individuals who hold the power in this world prefer you ignorant.

"But once I tell you what you need to know you will no longer have the protection of that ignorance. You will have stepped into a war that has been raging for centuries. You will have stepped across the battle lines and chosen a side. This will make you a target. It will make your families a target as well. I can offer you protection, and you will by no means be helpless. But the danger is grave and real."

Sid leaned forward, placing his hands on the table to emphasis his next words. "I need to know that you are ready to hear what I have to say. I need to know you are ready to have your minds blown and your lives put at great risk. I cannot tell you anything of substance until then."

"Is that it?" Vic asked, chuckling to himself.

This elicited a round of stares from everyone else at the table. Vic shrugged and laughed again.

"I think we're ready to listen," Gary said, though there was a tremor in his voice. The gravity of the situation had struck him finally.

Nods greeted the announcement. Most of the men voiced their willingness to listen.

"Most of you are ready," Sid agreed. "But not all of you."

The old man turned his icy blue eyes to the end of the table. Danny and Malachi withered under the gaze. Malachi looked down at his hands, realizing for the first time that he held them in a tight grasp. Danny leaned back in his chair and stared at the ceiling.

"I don't know," Danny said. "This just sounds so crazy. It's like a comic book or something. I mean, you seem normal and all. But what you're saying doesn't sound normal. There is a bit of cognitive dissonance I'm experiencing here and I can't just make it go away. This sounds all very suspicious and I'm trying to figure out your angle here."

"I assure you, there is no angle," Sid answered.

"Well, I just can't cut off this reasonable side of my brain and dismiss a lifetime of experience," Danny said. "I just can't ignore what they're telling me."

"And what are your experience and reason telling you?" Sid asked.

Danny smiled and shook his head. "Don't take this wrong way," he began. "But they're telling me you're a lunatic. They're telling me you have either got a touch of dementia or you've gone off your meds and you're trying to pull us into this fantasy of yours."

"Then what's the risk?" Sid asked, gesturing with his cane.

"What do you mean?" Danny asked for clarification.

"If I'm just a crazy old man then what's the risk in suspending disbelief for a moment and opening up your mind?"

"The risk?" Danny asked back, incredulity in his voice. His eyes got wide as his brow shot up in disbelief.

"The risk is that I'm gonna get fed a big, steaming pile of BS," he said. "The risk is that we might get pulled into your delusion."

"Oh, I'm sure you're too smart for that," Sid countered. "Surely, if I lay out for you my grand delusion you will be able to see right through it, and expose me as the fraud, or madman, that I am."

"Alright," Danny nodded in agreement. "You got a point there. I'll listen. But I won't be easily swayed."

Sid smiled across the table. "I would have it no other way."

"That only leaves one of you to convince," he went on to say. "But I rather think he may be a tougher nut to crack."

He looked across the table at Malachi as he said those last words. This time, Malachi was able to return the stare. He felt a wall rise up inside of him, a desire to resist this man to the very last no matter what.

"I'm afraid so," Malachi agreed.

A silent consent seemed to settle around the table. The matter had been decided as much as it could for the moment. All the men were ready to listen, except Malachi. That last little bit would have to be decided between the two of them alone.

"You said there were two things you needed," Giovanni pointed out. "You needed us to be ready to listen and something else. What was the second thing?"

Sid played with his cane again. This time, it was he who avoided the stares of the others. Malachi felt a tension rise in him. On some level he knew what Sid was about to say.

"I'm afraid this won't make me too popular," Sid began. "But I am going to need the number to be complete. I will need all seven of you."

"There's only six of us here tonight?" Danny pointed out.

"Yes, but seven of you received a sign," Sid answered. "That means seven have been chosen. We can't proceed without the full number."

Realization dawned on the men all at once.

"You can't mean Tres," Gary spoke up first.

Sid nodded. "I'm afraid so. He was given a sign. He was chosen."

"There's no way Tres can join this," Malachi said. "His son is critically ill. You know what happens when someone gets the Sleeping

Sickness. It's . . . It's a hundred percent fatal. You can't put this on Tres right now."

"He's not going to do it," Victor added, becoming serious for the moment. "There's no way he'll leave his family for this. He probably hasn't even left the hospital."

The heaviness that Malachi could feel on Sid came crashing back down on the old man. The eyes drooped and the lines on his face were suddenly deeper.

"I'm afraid your friend will be leaving the hospital soon," Sid announced gravely. "Soon, there will be nothing for him there but agonizing memories. Soon, he will be the most eager to leave everything behind and follow me."

Chapter 4 - The Funeral

It didn't take long before the message they all dreaded to hear was delivered to them. It was late Friday afternoon when the phones began to buzz, indicating a text message had come in. Each one of the Swordsmen knew what it was, each one had been expecting it all day. Over the course of the week, they had received updates about the Bettis boy and his deteriorating condition. The chances weren't good, they knew.

Even then, each of the men expected a miracle. After the signs they had received their faith had felt a renewal. They hadn't spoken of it yet, but each felt it. That surge of belief and the raw energy of new belief, the kind they hadn't felt in a long time, they felt again. The world was new. It radiated with a power that they could tell was the power that moved all things. A presence hovered close to their hearts, one full of mystery and promise; one full of hope.

This new surge of faith made the message they received all the more terrible. Miracles had become possible in the heart of the Swordsmen again. The impossible was possible. And if anyone deserved a miracle, it was four-year-old Owen Bettis.

"Swordsmen, I regret to inform you that the son of our beloved Brother Tresmond succumbed to his illness earlier this morning. Please remember him and your family in prayers. I will follow up with funeral details so we can all give him our support. Please forward me donations to help offset the medical costs the family has incurred."

One by one the message was read. One by one the men felt their dreams dashed and their faith shaken. They had never once uttered a word, even to themselves, that they had expected a miracle, but each one felt the shock of utter disappointment.

Giovanni Santos was in the middle of conducting when he felt his phone vibrate on the music stand. Normally, he wouldn't have had the device anywhere near him at this point in the day. But this week he had been expecting great news, news of a miraculous recovery.

Instead, he saw the message displayed on his home screen and felt his heart sink. The baton stopped in mid-stroke. The kids kept playing, focused on their music. One by one they noticed their conductor had stopped and the music fell silent.

Vic and Gary were at the firehouse together when they received the message. They were teaching a refresher class on emergency medicine for the circle of firefighters. For a moment, Tres and his troubles were far from their minds.

Vic pointed down to the CPR dummy lying at his feet. It was a rubber, human figure that was only a torso.

"Ok, we need to assess the victim and his condition," he said to the class. "What do we do first?"

"Check the breathing," came the answer from more than one voice.

"No," Vic said with a smile. "You find his arms and legs. I mean, look at the guy. That's his problem. His arms and legs are gone."

They had heard the joke a hundred times, but it didn't stop them all from laughing. Vic laughed along with them, always grateful when he could bring levity to the day. So much of life was so serious, so heavy, people needed some lightness to it.

Mid-laugh he felt his phone vibrate in his hand. The smile fell from his face as he locked eyes with Gary. This was one of those serious moments, the kind that weighed down men's souls. Except this would need a lot more than laughter to cure it.

Zachary Metts had just pulled off a set of brake pads when his phone vibrated in his pocket. I can't get it now, he told himself. It's because my hands are full of grease and brake dust.

Except he knew the real reason why he didn't want to read the message on his phone. He knew the words that would be written there, as surely as he could look at the uneven wear on the brake pads in his hand and tell the calipers were failing. He knew there was a message there telling him the miracle had failed.

Of all the men, Zach believed the most that a miracle was on the way. He just knew it was. His mother's voice in his head, reassuring him that with enough faith you could pray a miracle into existence. But it took a believing prayer from a righteous man.

"The reason your prayers ain't answered is one of two things," he heard her warn him once again as she had warned him countless times. "Either you ain't believing right or you ain't living right."

The words stung him as they had with every failed prayer in his life. It was his fault that the Bettis boy had died. He hadn't believed enough. He still clung to so many of the evil ways his mom had warned him of. It was his fault that Tres was going to have to bury a four-year-old son.

Danny Taylor had the opposite reaction from Victor. Instead of blaming himself, he blamed God. His phone was sitting face up on his desk while he hammered away on his computer. He continued to search diligently for the virus that had infected them the previous week, even though he knew he would find not the slightest trace of it ever being there. Still, the bosses wanted it found, so he looked.

Of all the Swordsmen, Danny had the least expectation of a miracle. He believed them, for sure, but didn't ever really expect them. Miracles were a part of the old story, maybe the old way that God interacted with the world. But his age was a more rational age, a different way of looking at and living life. God let things follow their natural course these days, allowed the laws and the forces to have their way.

Still, he couldn't help but turn his disappointment to God when he felt the phone vibrate beside him. A quick glance and he got the gist of the message. His fingers hardly paused in their work across the keyboard. Maybe a brief stumble, a mistype. Then, they continued their mad scramble in a search for data that wasn't there.

How could a God who claims he loves us let this happen, he asked himself. It was a dark thought, he knew. And though he was aware of the seriousness of such an accusation, even one in the depths of the heart, he was unaware of the contradiction it created in his belief system. If he believed in a God of natural law who didn't intervene in the world, how could he be disappointed when this God failed to act in the world?

For the time being, these contradictions coexisted peacefully. It was a lot like the contradiction of him working so hard on a solution he knew couldn't be found. Life can be a bundle of contradictions sometimes, or so it seems. The less we realize the better. But at some point, they will collide, and one or both will be destroyed. Sometimes they will destroy an entire world in the process.

While Danny worked away, unaware of the bundle of contradictions within him, he was also unaware of the collision course upon which they were set. Soon, these mutually exclusive ideas would shatter themselves against each other in a reckoning that was closer than he realized. Soon, his world would be destroyed, and Danny would have to begin the fretful work of rebuilding it all over again.

Of all the men who received the news of Owen Bettis' death, only Malachi thought to blame Sid Bickley. He was the first to receive the news. It came in a tearful call from Tres, informing Malachi of what had just happened. After hanging up, he walked across the parking lot of Medical Park Three to the main hospital, up to the ICU, where Owen had just breathed his last.

Malachi embraced his brother in faith as the man wept inconsolable tears. He knew there was nothing he could say, no words that could possibly touch this pain that Tres was feeling. He was helpless to do anything but stand with his friend.

So that's what Malachi did. He stood by, silent and unmoving, as his friend wept and cried out to his God. His wife, Grace, was there with her mother and her family. Unspoken questions lingered in the air, wondering where God was, how He could let this happen. A still more powerful question stirred within: how can we ever survive this moment? It pushed the very edge of human endurance and strength. The whole world was upturned with this one act. What should never happen had happened, and life would never be the same.

Hours later, when Malachi left the family alone to their grief, he sent the text to the Swordsmen, letting them know the awful news. As he sent the message, Malachi burned with a different type of anger, asked himself a different kind of question. His rage was directed at the mysterious man who, in Malachi's estimation, had started all of this.

After all, none of this had started until Sid Bickley showed up at their meeting. With his cryptic talk of dark powers and the will of God, promising signs and asking them to join his army. If he wasn't crazy then Malachi was certain the man was eaten up with pride. Probably a little bit of both.

Of course, Malachi had no idea how the man actually was responsible for all this. The Sleeping Sickness had begun ravaging the country about three months ago, and had reached the Tri-Cities by late March. Now, at the end of May it had claimed yet another victim. Certainly, Sid didn't cause the disease, and the rational part of Malachi acknowledged this. But he couldn't help draw the conclusion that it hadn't hit his circle until Sid showed up. The man was guilty by association.

A good part of his anger was directed at himself. He had let the snake into the garden. Despite his misgivings and the warnings that went off in his head, he still let the man join their group that night. He was the leader of the group and was ultimately responsible for what went on within, especially what was let in. Just as he irrationally blamed Sid for the Sleeping Sickness, he blamed himself for letting Sid infiltrate his group.

The funeral for four-year old Owen Bettis was held Sunday afternoon. Everyone there told themselves it was one the saddest things they had ever experienced. The church was full to bursting. From family to friends, from school mates and their parents to acquaintances of the family, everyone who had the slightest contact with Owen and his parents crowded into the church that Sunday afternoon.

The only one who was determined not to be there was Grace Bettis, the child's mother. Five minutes after the service was supposed to begin Grace sat in a chair in the church foyer, determined not to budge. The family waited nervously by the doors, waiting for their time to march in together. Tres was on his knees, pleading with his wife.

"We have to go in there," he said, his voice near to breaking.

"Why do I have to go in there?" she asked, saying "there" like it was a poisoned word.

"Because, we're laying our son to rest and I can't do it without you." He reached out to grip his wife's hands but she jerked them away.

"That is not my son in there," she insisted, pointing to the closed sanctuary doors. "I don't know who it is they cremated, but that is not our son. Do you hear me?"

"Please don't do this," Tresmond plead, his voice finally cracking. He buried his face in his wife's lap.

Grace seemed not to feel his touch. She turned her head away and looked towards the wall. Her mother broke off from the crowd of family and reached out towards her.

"Baby, we got to go. You hear me, it's time," she said.

"I don't have to go anywhere," Grace shot back. "Because my son isn't dead."

"How can you say that?" Tres asked, welling deep in his grief. "You heard the doctor. You know what he said."

"I'm his mother and I know," she said, her voice breaking for the first time. "You won't understand because you didn't carry him in your body, then feed him from your body. OK?! Tres, you don't know. But I do. I'm his mother and I know!"

These last words echoed through the foyer and out into the sanctuary beyond. The sanctuary doors opened and a concerned face peered in. The funeral home director stepped up to the family and gave them his nod. It was time to go in.

"Fine. Fine," Tres said as he stood up and straightened his jacket. "I'm going in there and saying goodbye to our boy. And I'm going to do it alone. You're going to regret sitting in here and not taking this chance. You hear me? You'll regret this. But I'm not going to listen to you bitch and cry when you realize what you've done."

He snapped his coat straight and turned around to join the family. With a nod from the funeral director, they took their places. The sanctuary doors were opened and the organ music swelled to the sounds of "A Mighty Fortress is our God." Tresmond and the family disappeared down the aisle as the congregation stood in honor and solidarity.

The doors closed and Grace Bettis was left alone in the foyer. Left to herself she let her grief in and she dropped her head to weep. Sobs wracked her as she tried to stifle the tears. She pressed a tissue to her face, as if she could stop the flow through force.

"Mrs. Bettis," a voice said to her as she bent down to cry.

She quickly straightened and looked up into the face of a handsome, elderly gentleman. He was well dressed in a dark suit and carried himself with an air of otherworldly confidence. Bright, blue eyes looked into hers as she saw instant understanding and sympathy.

"I'm sorry, I'm not going in," she said, mistaking the man for one of the funeral directors.

"Why aren't you going in?" he asked. "This is a service for your son, is it not?"

She grimaced and shook her head. "I don't care if you think I'm crazy, but my boy isn't dead. Those are not his ashes in there."

"I don't think you're crazy at all," the old man said, and Grace believed he meant it. It was the first person she had said this too that didn't immediately dismiss her as being mad with grief.

"Tell me," he said. "Why do you think your son still lives?"

She tried to wave him away. "I don't know. Maybe I am crazy."

The old man caught her hand and knelt beside her. Blue eyes that were soft a moment ago suddenly seemed intense and urgent. She found she couldn't look away.

Dimly, she felt her hand being lifted. The man began to speak, his voice deep and resonating all the way into her chest. Hands stroked the top of hers, drawing her into immediate relaxation. The weight of the last few days began to melt away.

"Mrs. Bettis," he said. "My name is Sid Bickley. I want to help you, but first you need to help me. Can you help me, Mrs. Bettis?"

That sense of deep relaxation washed over her until she felt she might even fall asleep. It was nice to be in such a strong and comforting presence. For a moment, the world even started to make a little more sense.

"Call me Grace," she said as her eyelids felt heavy.

Malachi and the Swordsmen sat in a pew halfway down the church. As the music began, they stood, watching the family process down the aisle. As Tres passed, he locked eyes with Malachi and reached out to take a comforting hand from him before continuing on to the front pews reserved for the family.

Every one of the Swordsmen had noticed that Grace was absent from the procession. Danny mouthed a question to Malachi which was answered with a shrug of the shoulders. They, along with the rest of the crowded church had heard the outburst from the foyer. Whatever was going on with Tres' wife, it was serious enough that she was going to miss her own son's funeral.

The congregation sat down as the preacher took to the pulpit to begin the service. It was a heavy service, the weight of a thousand unanswered questions swirling around. Even the opening scripture, a passage from Second Corinthians, urged the people to walk by faith and not by sight. There were questions that could not be answered, or at least answered by the human mind. Times like this would require faith.

As surprised as he was that Grace did not process with the family, Malachi was even more surprised when she walked in ten minutes later. Just as the pastor was concluding his opening remarks, the sanctuary doors opened up. Grace walked down the aisle, escorted by the slim and dignified figure of Sid Bickley.

Malachi whipped his head towards the other Swordsmen. A question was hissed out that everyman was thinking. Why the Hell was Sid Bickley escorting Grace Bettis down the aisle? When did he even get here?

No one knew the answer, and so they watched in silence as the two made their way to the front of the church. Sid looked straight ahead, his aristocratic features showing no discomfort at the scrutiny from every eye in the church, even the pastor. Grace held her head up high, a look of defiance on her thin features. She looked austere that day, though finely dressed in a black skirt. Her look was one who would suffer with endurance, and not let the suffering wear her down in the slightest.

She hugged Sid as the older man led her to the seat beside her husband. Tres looked surprised to see them both, then reached out a grateful hand towards Sid. The two shook with unspoken gravity and Sid walked to the back of the church where he stood for the remainder of the service.

All through the service Malachi could feel Sid's eyes boring into his back. He didn't know how he knew, but he was sure of it. The man was here to torment him. One time he even turned around to check. Sure enough, the icy blue eyes were looking right at him. Malachi felt accusation in that stare, or maybe it was a challenge. Whatever it was it only stirred up Malachi's suspicion and hatred of the man even more.

What was he doing here, Malachi thought to himself? Did he really think this was a good time to show up and prod the men towards his little quest?

What disturbed Malachi even more was seeing Tres' reaction to Sid. It should have been anger, outrage, for the intrusion. Instead, Tres actually looked grateful, thankful to see the man who had predicted his son's death. Not in so many words, but they all knew what he meant. What could possibly be going on in Tres' mind? Was he just delusional with grief?

Malachi wasn't sure, but what he was sure of was that he had to protect Tres and the rest of the group from this viper that had made his way into their midst. They might not see the danger, but he did. Even if it took everything in him, Malachi would not let this cryptic, old man tear them apart and lead them right to the gates of Hell.

"Not on my watch," he muttered, too low for anyone to hear.

After the service, the family filed down to the parlor to receive guests. The room was packed. Men in dark suits and women in dresses squeezed together in a line that wrapped around the whole room. They spoke in guarded whispers, careful that any sounds of joy might not reach the grieving family. The pungent aroma of flowers, wafting from no less than a dozen arrangements suffocated the room along with the crowds.

Much to Malachi's disappointment, Sid hung around long after the funeral was over. The Swordsmen formed their own contingent in the parlor, standing off to the side as the condolence givers filed past. Sid stood near them, but not with them. His eyes watched the lines with keen interest, looking for something only he saw.

As Sid watched the people Malachi watched him. He looked as if he could unlock the mystery of Sid Bickley simply by looking. While he stared, he silently wished him away, that he would leave them alone, at least for today. But the older man gave no sign of moving and no sign that he even tired in the least. He stood alone, watching the crowd, back perfectly erect and features still, belying a hidden strength. The longer Sid loitered, the more aggravated Malachi became.

It wasn't until the line of visitors had dwindled that Sid moved in the least. When the last of the condolence givers had expressed his sympathy, the last hand shaken, the last thanks given, the family was left alone with Sid and the Swordsmen. The funeral director came over with his last set of instructions, and so commenced that awkward moment when there was nothing left for the family to do but try and go back to their lives.

As soon as he was done with the funeral director, Tres locked eyes with the Swordsmen across the parlor and made his way towards them. Malachi could quickly see, though, that he was wasn't heading towards him, but towards Sid.

"I want to thank you again," Tres said, holding his hand out to the older man. "Whatever you said to my wife . . . for getting her in there."

"I didn't want her to regret not being there," Sid answered, taking the offered hand.

"Yeah, I said the same thing to her. Didn't seem to help."

"Sometimes words that come from an unfamiliar source are better received. It's just human nature." Sid shrugged at his own observation.

Tres turned to thank all the Swordsmen in turn. He embraced Malachi and expressed his heartfelt gratitude. Malachi could feel the tears begin to well up in his friend, but took hold of his composure again.

"So," Tres began after an awkward silence. "Mr. Bickley, is that offer still good? Do you still want our help?"

Malachi was floored by what he had just heard. It took a moment to shake the confusion from his head. Was he serious? Malachi couldn't see how Tres didn't completely deck the old man, much less take up his offer to join some insane quest.

"Tres, is that a good idea?" Malachi interjected before Sid could answer.

"I think it is," Tresmond nodded. He looked over at Malachi and he could see the that he was dead serious. Every bit of intensity that he possessed, the kind that made him such an inspiration to others was coiled and waiting for an excuse to be unleashed.

"Let's talk about this later why don't we?" Danny suggested, stepping in to Malachi's way of thinking. "You go home and get some rest and we'll talk about it later."

"I don't want to talk about it later and I certainly don't want to sit around my house and just think about this."

"But Tres, you just . . ." Malachi started to say. He found he couldn't finish the thought.

"I just what?" Tres asked. Malachi could hear the pain in his voice. "I just buried my son? Was that what you were going to say?"

"You need to grieve with your family," Malachi said. "They need you right now."

"My family was broken when my boy died," Tres answered. "My wife thinks he's still alive. The house is empty. And all I've got is the guilt of knowing I couldn't save him. You know what that feels like, Malachi? I'm his dad. I'm supposed to be able to protect him from shit like this. And I failed."

"You didn't fail," Vic reached out to say.

Tres jerked away from the comforting hand. His eyes held a challenge that no one wanted to meet at the moment.

"Maybe there was nothing I could have done," Tresmond said. "But there was more I could have done."

"You don't think that this might be a bad time?" Malachi asked as a last-ditch attempt to sway him. "Maybe wait for this to settle down."

"I don't want to wait," Tres said. He turned to face the gathered men. "Listen, ever since my boy died, I have been sitting around wondering what I have going for my life now that he's dead. Grace hasn't talked to me since Owen died. Work sounds like the stupidest the thing in the world for me to do. There's only one thing I can think of that will keep me going right now: find the sons of bitches who did this to my boy and make them pay."

His voice cracked at the last and tears pooled in his eyes. He turned away and took a deep breath to compose himself.

"It's all I've got," he said, his voice muffled as he buried it in his hands. "I got nothing else right now. Nothing at all."

Despair at his own helplessness stunned Malachi into silence. It was clear there was nothing he could say that would sway his friend. He was consumed with grief and rage right now, and they were both helpless feelings. At that moment he scrambled for somewhere to direct them.

"I don't think this is the answer," Malachi said. He looked over at Sid who was regarding him quietly. Throughout the whole exchange the old man hadn't uttered a word, but simply let the argument run itself out.

"Can we really believe anything he has to say?"

If Sid was offended by Malachi's challenge, he didn't show it. Somehow, that quiet calm only further infuriated Malachi further.

Tres turned back around and pointed at Sid. "So far, he's the only one that has any answers at all. And I've talked to everyone I could about this. Guess what? Nobody knows a damn thing. Nothing! The doctors don't know anything, the nurses don't know. I've talked to reporters, they don't know. I've talked to the Health Department, they don't know. I've even talked to the CDC and you what they told me? We have no idea. Not in so many words, but that's what it amounts to. Nobody knows anything.

"He's the only one that knows a thing. Maybe he's full of shit. I don't know. But I've got nothing else to go on. I've got nothing else to do. And if he gives me even the slightest chance of doing this one last thing for my boy, then I'm going to take it, and I will push aside anyone who tries to get in my way.

"And when it's over. If I'm still walking and breathing when it's over, I'm going to lock myself in a room and weep for my boy and never come out again."

Sid nodded and reached out to touch Tresmond's shoulder. "I accept your offer of help," he said. "But understand that this quest is not a quest of revenge. It is the reckoning we are after."

Tres threw up his hands in resignation. "Whatever you say, Mr. Bickley."

He turned back to the Swordsmen and wrapped them in his arms until they formed an impromptu huddle in the middle of the parlor. He looked each of them in the eye, sharing with them his contagious intensity.

"I'm going to do this thing," he said to them. "If Mr. Bickley over there can help me, then so be it. If he turns out to be crazy then I'm on my own. Either way, I'm doing it.

"What I want to know is if you're with me. I'll do it alone if I have to. But I want my brothers with me. I'm stronger with you. I know that for I fact. I need you. If you want, I'll get on my knees and beg."

Tears pooled again in Tresmond's eyes as he made his plea. The corners of his mouth trembled, battling the well of emotion. Malachi could feel the effect on every man in that circle. He knew what they were feeling because he saw his own emotions written clearly in their faces. There was no way they could refuse Tres when he laid it out like that. Against all of his better judgement, it looked like they were going to take this leap in the dark. And heaven help them, the only one to catch them would be Mr. Sid Bickley.

Chapter 5 - The Keeper

Sid Bickley lived in the historic part of town. Back among the neighborhoods that were built when the city was young and land was abundant, his was one that still possessed a sprawling yard and tall trees that spread shade out through their abundant branches, and roots that buckled the sidewalks. It was back far enough from the road that it could be easily missed, but once noticed, it stood out.

"That's a beautiful Queen Anne," Danny remarked as he pulled up outside the front with Malachi.

The mansion suited the man, Malachi thought to himself. The brick was faded with ivy crawling up its sides. The conical tower on the left side of the house gave it an asymmetrical feel. A deep porch with ornate metal carvings along its border cast a shadow over the front door. It was large and mysterious, just like the man who lived there.

Malachi let his eyes flow over the complex design, taking it all in. The gables and roof lines looked erratic, sprouting all over. Parts of the house jutted out, others sunk back, betraying a complex floor plan that one could easily get lost in. He gave up trying to determine exactly how big the house was. Like everything else about this endeavor, they would just have to trust Sid.

Danny sighed, feeling every bit of Malachi's trepidation himself. "So, you ready to do this?"

Without answering the two men got out and stepped through the iron gates and towards the porch. Old boards creaked beneath their feet, some so old they promised to buckle under the weight. A musty smell overwhelmed them, the lingering scent of neglect and long years untended. Malachi could even sense a sadness, or a longing coming from the bricks. This house had gone a long time since it had felt happy days.

The door opened before Malachi could knock. A tall man looked down at them, white hair slicked back over his head. He wore a dark suit and a decidedly neutral feature to his face. It was the look of a classic butler.

"Greetings gentlemen," he said in a deep and powerful voice. Malachi couldn't help but think of Lurch from the Adams Family. He pushed back the smile that wanted to break out.

"Master Bickley is waiting with the others," the butler said and stepped back to allow the men entrance.

Malachi and Danny were ushered through a house as antique on the inside as it was on the outside. Dark, hardwood floors sounded echoes from their steps. Wide moldings framed the doorways and windows. Furniture that proclaimed "old money", representing a variety of eras in their craftsmanship, decorated the rooms that the butler guided them through.

Despite its wealth, Malachi couldn't help but the feel the weight of sadness and neglect. The rooms smelled of dust and cleaner. It was obvious they had lain neglected for many years, and just now aired out and spruced up.

"Gentlemen, welcome," Sid greeted from the head of a long dining room table.

The other Swordsmen were already seated there. They nodded their heads in greeting as Malachi and Danny were guided to the last seats that were set. Malachi noted the real silver utensils and the China dishes that were placed at each seat as if they were preparing for a seven-course dinner.

"Thank you, Gerard," Sid said to the butler as he excused himself.

"Gerard has served the Keepers for many years," Sid noted when the butler was gone. "He will also be at your service as well."

"How quaint, you have servants in your house." Danny observed. There was noticeable disdain for the word servant. "Do you have a lot of servants."

"Do you mind if I smoke?" Sid asked, ignoring the question. Without waiting for an answer, he produced a cigarette and silver lighter and had blown out a first puff of smoke.

"Does it offend you that I have servants?" he looked to Danny and asked. "Are you that egalitarian that it hurts your feelings to see one man serve another."

Danny picked up a silver knife and twirled it between his thumb and finger. "What offends me is the idea that one man can think of himself so highly as to want to put other men beneath him."

Sid smiled, strangely amused by the comment. "I think you misunderstand service and servants altogether," he said.

"Really?" Danny laughed. "And what would you know about being a servant? Looks like you're lord of the manor."

"I know more than you might think." Sid pulled on the cigarette and let the smoke out slowly. "Let's not assume, shall we?"

At that moment Malachi knew exactly where Danny was coming from. His first assessment of Sid as an old aristocrat was only confirmed by being in his home. The old house, the antique furniture, the real silver and China dinner sets; it all screamed old world money and old-world values. Even Sid himself, arrogant and proud, looking down at everyone and everything with an air of superiority, spoke of an old-world attitude. It was clear he had come from a world of classes, with his class standing firmly on the top.

"Well, all I know is that there better be some Grey Poupon up in here," Vic chimed in, breaking the tension with his unusual brand of humor.

The table laughed, happy to break the serious tone it had taken. As they enjoyed the light hearted moment Gerard returned, pushing a serving table. Delicious smells wafted from the bowls arranged along its surface. Sid stubbed out his cigarette and sat up in his chair.

As if cued by some knowledge of their conversation, Gerard served Danny first. A knowing look passed between him and Sid, nothing more than a slight smile. Danny reddened as he watched the bowl of soup ceremoniously placed in front of him, knowing some sort of joke had been had at his expense.

After the soup was served there came a salad, then a course of roast beef and steamed vegetables. Sorbet was presented after the main course followed by a glass of brandy. Conversation around the table was trivial and deliberately avoided any reference to why the men were there at all. On the far end, Tres ate in silence, gathering about him a tension that every man at the table could feel, but none acknowledged.

When he received his glass of brandy, Sid thanked Gerard and leaned back in his chair. Producing the silver lighter, he lit another cigarette and looked over the men at the table. A silence settled over them, an unspoken cue that the light hearted moment had ended and it was time to entertain more serious topics.

"I want to thank all of you for your trust and faith in coming here today," Sid told the men. "I know it wasn't easy for all of you."

He looked over and fixed his eyes on Malachi and Danny sitting together.

"I wanted you to come here because this house has been a base of operations for my organization for quite some time," he continued after taking another pull off his cigarette. "It's very important to what we do.

You may notice that the architecture is late Victorian, but the house has older sections that go back much farther. In fact, the original house was built in . . ."

"Can we skip the history lesson," Tresmond interrupted.

Every eye at the table turned to the other end where Tres sat. He had been so quiet during dinner that he had been forgotten. All through the small talk of dinner he had suffered in silence. Now, he had reached the end of his patience. He glared across the table at Sid, eyes ringed with dark circles and red from little sleep. He still held his dinner fork in his hand, as if he planned on using it as a weapon.

"I apologize for what may seem like rambling to you," Sid remarked with a nod towards Tres. "But I assure you, this is all necessary."

"Why don't you just tell me who is responsible for killing my son and we go take care of it?" Tresmond asked.

"Because that would be the one thing to guarantee our failure," Sid answered.

"Just tell us what we need to know, then."

"These are things you need to know."

Tres shook his head in disgust. "I don't need to know a damn thing about your house. It's a big house. It's old. Let's move on."

Sid nodded and stubbed out his cigarette. Reaching into his jacket he removed another but did not light it. He nodded again, silently considering his next words.

"I know this must be difficult to you," he began.

"You don't know shit about what I'm going through," Tres cut him off. "So don't pretend like you do."

Sid gave him a tight-lipped smile. "Let's not assume, shall we?" he requested again. "About what I know or don't know.

"All of you listen and hear me well. I am about to tell you something that will challenge everything you believe about life and the world we live in. I am about to challenge everything you believe about what is possible and impossible. Your world will never be the same and you will never be the same. These are things the average man cannot hear. For if he knew the extent of the truth, he would not be able to carry on with his regular life.

"All of you have been called here for a different purpose, for a higher purpose. You will know things most men will never know and do things most only dream of. But in order for that to happen there are some things you must first know. If we go charging in with our old assumptions and beliefs about the world, we are dead before we begin. Do you understand that Mr. Bettis?"

Tres didn't answer. He continued his silent and angry glare across the table.

"Before you can have your vengeance you must learn a few things and acquire some new skills," Sid continued, unperturbed. "That will require some patience of you. But I cannot help you without that patience. Do you understand that Mr. Bettis? I need to at least get a nod from you that you do."

"Fine," Tres said. "I'll listen. If you can stick to what is important, and pertinent."

"Agreed," Sid nodded. "If you will acknowledge that I am the only one in this instance that knows what is important and pertinent."

Tres threw his fork down to the table with a clatter and sat back in his chair. "Let's do it then."

Sid nodded and tapped his cigarette on the surface of the table and lifted it to his mouth. The silver lighter clicked and a puff of smoke circled his head.

"When I first heard what I am about to tell you," Sid began. "I was twenty-two years old and in an Irish prison. I was facing a charge of murder and was scheduled to be hanged."

"Murder?" Zach asked. The mechanic looked like he wanted to bolt for the door.

"Yes, murder," Sid confirmed, nodding his head.

"Who did you kill?" Danny asked.

"The son of William McDonnell, sixth Earl of Antrim," he answered. Danny nodded. "Was it a duel?" he asked. "A matter of honor?"

"Yes, it was a duel," Sid answered. "And it was a matter of honor. But not what you suspect?"

"You mean it wasn't two aristocrats bickering over a perceived insult?" Danny shot.

That weight that Malachi had sensed on Sid came over the old man again. Something in the memory of what he was telling them put a heavy burden on him. It was a place, he could tell, that Sid did not visit often in his memory.

"No, it wasn't two aristocrats bickering over insults," Sid told them as he tapped the ashes off his cigarette. "The younger William, a viscount in his own right, had seduced my sister and gotten her pregnant. It would be a scandal for them as our family were employed as servants in the McDonnel house."

Sid looked over at Danny as he revealed his parentage. Danny could not meet that gaze, but looked instead at his brandy glass.

"To cover up his indiscretion the young viscount took my sister to a butcher that promised to remove the baby from her womb. In delivering that promise he not only removed the baby but killed my sister. Everyone was willing to move on and pretend it didn't happen. Everyone but me."

The story draped a pall over the room that had every man rapt with attention.

"So yes, I challenged him to a duel over a matter of honor. I had the misfortune of being a much better shot than the viscount. He winged me in the shoulder. My shot went straight through his head. Later that day I was arrested and given a speedy trial in which I was forbidden to speak a word in my defense and then sentenced to hang. It took all of three days to happen."

Danny scoffed, shaking his head in disgust. "That's the reason I hate the idea of servants and lords," he spat. "This kind of crap happens all the time. The powerful get to walk free no matter what."

"You have a point," Sid nodded. "But the reason for my hasty trial and hanging had nothing to do with the privilege of Antrim.

"The law was actually quite favorable to me as we had suitable witnesses to confirm the legality of our duel. And the Earl truly was an honorable man and would not have had me arrested in a fair fight. No, the person that was being protected in my hasty trial was not the young viscount, it was the butcher who killed my sister."

A shocked silence greeted this strange revelation. The men looked to each other, every one of them equally confused. None more so than Danny.

"Wait, are you trying to tell us that you were being hanged to protect some back-alley abortion doctor?" Danny asked incredulously.

"You see what I mean about challenging your world view?" Sid said through a puff of smoke. "After I had killed the viscount, I was getting ready to leave for Belfast to find that charlatan of a doctor who performed these back-alley abortions. That was the real reason why I was arrested."

"That doesn't make any sense," Gary said, speaking up. "Surely that doctor was operating illegally."

"Yes, by the letter of the law, he was," Sid told them. "But this was the moment when I was told that the world did not operate under the rules that I thought it did. Even the men I thought were in charge, men like the Earl, were not really in charge at all. Even the Queen, or Parliament in London were not the ones that held the strings of power. No, it was men like the back-alley butcher who killed my sister that were the real powers of the world."

The sense of confusion only intensified around the table. Malachi wasn't sure what to make of what Sid was saying. Since when did a back-alley butcher wield any power except fear and intimidation?

"Am I the only one confused here?" Giovanni asked to a chorus of head nods. "What kind of power did this doctor have?"

"This doctor was no ordinary man," Sid continued. "In fact, he was not a man at all. He was what we call an Elioud."

"What's an Elioud?" Vic asked.

"An Elioud is a child born from the sexual union of a human being, usually a woman, and a supernatural creature known as the Fae."

"Wait? What?" Giovanni asked. "Fae? Aren't those fairies?"

"Yes," Sid nodded. "They have been known by many names. Fae, Sidhe, Tuatha De Dannan, Dannae, Dagda, sprites, elves, lios alfar, and fairies among them."

"Fairies?" Vic questioned with a chuckle. "Is this Tinkerbell we're up against?"

Sid turned a decidedly unamused look in Victor's direction. The normally irrepressible humor was immediately quenched.

"I assure you; they are nothing like the fairies that Disney has portrayed to you in their children's cartoons," Sid warned him. "These are powerful creatures, capricious, unpredictable, and dangerous. Not all of them are evil, but not all think very kindly of human beings. Some help, some hurt. But in one way or another, all of them feed off of mankind. And that includes their Elioud offspring."

Another round of silence greeted this announcement as the men digested what they just heard. It was, as Sid promised, something that would challenge their view of life and the world around them.

Giovanni leaned forward. "So, this . . . doctor that killed your sister, he was an Elioud? A hybrid," he asked.

Sid nodded. "Yes."

"And he had the influence, or connections to see that you were arrested and hung before you could come after him?"

"He did."

"Okay," Giovanni said. "My question is why he was so worried about you? I mean, if he was so powerful, then why didn't he just decide to off you when you showed up?"

"He wasn't scared that I would hurt him," Sid pointed out. "This butcher was worried I would expose him. You see, before I went after the doctor, I made the mistake of telling everyone I was going to expose him for the killer that he was. I was going to report him to the authorities, shame him before his neighbors, then drag him through the streets of Belfast before I strangled him with my own two hands.

"Granted, I could little accomplish any of these things. But I was 22 years old and beyond the reach of sense, especially when my anger was up. This doctor, though he knew I was no physical threat to him, did not want his practice exposed. It meant a lot to him and he was doing good business those days. The last thing he wanted to see happen was some upstart son of servant force him to flee and set up elsewhere."

"I'm scared to ask," Vic began. "But why did this abortion practice mean so much to him? I hope it was because it made him a lot of money."

"It wasn't money he was after," Sid told them, a profound sadness in his voice.

Malachi felt a fear around the table to ask the question they all wanted to know but didn't want to know at the same time. But it had to be asked.

"What was he after?" Malachi asked in a trembling voice.

"You know when I said that the Elioud and Fae all feed off of mankind," Sid told them. "Many of the horror stories told about creatures eating people are true stories. Some painfully true."

"I think I'm going to be sick," Danny said, pushing himself away from the table.

A dark and desperate look had come upon Tresmond's features. He stared at Sid from across the table, his eyes wide and manic. Hands gripped the tablecloth, threatening to tear into it.

"That is not what happened to your son," Sid assured him. "Of that I am quite certain."

Everyone seemed to remember at once what was at stake. They turned to regard Tres whose face was racked with the conflict of pain.

"How do you know?" he asked in a trembling voice.

"I know because the Elioud are the only ones who feed directly off of people like that," Sid informed them. "Stories of vampires, monsters, werewolves, even succubi are almost all based on Elioud who feed on flesh and blood and . . . well other ways to feed off of people.

"The Fae on the other hand use other methods. They feed off of the essence of man, and they prefer to keep them alive."

"Wait, wait, I'm confused," Danny complained, interrupting the explanation. "Why do they have to feed off of us in the first place? And what is this essence they're stealing? And where do these creatures even come from?"

"They don't have to feed off of us," Sid clarified. "They choose to."

"Fine, why do they choose to?"

"To require that would require a demonstration rather than a lesson," Sid explained. "One that I hope to give you tonight.

"For now, I want you to start to realize what we are up against. The Elioud I was threatening was fairly low level in the hierarchy, but he had enough pull to have me arrested and sentenced to die. I was only saved when a man came to me and offered me a way out, as well as a chance at revenge. But in order to have that I would have to abandon everything I believed about the world as I am asking you to abandon everything you believe about the world. It will be much harder for you than it was for me I am afraid. The world I grew up in still believed strongly in spirits and spells and magic. Yours is a much more rational and materialistic one. I am afraid you are going to have to stretch a little bit."

"You're not that old, are you?" Gary asked. "You look about my dad's age."

"Remember, it was rural Ireland where I grew up," Sid pointed out. "And it was very long ago."

"How long exactly are we talking about?" Malachi asked, not sure he wanted to know the answer to this either.

"When I killed the viscount, I was twenty-two years old, and the year was 1877."

Another stunned silence greeted this announcement. It only lasted a moment and was broken when Danny snorted in disdain.

"You expect us to believe that?" he asked incredulously.

"I told you we were going to stretch that mind of yours," Sid promised.

"Yeah. But this?" he scoffed. "C'mon. If you were twenty-two in

1877 that means you were born in 1855."

Sid nodded but did not respond.

"Seriously?" Danny asked. "That would make you . . . 168 years old."

"167," Sid corrected. "My birthday isn't until September."

"Oh, well pardon me," Danny mocked. "Only 167. That makes a big difference."

"Well, you don't look a day over 160," Victor joked. He winked at Sid and held up his brandy glass in toast.

The table groaned and chuckled all at once. Giovanni balled up his napkin and hurled it across the table at him.

"Do you really expect us to believe this?" Danny asked. His mild skepticism had turned to open denial. "I know I said I would listen and I did. But frankly, I don't believe any of this at all."

"Are you saying he's making it all up?" Gary challenged. "He's lying?"

"I didn't say that," Danny was quick to interject. "Maybe he believes everything that is coming out of his mouth. I'm just saying that I don't"

"I don't expect you to believe any of what I have said at present," Sid told them as he stood up from the table. "For now, I only want to prepare your minds so that the shock is not too great all at once. Tonight, I will show you.

"Gerard will show you your rooms."

He turned to leave while the table watched in silence, too stunned from the revelations to say anything further. There was something about Sid's behavior that Malachi found extremely credible, though he couldn't put his finger on it. Maybe it was the way he presented his story, nothing like the crazy people he had dealt with in the past. The crazies always had a certain detachment from reality in Malachi's opinion. It was a whole package deal.

This wasn't Sid at all. He was rational, calm, collected; maybe too calm. Most of all he didn't seem to care at all what the other men thought of him. He only wanted to convince them enough to employ their help. Whatever opinion the men held of him didn't seem to matter to Sid in the slightest. And that is what Malachi found most believable of all - and frightening.

"Did you get your revenge?" someone asked Sid as Gerard held the dining room door open for him.

Sid stopped and turned to see who had asked him. It was Tres. The older man took a few more steps into the room to address the grieving father.

"I did," Sid told him gravely. "On November fifth, 1929 I snuck up on him at a rally in Germany. It was for a new, up and coming political party called the Nazis. I stuck a blade between his ribs and dragged him into an alley where he could bleed out slow and alone, contemplating his damnation before the judgement seat of God."

"That's a long time to wait for revenge," Tres noted.

Sid nodded. "It was. But I was not ready then for what I truly faced. I urge you patience, Mr. Bettis. Let's do this right and you will have satisfaction."

Sid turned and continued out of the room. He stopped and placed a hand on the doorway, turning his head to say one last thing.

"But by then it wasn't revenge I was after," he said. "It was justice."

Chapter 6 - Soulfire

After Sid departed Gerard returned to show the men to their rooms. They followed the servant to the north end of the house, through a twisting array of rooms and hallways that had the men completely lost in no time. The mansion was even larger than it looked from the road.

A spiral staircase on the other side of the kitchen took them to a hallway with rooms on either side. They were small and sparsely furnished. Each one held a bed, a chair, a writing table, dresser, wardrobe and stand with a bowl. A window in each room opened to pleasant gardens where the early summer burst vitality in a play of green life.

"Are these the servants' quarters?" Danny scoffed when he looked in at the sparse accommodations.

"No. The servants' quarters are the two floors below you," he pointed out, unperturbed. "These are the swordsmen quarters."

"Twelve rooms," Gary pointed out, counting six in either side of the hallway. "Are there supposed to more of us?"

"These are the just the quarters in the Keeper's house," Gerard told him. "When they must occupy the house for some reason. Sometimes a number stays on permanently for protection. But usually, they keep their own homes."

"Are there usually more of us?" he asked.

"The number of swordsmen has varied over the years. At one time we had as many as three-hundred worldwide. For the last thirty years we have had . . . none."

The men looked around the hallway that suddenly seemed much emptier than it was. Ghosts of happier, more prosperous times rose up. They could feel the presence of the hundreds of lives that had passed through there, slept there, hoped there. Voices, just out of range of their hearing, echoed the countless conversations that has rung through the halls.

"What happened?" Vic asked, awed by the enormity of the legacy that had just been passed down to him.

"It's a long story," Gerard answered. "But men's souls have grown weaker, more frail. They have become lost in the numerous distractions that your world offers. There are very few alive today that can take up the sword."

The butler sighed and reached out to touch the walls. Regret and longing mingled in that touch as he looked to reach out to a past filled with mistakes that could never be taken back.

"But that is a story Sid will tell you," he concluded before turning away. "There are bathrooms on either side of the hall. Take this time to rest and clean up. I will come get you just before sunset."

True to his promise, Gerard returned just as the sun was beginning to dip in the sky. A rich, golden hue had taken over the clear blue. Long shadows cast themselves over the garden as the day faded into the dim glow of twilight.

Malachi tried to rest, unsure of what the night held, or how long it would take. He lay down on the small, single bed, his arms resting beneath him. The musty smell of the room, full of the neglect of the years, was strong enough to be oppressive. The window opened with a few tugs, and fresh, garden air floated in.

Even then, he found sleep impossible. His mind reeled and whirled with the revelations of the day. Like Danny, he found it all but impossible to believe. But Sid had seemed unbothered by that and promised to prove it to them this evening. That prospect sent Malachi's heart racing with trepidation. What could possibly prove all these wild claims of fae and elioud, spirits and demons? As a Christian he had always claimed to believe in spirits and angels, and even demons were a part of the biblical canon. But to see that these things existed? Malachi was more than happy to confine them to a different level of reality, one to which he was not privy.

That was what bothered Malachi the most, though he only just admitted this to himself. He was an organized man that enjoyed an organized world. Everything had its place and purpose, and clear boundaries were set dividing things into the places where they belonged. Boundaries were good. They were what made organization possible. Without them everything jumbled and mixed together and made it impossible to get any kind of handle on the world.

This was true of his theology as well. He had read the stories of angels and demons, of the exorcisms of Christ and the temptations and machinations of the Devil. These were a tried-and-true part of the Christian world view. Malachi accepted them like he accepted the rest of the Bible, even the confusing parts.

But there were boundaries. The world of spirits and demons was the supernatural realm, and Malachi lived and worked in the natural. They may rub up against each other from time to time, but these worlds certainly didn't mix or get jumbled up. One didn't trespass the boundaries of the other. They just couldn't. Because if they did what would become of the order of the world? That would mean . . .

Malachi didn't follow that thought to the end. Even grazing his mind upon the idea made the pit of his stomach go cold and queasy. It was turmoil. It was chaos. And Malachi hated chaos.

Wasn't God the God who had tamed the chaos? Hadn't he looked upon that formlessness and void and brought it to order by his organizing light? Then how could such a God allow the chaos of world-mixing? Demons mixing with people? Spirits fornicating with humans? Then having offspring?

No, Malachi told himself. This couldn't be the case. God wouldn't create such a topsy-turvy world. He had made the world of men to be reasonable and orderly, and people like Malachi worked and lived in that world. That was his business. The world of spirits and demons and fae was the world of other creatures. And that world was none of his business.

What if it's not? That fearful and nagging question refused to be silenced. Does that mean your God was all wrong from the beginning? What will become of your faith then?

Malachi grunted and sat up in the bed. He got up and paced the small room, trying to ease the nagging and frightening thoughts stirring in his head. He would go and see this proof that Sid offered. It would probably amount to nothing. Danny would have a good explanation for it for sure even if he did not. In fact, by this time tomorrow they would all be laughing about it and wondering why they could have believed such a crazy, old man.

This thought gave him the comfort he sought, but still, he couldn't find sleep. As much as he tried to push the disturbing thoughts away, they stayed on the edge of his consciousness, remaining so close that it took all of his effort to keep them away.

This is exactly where Gerard found him when the sky was growing dark. He and the others stood in the narrow, white hallway and Gerard waited for the last of them to make it out.

Vic was the last to respond to the call and emerge out into the hallway. He stumbled out, straightening his short hair that had gone the classic salt and pepper color. Malachi could see the lines of sleep on his face and envied him the rest he had obviously been able to find.

"Is everyone ready?" Gerard asked. "We are going for a little walk."

"Where's Sid?" Gary asked.

"He will meet us there, "Gerard answered.

"Where exactly is there?"

"You will see when we arrive," was all Gerard offered.

The group followed the butler single file through the hallway and down the spiral staircase. They proceeded through a series of rooms and into the kitchens. From the kitchens they stepped outside into an old garden maze.

The fountain was dried up and full of leaves. Ivy and moss grew over the old stone walls. The flower beds bore the neglect of years. Still, the early summer filled the garden with green life and even some flowers bloomed despite the lack of loving attention.

As they walked over the paving stones, following Gerard in silence, Malachi couldn't shake the surreal feeling that came over him. The fading light of the sun cast an array of colors over the western sky. A wind blew through the garden, stirring up a clatter of dead leaves. A crow cawed on a nearby tree. The haze of twilight cast a pall over his eyes and his mind.

"You're traveling through another dimension," Vic said in his best imitation of the Twilight Zone. "A dimension of not only sight and sound, but of mind."

The group chuckled at the lighthearted attempt from Victor. As usual he was able to break the seriousness of the moment. It was something that more often than not irritated Malachi, but in that moment, he was grateful for it.

Gerard seemed most amused of all. He turned back and smiled at the group, as if he believed Victor's words were truer than any of them realized at the moment.

The iron gate whined as Gerard pushed it open and lead the group out of the garden and into the backyard. They made their way straight across the lawn to a line of trees at the far end. A portion of a stone wall stood at the edge of the trees. It looked like it had been knocked down years ago, and this jagged portion was all that was left. That and the faded wooden door that set into the wall.

Gerard stopped at that door, his hand upon the knob. It looked rotted and split. One kick probably would have splintered it off its hinges. The butler turned back to the men.

"Are you ready?" he asked. There was something in his voice that spoke of finality, as if once they passed through that door there was no going back.

"Where does this go?" Danny asked. He craned his head to see through the thin line of trees.

Malachi nodded his head, following Danny's eyes. The shadows made it impossible to see through the trees, but he figured they had to be close to the house behind them. Perhaps Sid owned that as well. Or maybe it went back further than he thought.

"Why don't we just go around?" Victor asked.

"That path begins here," Gerard pointed out. "I ask you again; are you ready?"

The men nodded their assent. Malachi shared a quick glance at Danny, wanting to see if he was ready to go through with this too.

"I guess this is what we came for," Malachi said.

With that Gerard turned the handle and pushed open the door.

Following the others, Malachi stepped through the doorway. As soon as he passed through the threshold, he felt a shift in the air around him. At first, the world just seemed darker around him. They had stepped into the small line of trees, so there would be the shadow that filtered out the fading twilight. But it was more than just a change in the shade of light.

A path opened up beneath his feet when Malachi stepped over. He didn't notice that before, but figured it had been hidden by the remnant of the wall. The group followed the path as it wound deeper into the trees.

That disturbing notion Malachi had tried to keep at bay all evening grew louder and louder as they followed the path. The trees around them grew bigger as the thin pines and scrub oaks gave way to older, even ancient looking trees. Thick arms of root knotted the edges of the path, sometimes large enough that they formed an archway the group had to duck under. Great sprawling canopies rose so high and thick as to almost make it complete darkness beneath. The only reason Malachi knew he was going the right way at all was because he followed the rest of the men.

"How far back does this property go?" Danny asked. He walked in front of Malachi, and clearly let his anxiety show in his voice.

Either Gerard didn't hear or didn't bother to answer. They continued deeper into the forest. The path inclined up as if taking them towards the peak of a hill.

"Something isn't right," Danny whispered to Malachi, reflecting his own fear.

"What do you mean?" Malachi asked. He knew exactly what Danny was feeling, but felt the need to ask why.

"There's no way his property goes this far," Danny hissed. Malachi could tell he was on the edge of a break down.

"Do you remember when we pulled in?" Danny asked. "There was another house behind this one. And I remember seeing other houses out the back window. And I promise you there wasn't this much space there."

"Maybe it's bigger than it looks," Malachi suggested. "Or we're walking between the houses. Something like that."

Danny shook his head. "We're close to the heart of the city. There is no wooded area this big. Plus, we've been walking uphill for the last five minutes. Pretty steep too. We should be able to see the city lights from this vantage point, even through the trees. But we can't. I can't hear anything either."

Malachi looked around. He strained his eyes and ears to pick up anything that he knew they should be able to make out. Lights from downtown buildings, from the nearby neighborhoods, even the ubiquitous hum of road traffic that was almost everywhere in the city. But Danny was right. It was as still and dark around them as the heart of the wilderness.

Strangely, Malachi found himself caring less the further they walked. The anxiety that had plagued him about Sid grew less the further they went. Instead, it was replaced by a vigor and excitement he hadn't felt in a long time.

"Danny, how are you feeling?" he asked.

"I feel good," Danny said. He stopped and marveled at his own words. "And I'm not even out of breath."

"Me neither," Malachi agreed.

He found that just as exciting as Danny's did. Of late he had been disturbed by a marked decline in his fitness that often struck men of his age. A sedentary job, middle aged weight, not having the time to exercise like he wanted to; all this took a toll on his health and fitness. He had seen it a lot recently. Even the trip from his car to the office had lately put him out of breath. Stairs were not even a consideration. It was a symptom he tried to ignore even as it got worse.

Something was definitely different here. Malachi breathed deep and reveled in the powerful rush of fresh air that filled his lungs. He felt it immediately energizing him. A surge of energy raced through him. Not only did he feel like he could walk the steep path in front of him, if someone dared him to a race he would run it without hesitation.

Once he noticed it himself Malachi could see that the same effect was over the rest of the men. They walked with lighter steps, stronger and more vibrant. Their talk was light also, joyful and full of expectation. There was even a thrill of excitement that they shared, as if they couldn't wait to see what would happen next.

It was something in the air around them. Wherever it was that Gerard was leading them, the air was different here. It was crisper, clearer. It reminded Malachi of that first cool autumn evening after a hot summer. You would wake up one day expecting the same still, humid air of August, only to find a crisp and breezy morning with a slight chill in the air.

This was the same feeling Malachi found walking the path with his fellow Swordsmen. There was something new and refreshing in the air. Even the smell of the earth around him rose up fresh and deep, untouched by the industry of modern man. It was the way he thought the earth ought to smell. And it even brought about a touch of sadness when he thought that he had never before experienced that in over fifty years of life.

Wonder turned to awe as the path crested the hill and ended at a broad, open peak. They stepped out of the cover of the trees and into the open night sky. Millions upon millions of stars shone down from above. They were brighter and clearer than Malachi had ever seen in his entire life. Even the Milky Way was clearly visible, and Malachi could make out the individual points of lights that made up the great streak of night light amid the deep expanse of space.

"Where are we?" he heard Danny ask beside him as they stepped into the clearing. Except this time there was no skepticism in his voice, only wonder.

Off to the east the moon began rising in a large, but slender crescent. It loomed over the horizon like a sickle made of delicate ivory, so close that Malachi believed if he stretched out just a little bit, he could touch it.

So taken was he with the sights around him that it took a while to notice that he could see none of the city lights that should have been visible to him from this height and perspective. There was no line of headlights winding through the city's highways. No towers rising up in perpetual light. No houses or neighborhoods giving their light to the nighttime.

Below the rise of the hill a dark valley stretched out. Malachi could barely make out a clearing, like a lake in the midst of the valley. Small, greenish lights danced over the water. It reminded of fireflies that he used to catch in the summer time. Above the valley another hill rose up higher than the one they were on. On top of that hill the ruins of a castle stood out against the night sky. Towers that looked broken and crumbling cast a sinister shadow towards them. Malachi shivered just looking at it, frightened of the place just by looking at its silhouette.

"I know someone has already asked this," he heard Vic say. "But where the hell are we?"   "You stand in a sacred place," they heard Sid answer from the crest of the hill.

Further above them, where the grassy hill peaked, a fire was lit, dancing in orange light. Sid sat by the fire, dressed in what looked like a white robe draped over his shoulder. A dog sat at his feet. Golden eyes regarded the men silently as they made their way to the fire.

"Come, sit around the fire please," Sid invited them.

Rectangular stone seats circled the fire. Each of the men took one, leaving five more unoccupied. Behind Sid, Malachi could make out standing stones that formed an old, and abandoned circle. Wherever they were it was nothing Malachi had ever experience in America.

"Alright, so sacred place, we got that," Victor said. "But where exactly is this sacred place. It feels like we left Kansas a long time ago."

Sid smiled back at Victor. "You don't know how right you are, Mr. Dodds. But I will explain that another day. For now, try to relax. I am sure all of you have felt an invigoration since we began our journey here tonight. Try to let that energy wash over you right now. Enjoy it. Save the questions for later."

The men took his advice and settled into their seats. They stared at the fire as it flickered before them. The hypnotic dance of flames, with the power mesmerize the minds and imaginations of the male species from time immemorial began to work its intoxicating influence over them. The night sky turned above them in its quiet regard. The fresh air of the woods and hills filled their lungs. The night around them pulsed with wild potential. They sat and stared until they were no longer businessmen and IT consultants, or managers, mechanics or any of the seneschals of the industrial world. They felt these titles and burdens stripped away from them by the fire and the night. They were stripped away until they felt again the primitive root inside them flare to life. The heart of hunters and warriors, poets and lovers awakened inside them. The deep passions of the soul that slumbered beneath the drone of civilized life stirred to new life. The fire of the soul that was washed out in the haze of digital lights began to burn bright again.

For the first time since any of them could remember, they felt like men. They felt without the slightest hint of doubt. It was not a thing they had to prove. It was who they were. As certain as the star shone and the bird flew, they were as they had been made. Every man knew himself around that fire. And each of them wondered how something so pure and powerful could ever be lost or forgotten.

Somewhere in the darkness around them a sound rose up, out of the forest just outside the clearing. It was dim at first, a low hum. It began with a single deep voice. A higher, female voice joined his, then others rose up to complete the harmony. They blended into a single note before drifting into the melody of a song.

It wasn't a song Malachi had ever heard before, nor could he make sense of the language in which it was being sung. It had an oddly Celtic sound to it, but then mixed with sounds he felt came from far away Asia, and even mixed with the sounds of Hebrew. He was tempted to say it was a combination of every language spoken on earth.

The song itself followed no identifiable melody. It rose and fell, sometimes sounding like it was a distinct theme. Then, it would break off and rise in another direction completely. Like the language, Malachi could pick out no particular style to the music he was familiar with.

Whatever the kind of music, it could not be denied how beautiful it was. The voices rose in perfect pitch, harmonizing effortlessly one with another. Sometimes you could pick out the individual voices, other times they melded into one, pure sound. The sound made Malachi's heart ache. As he listened, he longed for something he wasn't sure he could name, or if it even existed. It enchanted him along with the firelight, drawing him into an irresistible trance.

"Who is that? What is that song?" he heard Giovanni ask. He could hear emotion on the edge of tears in the music teacher's voice. He couldn't imagine what this like for a trained ear such as his.

"Those are some of the Fae," Sid told them. "And they are giving their song to us."

Distantly, Malachi wondered if he should be alarmed. These were the enemy, weren't they?

"These are allies in our fight," Sid explained to Malachi's unanswered question. "They help me tonight explain to you what it is we are up against."

Malachi felt himself irresistibly pulled into the current of the music. His mind relaxed, laying aside the hundreds of worries and concerns that always stirred there. He didn't notice how heavy the burden was he carried around with him until he began to put it aside for a moment.

Gerard rose up from the shadows behind Sid. He was shirtless, clad only in a linen skirt around his waist. Perfectly developed muscles stood out in the firelight, contrasting to the elderly figure he presented to them in the house. Malachi almost didn't recognize the powerful figure that hovered near the fire. There was definitely more to the man than he noticed at first.

In an air of ceremony Gerard lifted a clay amphora. It was painted along the sides in crude sigils of black paint. He poured crimson wine into a goblet he held in his other hand. Whispering over the lip of the cup he passed it to Sid.

Lifting the cup high in consecration, Sid bowed his head then took a drink from the cup. He passed it Victor on his right and watched him expectantly. Vic opened his mouth with a broad smile, like he was about to say something, then thought better of it. Imitating Sid he lifted the cup high then drank deeply from it. Rivulets of red wine ran down from the corners of his mouth.

"It's a very good year," he whispered, unable to resist some sort of amusing remark. A stern look from Sid wiped the smile from his face.

The wine cup passed to Vic's right. Gary followed the ritual of the others, lifting the cup high and drinking deep. It passed to Danny who hesitated, looking into the cup before deciding to drink himself. Then the cup was placed in Malachi's hands.

A distant part of him warned against drinking out of a cup which Malachi wasn't sure what it contained. Another Malachi would have questioned what was in it and why they had to drink it. But on the hilltop, with the purity of the air, the power of the stars shining above, the mystic music from the Fae, and the enchanting dance of firelight; all of these silenced the worried voice of Malachi. He took the cup, lifted it high and said a quiet prayer.

"Lord, help me," he whispered, and tipped the cup back to drink.

The taste of the wine was earthy at first. He could almost smell the soil and feel the sunshine that nourished the vines. A tanginess followed, stronger than any wine he had tasted before, almost like vinegar.

Once the wine had been passed around, Gerard filled it again. Sid drank and handed the cup to Victor who followed suit, passing it around the circle. Three times Gerard filled the cup. Three times they drank and passed the cup around circle. After the third drink a warmth had suffused through Malachi, relaxing him even further.

"Oh God who sees all things and knows all things," Sid began to pray after the wine was drunk. "Grant us eyes to see and ears to see. Open our hearts and minds. Enter into us Holy Spirit. Open the eye within that sees, and reveal to us the secrets of your creation."

Sid stretched out his arm and sprinkled a powder on the fire. Incense smoke wafted up and filled the hilltop with the rich, aromatic scents. Sid began to chant low, his eyes closed in prayer.

Malachi strained to understand what Sid was saying but could not make out the words. He spoke in a language that Malachi did not know, but the more he listened, the more he thought he did know the words, or at least he should. They were familiar, like a word that is on the tip of the tongue. His mind stood on the verge of knowing, just waiting for a push to understand.

Without warning, the push came. Sid's words went from foreign to familiar all at once. Malachi felt something move in him, a silent click of the mind, and he understood.

"When he established the heavens, you were there; when he drew a circle on the face of the deep, when he made firm the skies above, when he established the fountains of the deep, when he assigned to the sea its limit, so that the waters might not transgress his command, when he marked out the foundations of the earth, then you were beside him, like a master workman, and was daily his delight, rejoicing before him always, rejoicing in the inhabited world and delighting in the children of man. O spirit of God's wisdom, open thus our eyes."

Another rush in his mind and Malachi felt the whole world move beneath him. His whole mind and understanding stepped forward. A wind pushed him, lifting him up and carrying him. He reached out to the stone seat beneath him to reassure himself that he was still on solid ground.

A gasp went around the campfire as the men felt the same sensation as Malachi. They felt the rush of movement, the sensation of being drawn forward. They felt, and their eyes were opened.

Malachi had to shake his head at the strange vision that was now before him. It was strange, yet at the same time he knew it was real. It was more real than anything else he had ever seen. Without fully comprehending what was happening, Malachi recognized that he was looking at a deeper level of reality.

All around him golden fires were burning. He saw them clearly, inside the heart of every man around the fire with him, the Swordsmen and in Sid Bickley. Orbs of golden fire, twisting and flaring like miniature suns glowed inside every man. Tendrils of flame twisted off the little suns and filled the limbs and the mind. Malachi looked down and saw the same within him.

They were glorious to look at and beyond words to describe. He felt the light and power pulse from these fires, and he knew they gave fuel and life to everyone there. These fires were passion and life, faith and glory, goodness, courage, love and hope all in one. To think he carried such a fire in him made Malachi proud and ashamed all at once. He had this golden fire inside of him, yet what had he accomplished with it so far in his life? Nothing, he decided, that was worthy of such an awesome gift.

"What you see is the soul of man," Sid explained to them. "This golden fire, this little sun that burns within you; this is the soulfire. There is none like it in all creation.

"Look around you. Tell me what you see."

Malachi looked around and noticed the other fires that burned around him. He could see fire burning in the trees that surrounded the hill. This was a green fire that veined through the branches and leaves. He looked at the dog beside Sid, remembering him for the first time that night. Inside the dog a red fire burned, with tendrils of green flame twisting inside.

On the outskirts of the hill Malachi could see another type of fire altogether. Little suns blazed in the darkness, but these were orange flames bordered in blue fire. Without understanding how he knew, Malachi perceived these orange-blue flames belonged to the Fae. At a sight he could tell how different they were from him.

Turning his head, he gazed around, drinking in the new visions that opened up to his sight. He looked at the ground beneath him. There, like rivers beneath the earth ran flames of dark crimson fire. It pulsed like the lifeblood of the world.

Craning his head he looked up and his breath was taken away by the sight. The stars, brighter than they had ever been before, now blazed with even greater intensity. Each was twice the size that they had been a moment ago. Each burned so brightly that their auras took up the entire heavens. He knew then that the stars themselves were great life-fires. On their fringes he could see the same blue fire that burned in the souls of the Fae. He knew that he looked upon the sons of Heaven. Between the stars, barely discernible from the great light that blazed from them, a fire of dark violet streaked in the darkness of the deepest sky.

"Long ago, when man was young in the earth," Sid began to speak.

His voice carried out in power over the night. Malachi felt the voice penetrate his mind and burrow deep into his brain. The words trembled there, stirring an image that slowly came into Malachi's vision. A man appeared, hovering over the fire, the sun of his soulfire burned with an intensity that paled Malachi's own, and every man that surrounded him.

"He was given a soul breathed out by God himself. He was made in the image of the eternal and almighty. It was a stronger soul than what dwells in the heart of man today. It was the very pulse of life."

Malachi looked at the man, the image that turned to face each of them. He knew that the image was being produced by Sid's words, a phantom of sorts. But he also knew this was a reality of man long ago. His soulfire was brighter, the passion and power of his life stronger. Malachi looked at the man and envied him what he possessed, and a deep part of him mourned that humanity had lost this secret fire.

"When the Lord God created the heavens and the earth, and when he put men on the earth to work and keep it, he appointed Watchers, the sons of God to watch over and guard humanity and the new works that he had done," Sid continued.

Another image appeared over the man. This was a taller, stronger figure, robed in white with flowing white hair, but he did not look old. Another figure appeared beside him, a woman who looked the same. Her hair was white yet she appeared to be no more than twenty years old. Other, similar figures appeared, the Watchers of old. Inside each of them burned a white soulfire with blue flames on the edges, just like the stars.

"As the years passed, man began to regard these Watchers as gods, and bowed to them and worshiped them."

A woman appeared beside the man and they bowed to the Watchers. At first, these heavenly beings paid them no regard. But tendrils of man's golden soulfire began to snake off from their souls and wafted near the divine beings that stood over them. One of the Watchers pursed in his lips and sucked in the golden wisp of flame. His eyes widened in pleasure, glowing a soft golden color. He smiled and drank more deeply.

"Tasting the soulfire of man, the Watchers knew they drank what was forbidden to them, for in doing so they posed as gods. And divine creatures though they were, they were not God and should not have taken what belonged to God alone. But the more they drank, the more they craved. They took the mantle of gods, and demanded man give him his worship."

The solitary image shuttered and Malachi saw himself looking at a city. It was built of stone and mud houses. People walked the streets in tunics and robes, decorated with jeweled headbands.

A massive ziggurat rose in the center of the city. Crowds of people, dressed in linen skirts and ephods, bowed to the image that stood at the top. Malachi looked and saw one of the Watchers hovering above the idol. As the people worshiped, wisps of golden soulfire wafted up to the waiting god. He breathed deep and inhaled the aroma of adoration and praise. As he drank deeply of soulfire his eyes blazed with golden light, his mouth stood open in the throes of ecstasy.

"The more they drank, the more intoxicated they grew. Drunk on soulfire they forgot their role as Watchers. They remembered no more who they were. Some drew too close to man. Their hearts, corrupted from drinking this forbidden essence, filled with lust for the daughters of man."

Malachi watched as the floating Watcher looked down the steps of the ziggurat. His eyes fell upon a woman, who, naked except for her linen skirt, gazed up at the idol in adoration. The Watcher drifted closer, reaching his hands out to the kneeling woman. His eyes, filled with golden fire, narrowed with desire.

"The Watchers took for themselves human women for wives and concubines. To them were born the Nephilim, terrible creatures half-human, half-divine. They were the heroes of old, men of great renown. About them are much of our myths written. Out of their power and craft were birthed sorceries and witchcraft. Giants were made alongside of distorted monsters. Wars ravaged the land as they fought for power."

The image shuttered again and Malachi saw himself looking at a battlefield bathed in the light of a setting sun. Carnage and death filled the horizon. Men slashed at men in the brutality of warfare. Giants and monsters stalked the battlefield beside the men, dealing terrible death in their wake.

"Murder and rage took over the hearts of man as well as the sons of God. The earth cried out with the blood spilled and quaked beneath the burden of evil. God looked down and regretted that he had ever made man. His creation had been destroyed, corrupted, perverted. It lay in waste by the lust of gods and men. He resolved then to remake all things. He would start over. And it would all begin in a flood."

The ground in Malachi's vision cracked open. Great gouts of water erupted from the ground. In an instant the battlefield was flooded. Man and beast and giant wiped away in the surge of water.

A wall of water struck Malachi in the face. It filled his mouth and nose, dousing the light in foaming waves.

With a gasp he jerked his head back. The vision of water and war fled and he was around the fire again, surrounded by the other men. He saw others panting and holding their chests. Gary leaned forward, cradling his head in his hands. The images of the soulfire had disappeared. The world around them, amazing as it was, had returned to its normal appearance.

"Was that real?" he heard Danny ask beside him. His voice was weak, nearly a whisper.

"That was . . . more real . . . than anything you have ever known," Sid gasped.

Malachi looked up and saw Gerard helping the old man sit up. Sid had gone pale and his body slumped forward. His breath came in labored gasps as his limbs hung heavy and limp at his sides.

"What was it?" Gary asked, looking up.

"That was . . . the history . . . of our world," Sid said as he continued to breathe heavily. "It was . . . what happened long ago when . . . when the creatures of heaven first . . . tasted . . . of man's soulfire."

"Why would God ever let such a thing happen?" Danny asked in horror. Malachi could hear the strain in his voice. The vision had struck him deep, even deeper than Malachi. There would be a crisis of faith coming for him, he knew. He just hoped it wouldn't be fatal.

"Please . . ." Sid struggled to speak. "Let us talk . . . later. This has . . . this has . . . this has taken much from me."

"I just don't understand," Danny plead, ignoring Sid's weakness. "Why was the world ever allowed to get to that stage? What were the Watchers even protecting us from anyway? How did you make us see that? Did you give us drugs?"

"He said later," Gerard commanded. He spoke with an air of finality and authority, opposite of the deferential tone of the butler. There would be no arguing.

"Gentlemen, if you would make your way back to the house. We will continue this tomorrow."

The men were reluctant to leave. Despite the terrifying vision they all shared, there was still a magnetic draw to the place. They felt energized and alive like they hadn't in a long time. They felt a contentment to just be, without pressure or expectation. None of them wanted to give that up.

"Gentlemen," Gerard emphasized. "I must get Master Sid back to his bed for rest. I need you to return to the house."

"We can't stay here for a while?" Gary asked. "It's nice out."

"I'm afraid you cannot," Gerard warned. "It is not safe to linger in this place for too long."

Malachi turned and looked out into the dark. He could still see the shape of the castle that rose up opposite the valley below them. Flickering, orange light danced in its depths and he could make out some of the ruined battlements. Strange shadows cast along a portion of broken wall.

"Follow the path and it will take you back to the house," Gerard instructed. "Stay on the path and you will remain perfectly safe. Whatever you do, do not leave the path."

The air of finality in his voice left no option for the men. Reluctantly, they picked themselves up and made their way back to the path. Without a word they delved into the dark that surrounded them, leaving the open dome of stars and sky for the deep dark of the woods.

Malachi was surprised to find that he could make out the path beneath his feet. The moon and stars shone so brilliantly they even penetrated the thick canopy of ancient trees. He even guessed there was something about the air around them, something even about his eyes, that made it possible to see well enough in the dark that he didn't fear losing the path.

The path proved a great comfort as the men soundlessly made their way back. Often, they heard the movement of figures just out of eyesight. Branches snapped and leaves crunched under the passage of feet nearby. Every so often he could see a dim silhouette trailing the men as they walked back.

Even more sinister sounds echoed in the darkness beyond. Strange animals that Malachi could not identify called out through the trees. Guttural growls and high, almost shrieking whistles sounded nearby. One piercing cry sounded much too near, and the men froze in their tracks. It was a human sound, mixed with something primitive and bestial. The men exchanged a knowing and fearful glance before doubling their speed.

The promise of Gerard proved true. The men stayed on the path and after a hasty retreat in the night saw the doorway in the broken wall ahead. No one hesitated to pour through the door until Malachi, taking up the rear, paused on the threshold.

Looking back, he saw the thin pines and scrub oaks that he had seen when they first left that evening. Deeper still were the large and sprawling trees that made up the forest that somehow existed right where the rest of Sid's neighborhood should have been. He could barely make them out through a mist that had begun to obscure them so they stood as if veiled in fog.

Figures stood out among the trees. They were human, as far as Malachi could tell, and they regarded him from a distance. Moonlight shivered and shined on one of them. It was a man, or at least looked like one, tall, handsome and dressed only in a kilt of some animal skin. There was something mysterious and ethereal about the creature and Malachi knew that he was looking at one of the Fae.

The door creaked behind him and Malachi turned to make sure he was not going to be shut in. With one hand on the door, he turned back around to get one last peak at the Fae. But when he looked back again all he saw were the thin pines and scrub oaks, and the lights from the houses behind them.

Chapter 7 - Training

The next morning Malachi stood at the crumbling wall they had passed through the night before. With careful steps he walked around it, surveying its features and searching with his hands for any indication it may serve a deeper purpose. To all inspection it was just a crumbling section of wall with an old, wooden door set in its center.

Stepping through the door Malachi searched the wooded area behind the house. He couldn't see the trail they had followed the night before but easily made his way to the back of the property. About twenty yards through the thin trees he came to a rotting, wooden fence. He peered through a gap where one of the planks had fallen away. Behind the fence a perfectly manicured lawn glistened in the early light. It was just as he had expected it to be.

Thoroughly confused now, and more than a little disturbed, Malachi made his way back to the wall, determined to find something to explain their adventure from the night before. He walked around the wall, tapped on it with his hands. He shut and closed the door multiple times, hoping to trigger whatever properties it possessed.

"It's the wrong time of day," a voice called out from behind him.

Malachi turned to see Gerard approaching him from the house. The butler was dressed again in his dark suit, immaculately clean, looking every inch the dignified household servant.

"I was just . . ." Malachi started to explain before realizing he didn't even want to put the thought into words.

"Wondering how this door transported you to another world?" Gerard finished for him; a knowing smile crossed his features.

Malachi shook his head, still not willing to fully accept what had happened the night before. Except now he was beginning to feel stupid for his resistance. Still, there was something that refused to accept it all. It was just that . . .

"I just don't understand," he voiced to the butler. "How is it possible that we were just walking through the backyard." He gestured to the scrub oak and thin pines.

"The world is not what you think it is," Gerard said by way of explanation. "There is no other way to put it than that."

Malachi rubbed his temples, feeling overwhelmed. The world he had known was crashing down around him. The nice, orderly place that he enjoyed living in, the predictable, rational world that made proper sense, was being destroyed before his very eyes. What was rising in its place was a world far more frightful than the one he knew.

"I feel like if I could just make sense of it," Malachi said. "The maybe I won't feel so . . ."

"Afraid," Gerard finished for him.

Malachi nodded, unable to deny it to himself or anyone else. He was afraid. Everything about this business frightened him. And it started with the moment Sid walked into their Bible study. The man put a fear in Malachi he hadn't felt since he was a kid, and he hated him for it.

"Maybe you shouldn't try to make sense of the world," Gerard suggested. "And just live in it."

"How can I be expected to live in a world I can't make sense of?" Malachi asked, truly astounded by what lay ahead of him.

"I believe you will have enough sense of it to live well and without fear," Gerard assured him as they walked across the yard. "Just give it time."

"I guess what I hate more about this than anything else is that all this time I thought I had a pretty good idea about the world," Malachi said as they stepped back inside.

"And what bothers me the most is finding out I had no idea what I was talking about," he confessed. "Turns out I don't know a thing."

"That my friend," Gerard said. "Is what we call wisdom."

Around the breakfast table the men were quiet and sullen. Each was digesting the events from the previous night. After their return home they all fell asleep, suddenly overcome with a staggering exhaustion. The next morning, they had still hadn't found the words to talk about it.

Gerard laid out a magnificent breakfast across the dining room table. Eggs, bacon, hash browns and orange juice were piled up in abundance. The meal was crowned by the most exquisite coffee Malachi had ever tasted in his life.

"So, are we going to talk about what happened last night?" Vic asked.

When no one answered Danny spoke up. "I don't see a need to, really."

"What? Are you still doubting?" Gary asked. A hint of anger touched his voice.

Danny dropped his fork on his plate with a clatter and looked across the table. "No, I don't doubt. We asked for proof and we got . . . well we got something. I'm just not sure what it was."

"We looked into the soul of the world," Gary said. "He showed you a . . . a different level of reality. You saw it with your own eyes."

"Eyes that had maybe been tampered with," Danny said. "I mean, who knows what that drink was he gave us. Maybe it had LSD or mushrooms in it."

"Didn't feel like I was high," Vic interjected. "What? Like none of you know what I'm talking about. Danny, did it feel like you were high?"

Danny didn't answer at first. He pushed around his hash browns. With a shake of his head, he looked up at Victor.

"No, I didn't feel high," he admitted. "But I felt . . . I felt better than I have in over twenty years."

"Why can't you just believe?" Gary asked. "What more do you need?"

"I'm here, aren't I?" Danny shot back. "I'm here. I'm not going anywhere. OK? Just let me deal with it in my own way."

Gary nodded and the men settled back into their breakfast in silence. The only sound in the dining room was the clink of silver on plates.

"Did anyone else have a strange dream?" Giovanni asked, breaking the silence.

Danny froze at the mention of the dream. All the men looked up, as if remembering something profound.

"If by dream," Vic said. "You mean one so powerful that I couldn't distinguish it from reality. Then yes, I did."

The vision came crashing back into Malachi's memory. It was so powerful a dream, so potent and visceral that it left him shaking when he woke up. Never had such a lucid dream struck him in the night.

He had dreamt of a battlefield. The sky was dark overhead and a hot, blasting wind swept in from somewhere nearby. A red sun shined down through the smoke and clouds. The land was destroyed, ravaged to dust and ash beneath his feet.

Looking out across the vast plain Malachi saw an army marching towards them. As far as the eye could see, dark figures in black, distorted armor moved inevitably, unstoppably forward. They were gruesome figures, twisted in malice and hate. And they were beyond number, stretching even past the horizon. They were limitless in number and form.

Malachi sat astride a horse, dressed in brilliant armor. A red cross was blazoned across the white tunic that fell over his breastplate. In his left hand he hefted a shield with the same red cross painted on it. In his right he wielded a sword that blazed with a golden light.

Looking down the line Malachi saw other warriors with him, mounted and armored like he was. They looked like the calvary of the knights of old. All his friends from his Bible study were among the gathered calvary. Giovanni, Victor, Gary, Tresmond, Zachary and Danny were lined up next to him, arrayed for a mighty battle. He couldn't help but notice the smile they all had on their face.

Malachi smiled too. As he looked down at the forces arrayed against them, he saw they were so much more numerous than their own. Malachi and the others were facing overwhelming odds. But he wasn't afraid. There wasn't the slightest touch of fear in his heart. There was only one, powerful, unstoppable emotion that swept over him.

He felt joy.

Malachi almost laughed with the burst of joy inside him. There was joy in the day, and in the victory he knew was at hand. Despite the odds, Malachi knew they would win. Most of all, he felt joy because of the figure at their head who was leading him.

The figure sat upon a white horse, tall and majestic. He was turned away from him so all Malachi could see was his back. Dark hair, tied into a single band fell down from his shoulders. Instead of armor, the man on the white horse wore a white tunic. The edge was wet with a crimson spot of blood that dripped down. Malachi could see there was something etched on the outside of his thigh, almost like a tattoo. He knew without looking what was written there.

King of Kings and Lord of Lords

Strength and power coursed through Malachi every time he looked at the figure on the white horse. One look in his direction and Malachi had to suppress a laugh. Today would be a glorious day.

"I remember," Tres said, shaking Malachi out of his reverie.

He felt a reluctance to let go of the dream. The emotion, the joy he felt was so powerful that the world they lived in felt dull by comparison.

Tresmond went to explain the dream that Malachi himself remembered having. The men around the table nodded as they listened, affirming they had the exact same vision.

"I never felt so happy in my life," Tres said, then broke down crying.

An awkward silence fell over the table as Tres wept. The men were both unable and unsure of what to do with such a naked outburst of emotion. Giovanni, who sat next to him, reached out a comforting hand as the other men picked at their breakfast again.

"That is a dream that every swordsmen has," Sid told them as he stepped into the room.

The older man had recovered from the exhaustion of the night before, but Malachi could still see the strain upon him. His face was more haggard and paler than the night before. He leaned more on the silver-tipped cane and seemed to find his breath more difficult to get hold of.

"What does it mean?" Danny asked once Sid was seated.

"It means you were chosen," Sid answered. "Every one of you. You see, it is not my army you are joining, it is Christ's. I am just a soldier like you."

"Where were we?" Gary asked.

Sid lifted up a forkful of egg to his mouth and paused. He put the fork back down and looked thoughtfully across the table.

"It is a battle that will take place sometime in the future," he told them. "A battle all of you will be called to join."

The men silently digested these words as Sid began his breakfast in earnest. Malachi had never considered himself a fighting man, the army had never any appeal to him. Still, he found himself excited at the prospect of that battle. He couldn't wait for it to happen. Somehow, he knew, that day would be the greatest day of his life.

"For now, it is time to train," Sid informed them. "We have a smaller battle of our own to fight. It is time we get ready for it."

"Train?" Danny asked. "Like what kind of training."

"You are warriors," Sid told him. "You must learn how to fight."

An hour later they all stood before the most unlikely trainer they could imagine. Gerard escorted them to the training quarters of the mansion. It was a space that looked like a perfect and well used dojo. The space was wide with hard wooden floors. The floors were covered mostly in mats, most had seen better days. A few even padded the walls as well.

A sliding glass door was opened to let in the morning air. Even then there was an old smell of sweat that permeated the room. It told of countless hours of countless men working and training there.

Completing the look of the training room were the various weapons and equipment in stands along the wall. Malachi could make out padded armor and sparring helmets. Weapons consisted of bo sticks, swords, axes, polearms, nunchucks, and a few Malachi couldn't identify. Most of them were made of wood and bore the marks of many training sessions. Others looked like the real thing, made for actual combat.

Pacing the mat in front of them was a short man with long, grey hair pulled back in a pony tail. He looked to be of slight build and walked with strong and balanced steps. He wore a shirt with cut off sleeves and collar, tucked into grey sweat pants. A grey beard mixed with remnants of brown hair filled out his face. Light brown eyes looked the Swordsmen over who waited on the edge of the mat.

"Gentlemen, this is Master Sergeant Ronald Diggs," Sid introduced. "He will be training you in the art of combat."

Malachi looked skeptically at the older, slight man who watched them. He didn't look much like a trainer, and even less like a Master Sergeant. In truth, he looked like a hippie who had retired to start an organic farm.

"You're teaching us combat?" Tres asked. The doubt was clear in his voice.

"I am," Sergeant Diggs answered calmly without any sign of being provoked.

"Do you doubt I can teach you?"

"No offense," Tres said. "But you don't look like you know much about combat."

A smile crept over the lips of the Master Sergeant. "A lot of Rangers said the same thing to me before I put them on their ass."

"You trained Rangers?" Vic asked, clearly surprised.

"After serving 15 years in the Rangers I went back to teach hand to hand combat," he informed them. "I taught for nearly twenty years."

"But when was the last time you taught?" Tresmond challenged.

"Last week," Diggs answered. "I still give private lessons."

"Like I said, no offense," Tres reiterated. "But I'm a personal trainer myself and I think I need someone who could keep up with me."

"I assure you, the Sergeant is more than qualified," Sid stepped in to say. "I know it has been some time since I have acquired his help, but he has trained swordsmen before."

"I don't mean to be rude but I don't have the luxury of worrying about anybody's feelings," Tres said. "I just need to know he's up to it."

Sergeant Diggs shrugged his shoulders and stepped back. He held out a hand, inviting Tres to the mat.

Tres looked to Sid then to other Swordsmen. Vic shrugged, and no one else offered any guidance to him.

"Alright, if you think you want this," Tres said.

He took off his shoes to be barefoot like Diggs and approached the Master Sergeant. After a few stretches he assumed a boxer's stance, bouncing on his heels. Tres circled the Master Sergeant who looked him up from head to toe. Malachi had a bad feeling all of a sudden. Watching the expert way that Diggs assessed his enemy, Malachi could tell it was about to get ugly.

"I got to warn you," Tres said with a slight feint. "I used to teach kick boxing."

He sent a jab towards Diggs who ducked it without effort.

The younger man laughed and changed direction, circling the Sergeant.

Two more jabs were easily dodged as Diggs watched and waited. Tres feinted and the Master Sergeant didn't bite.

"Alright, you're not bad," he admitted. "But I need you to be good."

With that he leaned in with a darting punch. Diggs ducked the blow and swung out his leg in a wide circle, belying an agility greater than his years.

Tres cried out as his legs flew out from under him and he hit the mat with a thud. Without hesitation he popped up and charged in again.

The next punch was dodged and Diggs grabbed Tres' wrist and twisted. He kicked his legs out from under him again, still holding the arm. This time Tresmond cried out in pain as he writhed on the floor with the Master Sergeant twisting his arm back.

To his credit, Tresmond kept getting up. As often as he was thrown down, he jumped to his feet again. But never did he get close to landing a blow. Diggs blocked, dodged and swept aside kicks, lunges and punches. Time and again he threw Tres down, swept his legs out or buckled his knees. Over and again the younger man ended up on his back or grappled in an impossible hold or lunging at the air where Diggs was standing just a moment ago.

Eventually, his pride was worn down and Tres indicated he had enough. Gripping his left side with a grimace he limped back to the line of waiting men.

"Alright," he groaned. "I think he'll do."

Sergeant Diggs smiled. He was barely winded and didn't even look the slightest bit out of breath. If Malachi hadn't seen it with his own eyes he wouldn't have believed it.

"Does anyone else here think I can't train them?" Diggs asked.

Both Malachi and Danny raised their hands. Vic stifled a laugh as an inquisitive eyebrow shot up on the Sergeant's face.

"Really?" he asked. "Would care to test me as well?"

Danny held his hands up. "It's not that, I promise," he said quickly. "I have no doubt you can kick my ass. It's just that I'm 53 and I haven't exercised in twenty years."

"I'm 55," Malachi echoed. "And I never was the athletic type. If we get in a fight, I'm more likely to hurt myself more than anyone else."

The men chuckled at this admission. Malachi smiled too but meant every word he said. He had tried athletics in his day, just like everyone else, but quickly learned that was not his gift. He tried to keep up at the gym for fitness's sake without entertaining any illusion about his athletic prowess.

Sergeant Diggs smiled at their candor. "I'm 65," he told them.

A groan came from Tres at this admission. This sent another ripple of laughter through the men.

"But you've been doing this your whole life," Danny pointed out. "You're asking two old men to get their muscles to do something they've never done before. It's a whole different ball game."

"True," Diggs nodded. "You won't get to my level. But you can do more than you think. Your muscles, even as old as yours, are still capable of marvelous things. Let me teach you what they can do."

"Trust the Master Sergeant," Sid told them from his watching place on the edge of the mat. "Trust me. You've been called to this Mr. Green. You too Mr. Taylor. Put in the effort and you will become what you are meant to."

Danny looked at Malachi before shrugging in submission. Malachi shook his head, still not believing what he was getting himself into. Before he could answer, the dream he had the night before rose up in his mind again. He could see the armies of darkness arrayed out before him in dread and despair. He felt the sword again in his hand and the shield that guarded him. Most of all he saw the man on the white horse, and a surge of joy filled his heart again.

Malachi nodded, resigned to whatever God had in store for him. He knew then it didn't matter where he was called and what he was asked to do. If it was for the rider on the white horse, he would ride into Hell and back. And he would smile the whole way.

Two hours later the rider on the white horse was the furthest thing from Malachi's mind. And he definitely wasn't smiling. All he could think about was the pain.

"Alright, let's take a little break," Sergeant Diggs said for the first time that day.

Malachi thought he would collapse in exhaustion. Every muscle in his body cried out in pain. Even some muscles he didn't know existed were screaming at him. Making his way to the wall of the training room he collapsed.

"You did good out there," Sid told him. The old man had a knowing smile on his face. He reached down and handed Malachi a canteen of water.

Malachi nodded his thanks and took the canteen. After one sip he poured the cold water on his head. He sighed in relief feeling the cool droplets run down his face.

"If by good you mean flailing my arms and legs around while getting thrown around, then I guess I did pretty good," Malachi answered when he had gotten his breath back.

Even though he joked, it wasn't too far from the truth. The Master Sergeant was already driving them hard. He showed them punches, kicks and blocks, then demanded they repeat the motions over and over again. Just when Malachi thought he had gone as far as he could, Diggs would stand in front of him and insist that he demonstrate on him. Of course, none of Malachi's shots came anywhere close to hitting. The Master Sergeant slipped the shots and sent him tumbling to the ground.

Malachi consoled himself with the thought that none of the other men fared any better than him. Even Gary, big as he was, got tossed effortlessly to the ground by the trainer. After two hours Vic's jokes had run dry and Tres was breathing heavy and showed signs of exhaustion. It was the type of training none of them had ever experienced before, and it showed.

"So, what do you expect to happen here?" Malachi asked Sid. "With all this training, I mean. We're obviously not going to turn into some elite fighting force. Are we just doing this so we don't embarrass ourselves, or get beaten too easily?"

Sid smiled down at Malachi with an unreadable expression on his face.

"What makes you think you can't be an elite fighting force?" Sid asked back.

Malachi chuckled and shook his head. He took another big drink of water and wondered if it was even worth pointing out the obvious.

"Even if I trained for years, I would be mediocre at best," he said. "Maybe if you put us against ordinary people, or old women, we could do OK. But if we were to go against professionals, or even athletic people, we're getting our asses kicked."

"You sell yourself short, Mr. Green," Sid answered. "Surely, you know you can do better than that."

"I'm just being realistic here," Malachi pointed out. "Except for Vic, none of us are even ex-military. And Tres is the only one who has the physical tools for this. The rest of us are just regular guys with regular jobs."

Sid nodded and gestured to the other men behind him. "There's nothing ordinary about what you have stepped up to do," he pointed out.

"You know what I mean," Malachi insisted.

"And I hope you know what I mean," Sid told him, an earnest expression on his face. "You may be ordinary but you serve an extraordinary God."

"Speaking of regular jobs," Sid addressed the whole group before Malachi could answer. "I hope all of you have been able to take the appropriate time off of work. Two weeks is what we need to start with, though it will likely be more. If you need help let me know and I'll see what I can do."

"I don't plan on going back to work," Tres said. "I'm with you as long as this takes."

One look at his face said he was deadly serious. Determination and conviction were etched clearly on his features. Malachi could see he had thrown everything into avenging his son's death. The force of that conviction almost frightened him.

"Me and Big G had enough time stored up," Vic told them. "More than two weeks will be a stretch, but we got at least two."

"Summer just started so I'm good for a while," Giovanni said. "Of course, camps will be starting next month so I would have to get ready for that."

93

"I don't think I really have a job to go back to," Danny said. "When I asked for time off the brass said that was a good idea and promised to have a long talk when I get back. They need a fall guy for our system crash. Guess that will be me."

Sid nodded, taking in the information. "I'm sure we can find you something when this is all done.

"What about you Mr. Metts? Mr. Green?"

Zach shook his head. "I got a week, that's all. And boss man wasn't happy about that. I don't see being able to get any more than that."

"Same here," echoed Malachi. "Week was all I could pull."

"You'll need to take more than that," Sid insisted. "I don't have the connections I used to, but if any of you get fired, I can find you jobs that will be more accommodating to our line of work.

"Mr., Green, you should be ok at the hospital. I'll talk to Dr. Canta and see what I can do."

"Dr. Canta?" Malachi said, impressed with the name drop. It was a big one. "If you know Dr. Canta then you are well connected. He pretty much runs the hospital. Not in name, of course. But everyone does what he says."

"He's been a useful ally over the years," Sid told him.

"Hell of a doctor too," Malachi pointed out. "Never seen such a skilled physician. Even the nurses have taken to calling him the god of medicine."

Sid paled at these last words. He gripped his cane and looked down at Malachi, his face contorted and angry.

"What did you say?" he demanded.

Malachi recoiled at the sudden surge of anger in Sid. He had never seen the old man so fueled with emotion and it was more than a little frightening.

"The god of medicine," Malachi said hesitantly.

"Why would you call him that?" Sid asked through clenched teeth.

"I don't call him that, that's just what they call him."

"Who?" Sid insisted. "Who calls him that? Who?"

"I don't know, the nurses I think," Malachi said defensively. "It's just something people call him."

Sid straightened and wiped sweat from his brow. Malachi could feel the fear emanating from the man. Whatever he had said had just set him off in a dreadful way. Sid looked over at Gerard who wore the same worried expression.

"Get the car," Sid demanded. "Men, continue your training. I have a problem I need to tend to."

Chapter 8 - A Doctor's Visit

Sid watched Dr. Canta step into his office, oblivious to his presence. He sat in the chair across from the doctor's desk, looking out over the entire hospital complex, an exclusive view for someone who had reached the pinnacle of his career.

"Good afternoon, Doctor," Sid greeted, announcing himself.

Canta didn't even look up and acknowledge the older man sitting in one of the chairs across from his desk. He slapped the papers he was carrying down on the desk and took his seat. Swiveling the chair, he faced the expansive view from his office, his back turned to Sid.

"As usual, you announce your presence here like an air raid siren," the doctor said, templing his fingers.

"Quite a view you have here," Sid observed, ignoring the criticism. "You must be considered very important to get this kind of office."

"Is there something I can help you with, Sid?" Canta asked, swiveling the chair around.

Sid leveled a serious and accusatory glare across the desk. Looking at the doctor he looked for signs of what he feared the most. Like everyone else of his kind he was strikingly handsome and was shaped of what other men would call a perfect form. His tan face was finely chiseled in masculine angles. He had blonde hair cut short and combed close to his head and clear, blue eyes that drew people in magnetically. Doctor Canta was the very icon of what women wanted and men wanted to be.

None of these features mattered to Sid as he looked closely at the doctor. The charm, the good looks, the physique; he looked past all of these and tried to feel if a new energy had infected him.

"You know what I need from you," Sid told him after an uncomfortable silence passed between them.

Canta smiled, shaking his head. "Haven't we had this conversation before, Sid?" he asked in return. "It told you then, like I'll tell you now. I can't help you."

"I'm not asking you," Sid retorted. Just the hint of a threat hung on his words.

The smile fell from Canta's face.

"There's nothing I can do," he said. "Whatever is touching these kids is beyond me. Besides, I thought I was very clear about not getting involved."

"Right now, it's beyond all of us, but that doesn't mean it will stay that way," Sid pointed out.

Canta's head dropped and he shook his head. "I can't do that, Sid. This is serious. The Family won't let me meddle this time."

"Need I remind you of your oath?" Sid asked him.

Canta jumped out of his chair at these words. For a moment Sid thought he would attack him, but the doctor just stood up and began to pace behind his desk. Sid could see the anxiety that gripped him. He really was afraid of what was going on. But there was something else there. Not fear but . . . He couldn't put his finger on it.

"I think I've fulfilled that oath many times over," Canta argued. "Do you know how often I've put my neck on the line for you? Not to mention all your predecessors too."

"I wasn't aware that your oath had an expiration date," Sid observed as he watched the doctor grow more agitated. Something else was there. Sid could feel it working to the surface.

"Well, it probably should," Canta said as he paced. He rubbed the back of his neck in agitation. "Do you know how long ago that was?"

"Do you remember what is at stake?" Sid asked in return.

"Old news, Sid" Canta said. He leaned his hands on the desk, looming over Sid. "The world has moved on and it's times you did as well."

"I'm not asking," Sid warned. He could feel the conflict rising in the room.

"I can't help you, Sid. I'm sorry. You'll have to get someone else to be your errand boy."

Reaching into his pocket Sid held out a small piece of faded leather. It had been folded over and sealed up with a silver circle emblazoned with a cross. The surface of the leather was stained in crimson, like a drop of blood that had been spilled on it long ago.

It was a nondescript item that Sid held, but the result on Canta was noticeable. He paled when he saw it and swallowed hard. He tried to recover his demeanor with a forced smile. Sweat began to bead on his forehead.

"Sid, why would you do that?" he asked, the hurt obvious in his voice. "After all we've been through."

"Why would you make me do this?" Sid asked in return.

The forced smile returned to Canta's face. "Hey, why do you even need that old thing, anymore?" he asked. "Why don't I buy it from you?"

"It's not for sale," Sid answered.

"C'mon," he said, trying to lay on the charm. "There's a lot I could give you."

Sid could feel the effect of a geas on him, pulling at him, making him want to comply. It was the effect of natural charisma magnified to an inhuman degree. It had been so long since any enchantment had been thrown his way that he recoiled from the effect. Shaking his head he went from surprise to outrage.

"Are you trying to put an enchantment on me?" he asked, barely able to get the words out.

"Give me the charm," Canta demanded, holding his hand out towards Sid.

The power of the geas multiplied, slamming into Sid's consciousness like a sudden wave. A compulsion grew in him, demanded him to do as Canta asked. He felt like a tug inside of him. Canta was hitting him with all of his power.

"The charm," he demanded again, his face growing dark.

At that moment Sid could see all of his fears realized. Canta wasn't just reluctant to help him out of a sense of caution. Something darker had taken root in him. He had drunk of something forbidden and it had sent an intoxication through his soul.

Even knowing that as long as he held the charm then Canta couldn't harm him he still felt a quake of terror within him. He was being hit with a powerful enchantment that was trying to break down his resistance. He watched helplessly as his arm crept forward, ready to place the charm in Canta's outstretched hand.

The shock lasted only a moment. Sid recovered himself, pushing off the initial surge and remembered who he was. He remembered what he had been through. He had faced greater perils than these, resisted greater enchantments. He was a Keeper of the sacred flame of life, he reminded himself. A Keeper of the sacred image of God.

"Release me from this enchantment, Ercanta!" Sid demanded, pulling his arm back.

The doctor reeled at the sound of his true name. He fell back in his chair in a swoon. A hand went up to his head, gripping the temples. He looked like he was on the verge of passing out.

"Don't do this," the doctor plead. "Please, you don't understand."

"What have you done?" Sid asked. "What have you taken?"

Canta moaned and writhed in his chair. Sid stood up and walked around the desk. The doctor refused to meet his eyes, covering them with his hand.

"Just leave me alone, Sid," he begged. "Please."

"Do they call you the god of medicine?" Sid asked.

Canta cried out and shook his head, refusing to answer.

"Ercanta!" Sid cried out. "Do they call you the god of medicine?"

The doctor cried out again. His hands flew into his hair and he gripped it tightly.

"Just . . . some nurses," he answered, the words being forced out of him. "They just . . . they just . . . they just play . . . that's all . . . harmless. Ahhhhh!"

He screamed out at these last words pulling at this hair. He began to shake as the conflict of compulsion and his attempt at deceit tore him in two. A new concern began to frighten Sid. If Canta resisted too much then it could be fatal. Sid couldn't let that happen, at least not yet.

"Have you renounced the name?" Sid asked. He was answered by a new outcry of screams and writhing. Even his legs began to shake.

"Have you renounced the name?" Sid demanded, yelling at the tortured doctor.

"I can't! I can't!" Canta confessed in agony. "You don't understand! The taste! It is the taste of heaven. It is the breath of God! You don't understand!"

Watching the doctor subject to this agony Sid could feel nothing but pity for the creature. He was right, after all. Sid didn't understand. Probably never would. At least not to the extent Canta was talking about.

He sighed, realizing it didn't make a difference whether he understood or not. Canta, as a Fae, could not drink of the soulfire that was meant for God alone. It was what had corrupted the Watchers, had led to their downfall and the destruction of the world. As much as Canta was intoxicated by the worship, it would destroy him in the end.

"Canta," he said with genuine sympathy. "You know you can't do this."

The doctor began to weep. Covering his face with his hands he cried, racked with shuddering sobs.

"Don't make me do it," he plead. "Let me keep it, Sid, just for a little bit."

"Canta," Sid implored. "You can't. Renounce the title. You must."

"Let me keep it!" Canta snarled jumping from the chair.

He hurled a geas at Sid, even stronger than before. The older man recoiled, almost losing his footing. The compulsion washed over him again, this one mixed with a deep dread.

"He will not suffer thy foot to be moved," Sid quoted, taking strength from the words. Canta was pushed back into his chair.

"He that keepeth thee will not slumber. Behold, he that keepeth Israel shall neither slumber nor sleep. The Lord is thy keeper; the Lord is thy shade upon thy right hand."

When Sid was finished Canta was shaking uncontrollably. He looked as if the chill of a fever had taken hold of him. He looked up at Sid with pleading eyes, dark circles already formed beneath them.

"Help me, Sid," he plead, tears streaking down his face. "I can't do it alone. Help me, Sid."

Sid leaned forward and held Canta still. He could feel heat emanating from him. It almost made Sid begin to sweat.

"Ercanta," he said gently. "Renounce the title of God. I give thee strength of mine. Take it. Renounce the title of God."

"I renounce the title of God," Canta said through chattering teeth. "I renounce the title of God and all of the worship given to me. I renounce it and give it to the God whom it belongs, the King of earth and heaven."

"Say the shama," Sid implored him. "Finish it."

Canta opened his mouth, but no words came out.

"Shama yisrael," Sid prompted. "Ercanta, say the shama. Shama yisrael."

"Shama yisrael," Canta chattered after.

"Adonai elohaynu," Sid prompted.

"Adonia elohaynu."

"Adonia echad."

"Adonai echad."

With those last words the trembling slowed and a calm came over Canta. He looked even paler than he had before and the rings under his eyes darker. The hale and fit body felt thin and emaciated under Sid's touch. He was wasting away before his very eyes.

"I can't remain long," Canta said. "I can't hold this form. I am too weak."

"I know," Sid said, understanding what he meant. "Go back to

Annywyn. Rest up and come back as soon as you can."

"It will take some time," he said.

"I will find the strength for you," Sid promised. "We need you for what lies ahead."

Canta nodded. "I'm sorry, Sid. After all we have been through. I never should have done this."

"I'm not done with you yet, old friend," Sid told him.

Even as they spoke, he could feel Canta's body growing thinner and lighter. He watched as the skin grew translucent and the web of veins showed beneath. His breath came in labored gasps.

"Gather your strength, Canta," Sid told him as he faded. "I will cover for you here."

Canta nodded and closed his eyes. Sid lowered him to the floor before struggling to get up himself. He felt all of his years at that moment. The struggle with Canta had cost him, but at the same time had given him a new energy. It felt good to be in the fight again. He knew he should have never left it, no matter how desperate it had gotten. That was the worst excuse he could have given himself.

"Still got some fight in you, old man," he told himself. In truth, it just felt good to be doing what he was meant to.

Sid picked up his cane and sighed. Walking to the window he looked outside at the bright day. Millions of people outside in the world going about their business with no idea what was at stake every day. And that was what he fought for, he told himself, that they might go about their lives unafraid of the evil that hunted them.

Content for the first time in many years, Sid turned to leave. He paused to look down at the floor where Canta lay. There was nothing there now, and no indication at all that a body had been there just moments before.

Chapter 9 - Gunmen Too

After a grueling day of training and exercise, Malachi learned they were to be taught in more than hand to hand combat.

"Today you will choose a gun," the Master Sergeant told them Wednesday morning after breakfast.

They had discovered more depths to the house that morning. Over in what they had begun to call the swordsmen wing, was an indoor gun range. An impressive array of weaponry was laid out on the table just inside the range. Malachi didn't believe he had ever been near such a vast display. Everything he knew existed was there along with many he had never guessed. Pistols, rifle, shotguns, assault rifles, and many that looked like hybrids of different types were displayed.

"Every man has a gun that is best suited to his temperament," the Master Sergeant explained as the men looked over the weapons. "You will try out a variety today and we will find what suits you best. Have you all seen Harry Potter?"

All the men nodded except for Zach. He made a cross with two fingers as if to ward off evil. Many Bible studies had degraded into arguments over whether or not Christians should read the popular books about the boy magician. Zach, being the sole opponent, insisted they were the tool of the devil.

"Well, for those of you that have seen it," Diggs explained. "This is a lot like choosing a wand. The gun chooses you."

"This is nothing like that satanic trash," Zach muttered under his breath as he admired one of the many 9mm options on the table.

"You like the Sig?" Diggs asked when he noticed Zachary looking the pistol over. "The P210 might be the best one ever made."

Malachi looked over the array of weapons as the men openly admired them. Normally, he wasn't much of a gun man, but any break from their fight training was welcome to him. He had woken up that morning in excruciating pain. Every muscle in his body was sore and bruises covered his back and arms. When he tried to get up his joints protested, requiring several minutes of stretching and groaning to coax them into action.

"I thought we were the Swordsmen?" Vic asked as he handled one of the biggest handguns Malachi had ever seen. "Are we going to be the gunsmen now?"

"Sid wants you trained in the weaponry most likely to be used by the enemies you will face," the Master Sergeant explained. "Once upon a time that was swords. Today, for good or ill, it's guns. But don't worry, I'll teach you to use a sword as well."

After that brief introduction Diggs had all the men begin shooting with a variety of pistols. He insisted they try them all, whether they wanted to or not. As they shot, he looked closely at them, not correcting anything at the moment. What he was watching for none of the men could tell. Whatever it was, he looked intently, scrutinizing the grip, the stance, and even the face of the men as they fired.

A first round with every gun proceeded until the Master Sergeant had them all stop.

"If you had to pick just one of these, which one would it be?" he asked the men.

"The P210," Zach answered without hesitation. "That's the hottest thing I've ever held in my hands."

Vic chuckled and opened his mouth, unable to resist the invitation that Zach had given him. A stern look from Diggs and a sharp elbow from Gary silenced him before he could get anything out.

"Yes, you and the Sig seemed to bond there," Diggs observed. "I agree. Take it. That's your main sidearm now."

Most of the other men had a preference of their own. After shooting them all they had definite opinions of what gun they should carry.

To no one's surprise, Gary took the Desert Eagle. The large and powerful sidearm seemed to suit him well. Giovanni took for himself a Glock 9mm, while Victor attached himself to the 1911. Danny preferred a snub nosed .38 while Tresmond surprised everyone by choosing the .380.

"Are you sure about that?" the Master Sergeant asked. "A lot of people will pick that for a backup weapon. There are other options out there that have a lot more punch than that little thing."

Tres shook his head, undeterred. "The others are too bulky," he said. "I don't know what to say. This is the only one that felt right in my hand, that wouldn't slow me down."

The Master Sergeant nodded, conceding to Tresmond's reasoning. "I can see that. Maybe that is the right fit for you. Make sure you grab the Ruger. The new ones are outfitted with a twelve-round mag."

The only one of them who seemed to have trouble picking a sidearm was Malachi. Never a gun enthusiast, he had only moderate exposure to the weapons in the first place. All of them felt bulky to him and awkward in his hands. He seemed to be an adequate marksman, but didn't feel an affinity for any one of the pistols.

"Let's just stick to the Glock 9 for you as well," Diggs suggested. "If it doesn't work for you then we can keep looking."

The test with the rifles and shotguns were as equally daunting to Malachi. While most of the men took to one larger weapon over another, Malachi didn't seem to find one that fit him perfectly.

"Maybe you're just not a gun fighter," Diggs suggested, sounding a little frustrated. "I can usually fit a man with a gun pretty easily, but you are proving to be a challenge."

None of the other men proved to be a challenge at all. Gary latched on to the AR15 almost immediately. Giovanni chose the Beretta tactical shotgun with the pistol grip, while Zach preferred the more compact Tavor X95. Danny seemed to gravitate towards the HK416 and finally decided on that one. Tres was the only one that chose an AK style rifle and picked PSAK-47. To his own surprise Vic liked the M40 more than any other weapon.

"Never thought of myself as a sniper," he commented, admiring the weapon treasured by marines all over the world for its accuracy and reliability.

"Maybe they missed your real talent when you served," Diggs suggested. "Infantry?"

Vic nodded with a smile. "I think I irritated my CO's too much," he said. "They hoped I would be cannon fodder and out of their hair."

"Think?" Gary said incredulously. "I know you irritated your CO's. And everyone else you ever served with."

The Master Sergeant returned the smile with a wide one of his own. "Wouldn't be the first officer who couldn't see the forest for the trees."

Long after the other men had chosen both their main weapon and sidearm Malachi was looking over the vast array offered to him. None of them screamed out to him. None of them felt particularly useful to him either. Rationally, he knew that he might very well need one of these weapons, although he hoped it never came to that. But he couldn't seem to decide which one to choose.

"I guess I could use the AR," he finally suggested.

"You can't go wrong there," Diggs observed. "Don't worry, we'll find out what you are supposed to fight with my friend. I've never failed a soldier yet."

Once the long process of choosing was done, Diggs set about teaching them how to use the weapons. This time, when they shot, he was looking to correct stance and method. He was patient, aware of each man's skill level. Vic was, by far, the best marksmen, though Danny and Zach proved quite adept also.

The respite from their fight training only lasted until a few hours after lunch. Once they had a final round with their guns, Diggs had them fighting hand to hand again.

All the men groaned as they assembled at the training room, but none more vocal than Malachi and Danny. The two older men felt every bruise and sore muscle flare up again as they kicked, punched, blocked, whirled and fell on their backs. Malachi could tell he was slower, not faster than the day before. When he pointed this out to Diggs the Master Sergeant was undeterred.

"Your muscles have to get used to the activity," he explained to them. "You'll pick up speed, and agility. I promise."

Malachi kept swinging arms that felt like they had thirty-pound weights on them. It's Wednesday, he told himself. This can't last much longer. He never believed he would ever think longingly of work. But as he pushed his sore and beaten body to further and further limits, he found himself thinking of his boring chair and desk back at the office, and all the little spats and problems that used to drive him mad. He thought it looked a lot like paradise.

Chapter 10 - Preparation

Thursday evening Master Sergeant Diggs stood with Sid on the upper floor of the mansion. They looked out a window at the back garden below. The sun was setting, casting an orange light over the trees. Nearby they could hear the cicadas begin their night time buzzing.

Below them, the men exercised in the yard. Some worked alone, punching the air and swiping away invisible attacks. Others worked in pairs, jabbing and feinting and working through take downs.

"How are they coming along?" Sid asked as two men watched from the high tower room.

Diggs shrugged noncommittally. "They're learning," he remarked. "Tresmond shows a lot of promise. Victor as well. Surprisingly, Danny has showed some flare as a fighter. They shouldn't embarrass themselves in a fight but they aren't an elite unit or anything."

"But do they know enough?" Sid asked. "For the transformation. Do they know enough to make it stick?"

Diggs shrugged again. "That's more your area than mine," he reminded him. "Remember, I've only done this once before."

"I know," Sid nodded. "And this is the first time I've done this by myself."

A sense of loneliness came over Sid without warning. His mind thought back to all the men who had stood with him and stood before him. They had faced hard times together, but they had always faced them together. Never had he been forced to make decisions all on his own like he was now. Never had any Keeper, as far as Sid knew, had to stand alone in his dark hour. He sorely missed his friends.

The two men continued to watch the training below. Watching them go through their practice they did look a touch more competent than they were before, but they were far from ready to face any enemy. And they certainly weren't ready to face the enemy that waited for them. In truth, no human was. All the same, it was Sid's job to prepare them for just that.

"I guess we are as ready as we will be," Sid remarked with a heavy sigh. "You've done an excellent job Master Sergeant."

He placed a hand on Diggs' shoulder. The Master Sergeant still studied the practice going on below. A small chuckle escaped his lips.

"What is it?" Sid asked.

"Just a funny thought," he said, gesturing to the men working out below. "By this time tomorrow any of those guys will be able to manhandle me like I was a child."

"Let's hope so," Sid agreed. "By all that is holy, let us hope."

Friday morning came with a dose of good news. They would not be training that day. Malachi was ecstatic when he learned his weary body would be getting a rest. Though he wasn't as sore as he was Wednesday, his bones certainly screamed out for a break.

This was followed by a drop of less than good news.

"Wait, we're what?!" Zach asked in shock. "What did you say we were doing?"

"You will be fasting today," Sid repeated, hitting the men like a cement truck in the face.

"Fasting?" Vic asked. "Like in no food fasting?"

"Is there another kind?" Gary asked, seeming to enjoy Vic's discomfort.

"We can't fast now," Tres complained. "You've just been working us out, developing new muscle. We need nutrition, especially protein if you want that muscle to develop properly."

"I've never fasted before," Zach huffed. "I don't think I can fast. I know I can't fast."

"It's all a very important part of the process," Sid assured them. "It will only be until later this evening."

"We can't eat until tonight?" Zach exclaimed. "We're fasting all day?"

An edge of desperation had entered his voice.

"I can't go a whole day without eating,"

"I assure you, you can," Sid told him.

"Jesus went forty days without eating," Gary chimed in. Of all the men he seemed the least disturbed about the fast.

"I'm not Jesus," Zach whined. A groan came out of him as he held his hands over his stomach, already seeming to suffer from the coming lack of food.

"This is not a spurious exercise, I promise," Sid assured them. "This is a critical part of your training."

Sid paused and a knowing look passed between him and Gerard. Diggs stood behind them with his hands folded behind his back and his head down, unwilling to look any of the men in the eye. There was a secret between them, that Malachi could see well. It was something that saddened them? Frightened them? Malachi couldn't tell which, but it scared him as well.

"Tonight will be a critical . . . the critical part of your training," Sid continued. "It will also be the hardest part of your training."

He paused again and looked to the other men. It seemed he was looking for strength to continue on.

"What happens tonight?" Vic asked. "Are we getting branded or what?"

Sid allowed himself a small grin.

"You may wish that was all that was happening to you," he said ominously.

"Tonight, you will face your demons," he continued. "Tonight, you will face your mortality. It is the one test that a swordsmen must face. If you face it successfully, then you will be a warrior, a knight in the service of God, standing with the elite warriors that have served and fought and died for thousands of years. It is the most honored brotherhood a man can be a part of besides the Church."

He paused again and looked at the floor. One of his hands absently fiddled with the silver tip of his cane. Malachi felt a pit of dread rise up in his stomach.

"But there is also a chance that you may not survive the test," he told them.

It took a moment for the import of his words to sink into the men. That they would face danger was a certainty. But to possibly face death in training, and tonight? It was a blow that stunned them into silence.

"What do you mean, we may not survive?" Giovanni asked for clarification.

Sid looked at him with a weighty sadness.

"It means just what I said," he told them. "You may not survive the test."

The weight of those words sunk in as each man searched himself. The stakes were suddenly higher than they imagined.

"What kind of test is this?" Danny asked, his skepticism returning. "Is this even legal?"

"It is not the test that you think of when think of test," Sid explained. "This is the kind of test to refine you, to harden and complete you. But it is also dangerous."

"Like silver in a furnace," Malachi quoted.

"Yes," Sid nodded. "Exactly like that."

"I don't think we've been given enough training for this," Danny complained. "We've learned a little hand to hand combat and shot some guns. I don't think that qualifies us for a test of life and death."

"This does not test your physical prowess or your fighting skills," Sid answered. "This is a test of your faith and your trust. It is a test of character."

"Still, I can't say I'm ready for this."

"You are ready," Sid assured him.

"Yeah, well how can you be so sure?"

Sid gripped his cane and took a step towards the men. He looked them in the eye, one after the other. Malachi could feel an intensity emanating from that look, a power that belied the elderly exterior of the man.

"All of you are ready," he asserted with confidence and power. "I know because I did not choose you. All of you were chosen for me. You were chosen for this time, and for this task. The one who chose you is the one who equips you. The one who equipped you has made you ready. The one who has made you ready does not falter or fail. Trust in him. Trust in who he has made you, and in who he is still making you, and you will not fail."

Sid left them with the assurance that any of the men were free to leave before the test that night. They were to spend that day in prayer and fasting. If, after the time of fasting was done and any of them felt they were not ready, they would be released.

When they were alone all the men expressed their doubts to each other. A look of worry and consternation was on every face that looked at Malachi. All except Tres.

The grieving father showed not the least shred of doubt in him. If anything, he looked to have a peace about him, a calm that he hadn't showed since the death of his son. Malachi even feared he may be looking forward to the test that night, that he may even welcome the prospect of his death.

"What do we do?" Danny asked the group. He was answered by shaking heads.

"This sounds crazy," Giovanni said. "What kind of test could this be?"

"I don't like the sound if it," Zach echoed. "I certainly didn't sign up for this when we agreed to help."

"Well, what did you think would happen?" Gary asked.

"I certainly didn't think we would face some test that might kill us," Danny argued.

"Yeah, but we knew we might face that at some point," Gary countered.

"Speak for yourself."

"No, we all knew this going in," Gary continued to press. "Think about it. He asked us to be warriors, to help root out an evil that no one else in the world was able to face. Do you think that would come without any risk? Do you think we could do that without putting our life on the line?"

"Not in training," Danny pointed out.

"If there is no risk in training it won't prepare you for the real thing," Vic chimed in, speaking from his military experience. "You have to face this on some level if you want to be ready to face the real thing."

Danny shook his head and waved him away. "Do you really think we're ready to face something like this?"

"I'm ready," Tres spoke up. "Whatever it takes. I'm ready."

"Tres . . ." Danny began but found he couldn't finish the words.

Every one of the men seemed to remember why they were there in the first place. Tresmond had lost his son to a terrible evil, something Sid told them was beyond a mere disease. They had been called to stand with their brother. Now, that call was being put to the test.

"He told us today was for fasting and prayer," Tres said. "So, let's do that. We pray. We fast. We find out if we're ready for this. If you aren't, I understand. I won't hold you to it. Sid told us we have until the evening to decide. So, let's decide then."

The men all seemed in agreement with what Tres asked of them. Suddenly, Malachi was no longer aware of his hunger. Something else had settled in his stomach and it left no room at all for food.

Gerard guided the men through the mansion towards the south end, the part they had not been in before. At the end of a long, paneled hallway stood arched doors with thick, oak molding. He pulled these open and stood aside as Malachi and the men stepped into a small chapel.

It reminded Malachi of the chapels he visited in Europe, those housed in the castles all over the continent. It was made of stone, carved in ribbed arches that formed a dome over their heads. Stained glass windows let in colored light from the sides with one large window at the front. Biblical scenes were depicted in the glass, a still life from stories that Malachi immediately recognized. Six rows of short, wooden pews ran up each side of the chapel. An open Bible sat upon a stone altar on the raised dais at the front.

"You will prepare yourselves here for the trial ahead," Gerard told them. His voice echoed off the stone wall, giving weight and solemnity to his words.

"Is this a Catholic chapel?" Zach asked, noting the kneelers in front of all the pews.

Malachi groaned inside, not willing to fight this battle today. As Zach himself often said, he was from a tradition of "holy rollers" who had a natural distrust of anything that resembled the Roman Church. Although the Swordsmen were an inter-denominational group, Zach didn't consider Catholics part of that equation. Many Bible studies got distracted with his question of are Catholics even Christians.

"This is a Christian chapel," Gerard asserted, not claiming any denominational affiliation.

Zach nodded, satisfied with that answer. He did a quick look around the chapel, as if to assure himself it didn't have any statues of the Virgin Mary anywhere.

"I will come get you when it is time to go the ceremony," Gerard said before turning to leave.

"Wait, we're going to be here all day?" Vic asked of the retreating figure. He checked his watch to confirm his suspicion that it was still morning.

Gerard stopped and turned back to the men. He smiled indulgently at them but did not answer the question that had been posed.

"Take advantage of this time," he said. "I will see you this evening."

With that he turned and left the men in the chapel. Vic checked his watch again and threw up his hands in frustration.

"It's nine o'clock," he told them. "Are we supposed to sit here and pray for . . .ten hours?"

"Guess so," Gary patted him on the shoulder and said.

"What am I supposed to pray about for ten hours?" Vic asked to no one in particular.

"Pray for something to pray about," Zach asked. He chuckled to himself, obviously pleased with his joke.

"Haha, very funny," Vic shot back. He obviously didn't like to be the one to receive the jokes. "I need to pray to stay awake. Don't be surprised if you hear me snoring some time. And don't wake me up."

With no other choice the men settled into a pew and began their prayers. The silence settled over them with a sense of dread at first. All Malachi could think about was this trial, or ceremony ahead. Whatever it was it would put their lives at risk. The very thought set his imagination at work cooking up all sorts of scenarios where he died some horribly convoluted death.

It took him the better part of an hour to shake these thoughts out of his head and focus on the task at hand. I'm doing this or I'm not, he told himself. I don't have to go through with this trial if I decide not to. When Gerard comes to get us this evening, I will simply tell him I'm not up for it. I can't take the risk. Sorry, I'm not cut out to be a soldier. I'm an administrator at a hospital, not some demon fighter. No shame in that.

As soon as he had convinced himself of this Malachi was able to settle into a prayer. He closed his eyes and breathed deep, allowing a calm to wash over him. All around him he could hear the prayers of some of the men as they whispered in the echoing chapel. It kind of fell into a rhythm and Malachi felt himself being carried along by its currents. He forgot about his breath, about the task ahead, even about the chapel around him. Turning his mind to prayer he reached out for the presence of the divine that he found was always hovering near him when he reached out in faith.

All sense of time was lost as Malachi let the prayer take him over. Only dimly was he aware of what was going on around him. At some point a voice cried out in anguish, but they all stayed in their prayers. At another time Malachi heard weeping behind him. More than once, someone broke out in song or in loud prayers. But never once was the sense of being in prayer broken. Hunger and fatigue and discomfort all faded into the background. There was only the sense of the divine, hovering near, but never overwhelming. A presence, an undefinable power kept them in the state of prayer, drawing them deeper and deeper.

When Malachi had the sense of the chapel darkening, a song to play in his head. He didn't notice it at first, until at one point he realized he was singing. Quietly, and then with more passion as the words struck him and filled him.

This is my Father's world

And to my listening ears
All nature sings, and round him rings
The music of the spheres

As he sang, he was overcome with a deep sense of peace. He didn't worry at all about the trial that was coming ahead, nor the dangers it posed. An assurance came over him that he would be okay, that he would not only pass the trial, but that he had been called to face it. The same power that drew near in prayer was telling him, in no uncertain terms, that he was meant to face whatever test Sid had for him, and that he would come through the other side.

"Gentlemen, it is time," the familiar voice of Gerard told them.

Malachi opened his eyes, and straightened up, surprised to see how much time had passed. The chapel was in the first darkening of twilight. He looked down at his watch and it read seven o'clock. As Vic had predicted, they had been praying for ten hours.

A smile crossed his lips as he looked across the aisle and saw Zach get up from one of the kneelers. The self-professed holy roller looked down at the cushioned frame as if he were a little confused, wondering how he got there. Malachi saw the other men rub their eyes and look around with amazement, wonder on their faces as to how the time could have passed so quickly.

"Are you ready for the trial?" Gerard asked when they gathered at the door of the chapel.

A few nods answered the question. No one said anything out loud.

"I need to hear your answer," the butler demanded. "Before we go any further, I need to know you are ready for what lies ahead."

"How can we know?" Danny answered. "We have no idea what lies ahead."

The butler smiled and nodded his head. "Well spoken, sir," he said. "Do you want to continue? Is there anyone who wants to back out? I need to hear an answer."

Gerard locked yes with each man in turn. Each man he looked at he received the same answer.

"I'm ready," they all said.

Malachi was last. He wasn't sure up until that point exactly what he would say. That a sense of peace and acceptance had come over him during his prayers was undeniable. But it didn't change how crazy it sounded to Malachi to be accepting this vague challenge that came with a certain danger.

"The Lord is my strength and my shield," he heard himself answer.

"Whom shall I fear," the men answered in unison.

"The Lord is the stronghold of my life."

"Of whom shall I be afraid."

"Let's do this," Malachi said.

Once he had received all their answers Gerard lead them through the hallways of the mansion and out into the backyard. Like their last journey, it was sunset when the men approached the broken wall at the edge of the property. Just like the last time they walked through the old door and made their way through the path.

It didn't take long for Malachi to recognize the strange change in the environment. One step around a turn in the path and the trees grew larger and more ancient. The canopy of the old forest spread out over their heads, blotting out the waning light. The vigor returned to the air, along with that sense of magic and mystery that permeated the atmosphere.

Malachi smiled despite himself. It was an irresistible sense that wouldn't be denied. The vigor returned to him, the strength in his every step. It cleared his mind and filled him with confidence.

"It's nice to be back," Danny turned to him to say.

Malachi could only nod, taking in the forest around him. They walked through the winding path as the night grew dark. He noticed they took a different route from the last time they were there. Instead of going up they seem to skirt around the base of a hill, before winding down.

When the path began to descend the scenery changed around them as well. Instead of the thick forest, they started to pass through tall grasses. A mist settled down around them, so thick they couldn't see more than ten feet off the path. No one asked any questions. They were strangers here and relied on Gerard to guide them.

Their path led them through a stand of tall pines and cedars. They passed through their shade, feeling the air grow cooler the deeper they walked.

The stand of trees ended abruptly at a rocky edge. Malachi could tell it was the lip of a valley. The fog grew even denser here, almost impossible to see through.

Without hesitation Gerard led them through the path that wound down into the valley. The fog folder over Malachi and he could feel the chill of the air it brought along with it. He could hardly see Danny's back who walked in front of him. All around him he could make out the bare shadow of small, skeletal trees.

They continued to walk further into the valley and the fog began to lighten. The shadow of trees became actual trees themselves, but they had no more features. They were long dead, devoid of leaves, twisted and gnarled. They looked like hands frozen in horror, still gripping something that had long been torn from them.

Something moved among the trees, rippling along the branches. Malachi squinted and leaned closer. A dark mass hopped along the edge and he saw golden eyes peer out at him from the darkness.

They were ravens. Dozens of the birds clustered along the dead branches, like grim harbingers out of a nightmare. The one staring at Malachi flapped his wings and let out a guttural croak.

The path finally ended at an iron gate. A stone wall ran out from the gate, beyond Malachi's vision. Inside the gate, among the low clinging mist, tombstones stretched as far as he could see.

"A graveyard?" Vic remarked as they stood at the threshold. "You took us to a graveyard?"

Gerard pushed the iron gates open. They cried out in protest on rusty hinges, like a long, low scream that pierced the night. Malachi shuddered involuntarily.

Walking among the tombstones Gerard guided them deeper into the graveyard. Mausoleums and sarcophagi appeared between the leaning monuments of granite and stone. A chill, deeper than the cool air settled on them as they walked among the dead.

Malachi couldn't help but feel a cold dread as they traversed the graveyard. Like everything else he experienced in this place, the place Sid called Annwyn, the fear induced by walking among the dead here was much greater than what he ever experienced in the normal world. Just as the air was sharper, the earth richer, and the vigor of life stronger, so were the emotions that stirred in Malachi. This place was more terrifying than any graveyard he had ever been in. It was as if he could feel the spirits of the dead lingering nearby. At any moment he expected the gathering mist to coalesce into the form of a phantom and let out a terrible wail of anguish.

"Just don't tell us we have to dig our own graves" Vic remarked, trying to make light of the situation.

"I would never do that," Gerard said as they neared a domed building near the center of the graveyard.

They passed near a set of sarcophagi that looked newer than the others. They were plain, though carved of stone. Unlike any of the others, the lids had been pulled back to reveal an empty darkness within. Malachi quickly counted seven. The cold dread he had been feeling in the graveyard turned to ice.

"Why are there seven of those?" Zach asked. Malachi could feel the dread coming from his voice, echoing his own.

"I think that should be obvious," Sid answered from inside the domed building.

The men followed Gerard passed the open sarcophagi, and up the shallow steps into the marble building where Sid waited for them. It looked like a temple, open and round, the domed roof held up by pillars. A fire burned in the center of the marble floor from a pit that had been carved out for that very purpose.

Sid waited on the other side of the fire. Like the last time they came to Annwyn he was dressed in white robes. He held a wooden staff in place of his silver tipped cane. One hand was placed on a small marble stand that came up to his waist. The top carved out into a bowl.

The men gathered on the opposite side of Sid. A silence, born of anticipation and a touch of fear settled over them. The fire crackled in front of them, casting strange shadows on the domed ceiling. Outside, the mist hovered in the darkness, tracing itself along the cold ground. Moonlight illuminated the mist, giving it a silver glow. In the distance Malachi could hear the ravens continue their prophetic calls.

"Men, if you are here then that means you have decided to undertake this test," Sid began. "I thank you for your trust in me. It will not be easy.

"In a moment I will ask each of you to get into a sarcophagus. We will place the lid over you as well. It will be just like entering into a casket when you die. There, you will face your demons. There, you will face your own death. Trust in the Lord and you will conquer. Conquer, and you will emerge a new man. Do you understand?"

Danny shook his head and raised his hand. "I'm sorry, I don't understand. How long will you put us in that box and how will we face our demons?"

"You do not need to understand the process," Sid clarified. "All I need you to understand is what we will be doing and what is expected of you."

Danny looked back at the open sarcophagi. They waited as open graves, ready to swallow them up. Malachi could feel his own conflict reflected in his friend's features.

"I guess I do understand," he shrugged.

The old man nodded and bowed his head. His lips moved silently as he stretched his arms out wide. Malachi couldn't tell if he was mumbling or praying. With a deep breath he lifted his head and spoke aloud.

"Eternal God, in whom we live and breathe and have our being," he began. "Send us your Holy Spirit we pray. Cover these men with your protection, fill them with your grace and gird them for the task they have ahead of them."

Opening his eyes Sid looked at the men gathered before him. His face had grown stern and serious. His eyes blazed with an intensity that made Malachi rock back on his heels.

"Are you ready to face your darkness and death?" he asked them.

The men responded with a few nods. Some of them muttered a "yes."

Sid brought the staff down on the marble floor. The boom echoed in the chamber. Malachi felt it rumble in his chest. They jumped back at the sudden power and violence.

"I ask you," Sid thundered, his voice like a storm. "Are you ready to face your darkness and death? Answer me like men."

"I am," the men said together. Their voices range out in unison.

"Are you ready to face your darkness and death?" he asked again.

"I am," came the response again, louder this time.

"Are you ready to face your darkness and death?" Sid asked a third time.

"I am," came the third response.

"Are you ready to take up the weapons of light?" Sid asked them.

"I am," the men answered.

"Are you ready to give up your life as a sacrifice to the Lord?"

"I am," they answered without hesitation.

Each question Sid asked three times. With each time the answer grew stronger, more powerful, more certain. Malachi could feel the power of the response in him as he answered with his brothers. The conviction he felt during prayer multiplied and grew in him. His confidence soared. His doubt withered. This is what he was meant to do. Whatever came of it, he would face it with courage.

"Men, disrobe," Sid commanded them.

The men obeyed without hesitation. They all felt what Malachi had felt. A powerful spirit moved in them, uniting them and giving them strength. This was destiny they were walking into.

Malachi shivered in the cold mist of the graveyard as he took off his clothes. A wet chill crept over his skin, sinking deep into his bones.

"Just for the record," Vic said as he shuddered. "I want everyone to note how cold it is out here. So, no judgement, yeah?"

The men laughed at Victor's joke, probably a bit heartier than it deserved. The fear and the cold had them gripped in a tension they were all too eager to break.

When they all stood naked before him, Sid produced a glass vial. He walked to Gary, the first in line. Tipping the vial a stream of oil fell over his head. Sid touched his head and blessed him.

> *Dwell in shelter of the Most High and abide in the shadow of the Almighty. May the Lord be thy fortress and the God in whom thy trust. He will deliver you from the snare of the fowler and from the deadly pestilence. He will cover you with his wings and you will find refuge. You shall not fear the terror of the night nor the pestilence that stalks in darkness. A thousand my fall at your side, ten thousand at your right hand, but it will not come near you. Because you have made the Lord your dwelling place no evil shall be allowed to befall you, no plague come near your tent. He will command his angels concerning you to guard you in all your ways. On their hands they will bear you up, lest you strike your foot against a stone. You will tread on the lion and the adder; the young lion and the serpent you will trample underfoot.*

Sid anointed each man with oil as he blessed them. Another surge of power pulsed through Malachi as he felt the oil run down his head. The aroma of strong scents emanated from the oil, frankincense and myrrh and the extracts of sacred oils.

After their anointing the men were led each to an open sarcophagus. Cold mist swirled around them but they did not feel the cold. Each man stood by an open tomb. Naked as they were born, they were ready to descend into the silence from which they came. Not a trace of fear could be seen on their faces, only the resolve to face whatever lay ahead with courage.

"I thank each of you for your trust," Sid told the men. Malachi could detect a touch of sadness on Sid's voice, as if he already felt regret for what he was about to do.

"I ask you to trust me again," the old man continued. "You stand beside the grave of your old self. Enter now, and be made new."

Malachi nodded and climbed inside the stone sarcophagus. A chill ran through him as his naked skin touched the cold marble. He could see the stars of Annwyn shining bright and clear above him. They shined down on him like a benediction, gracing him with the light of heaven.

"I'm going to need it," Malachi muttered to himself.

"Try to relax," Gerard said as his face loomed in the opening of the sarcophagus. "I am going to close the lid. You may feel panic, but try not to resist. Everything will happen as it should."

Malachi nodded, feeling his resolve weaken and his uncertainty return. Stone scraped on stone as the lid of the sarcophagus was dragged over him. The last light of the stars disappeared as the darkness of the grave covered him.

The darkness was total. Malachi could see nothing, not even his own hand when he passed it in front of his face.

The silence was as total as the dark. His breathing echoed in the small chamber without any other sound to compete with. Soon, his own heartbeat echoed in his ears.

As he waited Malachi grew more uncertain. A vague sense of fear replaced all the resolve that he had just moments earlier. He was alone in the dark and silence, and a cold chill was creeping through his bones.

It wasn't just getting colder in the sarcophagus, Malachi noticed. It was wet too. His back and shoulders and legs felt ice cold water on them. Was it there before, he asked himself as the vague fear grew to a certain dread.

When he felt the water rise that dread gave way to panic. It was ice cold water and it was getting higher. It wasn't just his back that was wet now, the sides of his arms were submerged. The water was still rising.

"Hey!" Malachi called out. "There's water in here! Is that supposed to happen?"

No answer came to his question except more of the dark silence.

"Hey!" Malachi called out again, beating on the back of the stone lid. "It's filling with water!"

He couldn't see the water, but could feel it pooling beneath him. It rose higher and higher, covering him with its dread chill. It covered his feet and chest and continued to rise. He felt it rise past his ears and touch the sides of his cheek.

"Hey! Help!" he cried out, banging on the lid. "Sid! It's filling with water!"

No answer came from his desperate cries. He began to shake as fear and cold washed over him. The iciness of the water was unforgiving, and it sapped the heat from his bones.

"Sid! Gerard!" he yelled out in vain.

The water covered his face and Malachi tried to sit up to find air. Pain shot through his head as it struck the unyielding stone. He felt out with his hand to find the top then leaned up as far as he could. He felt a streak of warmth flow down his head and he knew it was his own blood.

"Sid! Help! Gerard!" he screamed as he hammered on the lid of the coffin.

The water continued to rise and Malachi gave full vent to his panic. He thrashed and beat at the lid, the walls, anything his hands or feet could touch. He didn't notice the cuts from the stone, nor did he feel it when he broke the bones in his hands.

The water filled the sarcophagus, taking all the air with it. Malachi continued to struggle even as he knew it was in vain. He lacked the strength to save himself. This was the moment he had feared his whole life. The cold settled into him along with the silence and dark.

Malachi felt his lungs burn and knew that the end was coming. A new calm came over him as he struggled, even a sensation that could be called peace. He felt his struggle cease, his body still. The quiet and dark washed over his senses, his body, and then his mind. With the last of his resolve broken, Malachi let go.

Outside the sarcophagus, Sid and Gerard stood in the graveyard and listened to the muffled screams and struggles that were going on within. A pained look of conflict contorted Sid's face. The butler looked calmer as the thumpings and cries for help slowly silenced, then faded completely.

"I don't think I'll ever get used to this," Sid confessed when the graveyard went completely quiet.

The stillness felt heavy now as if it had its own weight. The blue light of the moon shimmered in the swirl of mist. Somewhere beyond the graveyard a raven croaked, his sound like an opus to the dead.

Gerard looked up at the old man with sympathy. "If you did get used to it, I would worry about you," he said.

The two men walked over to a pool of water that stood next to the row of sarcophagi. It was built into the ground with stone steps leading down into it. It was a small pool, a rectangle just large enough for a big man to lie down in.

"Yes, this is the worst part of it all," Sid continued to muse. "Having to stand here and listen to them die."

Chapter 11 - Facing the Demons

Malachi gasped and his eyes flew open.

Light and air filled him with a sudden intensity. He flailed his arms, searching desperately for purchase, for anything that could pull him out of the sarcophagus.

Realization came back to him as the panic subsided. He could breathe again. He could see. Malachi took in another deep breath to take stock of his environment.

He was in a long hallway with a red carpet running up its length. Unadorned beige walls stretched out on either side, with wood paneling that rose waist high.

Relief poured through Malachi as he touched the walls and continued to breathe deep, refreshing air. With the relief he remembered why he was there. This was a test.

Looking around him again his relief became short lived. Water poured down the walls of the hallway. The carpet was already soaked beneath his feet. It wouldn't be long until it filled up completely.

Already feeling his panic rise Malachi plowed down the hall. At the end he could see two doors waiting. One of them, he hoped, was a way out.

After a quick pause before the doors, Malachi chose the one on the left. It opened without resistance. Surprise struck him as he recognized the room beyond. It was his grandmother's house.

There was no mistaking the old family home. Wood floors topped with that fading Persian rug, so old that it was frayed with holes worn in spots. All the same his grandmother loved that rug and refused every entreaty by the family to replace it.

Old, family furniture, including a blue sofa as faded as the rug decorated the room. Family portraits hung on the wall. Malachi could see his own senior picture on the other side of the box television set, antennas sticking out wrapped with aluminum foil. Outside he could see Swansea Middle School across the street.

It was all just as he remembered it, like he wanted to remember it. Before his grandmother died and they had to sell the house. Rather, his uncle sold the house, bringing untold pain upon the family.

Still, it was a good memory. Just seeing the old place filled Malachi with warmth. Even better, he could escape the rising waters and walk right outside.

"Look who showed up," a gravelly voice called out, filling Malachi with a deep and primal dread.

A familiar figure looked up from the antique rocker in front of the TV. Hands that shook just slightly lifted up a glass with a red painted rooster on its sides. Malachi didn't even have to look to know that Old Crow bourbon filled that glass.

"Uncle Ray," Malachi whispered in shock.

It was one of the last people he wanted to see.

Uncle Ray was a Vietnam Veteran, scarred in deep ways from the war. Or at least that is what his mother always told him. At least he had been.

Ray was one of the veterans who really never returned from the war. Alcoholism, depression, drug abuse, unremitted rage; all the classic signs of PTSD that went undiagnosed and unrecognized plagued Uncle Ray. He struggled to hold down jobs, or relationships. Lifestyle and circumstance forced him to live with his mother until she died. Two years after that he sold the house and moved into a veteran's home, that is until he decided to end it all with a .45 stuffed into his mouth. To this day, Malachi could honestly say Uncle Ray was the meanest bastard he had ever known.

"Whiteys come to see us," Uncle Ray shot at Malachi through bleary, blood-shot eyes.

That was Uncle Ray's name for Malachi as far back as he could remember. He didn't know how he got that name, except for his skin being lighter than Ray's, though not the lightest in his family by a long shot. For some reason, Uncle Ray had fixated on Malachi some vague and unnamed hatred.

"Ain't nothin' worse than a black man parading around as if he's white," Uncle Ray spat and sipped his bourbon.

"Why you keep crawlin' around here as if you one of us?" Ray asked him. "You don't belong here, Whitey. Hear me? You run along with your white folks."

Memories came crashing in on Malachi as he listened to his uncle hurl the familiar insults his way. He was a child again, subject to the anger of an older, stronger man. It was a helpless fear, for he had no recourse but to endure.

123

"Uncle Ray is just angry," his mother would explain whenever Malachi complained about it.

It would be years later until Malachi realized Uncle Ray was terrible to everyone. In some way, they were all equally helpless. But as a child all Malachi could understand is that Uncle Ray hated him and no one did anything about it. He was left to confront that fear and anger all alone.

"Your mama should have smothered you," he would say when no one else was noticing. The smell of bourbon always hung thick on his breath. "But I will. When she ain't lookin, Whitey. Gonna put the pillow over your face and squeeze it until there ain't no more breath in you."

"Why you still standin there, Whitey?" his uncle asked as Malachi stayed rooted in the threshold. "You ain't coming in here."

Malachi watched his uncle sip at his bourbon. He rocked in the chair, watching something on the old television set Malachi couldn't make out. Dimly he was aware of the water rising up to his ankles.

After twenty minutes Sid checked his watch and looked at Gerard. They both looked down at the pool of water at their feet. Its surface remained undisturbed.

"Any minute now," Sid remarked.

Most of the time, it took about thirty minutes for the men who would get through the test to see it to the end. The fastest Sid had ever witnessed was twenty-five. Any longer than forty-five minutes and the chances were rare for getting through. No one had taken longer than an hour and made it.

"Who do you think will be first?" Sid asked, more to occupy his mind and keep it off his worry than anything else.

Gerard thought for a minute. "I would say Victor," he answered.

Sid scoffed. "What? Mr. Dodds? No way."

"He has a good sense of humor," Gerard noted. "There's a lightness to him. That will get him through."

"Unless it's a cover," Sid pointed out. "Then he could take the longest. My money is on Gary. He's got the faith to get through."

Gerard considered this and nodded. "He may. I still say it will be Victor."

"Care to make it interesting?" Sid asked. "I'll put twenty on Gary."

Gerard smiled and shook his head. "You know I have nothing smaller than a fifty."

Sid smiled and looked down at the pool of water at his feet. It still hadn't moved, nor had the surface been disturbed in the least. A knot of worry began to grow in his stomach. What if no one made it out? That was unlikely, but it had been so long since he had inducted new swordsmen. And so much had changed since then. People had changed so much since then. So much of human virtue had grown cold. The nobility and courage, the faith and hope, even the love - especially the love - that fueled the hero's heart was lacking in today's men.

Forcing himself to shake away those doubts Sid pushed the worry away. He had not chosen these men, he reminded himself. Someone far wiser had made this decision, had gathered this group and made the call. He would be faithful and true. If for some reason only one, or none of them, emerged from the trial, it would all be according to a higher wisdom.

Lost in these thoughts Sid didn't notice the surface of the water stirring. It rippled at first, as if the ground had shaken it. They began to appear all over the surface, colliding with one another as the water was agitated.

Hope flared in Sid again when Gerard nudged him and pointed to the pool. Bubbles broke the surface. A hand reached out, grasping for any hold. With one last churn a head emerged, followed by the rest of the body.

Sid and Gerard both exchanged a surprised look as they recognized the form struggling out of the water. Giovanni took hold of the steps and was able to pull himself to the edge. Exhausted, he collapsed on the stone edge of the pool, half of his body still in the water.

"Giovanni," Sid mused, looking down at the breathless figure.

Gerard shrugged and leaned down, grabbing the man beneath the arms. He gently pulled Giovanni out of the pool as he struggled to get his bearings again. Sid could see on his face the confusion and disorientation that were the hallmarks of coming out of the Pool of Awakening. He shook as water dripped off of him, the cold air shocking the already travailed body.

"Lay him down," Sid instructed.

The butler lay the shaking Giovanni on the ground next to the pool. His breath calmed as he looked around. Recognition dawned on his face looking up at Sid and Gerard.

"The test," Giovanni muttered.

Sid nodded. "You passed the test," he said.

Giovanni let his head fall back onto the ground. He took in one big breath, this one a sigh of relief.

"That was terrible," he remarked. "Tell me I never have to do that again."

"Never again," Sid promised him.

Leaning down Gerard offered Giovanni a hand up. The other man rose to his feet and the butler wrapped a blanket around him. He looked around the otherwise empty graveyard.

"So, I'm the first?" he asked.

Sid nodded. "You're the first. Congratulations."

Nodding in return Giovanni looked around again at the emptiness of the graveyard. He pointed to the sarcophagi, the ones they had been lowered into just moments earlier.

"I remember it filled up with water," he said. "Was that supposed to happen?"

"It was," Sid told him. "That was part of the test you undertook."

Giovanni looked with wide eyes at the sarcophagus. The reality of what truly had been at stake hit him, what could have happened.

"I could have died there," he remarked. His head rocked back in disbelief.

A knowing look passed between Sid and Gerard; a heavy silence pregnant with meaning. The butler took Giovanni by the arm and lead him towards the temple where a fire and wooden benches waited.

"This may be hard to hear," Sid began when Giovanni sat by the fire. He wrapped the blanket tighter around him.

"You didn't almost die in the test."

Giovanni chuckled. "You weren't in there. No, when the water filled the casket . . ." He trailed off, finding it difficult to gather his thoughts.

"I was sure I was going to die," he finished.

Sid placed a comforting hand on his shoulder. "That's just it, Mr. Santos," Sid told him. "You did die."

The water rose to his knees. Uncle Ray just laughed, watching the panic spread across Malachi's face.

"What's the matter, Whitey?" he asked. "Your smart ass ain't got the answer, do you? Think you know everything?"

"Uncle Ray, please," Malachi begged.

He could feel the pressure build behind his eyes. A lifetime of shame and doubt gathered there, pushing on the edges of his self-control.

Feelings he had long pushed down came raging back into his heart and mind.

"You don't belong here," Ray spat, gesturing at Malachi with his whiskey glass. Brown liquid splashed out of the cup and onto the old rug.

Malachi shook his head, unbelieving. He stepped back from the doorway leading to his grandmother's house, turning to face the other door. Placing his hand in the knob he turned it and pushed the door open.

The smell of cheap incense and sweat poured out the door along with a dozen other scents. Even before the dim light brought the room into view Malachi knew exactly where he was. Old and mildewed paint peeled off the ceiling. The walls were covered in posters, mostly celebrating beer and women. Directly opposite him, right beside the door with the hole kicked in the bottom, was the poster of the three girls in the Budweiser bathing suits.

Malachi remembered that poster more than the others. Not just because of the girls; platinum blondes who lay just touching each other, their bathing suits forming the beer logo. It was because it was what he saw every day when he left his dorm.

"What's up AA," a familiar voice called out in greeting. The greeting was anything but friendly.

If there was one person Malachi wanted to see less than Uncle Ray, it was Kevin Whitmer. From his swivel chair - the ragged beige chair whose one virtue was that it could spin around a full 360 degrees - he dominated the common room of the four-room suite that Malachi shared with him and seven other guys during his years at Lander University. Next to Uncle Ray, he was the biggest asshole Malachi ever had the misfortune of knowing.

"AA, didn't expect to see you here again," Kevin laughed, swiveling back and forth in the beige chair.

Just like Uncle Ray, Kevin sat in front of the TV, sipping a drink and guarding the room. His was a can of Busch Light, never far from his hand when Malachi knew him. Hard core pornography played out on the screen of the beat-up TV/VCR combo. Kevin had seemed to possess an endless supply of the stuff, and loved to play it constantly, despite the objection of Malachi and a handful of the other guys. The only time Kevin ever relented was when a parent was supposed to be coming by.

Taking a step away from the room Malachi felt the rising water touch his waist. Time was running out.

"Kevin, I need to get through here," he said.

Part of him didn't know why he was asking Kevin if he could pass through the common room. It was just as much his room as it was Kevin's. Another part of him knew exactly why he was asking Kevin.

"You want to come in here, with us?" Kevin asked, gesturing around the room although he was the only one in it.

"Come on," he said. His face lit up with that malicious smirk Malachi had grown to despise with all his being. "You know you don't belong here, AA."

AA. The name stung him like it had all those times Kevin called him that. It was a name of Kevin's own devising, and he was endlessly proud of it. When most people heard it, they assumed Kevin was calling Malachi an alcoholic. But Kevin didn't mean AA in the way of Alcoholics Anonymous. His was more sinister.

"Affirmative Action," Kevin snickered, turning back to the smut on the television screen. He burped and crushed his beer can and hurled it against the wall. The crumpled aluminum bounced off the smoke-stained Union Jack and tumbled to the floor.

The minute Kevin had found out that Malachi was the recipient of the South Carolina Young Black Scholars Award, and that it covered a full ride to Lander, he had become convinced that Malachi was only there because he was black. It didn't matter how many times Malachi had pointed out that the scholarship was only for students with a 4.0 GPA in math and science. Kevin fell in love with the idea and ran with it.

"You know, some of us had to work to get where we are," Kevin said. Another Busch Light somehow appeared in his hand.

All the silent and bottled-up rage rose up again in Malachi. It was followed by his shame and disgust at himself for his lack of action. Countless times he had asked himself why he didn't just pummel that idiot. Or at least one good shot to the jaw to shut him up. But he never did. He scowled and hated Kevin for his insults, but never did anything about it.

Of course, Malachi knew the answer. He let Kevin carry on with his insults the same reason he let Uncle Ray. A part of himself believed what they said.

"You don't belong with us," Kevin went on, bobbing back and forth in the chair. "You should stay with your own kind. It's better that way."

I don't belong anywhere, the thought echoed in Malachi's head. I don't have any kind. It was something he had learned to live with, but he had never gotten over. *I don't belong anywhere.*

The water rose up again. Malachi could feel the cold and wet rise up just over his stomach. Behind him he could hear it churn angrily in the hallway. A light flickered and he felt the chill settle into his bones.

Gerard grabbed Vic under the arms and eased him out of the pool. The trembling, naked figure looked around frantically, trying to find some way to ease his disorientation.

"Easy," Sid calmed him as Gerard wrapped him in a blanket.

"Next to the last," Gerard pointed out. "Who did you say would be first again?"

The attempt at humor tried to cover the anxiety that both of them were feeling. Sid glanced down at his watch. Fifty-five minutes had passed. Malachi was still inside the trial.

Vic had taken a long time to emerge out of the pool. An hour was as long as Sid had seen anyone remain inside. As far as he knew there was no upper limit to how long a person could take. But in his experience . . .

Shaking his head he pushed that thought away and checked his watch again. The others had helped Victor to the fire and were easing him onto the wooden bench. Gerard came to stand by Sid again. They both glanced down at the pool. Its surface was still, undisturbed by any signs of motion.

"Come on, Malachi," Sid urged, the feeling of dread gripping him like an icy hand.

"Uncle Ray, you've got to let me in," Malachi begged.

He had turned back to family, hoping his pleas would move someone he was related to. Ray remained implacable.

"This is not your place, Whitey," he snarled. "Go with the other kind you love so much."

If anything, Ray had become more hateful than Malachi ever remembered. His bloodshot eyes were almost completely red. Spittle flew from his mouth as he yelled at Malachi. A sheen of cold sweat covered his face.

"You think you're better than us, huh?" he yelled out. "You think you're hot shit with your white ways and white talk. You ain't black. You ain't one of us, Whitey. Move on!"

"Uncle Ray!" Malachi cried out.

"I ain't your uncle, boy," Ray screamed out, his breath coming in ragged and hoarse.

Malachi could feel the water rise up to his chest.

An hour and five minutes.

Sid checked his watch again, shaking his head. Gerard looked at him from the other side of the pool. The hollow look he gave said it all. Time was running out for Malachi.

"Where's Malachi?" Giovanni asked as he came to stand beside them. He still had the blanket pulled tight around him.

"He's not emerged yet," Sid told him.

"How long does he have?" Tres asked as the others got up from around the fire and stood by the pool.

"It takes as long as it takes," Sid told them. Even as he spoke, he knew he couldn't keep the anxiety out of his voice.

"How long does he have?" Danny asked, repeating the question.

"There is no limit set on the time it takes to finish the trial," Sid remarked, though he couldn't look them in the eyes.

"What aren't you telling us?" Gary stepped up to ask. "There's something you're not telling us."

Sid exchanged a look with Gerard. He knew what the butler thought, and he was right. It would be pointless to keep anything from them at this point.

"There is no time limit on the trial," he said again. "But an hour is about as long as it has taken for anyone who eventually passed."

"How long has it been?" Vic asked.

Sid glanced down at his watch. "An hour and ten minutes."

The enormity of the words took a minute for the men to process. They looked down at the pool, its surface still undisturbed. Malachi was caught somewhere in the trial, and his time was running out.

"I guess we have to help him," Tres said, throwing off his blanket.

Without hesitation he jumped back into the pool. Sid and Gerard watched and let the man try, knowing how futile his efforts were.

When Tres landed and the water only came up to his waist he looked back up, confused. Reaching down he searched with his hands and even dove under the surface.

"How does the bottom open?" he asked.

"The bottom doesn't open," Sid told him, shaking his head.

"Then how did we get in here?" he demanded. "How did we get from those coffins to this pool over here?"

"You just did," Gerard said. "It's the way the trial works. He either comes out of there or he doesn't."

"We're not leaving him behind," Tres said. "How do we get him out?"

"We can't" Sid reiterated.

"Then we just get him out of there," Gary said. He moved towards the sarcophagi.

The butler reached out and placed a hand on Gary's chest. As big as he was, Gary stopped in his tracks. He looked down at the hand holding him back. It was small compared to his, and even looked frail. But Gary felt as if he were walking into a mountain.

"You do not touch the graves," Gerard said, leaving no doubt at all.

"We have to do something," Gary plead. "We can't leave him there."

Gerard nodded, feeling the struggle and agony the other men felt. "You can pray," he told them.

It seemed to take a minute for Gary to process. He could discern that Gerard meant them in a way that most people did not when they said those words. His offer to prayer was not mere sentiment or an empty attempt at comfort. It was a serious suggestion.

Gary nodded and went to stand back with the other men. He put his arm around Victor and they both looked into the still waters.

"That," he said. "We can do."

Indecision wracked Malachi. He could feel the water rise up, almost touching the bottom of his chin. It continued to pour down the walls even faster than before. He could hear it roaring now, as if angry.

Turning back to the old dorm common room his hope sank further. Kevin sat with his back to him, sipping Busch Light and lazily watching the pornographic scenes on the battered television.

"Don't even think about it AA," he yelled out. "This place isn't for you, and you know it."

"It isn't for me?" Malachi yelled back. "You're the one that got kicked out."

"Wasn't my fault," Kevin argued, still facing the TV. "It was bullshit and you know it."

"It was date rape," Malachi retorted. "How is that not your fault?"

Kevin swiveled the chair around, his face contorted in rage. "Like Hell it was! That bitch made it all up!"

"Then why did they kick you out, Kevin?"

"It was politics," he said. Kevin had composed himself almost immediately. Sipping on the beer he swiveled back and forth on the ragged chair.

"It was to satisfy the girl's family," Kevin went on to explain. "They were big donors and didn't want to believe their cute, little girl was actually a RAGING SLUT!"

Screaming out these last words he slammed the can on the floor. Foam and cheap beer spilled out, splashing all over Kevin's face.

"Wrong again, Kevin," Malachi answered. "It was because hers was, what? At least the third girl to complain about you."

"What's your point AA?" Kevin asked. A new beer had appeared in his hand and he sipped at it casually.

"You're the one who doesn't belong," Malachi argued. He tried to sound confident but couldn't keep the desperation out of his voice.

Kevin threw back his head and laughed. "You don't get it, do you?" he said through an arrogant smile. "It doesn't matter AA. See, you've got this idea stuck in your head that it's about what you do, or what you say, or how you dress, or what kind of job you get. None of that matters, AA. None of it. Nobody cares about your grades or your family or your accomplishments. You don't belong. Simple fact, man. You can't change that. This is my world. You belong in your world."

Desperation rose in Malachi along with the waters. His fight with Kevin was a last-ditch effort, and he knew it. The truth struck him with a finality that resonated deep inside him. Kevin was right. Uncle Ray was right. He didn't belong.

Tilting his head back Malachi struggled to keep his head above the water. Part of him wanted to let it drop. There was no point to the struggle now. He didn't belong anywhere. Uncle Ray wouldn't let him in. Kevin wouldn't let him in. Malachi would be left to the waters and their indifference, as cold as the two men who opposed him.

"This is my world, AA," Kevin laughed, turning back to the TV.

Kevin's world. The arrogance galled at Malachi more than anything else. The people who thought they were the masters, the owners of the world, the ones upon which everything rotated; this kind always galled Malachi. He hated them, deeper than he wanted to admit. Deeper, even than he thought he should. Men, and many women too, who acted like it all belonged to them, like they owned it all, were the great stains on society in Malachi's opinion. He wanted to scream at them; to shake them and tell them it wasn't their world at all. It was his father's world.

"My father's world," Malachi whispered to himself.

The sound of a hymn began to play in his head. It was the same hymn he found himself singing during his prayers in the chapel. It was a simple tune, and a simple message. But in that moment, it struck him as a most profound truth.

"This is my father's world," he said again, feeling empowered by the words.

A surge of energy and hope flowed in him. He felt it emanating from a place deep inside of himself, even deeper than the rage and doubt and insecurity. It was a place older than any childhood trauma or guilt. It was already an old place and a deep place when he first felt it.

"Your father is the king of heaven and earth," his grandmother told him one day. Malachi couldn't have been more than five years old, and this was one of his first memories.

"No matter what happens to you, don't forget that," she said, sharing with him the immense faith that had carried her through life.

How such a wonderful human being could have spawned something as awful as Uncle Ray always amazed Malachi. But such were the mysteries and vagaries of human life. Out of beautiful things can rise ugly things. And from dark and dreadful places can emerge objects of wonderful and sublime beauty.

"You are the son of the king."

"My father's world," Malachi said again as he felt the water touch his lips. He no longer feared the water, or anything that lie in his way.

"What did you say Whitey?" Uncle Ray asked as Malachi turned to face the door that led into his grandmother's living room.

"This is my father's world," Malachi repeated as he gripped the sides of the doorway.

"What did I tell you, Whitey?" Uncle Ray said as he rose from his chair. He towered over Malachi in all the fear and terror he remembered. His was an immovable power that Malachi was always helpless against.

But not today.

"You don't belong here," Uncle Ray fumed.

"This is my father's world," Malachi said as he pulled himself out of the water and onto the threshold of the door. He faced off against the figure of his uncle who loomed over him, fists clenched in fury.

"Wherever my feet tread, there I belong."

As he spoke these last words the water exploded behind him. A wave hit him in the back, throwing him to the ground. Churning foam filled his grandmother's living room. Uncle Ray was knocked aside along with all of the furniture, the pictures on the wall, and even the wall itself.

The current of water overwhelmed Malachi and threw him down. The world tumbled as he was flipped over and pummeled with water. He flailed out his arms, searching for purchase, scrambling for balance in the churning water.

Detritus from the torn house floated all around him. Remnants of the dorm room churned past. The poster of the beer girls fluttered in the current and then was swept away. Below him he saw the still bodies of Ray and Kevin, their arms spread out, sinking deeper into the water. A dark and gaping abyss waited for them, impenetrable and complete.

Thrashing around Malachi turned from the doomed bodies and struggled upwards. Above him he could see a light shimmering, promising release from the all-consuming water. He kicked up and threw out his arms, swimming for the surface.

As he rose up, he felt the weight of his terror leave him. He knew the bodies of Ray and Kevin were sinking further, down into the inky blackness of the deep waters. As they sank, he felt them losing their grip on him. With each thrust of his legs, he felt lighter. With each push of his arms, he swam further away from that doubt that had haunted him his entire life. He was swimming to freedom.

With one last push, just as his lungs were burning for air, he felt his hand break the surface. A cry came out of his lips as his head followed. Light burst into him, all-consuming light. All of his fear and agony broke away as he emerged from the water. All he could feel in his heart now was joy. Deep, powerful and perfect.

He was reborn. This was his father's world. And he was a son of the king.

"This is my father's world," Malachi cried out, racked with sobs. "My father's world! My father's world!"

"Yes, it is," he heard someone say. "This is your father's world."

Strong arms lifted him out of the water and onto the ground. Cold came shuddering into his bones. It was a chill deeper and more complete than anything he had ever felt. The trembling took over his limbs and his teeth chattered together.

"My father's world," he said again. The joy of the realization wouldn't let him stop. "This is my father's world. My father's world."

A warm blanket was wrapped around him as his sense slowly returned to him. Gerard loomed over him, wrapping up his still trembling body. Other faces came hovering nearby. Concern and relief washed over their expressions.

Sid stood apart from the others, just outside the mill of looking faces. A strange smile crossed his features. Malachi thought he could also see relief as well.

"You scared us there, brother," Vic said, clapping him on the shoulder. "What took you so long?"

Malachi chuckled and closed his eyes. For the first time since he could remember he felt at genuine peace. He was naked and cold and still dripping wet, but he felt none of these as deep as he felt his peace. He was alive. He was here. He was surrounded by his brothers. Most of all, this was his father's world. Anything else he could handle.

Chapter 12 - Explanation

The fire crackled under the dome of the temple. Silence dominated, interrupted only by the sound of the flame as it cast shadows along the pillars and the marble floor. All seven of the men had emerged from the pool. Each one sat huddled in a blanket, his thoughts a million miles away. Gerard and Sid stood nearby on the other side of the fire, watching over the men as they processed what they had just experienced.

"Gentlemen," Sid broke the silence. "The night grows long and I know you have many questions for me. Ask, and I will try to answer the best I can."

At first, no one took him up on the offer. They had long recovered their temperature, but their minds still reeled from the experience. There were questions, but perhaps too many to be asked at once.

"What happened to us in there?" Giovanni asked. Being the first out of the pool, he was the first to fully recover his senses.

Sid breathed deep, collecting his thoughts. "As you were told before, this was a trial, designed to make you face the deepest fears and insecurities you carry around with you, as well as your own mortality."

"But how did it happen?" Giovanni pressed. "All you did was seal us up in sarcophagus and fill it with water."

"What was that for?" Gary asked. "You could have warned us about that."

"If I had warned you, would that have helped?" Sid asked. "If I had told you what was actually going to happen to you, would you have even done it?"

When Gary didn't answer Sid smiled and looked down at the staff in his hands. He eased himself onto a stool and looked at the men over the fire.

"I have told you before what a serious undertaking you have volunteered for," Sid reminded them. "To face the enemies that you will face requires incredible skill, strength, and above all, courage."

"Which we have neither," Vic chuckled, some of his humor returning.

"I disagree," the older man said. "In fact, I disagree vehemently. I see seven men of incredible courage. Men with courage enough to face their greatest fears and even their death."

"Except we didn't know we were facing our death," Gary argued.

"Ah, but you did," Sid argued back. "Each one of you knew the risks involved. Sure, you didn't know that the casket would fill with water, but you knew what you were doing carried with it a risk of death. This you faced. All of you. And you did it without hesitation.

"Moreover, you all faced some of your greatest fears and doubts. You faced the shadow that lies within. Very few could have done what you did. Believe me, very few would have even dared."

"And our skill?" Danny asked, his most pressing concern. "You talked of strength and skill. Speaking for myself, I am an over the hill programmer who has left the best days of his skill and strength behind. And even then, it wasn't that great."

Sid tapped his staff on the marble floor, an almost absent-minded gesture. "That . . ." he said, letting the word trail off. "That has been taken care of better than you know."

"What is that supposed to mean?"

"That I will have to show you," the older man shrugged. "I promise I will, tomorrow morning. I will show you how skilled you are and make a believer out of you yet. You have been remade. Reborn."

"But how?" Giovanni asked, repeating his initial question. "How did all of this happen?"

"It is the power of the graveyard," Sid answered. "That is the best way I can tell you. It was what this place was created for, long ago, long before my time. It was made that men would face their fears, their doubts, and either come out the other side, or . . ."

He let the idea trail off. There was no need for him to reiterate the risks. They had all faced them and had all survived.

"It's magic," Zach said bluntly.

Malachi had only been half listening to the conversation around him. His mind had been distant, distracted. It was focused on no idea in particular, simply spinning out into that strange ether where daydreams are caught and random thoughts reside.

When Zach mentioned magic, an instinct Malachi had honed over the years of knowing the man woke up and took notice. Any mention of the occult or the supernatural was likely to evoke a suspicious and angry reaction, accusations of witchcraft and sorcery, and promises of the fiery punishments visited upon any who would dabble in those dark arts. Malachi braced himself for the outburst soon to come.

Strangely, it did not arrive. Zach did not offer any condemnations, no warnings, not even a protestation about associations with demonic powers. He continued to stare into the fire, a contentment on his face that Malachi had never seen before. Like the rest of them, Zach had found a peace with whatever had been haunting him. He had faced his own demons, and emerged out the other side victorious.

"You good with this?" Gary asked, giving him a playful nudge. "I know Mom would disapprove."

The bare traces of a smile crept over Zach's face. "I'm thinking maybe Mom didn't know everything."

A chuckle danced around the fire. In a way, Zach had said it all. Each of the men had to let go of a part of themselves, a part of their past. They had to accept what they had been, what they were and what had happened to them. In doing so, they had overcome it.

In the same way they had to accept that something strange had happened to them. Though a million questions still lay unanswered in Malachi's mind, he felt that he didn't need to know the answers. He doubted that Sid even had them. He could spend all night hammering the old man with his questions, and at the end of the night would not understand what was going on.

For the first time he could remember, he was ok with that. Malachi could genuinely and honestly say that he was ready to accept what was happening, accept his lack of understanding, accept his lack of control, and he felt good about it. It appeared to him as the illusion it was. He never really had control of anything, just the barest appearance of control, just enough to satisfy himself.

None of that seemed to matter now. He was changed. He was transformed. How much so was yet to be seen. The peace inside him was not ready to be disturbed with those questions. For now, he would let it be.

"You said something to me when I first came out of the pool," Giovanni said. Apparently, he had at least one more question to be answered.

Sid nodded as if he knew what was coming.

"I said that I could have died in there, we could have almost died," Giovanni explained. "You told me that I did die. What do you mean by that?"

Sid nodded again, collecting himself. All the men around the fire looked expectantly at him. They had all received the same cryptic words when they questioned him at first, and all wanted at least an answer to that.

"This may be hard for you to understand," he began. "But it means exactly what it says. Each one of you died in that sarcophagus."

"You mean metaphorically," Danny said to clarify. "We died metaphorically."

"Have you ever heard of anyone dying metaphorically from drowning?" Sid asked.

Danny scoffed. "Yeah, but you stopped the waters when we lost consciousness, right? Or the water was an illusion. It was something we saw in our minds, just like . . ."

Danny trailed off, his eyes taking on a distant and unfocused cast. He shook himself out of it almost immediately.

"Well, just like everything we saw and experienced there," he finished.

Sid shook his head slowly. "I'm afraid not. The water was very real."

"But . . ." Danny began but couldn't find the words.

"All of you died," Sid told them. "Not metaphorically. Literally. In body, for absolute certainty, you died. It was in death that you faced the demons that haunt you, and in facing them you emerged to new life. That is the only way to understand it. That is the only way that your transformation could be complete."

"Are these new bodies, then?" Vic asked, looking down at his own hand in disbelief.

"Yes and no," Sid answered. "You will notice that your bodies and faces look very much like the one you had before. Your loved ones and friends will have no trouble recognizing you.

"At the same time, it is different. It is fitter, stronger, more durable. It is more capable of fighting off disease and healing itself, and can take more damage and accomplish more than your old body ever could."

Despite having already noticed changes in himself Malachi could hardly believe what he was hearing. As he sat around the fire and allowed his body to warm up again, he had noticed that the paunch that had been gathering around his middle was noticeably smaller, even absent. His arms felt stronger, his legs lighter. He had yet to test these out, but had thus far attributed these feelings to a new surge of energy after his battles. But if Sid was right, then he was different altogether.

"Are they resurrected bodies?" Vic asked. "Kind of like the ones we

139

will all receive one day?"

"No," Sid answered. "They are not resurrected bodies. There is something that you must understand about all this. I don't mean to be vague on purpose but I don't completely understand it myself. They are new bodies but they are still connected to your old ones. They are of your old flesh but new flesh at the same time."

"Wait, wait," Gary gestured for Sid to slow down. "What do you mean connected to our old bodies? You say that like they're still around."

Sid poked at the fire with his staff as he gathered his thoughts. Looking up he pointed to the tombs and crypts of the graveyard outside the temple.

"Gentlemen, if you were to open that sarcophagus, the one you laid down in just hours ago, you would find a body. It would look familiar to you because it would be your own. It would be a pale figure, cold and lifeless, and just as dead as the countless corpses that lie here in this graveyard. I tell you this because you are expressly forbidden from doing that, no matter how you may be tempted to do so. For the minute you look upon your corpse you will rejoin it. And this time you will stay dead until the Lord returns."

Stunned silence greeted these last words. Malachi felt his head rock back, just as if someone had punched him in the face. A surreal sensation, almost like floating from his own body settled over him. His body? His dead body? It was lying in a tomb just feet from where he sat up and warmed himself by the fire.

"I don't get it," Danny spoke up. "If our body is in that crypt, what is this?" He gestured to his own, upright and living body.

Sid shook his head, frustration beginning to show on his face. "I don't really know" he said. "It is in the power of this place to make new men, to make swordsmen. It had been this way for thousands of years when I first learned of it. Men who have taken up this call lie down in a coffin or grave. Their bodies perish as mortal bodies do. If they pass the trial then they emerge out of that pool a remade creation. It is similar to the body that still lies in the grave, but different. As I said before, it is stronger and faster and more durable than the other. Your life expectancy has greatly increased as well.

"But despite this, it is still connected to the body in the sarcophagus. Something of your old self, some essence or piece, I suspect, was made to fashion this new one. That is why you cannot look upon your old body.

140

It must stay in its tomb for now. When you do die, there will be no body to bury, for you will join that corpse that waits here today. Does this make sense?"

Vic laughed as the other men shook their heads. "Clear as London fog," he quipped.

"I'm sorry," Sid apologized. "There is no better way for me to explain this. Part of it will never make sense."

"It makes sense to me," Tresmond spoke up for the first time.

He had been quiet for so long that his voice surprised Malachi. Looking over the fire he noticed a deep and longing expression on his friend's face. He saw the pangs of grief that had been there for the last two weeks. But there was something else there as well. Malachi felt it because he saw his own feelings reflected in Tresmond's eyes. There was a calm in the midst of the storm that had become his heart.

"You see, when my boy died, I knew I would never have peace again," Tres said. He looked up and Malachi could see tears glistening in the firelight.

"Not until I died," he continued. "I knew that no matter what happened, even if I got better, there would be no peace. Not until I was dead. As soon as I heard he was dead I knew I would never have peace again in life until I was dead too."

Looking down Tres picked at the blanket wrapped around him. He bobbed his head, acknowledging something unspoken. When he looked up again tears were streaming down his face.

"Well, I feel peace," he told them. "I still hurt, but there's a peace. So, I know. I had to have died. Because I have some peace, you see. So yeah, I can't explain it. But it makes sense to me."

Gary reached out and put a comforting hand on his friend. He didn't say anything, nor did anyone else. They simply let the moment be, and in their silence communicated an understanding and a mutual sharing of a burden. The silence said it deeper than any words could.

"Gentlemen, I know you may have more to ask, but you need your rest," Sid stood up and told them. "These new forms, though strong, have to rest from the trial it endured."

As if on cue Malachi felt exhaustion wash over him. Rather, he noticed it as soon as Sid pointed it out. It was set deep inside him, and demanded a long and peaceful rest.

"You will sleep here," Sid announced. "The air and earth of Annwyn will restore you more completely than at the mansion. There is a grove nearby where you can sleep. Gerard will bring you some bedding."

"Wait, I thought we couldn't be here at night all alone," Danny pointed out. "You said this place was dangerous to us at night."

"You no longer have to fear the darkness of Annwyn," Sid told them "Nor the evil things that stalk here at night. In fact, you don't have to fear the darkness at all. From this day forward, as long as you remain faithful, the darkness will fear you."

Chapter 13 - The New Men

Early the next morning the Swordsmen gathered in the practice room. Gerard had been waiting for them when they woke up the next morning. The dawn rose bright and clear over the grove. A late mist gathered on the grass of the clearing where their bedding had been set. Dew covered their blankets and sent an early chill through them. Despite this they all woke up feeling invigorated and clear headed. In fact, Malachi couldn't remember the last time he had woken up feeling this full of energy.

After returning through the gateway and back to the mansion they had just enough time for a quick breakfast before they were called to the training room. Master Sergeant Diggs was waiting for them when they arrived, dressed in loose fitting pants and a sleeveless shirt. His bare feet paced the practice pad as they stood in front of him.

"Gentlemen," he said with an excited smile in his face. "Believe it or not, today is the last day that I will train you. After today you will have moved beyond my skill level and ability."

No one laughed at what Diggs had just said. Nor did they believe him. Vic looked up and down the row of men, with his own smile as if to say, "Is everyone hearing this?"

"You may not believe me," Diggs said. "But I assure you it is true."

Danny raised a hand. The Master Sergeant pointed for him to speak.

"You're right, I don't believe you," Danny said. "I know Sid told us that we would be stronger and faster, but the gap between us is pretty big. I doubt we are even close to your skill level. At least I know I'm not."

Diggs shrugged. "You don't have to take my word for it. But you do have to believe it. Why don't I show you?"

He gestured for Danny to join him on the mat. Danny tried to protest, but Diggs made it clear that he wasn't making a request. With a resigned sigh he shuffled out to the center of the mat to face the instructor.

"I want you to relax," the Master Sergeant said when Danny assumed a fighting stance. "Let's not tense up yet, just relax."

Following Diggs' cue Danny took a deep breath. He rolled his shoulders a few times and let his arms drop to their sides.

"Focus on your breathing," Diggs said, instructing Danny through several deep breaths. "Let the air flow into you and don't think about fighting. Relax, and let your instincts take over and guide you."

After a few deep breaths Danny opened his eyes. Diggs nodded to him and both the men assumed a fighting stance. Circling each other they waited and watched. Already Malachi could see a difference. Danny was holding himself differently, more poised, full of coiled energy.

Diggs threw out a quick punch. Danny slipped it and stepped to the side. Another one came that he backed away from. Two more quick jabs followed which Danny was able to stay away from.

"Not bad," Diggs commented.

Throwing two quick jabs Diggs leaned into the attack as Danny backed away. Once he closed in the Master Sergeant grabbed Danny's arm and threw him over his back, sending him landing on the mat with a thud.

"C'mon," Diggs chided. "I know you can do better than that."

"If you say so," Danny said with a groan as he picked himself up.

"Don't think," the instructor told him. "Let your instincts guide you."

The Master Sergeant unleashed a flurry of punches. Incredibly, Danny began to block them. To the face, then the body, Danny swung his arm around interrupting the shots. Diggs ducked down and swept his leg out. Danny's own flew in the air as he landed on his back again.

"Stop thinking," Diggs told him, gesturing for him to get up.

Again, the men went at it. The Master Sergeant throwing punches and Danny desperately trying to knock them away. Four, five, six punches were blocked in a row. The Master Sergeant dropped to a knee a delivered a blow to his stomach. This time, Danny doubled over in pain.

"That didn't hurt you," Diggs goaded, circling around for another attack.

"Yeah, what do you know?" Danny shot back. Deep red began to infuse into his cheeks. He straightened up again and prepared to face another attack.

"I know you can do better than that!" the Master Sergeant yelled.

The men fell to it again. More punches thrown. This time, it seemed like Danny would avoid them all. Once again, he was undone by a change of pace. Diggs grabbed his arm and twisted. He kicked out and swept out Danny's legs, sending the other man to the ground with a thud.

"Stop thinking! Instincts!" Diggs yelled, pointing in Danny's face.

"I am, damn it!" Danny yelled back as he got up again, fury was written across his face.

"C'mon," Diggs goaded. "Instincts!"

It took a moment for Malachi to notice, but once he saw it the change was unmistakable. Danny was angry and he wasn't backing down. The old Danny, the Danny that Malachi knew would have indulged the Master Sergeant for only a moment. After getting beat a few times he would have bowed and slunk back to the line and admitted that he couldn't win.

This Danny was having none of it. Every time Diggs threw him down, he popped back up. After every blow and take down he saw a deeper determination etched on Danny's face. Consciously, Danny may not have believed he could beat Diggs, but some part of him did. As Malachi watched the demonstration stretch on, he saw that part of Danny grow stronger and stronger.

The blocks came in with more confidence. The reaction time was quicker. An intense concentration etched his features. Danny moved faster, but at the same time seemed less strained. He grew focused, and more at ease.

Diggs shot out a leg to sweep Danny to the ground again. This time, Danny was ready. He saw the sweep and jumped out of the way. He landed and shot out an open-handed blow to the Master Sergeant.

A resounding smack echoed in the training room. Digg's head flew back and he landed hard on the mat.

Dead silence dropped over the room. Malachi couldn't quite believe what he had just seen. The way Danny looked down at his own hand in amazement, Malachi could tell he didn't quite believe it either.

A slow clap sounded somewhere behind them.

"Congratulations, Mr. Taylor," Sid said from behind them.

They had been so engrossed in the fight that no one noticed that Sid had stepped into the room. The older man walked to the mat and gestured to the stunned Danny with his cane.

"This is the just the beginning of what you are capable of, Mr. Taylor," Sid told him. "From now on, I cannot allow you to train with Master Sergeant Diggs any longer, for fear you may harm the man inadvertently."

"Did he just slow clap us?" Vic asked. He was silenced by an elbow from Gary.

A stunned Danny reached out and helped Diggs to his feet. The Master Sergeant smiled as he rubbed his cheek. He patted Danny on the shoulder and went to stand with the other men, leaving Danny on the mat by himself.

"Why don't we see what the rest of you are capable of," Sid suggested. "Malachi? Would you indulge us? Spar with Mr. Taylor, would you?"

Malachi surprised himself by being excited at the opportunity. A part of him had even been hoping he would be called on next. Some new part of himself, something reborn, was eager to prove himself.

It didn't start out pretty. Despite his new enthusiasm, Malachi had not yet unlocked that part of himself that Danny had. Time and again he was thrown to the mat, struck down, hit, kicked, hurled and tied up in binding holds. Each time he was thrown down or hit it seemed to hurt less. Each time he got up again, he felt his energy rising rather than being discouraged.

By slow degrees Malachi began to match Danny. The hits scored less, took longer. A flurry of blows came out of him, blindingly fast. Malachi batted each one away. Danny came in with a wide swing at his head. Malachi ducked it and threw out a punch to the ribs. He felt it connect as Danny was thrown back, crumpling over in pain.

Applause rose up from the watching men. Malachi smiled and turned to them, remembering finally that they were there. As he fought, they had faded from his mind. A razor-sharp focus had him honed in on the fight, and only the fight. Self-consciousness washed away in the purity of combat. It was only the two men squaring off, pitting skill against skill.

Just as surprising as the new skill was the new level of fitness that Malachi had seemed to acquire. When they were finally done sparring, Malachi was breathing heavy and sweat glistened off of his face. Unlike his unusual forays into the gym, where a little exercise would have had him panting in pain, this breathlessness was energizing. It made him feel good, not strained, to breathe deep. He felt his lungs open in joy, and his heart thumping in shared excitement. Even the sweat that beaded down his cheek was a celebration, a sign that he was alive and thriving. He felt like a boy again. A boy who couldn't help but run, and every cell in his body rejoiced when he let them run free.

Despite these advantages, it seemed that Danny retained an edge in hand-to-hand combat. For every one time that Malachi took him down or scored a hit, Danny scored two. Once this became obvious Malachi was called back to the side and a new fighter was invited to face off with Danny.

Tresmond came next. Predictably, he unlocked his skill quicker than Danny or Malachi had. Having the benefit of starting younger, and beginning with more skill, he adapted quickly. Danny had only taken him down twice when Tres responded in kind. Danny shook his head as he picked himself up and entered into the fray again.

Watching the two combatants mesmerized Malachi. They moved seamlessly and impossibly fast. Punches and kicks, combinations came hammering at each other. They were all blocked, dodged and slipped. It was like watching a dance. And even though it was tinged with violent energy, there was something beautiful in it as well. His entire life Malachi had never enjoyed violence or violent sports, but watching the two men range over the practice mat, exchanging blows with artistic precision, he gained an admiration for it. This was nobility in motion, he decided. Courage, strength, skill; all of these were on display, and no man could help but admire what he saw.

It was Tres who broke the impasse. He did so in a most improbable way that stunned everyone there.

The fight had moved to the middle of the mat. Tres had just delivered a wide hook that Danny was able to duck. In one fluid motion, as he ducked the punch, Danny spun and shot out his leg to sweep Tresmond's feet out from under him.

This is it, Malachi thought as he watched the combat unfold. Tres barely had time to respond. Even as Danny's foot was coming around in its circle, Tres remained rooted to the ground. The momentum of his wayward punch still had him leaning forward. There was no way that Malachi could see that he could avoid the take down.

When it happened, Malachi wasn't even sure what he was looking at. Danny's foot had almost made contact. Tres was still leaning forward. But with a quick bounce, a half bend of the knee and a push off with his toes, he was in the air.

This was no ordinary jump. Tres lifted himself in the air and flipped his legs over, catapulting over Danny. Pulling out a move Malachi had only seen gymnasts use, Tres flipped and twisted over Danny and landed cleanly on the other side of his assailant.

Now it was Danny who was exposed. The sweeping leg caught only air as he spun around. Tres landed and wasted no time in his counter.

The open-handed blow landed on the side of Danny's head. Stooped down and off balance he fell over in a heap. The smack of the blow resounded through the training room.

The room watched in stunned silence. No one could quite believe what they had just seen. It was the kind of move that you attributed to special effects when you saw it in a movie. There had to be a cord connected to a stunt man. People didn't just move that fast in that way.

Except he had moved that way - and that fast. The men exploded in cheers and cries of disbelief.

"What the Hell was that?" Vic exclaimed.

"Where did that come from?" Giovanni asked.

No one seemed more surprised than Tres. He smiled despite himself then offered a hand to Danny. The other man pulled himself up as he rubbed the side of his head.

"That wasn't fair," Danny complained, but the complaint was good natured. "I don't think I can fight you anymore."

The only ones who didn't seem surprised were Sid and the Master Sergeant. They exchanged a knowing smile. Diggs nodded to himself as this is exactly what he had thought would happen.

"Looks like we have discovered our first talent," Diggs exclaimed.

When the men answered with questioning looks, Sid offered to explain.

"Besides your increased speed, strength and skill," he said. "Each of you has been gifted with one unique talent. A special skill that will enhance your ability as warriors."

"You mean we can all do triple axles?" Vic asked.

Sid shook his head. "I'm afraid not, though I can't rule it out. The gift you have been given is unique to you, though others may have it was well. What I mean is that is not a common gift of all swordsmen, it is a special gift. Mr. Bettis here, it seems, has the gift of . . . what would we call it? Acrobatics? Agility?"

"How do we figure out what ours is?" Danny asked, still rubbing his cheek.

Sid shrugged his shoulders. "That same way Mr. Bettis has discovered his. You do what swordsmen do and it will emerge naturally. When you discover your gift there will be no doubt."

"Yeah, but me and Malachi fought for a while and neither one of us unlocked a super power," Danny pointed out.

"It's not a super power," Sid corrected. "It's a gift. And you have to bear in mind that some take longer to manifest than others. Also, it may be a not combat gift. Swordsmen have also been given gifts of strategy or building or leadership, things like that. Don't worry, you will find yours and it will be exactly what you need. It will serve the swordsmen and their mission in a unique way that will be indispensable when the time comes."

The next to discover his gift was Gary. After being taken down, Danny decided to let Tres be the one to unlock the skill of the others. Vic faced off against him next.

It wasn't long before Vic looked the part of the professional. His military background helped, along with his previous training. He was faster and had honed more instincts. As he fought Tres it was obvious. Still, he was no match for the dexterity and speed he was facing.

Their fight had them ranging all over the training room. It had even carried them off the mat at one point. The men watching had to scatter out of the way as Vic pressed an attack that had Tres on his heels. The kicks and punches came in quick succession, almost too fast to follow. A smile crept over Vic's face as Tres backed up against the wall. He was out of room.

Tres countered with a combination that caused Vic to take a step back. He held his ground, determined not to give up his advantage. But a step was all Tresmond needed.

With a swinging kick Tres spun around. Vic ducked the blow. Sensing Tres was off balance he charged in with a scoring punch. But Tres didn't finish the spin. Halfway around, while he was still facing the wall, he used his momentum to leap towards the wall - and up it.

As it unfolded Malachi could see what was happening. And he could also see that Vic could do nothing to stop it. As Vic leaned in for what he thought was a final shot, Tres was running up the wall. Two steps up the vertical platform and he launched himself back, flipping over Vic as the other man was swinging at air. His momentum carried him almost to the wall. Landing hard, Tres grabbed Vic by the waist and slung him to the ground.

"I think that's cheating," Vic groaned. "That's definitely cheating."

When Gary stepped up, he proved to be a much more cautious fighter than Victor. It took a few good solid hits, but by now the men all believed, and he unlocked his skill quickly. With surprising speed for a man that large, Gary proved a good match for Tres. He absorbed the shots he was given and focused on a measured defense. Still, every attempt at contact only met with swiping at air or grabbing at nothing. Tres spun and dodged, flipped and even stood up on one hand to avoid being tagged by Gary.

Still, Gary kept on, determined. Sweat glistened on his forehead as he concentrated, watching every move Tres made. He blocked and stepped back, all the while his eyes followed the faster man intently. He was waiting, careful and deliberate.

Finally seeing his chance Gary whipped out his hand as a punch flew toward his stomach.

"Gotcha," he smiled, catching Tres' wrist in his hand.

Twisting his body he threw his opponent. Tres flew across the room, screaming out as his arms flailed in the air. He crashed into the weapons stand, splitting open the wooden shafts of spears and bo sticks.

"What the?" Gary gasped, staring at his empty hand.

The men stared in stunned silence. Vic and Danny actually stood with their mouths open, looking to Gary, then back to the crumpled figure groaning among the broken weapons.

"Tres," Gary gasped, the first to find his senses again.

Running over to the broken weapons stand, Gary dug through the splintered wood and spear heads. The other men were close behind, running to check on their fallen comrade.

"Hey man, you okay?" Gary asked as he tossed aside the broken top of the weapons stand.

The other men quickly cleared out the rest of the detritus. Tres groaned, rolling onto his side.

"Dude, you threw me across the room," he said as he winced.

"I'm sorry man, I swear," Gary said. "I just thought I was throwing you down."

"It looks like another one of you has discovered his gift," Sid said from behind them. "You seem to possess an inordinate amount of strength, Mr. Walsh. Be careful. Your gift is a good deal more dangerous than some of the others."

Gary looked down at his hand as he contemplated the words. Being a bigger man than most, he had always had to be aware of his strength. Now, he paled and seemed down right frightened of himself.

"Don't worry, Mr. Walsh," Sid comforted. "You will notice that these are gifts you can control with easy effort. Your strength will activate when you want it to, when you put the effort in. You won't accidentally crush babies."

"Oh, this isn't fair at all," Vic complained. "He was already stronger than everyone else. Now he's the Incredible Hulk."

"Fortunately, you are all more durable than you were before," Sid told them as they eased Tres onto his feet. "Give him a few moments and he will be fine. A little bruised perhaps, but none the worse for wear."

True to his word, Tres was able to walk on his own. He tested out his shoulders, lifting his arm in a circle. A small grimace was the only evidence of any pain. He gave a tight nod to the other men to show he was indeed okay.

After they had all assured themselves that Tres was not seriously injured, they returned to their training. Vic took over on the training mat, sparring with Giovanni, and lastly, Zach. Both of the men quickly unlocked a dazzling array of skills. In no time at all they pushed Vic to the edge of his ability. Giovanni was even able to outmatch him consistently. But neither of them displayed a special or unusual gift.

"Don't worry, gentlemen," Sid assured them. "Your gifts will come in time. In fact, it is rare that most are displayed so quickly. In the course of your mission, you will discover them. Often at the perfect time."

"There is one more skill we need to teach you," Diggs said from beside Sid. "Or rather, one that you have and we need to make you aware of."

"X-ray vision?" Vic asked, his brows raised in expectation.

"Better," the Master Sergeant said with a shake of his head.

"What can be better than X-ray vision?" Vic asked back. "I mean . . . just for general life purposes."

"How about dodging bullets?" Diggs suggested.

His words were met with stunned silence. Malachi was certain he hadn't heard him right.

"Dodging bullets?" Zach asked. "Are you serious?"

Diggs nodded with a satisfied smile. "What warrior would be complete if you can't neutralize the most effective weapon in the world today? Yes, dodging bullets. All of you possess the innate capacity. You just have to know what to look for."

The excitement among the men was palpable. That day all of them had been transformed, and as the reality was beginning to sink in it was filling them with a raw energy they hadn't experienced since childhood. It was as if all their daydreams and fantasies of youth were coming true.

Ten minutes later, they weren't so sure. Diggs had the men bunched together in two groups in the indoor shooting range. Except they were downrange. They stood on either side of a paper target, twenty yards from Diggs who was loading a 9mm.

"Are you sure about this?" Danny asked, expressing the anxiety all of them felt, his voice echoing in the range.

The men looked at each other warily. They were uncomfortably close to the target, just two feet away. At first, they stood a comfortable distance away, though still wary being downrange from the shooter. But Diggs had insisted they get closer, motioning them to clump together and move close to the target.

"This is pretty close," Gary echoed. "Can't we take a few steps back."

"No," Diggs answered as he donned his earpieces. "In fact, I would like you get closer. I promise I won't hit you."

"Can you promise you won't sneeze?" Vic asked. The nervous tension sent laughter through the men who felt anything but amused at the moment.

"Watch the path of the bullet," Sid instructed. "See if you notice anything unusual."

"Stay still," the Master Sergeant warned.

The boom echoed in the range as Diggs fired. All the men jumped and leapt back, away from the target.

"I said stay still," Diggs ordered.

"Well quite shooting at us," Zach yelled back.

He fired two more shots. The men covered their ears and cowered back, but didn't jump away this time.

"Did you see anything?" Sid asked after those two shots.

"Just my life flashing before my eyes," Vic yelled back.

"Relax and concentrate," Sid instructed.

"Said by the guy on the other side of the gun," Gary muttered under his breath.

Diggs fired two more shots and the men began to relax a little more. Malachi thought he had seen something at the last shot, but wasn't sure. He straightened up, and watched closely. Two more shots came by and Malachi was certain this time, there had been something.

Feeling something click in his head, Malachi forgot for a moment that he stood dangerously close to the wrong end of a discharging firearm. The world went still around him. A preternatural focus sharpened his senses, awakened his mind. He felt the air stop moving and almost as if he were slipping into a place between two seconds.

Diggs squeezed the trigger again. A red streak shot out from the gun. Bright red and impossibly fast it flared to life, streaking towards the paper target. Except for its color, it reminded Malachi of a shooting star.

"What was that?" Tres breathed, seeing what Malachi had seen.

Diggs fired four more shots. Each one was accompanied by a red streak that flared out of the gun's muzzle and streaked towards the target. By this time, all the men had seen it.

"What you are seeing is the path of the bullet," Sid told them. "This is what will enable you to dodge the shots."

"We can't dodge that," Tres pointed out. "No way we're that fast."

"Watch closely," Sid instructed. "You will notice the red streak comes just before the bullet. It shows you where it will go. You have a split second, nothing more. It is just enough time to step out of the way before the bullet follows."

More shots came, each one with a red streak. Malachi watched closely and he could see Sid was right. The red, flaring streak came just before the bullet. Each time it seemed the bullet followed the path of the streak.

To make sure he turned to face the target. A red streak shot through the right shoulder of the silhouette. Less than a second after he saw that same spot blossom into a bullet-sized hole. It happened again on the head, then the torso, then just off target over the left shoulder. Each time he saw a red, flaring streak hit the target a hole appeared where the bullet passed through.

"How is this possible?" Danny asked. He too had turned toward the target, watching the red line of light flash past just before the bullet. Like the rest of the men, they had temporarily forgotten their fear and were marveling at this new ability.

"I don't rightly know," Sid answered, his voice echoing off the range walls, interrupted by pistol shots.

After the exercise they gathered back in the training room. Sid tried to explain to them what they experienced and how to use it.

"I don't have this ability myself, so it's hard to explain," Sid told them. "And it is one relatively new to the swordsmen. Or at least newly discovered. The gun had to be invented first, of course. The best we can tell is that just before a shot is fired, when the shooter has made the decision to shoot and squeezes the trigger, then the path of the bullet is determined. Somehow, with your new abilities, if you are close enough to the intended path you are able to see it. I think it is a glimpse into the near future, a variation, if you will, of the prophetic gift. It's God-given, what else can I say about it?

"I do know it works. For many years now swordsmen have used it to effectively dodge bullets and avoid being shot. With the speed you have been given you have just enough time to get out of the way. But be aware, it is not foolproof. With enough shots coming in fast enough even you will not be able to dodge them all. And though you are tougher and can heal faster than you could before, you can still be hurt and still be killed. Learn to look for that red streak. Anytime you see it means a bullet is coming close."

"What about machine guns?" Zach asked. "Can we dodge those as well?"

"Theoretically," Sid said with a shrug. "Of course, automatic fire comes much faster and would require quicker reactions. If the initial cluster of shots were close enough you could probably get out of the way. But I wouldn't imagine your odds were too great against automatic fire."

"Any advice on what we could do if we came against one?" Gary asked.

"Find cover," Diggs broke in to say. "As fast as you can. Return fire from a safe position. You're strong, all of you. But you're still mortal."

Diggs led them back to the practice room as the men took all this in silently. The words were meant to sober them up. After unlocking their skills and energy, then learning they could dodge bullets, they were full of enthusiasm.

"Who wants to go next?" Vic asked, smiling at the men as soon as they got back to the practice room. He jumped from one foot to the next.

"What about you, big guy?" he asked Gary, feinting punches while he danced around him. "Huh? You think you can throw me around? Got to catch me first."

"I caught Tres, you think I can't catch you," Gary answered taking a swipe at Vic which was easily ducked.

"Missed me, haha," Vic teased backing away from the big man. "Whoo! Come on, let's see what you can do."

With a smile Gary stepped up to the challenge. Vic let him step in close and take the first shots.

"Whoo! Missed again," he said as he dodged, goading the much bigger man. He turned to the side and shuffled his feet while feinting in and out.

Three more punches came after Vic who slipped each one. With every miss he laughed and leaned in closer, daring another shot.

"Can't catch me, big guy," he taunted, slipping away from a punch. "Much too fast for you."

Growling with impatience Gary leapt towards Vic, his arms outstretched wide. Vic only had time for a howl of surprise. By the time he saw what was happening he only had time to jump back.

The move came too late. Gary circled the smaller man in his outstretched arms and grabbed him in a bear hug. Effortlessly, he lifted Gary off his feet and squeezed.

"Whose too slow now you little twerp?" Gary asked with a satisfied smirk.

Vic struggled vainly against the arms that had wrapped him up. Grunts came coughing out as Gary applied pressure, making Vic's face go red.

"You give?" Gary asked, squeezing harder. "I can wait for you to pass out and drop you?"

Vic smiled despite his situation. He looked down at Gary with a face growing purple. He puckered his lips and leaned down, landing a kiss on Gary's cheek.

"Damn it, Vic," Gary said as he recoiled. He dropped the smaller man who landed in a breathless heap.

"You need to shave," Vic groaned as he gasped for breath.

The playful banter soon infected the other men. Goaded themselves by the surge of energy they paired off to practice their new skills. With no object except to exercise what they could do the men fell to a strenuous but effortless workout.

Malachi himself lost track of time. He fought with Danny first, then Giovanni. He ran a few rounds with Gary, then Tres. Exhaustion didn't touch him nor did the strain of the activity. It could be said that they played more than exercised. They had become like boys again, full of the strength of life and eager to display it. They didn't care if anyone saw or noticed, for the exaltation of their bodies was a joy in itself. To exert oneself was happiness. It was done for no reason except that it could be done. For the moment, it was enough.

Sid and the Master Sergeant watched the men practice with unrestrained joy. It was their own joy to see them come together as they were, to find their abilities and celebrate them. Like Malachi, it had been a long time since Sid had entertained his present feelings. It had been a long time since he been able to feel hopeful. For years it all seemed lost, desperate. He had been waiting for death to deal him that final defeat, then usher him in to meet his Maker in shame and failure.

Now, he felt that deep and pure sensation known as redemption. All wasn't lost after all. Even though it was only him, Diggs, and seven warriors who had just unlocked their skill, it was something. It was more than he had before. It was a start. Perhaps, he wouldn't die a miserable failure. Perhaps, he could honor the sacrifice made by those other brave men, the ones who used to stand beside him. Perhaps, their deaths wouldn't be in vain.

The lights flickered inside the training room and broke the spell. They only fluttered a moment, but seemed to presage something bigger. The men looked around in wonder, still breathless in exertion. Each man felt a presence move in with the blinking of the lights, as if the darkness they caused brought a deeper, more sinister darkness.

Malachi felt his stomach sink when the lights flickered. He looked around, expecting something foul and terrible to come charging into the room. A nascent fear crept over him, one he couldn't explain or justify. Every cell in his body screamed out warning, yelled out him to watch out, for something evil lurked nearby.

A hum went through the room as phone vibrated all at once. Malachi walked over to his and looked down at the device. It buzzed in his hand and a picture of a man in sepia tones appeared on the screen. The phones crackled and old music, like from a record, began to play from each one. A single baritone voice sang out in French.

> *La mer qu'on voit danser*
> *Le long des golfes clairs*
> *A des reflets d'argent, la mer*
> *Des reflets changeants sous la pluie*

"What is that?" Vic asked looking down at his phone. His face had gone pale and his irrepressible sense of humor silenced.

"That is what we are up against," Sid told them, confirming the suspicion each man felt.

The sliding glass doors of the training room shuddered. Malachi turned at the sound. Through the glass he could see the day had grown dark. He glanced at his watch to see it read three PM. Outside, it looked like midnight.

The doors shuddered again, then exploded. Shards of glass flew into the training room. A wind roared in, pushing the men back. The lights flickered again then blasted apart in a shower of sparks, plunging the room into darkness.

"Be still," Sid's voice rang out in the dark. It carried with it the sound of unmistakable authority. "You cannot be harmed here."

Wind continued to howl outside and rush into the room. Malachi held up his arm to shield him from the blast and saw Sid's figure move towards the shattered door. He stood tall and erect, unafraid and unruffled by the wind.

Malachi followed Sid outside, the other men close behind. Looking up he could hardly believe what his eyes saw. The clouds that roiled above him were as black as the pit of night. A deep rumble sounded from within, like the growl of a primitive and hungry beast.

Dark clouds swirled above, creating a vortex that formed right over their heads. Lightning flashed in the clouds, revealing billows of thick smoke that stretched out towards them like angry hands.

"Is that a tornado?" Danny asked, stepping back towards the house.

"This is a message," Sid yelled over the wind. "Believe me, no one else can see this but us."

Malachi stared up at the angry storm, transfixed. He could hardly believe what his eyes were seeing. Never had he witnessed a storm this complete, this dark, one full of such dread and fear.

Lighting flashed in the clouds again, illuminating the dark. In the center of the vortex, a face loomed towards them, shaped out of the dark billows. Malachi gasped and took an involuntary step back. The face opened its mouth and howled with the screech of the wind. Fury and evil were carried on that wind, directed at Malachi and Sid and the men who gathered around him.

"What's the message?" Malachi heard himself ask, not able to take his eyes off the angry churn of the storm above him.

"They know you're here," Sid answered. "They have felt your awakening."

A chill came on the wind that felt like the deep of winter. Malachi shuddered, finally understanding what it was they were up against.

"Men of God awaken, and the deep trembles," Sid announced, spreading his arms out against the fury of the wind. "Training is over, men. The war has begun."

PART II - THE ISLAND OF FIRE

Chapter 14 - Alicia Wyatt

Kristina Wyatt looked down at the Facebook post for what must have been the tenth time that morning. Shaking her head she scrolled on, not wanting to face that particular one yet. It was still early and she wanted to enjoy what was left of her coffee while it was still hot.

The morning sun slanted through her kitchen window, throwing a golden beam over half of the breakfast table. She sat with phone and coffee, scrolling through posts to catch up on what had transpired during the night. Outside, the day was coming to full life. Her backyard, freshly cut and edged, sparkled with dew and seemed to be cast over with a special magic of the early day. This was truly her time. Or at least it had been.

Thumbing back to that earlier post she looked over it again. If anyone was able to ruin her morning it would be Becca Martin. And there she was, at the top of her feed, being . . . being Becca Martin.

Determined once again to ignore it Kristina scrolled down, searching out some better news in her social media world. There was plenty to be had. Updates abounded about children, work and school. A girl she knew from college was getting married for the third time. That guy she worked next to all those years ago at car rental agency penned a long rant about the Republicans. Carol from the play group reminded everyone that she was still planning to host that afternoon. About a dozen of the women she followed posted messages about how wonderful their husbands were. Kristina always smiled at these, knowing that at least half of those very same women were on the verge of divorce.

"Mommy, am I going to school today?" a small voice asked beside her.

"No baby," Kristina answered without even looking down.

Alicia Wyatt, four years old, still dressed in her nightgown - the one with the faded rainbow on the front and the message "Without Rain there is no rainbow" - watched her mother continue her morning routine. She had seen it countless times before. Her Mom would be absorbed in this for more than half the morning, only coming out if something demanded it. Alicia hated the way her mom snapped at her while she drank her coffee. Still, she had the persistence native to little children.

"How come am not going to school?" she asked.

"I told you sweetie," her mother said without looking away from her phone. "It's summer. We don't have any school in the summer."

Alicia walked to the window to look outside while Kristina faithfully continued to scroll through Facebook. She flipped back to Becca's post, wishing she could just ignore it.

"Am I going to play group?" she heard her daughter ask.

"I don't know sweetie," Kristina answered as she found the post again.

"Why not?" Alicia wanted to know.

"Sweetie . . ." Kristina began, but didn't finish the thought.

She and Carl hadn't quite decided how they wanted to handle this yet. For once, her husband didn't seem to have an answer, and truthfully looked as worried as she was about it. Normally, nothing seemed to shake him. But this had disturbed him in a way that made Kristina that much more afraid.

Sleeping Sickness. It had been all over the news again. In Kristina's opinion school had ended just in time. If it hadn't, they would have had to seriously consider pulling Alicia out for the rest of the year. Of course, the school and the CDC assured them this wasn't an infection that could spread like a normal disease. They seemed very insistent on that point.

Then again, as Carl was quick to point out, they didn't know what it was or how it spread. For all they knew it was some kind of new germ, or something they had no way of detecting. The fact that they knew so little made any assurances the government gave them worth about as much as the paper it came on. All they knew was that this thing was fatal and it hit small kids.

It was enough to make Kristina forget all about the little worries in her life. So what that Becca was at it again. That was the way she had been since college. There was nothing that Kristina could do about it now.

"I just don't know," she finished her thought to Alicia. "We'll have to see, okay?"

This time, when she turned her attention back to Facebook it was because she didn't want to think about the Sleeping Sickness. A heavy sigh came out of her, more aggravated than anything else as she scrolled back up to the top of her feed. She was going to have to say something. Becca was quite insistent. Normally, she would ignore a post like this. If it was anyone else, she would just let it go. But Becca wasn't just anyone else.

"Can I watch Tooney Town?" Alicia asked, turning away from the kitchen window.

"Of course, baby," her mother answered, already forgetting about her anxiety of just moments ago.

As Alicia padded into the living room Kristina looked over Becca's post again. Great opportunity, it had read. This is the path to financial independence. Most all, it's fun. Kristi, we'll have a blast, trust me. And we'll make a killing too.

If Kristina had a dime for every time Becca had made such a promise, she truly would be financially independent. This is what Becca had been doing ever since they got out of college. Never content with a normal job, Becca insisted on taking up independent sales jobs that never seemed to go anywhere. At the same time, she never tired of them as well.

At first it was Mary Kay. That had been somewhat successful and Kristina wished that she had stuck with it. But Becca was all about burning bridges, and she managed to ruin a good thing when they found out she was signing people up under her that never volunteered to sign up. After that she tried a few pyramid schemes. Then there were the essential oils. Last time, it was face wash and non-chemical cleaners. That one Kristina actually liked. Of course, that meant Becca didn't like it.

The sounds of Tooney Town came echoing from the living room and into the kitchen. Without realizing it Kristina began to sing along to the opening song.

> *Tooney Town, Tooney Town*
> *That is where the fun is found*
> *Up and down*
> *Round and round*
> *We all have fun at Tooney Town*

As much as she hated the show Kristina had to admit that without it, she may have lost her sanity a long time ago. Some days, it was the only thing that kept Alicia out of her hair so she could get something done. With the sound of cartoon children in the background, Kristina let her attention return to Becca. Always with Becca. Needy, dependent, begging for help Becca. Except she always made it sound like she was helping you.

It wasn't that Kristina wanted to discourage Becca. But why, oh why, she asked herself, did Becca always have to try and include her all the time in her selling schemes? Every time she got a new job Kristina knew an email or post or some kind of request or invite was coming. This one was no different. This time, though, Becca had crossed the line.

Poring through the post again Kristina wanted to make sure what it was Becca was selling. She said it was "relationship aids." Kristina was pretty sure that meant something else altogether.

A quick look at the company's website confirmed her suspicions in the worst way. Even sitting by herself, looking over the products they sold made her face go hot as she felt a deep flush wash over her cheeks. Becca was selling this? And she wanted her, Kristina, to host a party at her house so Becca could peddle these . . . these things?

Thankful again that Tooney Town was holding Alicia's attention, Kristina quickly closed the page and tried to calm herself down. There was no way she was hosting a party to sell any of that stuff in her house. Didn't Becca know her husband was on the Building Committee at church? And she was on the Missions Team?

Of course, Becca knew that. She even told Kristina she could invite her friends from church to her sales party. It would spice up their marriage, she said. Just because you've been married for a long time doesn't mean you can't have a little fun, Becca told her.

Blushing all over again Kristina imagined how it would go over if she were to ask Phyllis Rigby to such a party. Or the look on her face when she found out what was being sold. Kristina would never be able to show her face at church again. Of course, Carl would never her let her host that kind of party at their house. Kristina couldn't imagine what he would say if she purchased one of those "relationship aids."

The flush and heat came pouring into her cheeks again at the very thought. Her mind even took a turn into some unexpected directions. Shaking these out of her head she determined that this time she would have to put her foot down with Becca. No more indulging that girl. She would have to grow up and get a real job. How she had survived this long was a mystery to Kristina, and everyone else who knew her.

Of course, she would have to let her down gently. She couldn't come right out and tell her she would never let that trash into her house. Even if Carl would allow it, she would never do such a thing. Would she? What if Carl was open to the idea? That would be awkward, of course.

Then again . . .

Before she could finish that thought she glanced at the time on her phone. Ten thirty already? She groaned and dropped the phone to the table, hating herself for getting wrapped up in it all morning long. She would have to make it up to Alicia. Maybe not play group, but a movie perhaps. Or the park.

As soon as her mind turned back to Alicia, she felt a prick of fear in her stomach. Something was wrong. It was a maternal certainty, something she felt without a doubt.

Turning to the living room she could still see the TV on. It had gone quiet, but the home screen of Tooney Town was still displayed. The seven main children, drawn in cartoon and respectfully representing every race and gender, smiled down at Alicia who sat perfectly still. Their too-wide eyes and drawn smiles had always looked a touch creepy to her. Now, they appeared downright sinister.

"Alicia," Kristina called out cautiously. The fear already showing in her voice.

Had she fallen asleep, Kristina asked herself. Oh please, let her be asleep. Let her be asleep.

"Alicia," she called out again, putting a hand out to her daughter.

As soon as she touched her, Kristina recoiled. The girl was as stiff as marble. It didn't feel at all as if she were touching flesh and blood, but something made of colder stuff.

"Alicia," she cried, her voice cracking.

Alicia Wyatt stared at the television with vacant, unfocused eyes. Her mouth hung open, still and soundless. The Tooney Town crew shined pale light on her slack features, mocking her with their own imitation of life. Blank eyes reflected the digital light, but gave no light of their own.

Chapter 15 - Investigation

The morning after the dark cloud arrived the Swordsmen gathered in the mansion study. Or at least that is what Sid called it. Malachi would have called it a library, for the walls were lined with books. There was even an open second floor, ringed with a walkway that accessed another level of books. It was more than he had seen any one person possess. The volumes ranged from shiny, new hardback spines to leathery folios that were nearly crumbled to dust. Sid even mentioned owning some volumes that were in scroll form.

Still, he insisted that it wasn't a library. It was too small, he said. The library of the Keepers was much bigger than this. These volumes were only of immediate necessity.

Eventually, Malachi had to concede that the room was more appropriately a study, though a vast one. The room itself was long, holding small tables around the perimeter. In the middle stood a larger, oaken table, what Malachi would assume would be in a conference room. A rolling chalkboard had been pulled over to the large table.

"Gentlemen," Sid addressed them as the men took their seats around the large table. "It's time to begin what you were called here for."

Malachi sat across from the large French doors that opened up on the second story veranda. Outside, he could see the woods that they had traveled into on two different occasions. From his vantage he saw just what he expected to see: a line of thin scrub oaks and pines, beyond which rose the rooftops of nearby houses. Nowhere could he make out anything that indicated the place where they had actually journeyed.

"It's time to get the guys who killed my boy," Tres said. He leaned forward on the table, his whole body coiled and ready for action.

"Indeed," Sid answered. "That is our objective, and to put an end to this horrible affliction. But first, we need to find out how they are doing it and who exactly is behind it."

"I thought you already knew who was behind this," Danny raised his hand and said. "Didn't you say the Fae were the ones who did this?"

"That's what you told us," Gary echoed.

"I did tell you that," Sid confirmed. "And that is who is behind this. But there are a few other things you must know about the enemy before we can effectively hunt them down."

The door to the study opened and Gerard stepped in. He carried a box overflowing with files and papers. Setting this down on one end of the table he pulled the chalkboard over to where Sid waited.

"As I have mentioned before," Sid began. "Our enemy is not a natural enemy. This disease known as the Sleeping Sickness is not of natural origin."

Pausing he reached up and wrote "Fae" at the top of the blackboard.

"Our enemy is a group of supernatural, spiritual entities called the Fae," he continued. "They are also known as the Sidhe, or Fairies, daemons, even some have been called gods from time to time. We divide these into two basic groups. There is one that is good and operates as an ally in our cause. We call them, 'The Good Folk.' The other is the group that is behind the evil we are looking to stop. These have been an enemy to mankind and called different things at different times. Today, the evil Fae and their human allies call themselves 'The Family.'

"What you need to know is that these entities are not human, though they can take human form and interact with the physical, natural world. The second thing you need to understand is that they feed off of human beings."

Before Sid could get any further Danny raised his hand. Sid nodded and motioned for him to ask his question.

"Yes, who are they exactly?" Danny asked. "I assume they are the Watchers that you showed us the other night?"

Sid tossed the chalk around in his hand. "That may be a longer story than I have time for today," he said. "And even then, I doubt I could answer that question to your satisfaction. Let's just say they come from spiritual entities that once were entrusted with a job. They were agents of God, just like the angels are. These Fae that we encounter today are the offspring of those entities, a younger generation. Some, as you know, are evil creatures that feed off of mankind, others are helpful and have still remembered their original purpose."

"So, they aren't the Watchers?" Danny asked.

"Correct," Sid answered. "We believe they are the offspring of those original entities. We cannot be sure, but that is what we think."

"Yes, but how did they become evil?" Danny asked. "If they were spiritual creatures, if they were made as servants of God. How did they become evil?"

"What made you think that spiritual meant only good?" Sid asked back. "Just because something is spiritual doesn't mean it is good. There is spiritual evil as well as spiritual good."

"No, but they weren't made evil, were they?" Danny argued.

"I don't see your point," Sid shrugged.

"If they weren't made evil and there was nothing evil yet when they were made, then how did they become evil?"

"Do I look like I have the answer to that?" Sid asked back. "I'm old, Mr. Taylor. But not quite that old. I know what you want to know. But I'm afraid that answer isn't one I have. Why and how they were tempted to evil I don't know. All I know is that just as human beings decide to do something contrary to the will of God, so have other spirits it seems. The how or the why or the mechanics involved is something that I don't know nor do I think that I could understand. Is it enough that it just is?"

Danny had a troubled look on his face and Malachi could tell he was anything but satisfied. Knowing Danny, he would probably spend most of the day and night pondering the question. It was one that had taken up more than one Swordsmen discussion.

"What we know is that this is what they are and they feed off of us. That is how they maintain their power," Sid told them. "Now, there are several ways that the Fae will feed off of soulfire."

Scratching on the board again he wrote out "worship."

"This is the most direct way that the Fae feed off of man," Sid explained. "They will induce him to give worship. To praise, believe in, have faith in. Sometimes they will pose as gods. Other times they will promise favors. They also have the ability to connect with idols so that when an idol is worshiped or adored then the spiritual energy from that worship goes to the Fae connected to it. This is the most traditional and direct way that man is fed off of."

"I guess that doesn't happen anymore today?" Gary said.

"Why wouldn't it?" Sid asked.

"Well . . ." Gary looked around, uncertain for a moment. "We don't really have idols anymore, do we? We've become a godless culture, not believing in anything. I would think the Fae would be pretty hungry these days."

"The Fae are fat and glutted today," Sid told him. "They are better fed now than they have been in a long time."

"Yeah, but how? Where are the idols?"

"Every car that drives by this street will have a symbol on it, will it not?" Sid asked. "Every one of your clothes has a symbol embroidered on it. Every purse is decked out in symbols to let everyone know where it was purchased. Even your coffee cups are covered in idols."

"Yeah, but we don't worship those," Vic pointed out. "Don't get me wrong, I like a pumpkin spiced latte, but I've never prayed to one."

"Perhaps not," Sid agreed. "But that may not be your poison."

"Does anyone pray to their latte?" Vic asked.

"You don't have to pray to something for it to be an idol," Sid pointed out. "Or to give it worship. There are more ways to worship than through prayer. Do you think the woman who carries the name brand purse really loves that purse because of the quality materials that have made it, or the way it makes her feel when she carries it?"

Vic thought for a moment then shook his head. "Because it goes well with her shoes," he answered.

"Yes, the shoes too," Sid agreed. "The skirt, the blouse, the hair, the earrings. All of it blending together to create an image that she has carefully crafted. And it is the objects, all connected to a symbol, that convince us they can give us prestige or beauty or desirability. And to complete that image we sometimes add the cup of coffee from just the right place.

"And we do this in many different ways. We feel a sense of satisfaction driving the electric car that has the right symbol on the front. Or we love our phone with its own status symbol connected to it. And just in case you think that you men who care little for these things are free from this temptation, how many times have you screamed with breathless enthusiasm for a team because they were wearing the symbol on their helmet that you love and adore? How many times have you felt exaltation because of their victory? Or ever thought yourself superior to those poor bastards wearing the losing jerseys?"

"Wait a minute," Vic interjected, making the time out symbol with his hand. "Time out here. Are you saying if we watch college football then we are worshiping an idol?"

A smile crept over Sid's face as he looked down at Vic. "You tell me. Can you watch college football without worshiping an idol?"

Vic breathed out a sigh and leaned back in his chair. "Man, you just blew my mind."

"Understand this," Sid told them. "Behind every major symbol in the world, be it corporate or sports or whatever, even symbols of your beloved political parties, all of them are connected in some way to the Fae."

Sid began to write on the board but was stopped again by Gary's raised hand.

"If what you you're saying is true," he began. "Then that would mean our whole lives we've been feeding the Fae."

"That's exactly what I'm saying." Sid confirmed.

An unsettling silence descended over the table. Gary looked down; his face full of concentration. Malachi himself thought about all the things he owned, and all the symbols that he was drawn to, attracted to. He couldn't help but wonder how much of himself he had already given to these dark entities.

"Bear in mind, just because you buy a product with a symbol on it doesn't mean you have given your worship to that thing," Sid told them.

"Then how do we know?" Gary asked. "How do we know if we're just buying the phone because we need it or because we're worshiping that apple on the case?"

Sid looked at him and seemed to stare into his soul. "Only you can answer that Mr. Walsh. Only you can tell me if you are buying a handy tool for life in a hectic and modern world, or worshiping an idol you hope will bring you happiness and peace."

Without waiting for another response Sid turned back to the chalkboard. Under worship he wrote out "fear."

"This is another fairly direct method of feeding," Sid told them. "Whenever we fear we are emanating spiritual energies. The power here is corrupted and not as pure, but this method has the benefit of being free to any creature in the area. Disasters, wars, neighborhoods full of crime will often be haunted by certain Fae. They have even been known to induce fear through their powers, possess and haunt places, things like that."

Beneath, fear, Sid wrote out "Consumption."

"Besides these methods whereby the Fae will draw the soulfire out of a person, there are also other ways they can feed," Sid explained. "These involve rather crude methods, usually direct interaction with the flesh. Not many of the Fae use these methods. Most of the time the Elioud, which are the offspring of Fae-human intercourse, resort to these types of feeding. This can range from anything to feeding off of sexual energies to actually devouring human flesh and blood."

"They feed off of sex?" Vic asked.

"Indeed," Sid answered. "During sexual activity a high degree of spiritual energy is released. Most of this is released by the man, so you don't really see the male Fae using this method. This is almost exclusively employed by the female Fae or Elioud."

"What about humans?" Vic followed up. "What happens to that energy when humans have intercourse?"

"What do you think would happen?" Sid asked back.

Vic shrugged. "I guess the woman would get it."

"Precisely," Sid agreed. "The Fae and Elioud are not the only creatures that feed off of spiritual energies. Human beings do this all the time. Because of our temporal nature we don't feel it the same way as spiritual creatures do nor can we live off of it or become powerful from it. But it touches us all the same. We can feed off of it. And we can even become addicted to its power."

Danny chuckled and shook his head. "What? Are you saying we've got spirit junkies out there?" he asked. "Or would you call them soulfire junkies?"

"That's a rather interesting way of putting it, but yes, that is precisely what I mean," Sid told him. "Just as the Fae can become hooked on feeding off of the spiritual energies of others, so can man."

"For example?" Danny prompted, still unconvinced.

"The sexual energies we were just talking about," Sid pointed out. "There are many women who derive a sense of pleasure over their sexual powers that have nothing to do with the physical pleasure of sex. They enjoy seducing men, having men stare at them and ogle them. They revel in the power they have in making them do their bidding and reducing them to a state that is dangerously close to worship. Sometimes, it even crosses over to worship. That's quite a rush for many women. In fact, the real draw behind the sex industry, especially ones like these pay to view websites is not the money being made off of them, but the adoration the women receive from so many men who come to stare at them and adore them. It's irresistible to many and highly addictive."

"What about men?" Zach asked. "Are we just food for women? Do we get anything out of it?"

"Not entirely," Sid clarified. "True, that in sexual activity and in certain instances of seduction, the energy goes from male to female. You must understand that this is also by design. That spiritual energy that is transferred from a man to woman is what fuels conception and the growth of human life. Especially the spiritual side of that life.

"But there are other ways that we share spiritual energy. Encouragement is one of them, and a very good one. When one person encourages another we naturally feel a boost of energy. Faith and trust are another, especially if we believe in something that can truly give us good strength. Gratitude is a powerful form of energy. And of course there is love, the most potent of all.

"These are all ways that we are meant to strengthen and build up one another, and they all can be used for good. But all of these can be used for evil. Not just the Fae, but human beings have used these methods not to share energy, but to feed off of other people. The arrogant, the egotistical, the self-centered; people who manipulate and denigrate others, people who enjoy exercising power over others, or causing fear and pain. When people do these things, they feel that rush of power because they are feeding off another person. Even good people find themselves doing this sometimes. It's all a part of being fallen creatures in a fallen world.

"So, yes, men can feed off of sexual activity, but in a different way. In a healthy relationship it is the exchange of mutual affection and love. In an unhealthy one there is manipulation or abuse or some sort of power trip-men who enjoy humiliating women or using them to make themselves feel powerful or important."

"So, what you are saying is that we have this system, this natural system, where man helps his fellow man, and the Fae, and the Elioud, and even just regular people, can manipulate it and use it for evil," Danny summed up.

"Precisely," Sid agreed. "In fact, nearly everything that is evil in this world is a corruption of something that God had originally meant for good."

"That sucks," Zach muttered.

"In more ways than one," Vic said with a satisfied smile on his face.

"You get it?" he prompted when no one else shared in his amusement. "It sucks. You know, like the energy getting sucked from us. It sucks. Right? Sucks."

A chorus of groans rose up from the table as the men realized Vic's joke. Gary dropped his head in his hand. This reaction only seemed to make Vic more satisfied.

"I tell you who's sucking energy from us," Gary complained. "Hey Sid, can you also write up there stupid jokes. That's how Vic feeds off of us."

"I'm giving of myself," Vic said. He put on the face of a selfless martyr as he placed a hand upon his chest. "I'm sorry if no one appreciates this gift I am giving you."

"That's right, Saint Victor," Gary retorted. "Just doing it all for others."

The other guys around the table chuckled at the exchange. Before Vic could counter with something of his own, Tres broke the levity.

"Do you mind, guys?" he asked, his voice full of tension.

The grief on his face was barely restrained. Malachi thought he could see desperation written across his features. A clenched fist had snapped a pencil in two but Tres didn't seem to notice it.

"I don't want to be a downer for everybody," he said. "But I'm ready to get down to business."

Looking down Vic nodded his head and reached for a pad and pencil. The other men made themselves look busy, or at least look like they were ready to get down to business.

"Certainly Mr. Bettis," Sid agreed. "The point I wanted to make here is that the Fae, and their motivations have historically been directed towards one end. Like every other monster, they live to feed. Especially off of anything that is good.

"That being said, remember that there are allies amongst the Fae and Elioud that are here to help us. They also must feed off of human soulfire. But unlike their more dangerous counterparts, our allies maintain a healthy relationship with us. They only take what is given, and that is usually in the form of love and gratitude. In return, they aren't corrupted like the other Fae."

"Corrupted?" Malachi asked. "Corrupted how?"

"To feed off of fear and worship and human essence in the way they do is evil," Sid stated bluntly. "They take evil food and it turns them even more wicked than they already are. With each passing year they fall further from grace and further from the ability to repent of what they have done and at least hope to be restored. Their minds are blinded, their wills destroyed, and their essence turned to something dark and ugly. Naturally, the Fae are quite beautiful. In fact, they are wonderful to look upon. But for the Fae that have been corrupted by evil this appearance is an illusion. If you were to look upon their natural form you would see something hideous and distorted. You would see the origin of every horror and monster story that man has ever told. In short, you would see the face of evil. You would remember what makes evil so bad and good so wonderful. I hope you never have to, but if you do, be prepared for what you will see."

Sid allowed those thoughts to sink in around the silent table. Malachi thought back to the storm that had swirled overhead the previous day. The darkness held something sinister within, something worse than black clouds. There was an evil he had never confronted before in his life. It was like his worst nightmare, but alive and walking before his very eyes.

"It is critical that we remember this as we look into what has been happening around the country to our children," Sid continued. "Remember what it is the Fae are after. This is key to figuring out what exactly they are doing."

Gerard began to pull folders out of the box and set one in front of each of the men. Malachi opened his and immediately recognized the distinct look of medical records.

"Two days ago, a five-year-old by the name of Angela Wyatt was admitted to the hospital for symptoms of Sleeping Sickness," Sid told them as they looked through the records. "That brings the total in the Tri-Cities area to six cases. Nationwide, we are up to seventy-two. In your files you will find the medical records of each of those children from our area. If we need to reference others in the country, I could probably arrange that. But this is where we start."

Malachi had to admit he was impressed. It was hard to get medical files. Even though Medicaid and Medicare swindlers always seemed to find a way, it was actually hard to do. That Sid could do this meant he had a far reach, and some friends in high places ready to take risks for him.

Peering through the file Malachi saw the name Barry Coles printed in the top of one of the bulk of papers. The file was massive. Over the course of their hospitalization each of the children had been visited by dozens of specialists and health officials. All of them had made copious notes in the medical chart. It would take hours to even get a handle on all the information contained in them.

Hoping to organize his search Malachi looked for the admission paper work on the newest case. Alicia Wyatt. Five years old. No known allergies. No hospitalizations. No known medical conditions. At four years old she had cut open her chin in a fall off a slide that required stitches. Two months ago, she had tubes put in her ears to control chronic infections.

Skipping over to the narrative, Malachi found out Alicia was at home with her mother when symptoms first came on. She was watching TV when her mother noticed that she hadn't heard from her in a while. When the mother went to check on the child she found her awake but unresponsive.

"Why don't we tackle this methodically," Malachi suggested, looking up from the file.

"You're the organizer," Gary pointed out. "Tell us what to do."

Malachi nodded, feeling every bit in his element. This is what he could do. It felt good to organize, to bring chaos to order. It felt right.

"Let's each take one and see if we can find something similar," Malachi instructed.

"Don't you think the CDC has already done this?" Danny asked. "What do you hope to find that they haven't?"

"It's not what we can find, it's what we want to find," Sid told them.

"What?" Danny asked incredulously. "Do you think the CDC is a part of this? That they're in on some conspiracy?"

"In a manner, yes," Sid answered. "I wasn't exaggerating when I told you the Fae were behind every corporation and bank and political institution in the West. Not everyone is a part of it but they have enough clout to keep people looking in the wrong direction. And if anyone insists on looking, they can make them stop - or go away if they won't."

It seemed surreal to Malachi to be seriously considering what sounded to him like a conspiracy theory that circulated on the internet. One of the ladies in his office seemed taken with a new one every week. Kathy Riles was always making comments about some shadow group, or conspiracy about vaccines, or the emergence of a one world government masterminded by the Freemasons.

"Crazy Kathy" would be right at home in this conversation, Malachi thought. But if what Sid was saying was true, then Crazy Kathy would be more right than anyone would have guessed. Malachi even wondered if Kathy herself would be shocked to learn how deep the conspiracy actually goes, a hell of a lot worse than the CIA or the Vatican.

"Alright, well let's see what we can find," Danny conceded.

Malachi assigned each of the cases to one of the men and began weeding out information. He stepped up to the board and Sid handed the chalk over to him. A queer smile played over his face as he watched Malachi work.

After erasing the notes Sid had made, Malachi wrote each of the children's first name at the top of the board. Alicia. Owen. Jeremiah. Barry. Jennifer. Kalisha. Below each name he wrote the gender of the child. So far it was perfectly balanced, three boys and three girls.

"Alright, let's look at the ages," he said next.

The ages seemed pretty well distributed as well. Alicia, Owen and Jennifer were all four years old. Barry was five. Jeremiah was the oldest case at seven years old, while the youngest in the TriCities area was Kalisha Thompson at three.

"Okay, we have the youngest at three and the oldest at seven," Malachi pointed out. "Is there any way we can confirm that this is normal for the rest of the country? I would think that kind of information would be readily available. Shouldn't have to pull any strings for that."

"I'm on it," Danny said, reaching underneath him to pull out a laptop.

"If you look on the intake forms it should note any allergies that the kids had," Malachi instructed the men. "Let's see what we have there."

Like the ages, allergies seemed to be random and well represented. Alicia, Owen, Barry and Kalisha all were allergy free. Jeremiah was allergic to peanuts and Jennifer had a previous reaction to amoxicillin as a toddler.

"Three to seven," Danny announced after they had found and listed the allergies. "What we have here is the same as the rest of the country. Actually, the youngest victim was three weeks away from his third birthday. Lives in Cleveland. The oldest is another seven-year-old. Seven years and eight months according to what I found. So yeah, three to seven years old."

"Okay, pretty much what we knew but a lot more specific," Malachi noted. "All victims between three and seven."

"What about race?" Vic asked. "Should we note that as well?"

"Let's do it," Malachi agreed.

Besides Kalisha who was Black and Barry who was noted as biracial, the other victims were White.

"The racial distribution seems to be equal nationwide," Danny confirmed, checking with the few public statistics on the disease he could find. "Seems to be an equal opportunity disease. Except . . ."

The last thought trailed off as Danny plugged away at his computer. He seemed he had forgotten that he was in the middle of a thought when he got lost in his research again.

"That is a bit odd," he said to himself, just loud enough for everyone to hear.

When he didn't follow that cryptic statement up, Gary stepped in to prompt him.

"You want to tell us what's so odd?" he asked.

Danny shrugged and didn't say anything at first. He wrote something on his notebook and went back to the laptop.

"Let's go on," Malachi suggested. "Danny will share with us if he finds something."

Next, was hospitalizations and prior conditions. Alicia had tubes put in her ears at one point and Jeremiah was admitted once for a reaction to peanut butter. Other than that, there was generally a clean bill of health for all the children. Kalisha had been looked into for a heart murmur as an infant but the symptoms cleared up by her second birthday.

"Definitely odd," Danny said. He jotted one last thing down on his notebook and pushed his laptop away.

"Okay, you know how I said that this disease was equally distributed among the races," he began. "Well, it turns out that it is almost perfectly distributed among the races."

"Why would that be odd?" Giovanni asked. "Wouldn't we expect that to happen?"

"Somewhat," Danny answered. "But not this perfectly. Just listen to this. The White population in the US is 59.3% according to usafacts.org. If my math is correct then the number of White victims of Sleeping Sickness is just at 60%."

"I agree with Gio," Gary spoke up. "What's so odd about that?"

"Ah, but it goes on," Danny continued, holding up a finger. "The number of Black victims is at 10%, and according to data they represent 12.6% of the population. The number of Hispanic citizens stands at 18.9% of the population and the victims is right at 20%."

"Yeah, I'm not seeing what you are stirred up about," Gary said. "It's sounds pretty random to me."

"Except real random never looks random," Danny pointed out. He picked up his computer again and began to type feverishly.

"Random, real random happens in clusters," Danny told them. "And disease is no different. While you expect the White population to have the highest number of infections, you wouldn't expect them to have near perfect representation with their racial percentage. And here, look at this map."

Danny turned the computer so the rest of the table could see the screen. On it was displayed a map of the United States. Red dots represented incidences of Sleeping Sickness. Just as Danny had told them, there seemed to be red dots equally distributed across the country.

"Look at this geographical representation," Danny told them. "Just like the racial, it's equal. No clusters that you get from random disease. There is a little bit of concentration in high population areas, but not much.

"And think of this as well. You would expect to find more cases of Hispanic children falling sick in areas with greater Hispanic populations, like Texas and California. Same for the Black population. You would expect to see more cases in the South and in the major northern cities. Once again, this isn't the case. You have just as many cases of Hispanic children falling sick in Montana as you do in Texas. There are as many cases of Black children getting sick in Maine as in Louisiana. This is what I mean by odd."

"So, what does it all mean?" Vic asked. "I agree, it sounds strange, but I just don't know what to make of it."

"I don't either," Danny shrugged. "But what it says to me right off the bat is that this looks like it is deliberate, not random. It's like whoever was behind this wanted a perfect sample of the population in terms of race and geography. And I bet if I did a little more digging, I would find it perfectly represented in economics as well."

"Okay, I'm with you," Gary chimed in. "But I hate to agree with Vic here and ask, what does it mean? Sid, what do you make of this?"

The older man thought for a moment and shook his head. "I can't say as I know."

"It's almost like they're experimenting," Giovanni spoke up. "You know, like a science experiment. They want equal representation and distribution."

"Is that something the Fae do?" Vic asked. "Sid, you said they feed. This sounds like something a lot more sophisticated than feeding."

"Their intentions may sound crude but the Fae are very

sophisticated," Sid answered. "In fact, they have been quite adept at fitting into the modern world."

"How does this help us?" Tres interrupted. Malachi could sense that boiling tension in him again. "Experiment or no does this get us any closer to finding them?"

"Definitely," Danny answered. "This is data. And data doesn't lie. And I have to admit that I was still a bit skeptical of what was going one here, but looking at these numbers I can't deny it. This isn't natural."

"Alright, we're making progress," Malachi said, bringing them back to the task at hand. "What's next? What about onset of symptoms? When did they start for all the kids?"

"Kalisha Thompson was watching TV when her mother noticed she was unresponsive," Danny said, leaning over to look at the file he was in charge of.

The same was true for Barry and Owen. Jeremiah was on the family computer when he went comatose. Jennifer Stokes was playing games on her phone.

"What about the latest?" Malachi asked. "I think I remember a mention of it in her file."

"Yep, it's right here," Zach announced, holding a hand up. "Says she was watching Tooney Town when her mother noticed something was wrong."

"What's Tooney Town?" Malachi asked. "Is that a game or something?"

"What? You never heard of Tooney Town?" Tres asked, more than a little surprised. "C'mon, I thought everybody has heard of Tooney Town."

Tres laughed and shook his head at the other men. Malachi could see genuine happiness written on his face. It was a happiness that was born in better times.

"Owen loved that show," Tres said as the smile grew sad. "It's a show about these kids at a daycare. But they have this play town there, you know a whole city in miniature. The kids can jump into the town and they have all sorts of fun there. You know, it's funny, Owen even asked if he could go to daycare. I said, 'Why do you want to go to daycare Owen?' He said, 'So I can go to Tooney Town, Dad.' Yeah, he thought daycare was a place where, you know, kids get to jump into toy cities. It was funny. He was funny."

The pain in Tresmond's voice came out as the happy memory reminded him of what he had lost. Malachi thought he was on the edge of tears. He could hear the strain in his voice, could hear the emotion that was being barely held back. To his surprise Tres let none of these out. He nodded his head then a mask fell over his face. Once again, he was the determined father out for justice.

"You don't happen to know if Owen was watching that show when . . . when he got sick?" Danny asked.

Tres shrugged. "I don't know. Grace just told me he was watching TV. It could have been Tooney Town. He watched it all the time."

"Do you think you could find out?" Malachi asked. It was a long shot, but worth it in his opinion.

Tres shrugged again and looked down at his phone. Another pain seemed to strike him then. He held his phone as if he were afraid of it, or afraid of what might happen if he used it to call his wife.

"I can try," he said standing up and walking out of the room.

"You don't seriously think a TV show caused this?" Giovanni asked. "That doesn't add up at all."

"We're just establishing a pattern right now," Malachi reminded them. "What if it does turn out that all of them were watching the same show? That would mean something, wouldn't it?"

"How can a TV show cause a sickness?" Giovanni continued to express his doubt. "And don't you think this is something that someone else would have picked up on?"

"If they were looking for it," Zach reminded them.

"Yes, but TV shows don't cause illnesses," Giovanni argued.

"He's got a point," Gary agreed. "Even if they were watching the same TV show, which they weren't, how could a show cause coma and then death?"

"You can't think like a physician," Sid added. "I believe Malachi is on the right track. Let's see if there is a similarity and then go from there."

"But there isn't," Gary insisted. "Not all of them were watching the same show."

"How can you be sure?" Malachi asked.

"For one, Jeremiah was on a computer, not the TV," Gary pointed out.

"You can watch shows from the computer," Vic said. "I watch most of my TV from my laptop."

"But according to these records Jennifer Stokes was playing games on her mom's phone when she got sick, not watching TV," Gary told them. "She wasn't watching the TV show that magically causes illness."

"There's a Tooney Town game," Danny said. He turned his laptop around to show them the homepage of the Tooney Town show. Besides the cartoons kids jumping out of a miniature city, there were banners for the Tooney Town game, the Tooney Town app and even the Tooney Town educational aid.

"Looks like they were into a little bit of everything," Malachi noted.

"But that doesn't prove anything," Giovanni said. "I'm with Big G. Doubtful a show caused this."

"Well, it is something to look into," Sid told them. "We should probably reach out to the other families and see what exactly the kids were doing or watching when they fell sick."

"Let me see what else I can find out about the show," Danny said, hammering away at the laptop.

Before they could continue Tresmond slipped back into the room. He held up his phone and a gave a nod to everyone.

"He was watching Tooney Town," he said. "According to Grace he watched that show the same time every day. It's what he was doing when she found him."

"That's two of the kids watching the same show when they developed symptoms," Malachi said, making a note on the board. "And we have a possibility that the others may have been engaging with some media around the same show."

"You really think it could be that show?" Tres asked.

"I don't," Gary answered. "We have no idea that any of the other kids watched that show or were playing a game associated with it or anything. Besides, my original point, how could a show make anyone sick?"

"Right now, it's the only link we have," Malachi said. "Danny, have you found anything out about the show?"

Danny shrugged as he continued to search his laptop.

"Nothing extraordinary," he said. "According to records the show is produced by a company called Catalyst Productions. Anyone heard of them?"

Head shakes answered Danny's question.

"Yeah, me neither," Danny agreed. "That's no surprise. Apparently, Catalyst is owned by TriCorp."

"Isn't everything owned by TriCorp?" Zach pointed out.

"Yeah, no surprise there. Let's see. Nothing else really stands out. Some affiliation with Star-Crossed Talent Agency. The Destiny Group is involved somehow. Never heard of them either. Also, something to do with Rip Starr Entertainment.

"Why do these shows always have so many companies associated with them? I can never make heads or tails of it."

"That's probably on purpose," Vic suggested. "You know, easier to cover up the trail." He rubbed his fingers and thumb together in the "money" sign.

Malachi didn't notice that Sid had walked over to the table until he was leaning against it towards Danny. When he did see him, he noticed his face had gone pale.

"Who did you say was involved?" Sid asked, a tremble in his voice.

Danny looked back at the screen without noticing the fear on Sid's face.

"There's a few," he said. "Which one were you interested in?"

"Rip Starr," Sid uttered. "Spelled with two R's, correct?"

"Yeah, how did you know?" Danny asked, looking up.

By this time the rest of the men had noticed the fear on Sid's face. A quiet descended upon them, one of uncertainty and dread. They all looked to him, wondering what could have elicited this show of fear.

"I'm afraid our suspicions are correct," Sid told them. "I can all but guarantee you that this show has something to do with the Sleeping Sickness."

"How do you know?" Gary asked. His skepticism had not been broken, but was seriously challenged.

"Rip Starr. That's a name I was hoping to forget," Sid muttered to himself. "But I guess all of our buried demons rise up again at some point, yes?"

He rapped the table with his knuckle. Apparently, he had come to some resolve within himself. The look of fear had been replaced with firm conviction.

"Swordsmen," he said. "I believe now is the time for action."

Chapter 16 - The Studio

An hour later the men were making their way to the far side of town. Sid had them hastily equipped. Each one was given the pistol he had chosen during training with some attempts at concealment. Gary's Desert Eagle proved difficult to hide. He eventually had to settle on a shoulder holster and put a jacket over it.

"It's too hot for this," Gary complained. "I'm going to die with heat stroke."

"That's what you get for picking a hand cannon," Vic quipped. "How did you expect to carry that anyway?"

"The other guns were too small," Gary explained.

Besides the pistols, each man was given a knife to strap on to the inside of his leg. Sid apologized for the meager equipment but insisted that time may be of the essence. Once hastily armed they loaded into the back of a van. Danny brought along his laptop while Gerard took the driver's seat with Sid beside him.

"This thing definitely has some child molester vibes going on here," Vic said as he slid inside the back of the van, noting the blacked-out windows.

"Especially with you in it," Gary retorted to the delight of the other men.

"My uncle used to have a van like this," Danny said as they all got situated. He looked over the interior with something that bordered on admiration.

"That just got creepier somehow," Vic pointed out.

"No, Randy was really cool," Danny insisted.

"He was a dude named Randy?" Vic asked incredulously. "And he had a van - and you didn't notify the police immediately?"

"No way," Danny said, undeterred by Vic's mocking and the growing laughter around him. "Randy was the man. He even had a little round bed in the van, and it would rotate. There were beads hanging down the back door. Oh, and he had this awesome system in there. Eight track and everything."

Vic had been stunned speechless. He looked at Danny, eyes wide, unable to even shake his head. The other men were besides themselves with laughter. Even Sid was infected in the passenger seat.

"Let me guess," Vic said, finding his voice. "He had long hair and a moustache."

Danny looked genuinely taken aback.

"How'd you know?" he asked.

"Oh, just a guess," Vic shrugged. "Gonna definitely need a shower when we get back."

"He was tall too," Danny continued to reminisce. "And skinny. Taller than Big G even."

"Heads up boys," Sid commanded from the front. "Danny, where are headed?"

Danny looked down at his laptop and began to give driving instructions. They had discovered the studios for Catalyst Productions was in nearby East Anglia, and Sid had insisted they check it out.

"What exactly are we going to do when we get there?" Malachi slid up to the passenger seat to ask. "What's the plan?"

"We'll have a look around," Sid answered.

"That's the plan?" Malachi asked, aghast at such a flippant suggestion. "We're just going to look around?"

"It's what is needed," Sid explained. "We have a suspicion that this Catalyst Productions may have something to do with the Sleeping Sickness. Our suspicions need to be confirmed or denied."

"Yeah, but to just show up and try to look around. What kind of plan is that?"

Sid turned to look at Malachi. "What do you suggest?"

"I doubt they'll just let us in," he argued. "Especially if they really are up to something."

"Won't know until we try," Sid pointed out.

"Yeah, but . . ." Malachi began. He was having a hard time formulating his thoughts. Or was it his fears?

"Do you have a better idea?" Sid asked.

Malachi shook his head. "Not really, but I would feel a lot better if we had some sort of strategy here. What if things go wrong?"

"I fully anticipate things to go wrong," Sid surprised him by saying. "That's why we brought the weapons."

Malachi was stunned into silence. Normally, he didn't even like to get into his car without his route preplanned, examined for traffic stoppages, an alternate route planned if the first presented too many difficulties. And this had to be done before he even started his car.

What Sid was proposing was pure insanity. To just charge in there without any semblance of a plan, with the expectation of danger, was beyond madness. Anxiety bubbled up in him and threatened to overtake him completely. He felt his breath quickening and his heart thumping in the inside of his chest. Sweat began to form on the palms of his hands and he even felt dizzy with fear.

"Malachi, you know what I've noticed about men with a gift for planning?" Sid asked, reading the anxiety on Malachi's face. "Sometimes, instead of the plan being a gift whereby they can control the world around them, the need for planning controls them."

With that Sid turned around and faced the front again. Malachi slumped back in his seat, not the least bit consoled by the older man's words. It wasn't the first time he had heard that he relied too much on planning, or maybe had a bit of a control streak. Not that he agreed at all. Plans were always good in his estimation. Anyone who thought differently just courted disaster, or was lazy. Or both.

"There are times for planning," Sid spoke up without turning to face him. "And there are times when you just need to act. A key part of leadership is knowing what the moment calls for."

Malachi didn't respond. He hardly heard what Sid said at all. The situation was already feeling out of control in his opinion. He dreaded what would come next. Some disaster, no doubt, and as usual he would be tasked with picking up the pieces.

For the rest of the ride Malachi stewed in silence. He didn't hear the banter of the men around them, nor did he pick up on the anxiety that underlined it. The men were putting on a brave face, but all shared Malachi's reservations to some extent. They were plunging into the unknown. Part of the feeling was excitement to be doing something, something more meaningful than they had ever done before. But this did not temper the fear of the unknown and what they might be facing.

The only one that didn't seem to fear at all was Tresmond. A calm and resigned look rested on his face. He stared off into space, but for vastly different reasons than Malachi. If Malachi had been able to look past his own fears, he would have noticed a resolve and determination on the grieving father's face, and all with an intensity that would have frightened him as well.

After a forty-five-minute drive the van turned off the main highway and onto a smaller road. A covering of trees stretched over them like a vaulted ceiling. Danny continued to give out directions. By instinct the men knew their destination was looming closer, and they began to feel their anticipation intensify.

"This next right should take us where we want to go," Danny instructed at last.

The final turn looked like it would lead anywhere except for a TV studio. The small, barely two-lane road was deserted. Trees lined the road on every side. There was nothing at all to indicate a thriving business was anywhere up ahead. There was a stillness on the road that was unsettling in its own right.

"You sure this is right?" Giovanni asked, peering through the front window.

"According to Google maps it is," Danny said.

The empty road continued to stretch out in front of them. Gerard slowed down, peering cautiously around him. The only sound on the road was the rumble of the van's engine. A wind blew and shook the trees. Branches rattled like a primitive warning. In his mind Malachi imagined a witch doctor shaking his feathered staff at them to ward them away.

"Here we are," Sid announced as the van crested a rise.

The men crowded up to look out the front dash. A valley stretched out before them that had been cleared and paved for the vast studio lot. A three-story building of long glass windows and metal frames stood out in front. Behind this main building they could make out three long, white domed buildings they assumed to be the sound stages where all the shows were recorded.

Gerard stopped the van at the top of the hill while the men inside surveyed the view from within. The same eerie quiet that dominated the road up to the complex still dominated. It was an utter and complete quiet. Clouds passed over the sun, casting a gray pallor over the world.

"Where is everybody?" Danny asked.

From their vantage point they could see no one moving below. There were no cars parked in the vast lot out front. No people moved between the buildings, hurrying about the endless business of making movies and shows. From their vantage point it could have been a model that someone built to admire, but never to be used.

"Am I the only one that is truly weirded out by this?" Vic asked. "Should it be this empty."

"Maybe everyone has the day off?" Zach suggested in the form of a question.

Gary shook his head. "No way. They still wouldn't leave the place deserted. You would have guards or something."

"Not to mention, at a studio someone is always working. I don't care what day it is," Danny said. "There's no reason it should be empty."

"Let's not assume it's empty at all," Sid told them. "Appearances, as they say, can be deceiving."

Gerard edged the van forward again with the men still crowded near the front. Silent awe dominated the interior of the van. Gerard pulled all the way up to the front gate and shut the engine off. With this last sound gone the silence became deafening. The men peered out cautiously, wondering what this emptiness could mean. Any excitement they felt at their first touch of action had been suffocated by the eerie silence they encountered.

"Well, gentlemen," Sid began as he unbuckled his seat belt. "We didn't come just to look."

"I guess we're doing this," Giovanni said.

Malachi nodded, feeling that this moment was the beginning of something they could not undo once it was begun. It was a moment that needed to be acknowledged.

"The Lord is my strength and my shield," Malachi said.

"Whom shall I fear," the men answered in unison.

"The Lord is the stronghold of my life."

"Of whom shall I be afraid."

Once they had begun properly the men all stepped out of the van and went to stand before the front gate. The chain link fence looked as new as everything else, shining almost silver in its galvanized coating. The gate that secured the fence was the kind that slid back and forth on wheels and was secured with what looked like a heavy electric lock.

"Looks like this thing has juice," Zach pointed out. He showed the others the strands of steel wire running vertically through the fence, as well as the row that protected the top.

Three signs all indicated the fence was electrified. One was the standard "High Voltage" warning. Another announced the installation by a company called, Watch Dog, complete with a menacing German Shepherd. The final sign gave the universal words of, don't touch this, in yellow, with a hand surrounded by lightning bolts.

"Guess it has electricity in it," Vic pointed out blandly.

"Gentlemen, how do you suggest we get in?" Sid asked as he surveyed the fence and gate.

"Wait, you're not suggesting we break in?" Malachi asked, aghast at the mere thought.

"How else would we get in?" Sid asked as if this were the stupidest question in the world.

"That's called breaking and entering," Malachi informed him. "And it's against the law."

"It's also against the law to develop a disease that strikes at defenseless children and first renders them unconscious before finally taking their life," Sid countered. "Is it not?"

Malachi tried to say something but quickly closed his mouth. A quick look at Tres told him that any argument against what Sid had said would not only be fruitless, but possibly hurtful. Of course, what Sid pointed out was right. Still, the idea didn't sit right with him.

"We could probably just drive through the gate," Vic suggested.

"That would set off an alarm," Zach told them. "I got a buddy that works for one of these companies. Any break in the charge will set off an alarm. Cops will be here in minutes."

"I don't believe we have to worry about the police," Sid assured them as he stepped back to look at the lay of the land.

"How confident are you in that assessment?" Malachi asked, horrified he was even entertaining this notion.

"About seventy percent," Sid shrugged. "How do you access this gate? Does anyone know?"

"Seventy percent?" Malachi repeated back, aghast. "So, you're thirty percent certain the cops will be here at some time to check out our little field trip here."

"It's this panel here," Danny answered, pointing out the post in front of the gate.

A box was attached to the top of the post, at just the right height for a car that might pull up to it. Danny opened up the door of the panel to reveal a keypad.

"Numeric keypad," he said.

"Thirty percent isn't bad," Sid insisted as he came to stand beside Danny. Together they inspected the keypad with no incoming revelations.

"I guess we can't cut the fence wire or anything," Gary suggested.

"Right," Danny confirmed. "If the current is cut off or even the voltage changes, or there is sudden variability in the current, anything like that would likely set off an alarm."

"I think we need to rethink this," Malachi said, trying to bring the men back to the threat they faced. "This is obviously more than just a walk up and see what is going on."

"I agree with Malachi," Giovanni spoke up. "Not sure we should be breaking in."

"What other options do we have?" Sid asked, seeming to ignore the objections of Malachi and Giovanni.

Then, turning to the other men. "The individuals who have perpetrated this thing work outside of the law in every way you can imagine," he reminded them. "They not only hold influence over our political and legal system, but have no scruples in breaking every ethical and moral code of our society. We can't always play nice. And we certainly can't play by the rules."

Vic stepped up to the fence, the portion beside the gate and held out his arms as if measuring something.

"What if we used jumper cables?" he asked. "If we clamped one side here and the other one just a little bit down the way. Would that keep the current going?"

"What for?" Danny asked.

"We could cut the fence then and crawl through," he suggested. "The cables would keep the current running. I don't know. Might work."

"If we keep breaking the rules does this make us any better than them?" Malachi argued. "And aren't we even commanded in the Bible to obey the laws of our land? That makes it an issue of faith for me."

Danny shook his head considering Vic's option. "I don't think that would work."

"Why not?" Vic asked.

"For one, you would need a set of cables for every wire we cut," he said. Coming near the fence he pointed out the wires that ran through the chain link. They were laced in the galvanized metal every foot starting from the bottom.

"Just to crawl through we would need to cut three of those wires, needing at least three cables."

"How many cables we got in the van?" Gary asked.

Danny shook his head again, dismissing the idea. "That's only one reason it won't work. We also have to consider that the same voltage and current needs to go through these wires to keep an alarm from being tripped. I doubt a set of jumper cables can do that. Plus, these wires are all taut. Any replacement we put on here would have to have the same amount of tension. Otherwise, the flow would be disturbed and the alarm set. A set of cables dangling on the ground so we can crawl over them wouldn't do the job. If we do that we may as well just drive through the gate."

Gary shrugged, warming up to that idea. "Maybe we just drive through and get it over with."

"Is everybody listening to the same suggestion I am?" Malachi asked, the incredulity clear in his voice. "We seriously want to break and enter, destroy public property in the meantime, and go ahead and throw trespass on top of it as well?"

Sid turned to face Malachi. His blue eyes blazed with an intensity that Malachi had forgotten was there.

"What do you suggest?" he asked. "Our enemies have likely hidden important information behind those gates, information that could be life and death for more children who will be attacked in the future. How do we legally and ethically obtain that information and stop them from hurting more? Tell me Mr., Green. What method could we possibly employ that will satisfy your conscience?"

Malachi felt the power emanating from the words as the older man spoke. Each one dug into him like barbs, as if arrows were being shot into his heart. He knew Sid was right. There was no way that they could get what they needed in a legal manner. If what he said was true about the Fae, that they had the governments and systems of the world under their sway, then there was no authority, no power they could turn to for legal help. They were it. A great evil, if indeed they were right about all this, was being perpetrated under the auspices of the law. The law would not help them here.

Still, knowing this, and being fully aware of this truth, did not stop the uneasy feeling all of it inspired in Malachi. It went against everything he was raised and was taught to believe and do. You respect the laws of the land. If you wanted to change something you went through the proper channels. You did all things in good order.

There was another fear that haunted Malachi, one he was dimly aware of but not ready to face yet. The moment he broke into this place, the second his foot trespassed this property line, he would be crossing a line himself. He would be pitting himself against the all the powers and authorities of the world he lived in. As flawed as they were he always worked within their boundaries.

But once he stepped through the line of that fence he would be working outside their boundaries. He would become an outsider, a renegade. The very thought made him sick to his stomach. He desperately wanted another way, a better way. For the life of him he couldn't think of what that could be.

"Mr. Green, I don't want to trouble your conscience," Sid told him, reading the distress in his heart. "But there are times when we must break the letter of the law in order to follow the spirit of the law. I think this is one such time."

Malachi shook his head. He knew Sid was right. All the same, he didn't like it. It invited chaos into life, disturbed the good order that God had ordained for all creation.

"How do we know the difference?" he asked, using what he knew was his last line of defense.

Sid smiled and tapped his head. "You have to use this thing God gave you and think."

Knowing Sid was right Malachi let the matter go. He looked to Giovanni who didn't seem as bothered as he did. All he got was a non-committal shrug.

"Maybe we hack into the access panel," Zach suggested. "You know, hotwire it so the gate opens."

"Do you know how to hotwire the panel?" Danny asked.

Zach answered with a shrug. "Just an idea."

"I think we should just plow through it," Gary suggested again. "There's no way we can get through this without them knowing we are here."

"They may already know we are here," Sid echoed, seeming to side with Gary's idea.

"There you go," Zach pointed out. "If they already know we are here then we may as well bust open the fence."

"Shouldn't we at least try to get in without being detected?" Vic said. "Besides, we don't know if they know we're here. I haven't seen any cameras yet. Which I must also say is a bit weird. Why wouldn't they have cameras? I don't see a single one out here."

"The Fae have an aversion to cameras," Sid told them. "Even the early, primitive cameras they don't like."

"Do they believe it will capture their soul, something like that?" Danny asked.

Sid shook his head, smiling. "Nothing like that Mr. Taylor. No, the cameras can sometimes catch the Fae as they really are, not as they appear. Out of caution they will avoid them altogether. The fact that we see no cameras here confirms my suspicions that this is their operation."

"Hey, that gives us a real good chance of not being seen yet," Vic piped in. "I say we don't announce our presence by plowing through the front gate."

"You got a better idea?" Gary asked.

"Any idea that doesn't involve destroying the gate is a better idea. If you want, we could just call them now and tell them we're here. Sid, do you have the Fae's number? I know you at least follow them on Instagram. We could even do a selfie beside the mangled gate and send it to them."

"Too bad sarcasm can't open the gate," Gary shot back. "I have yet to hear a better idea."

"We go over the top," Tres said, breaking his silence.

"That's a ten-foot fence," Vic pointed out. "How would we get over?"

"We back the van up to it," Tres said.

Pointing up at the top of the fence he indicated the posts that held up four rows of wire, sticking out at an angle. "With the van close enough, we can get a hold of those posts and vault over."

"Vault over?" Malachi asked, incredulous. "Do you think we can vault over that."

"I know I can," Tres answered. "And I'm pretty sure you can too."

"Have you forgotten about the electricity?" Danny asked. "As soon as you touch that post you will wish you never had. Not to mention, you will set off whatever alarm they have."

"There's a rubber mat on the floor of the van," he reminded them. "We drape it over the wires running across the top, right there where the support post is. We back the van up to the fence. With the mat over that post, we should be able to get a good grip on it and use that to vault over the fence."

Danny though about it for a moment, obviously trying to find a flaw in the plan. "I'm with Malachi, not sure I could vault over," he said. "But

. . . It may be the best we have,"

"I think it's worth a shot," Gary chimed in.

"I think it's better than destroying the front gate," Victor added.

"Shut up, Vic."

"It's a good idea," Sid told them. "And perhaps the best we have. However, my days of vaulting over a fence are long over. You will just have to do your investigations without me."

"Maybe not," Danny suggested. "There's another control panel just inside the fence. It's possible that one is not coded like the one on the outside."

Finally decided on their course of action, they set the plan in motion. Gerard backed the van up so it was almost touching the fence. Tres climbed on top, sizing up his angle and getting his balance. The top of the van gave a metallic thump as it buckled under his steps.

Gary handed him the rubber mat from the back. Just as easily as if he were arranging the curtains in his house, Tres draped the mat over the top of the fence, where it was guarded by four strands of high tensile, electrified wire. After draping it over he reached up and adjusted it, to make sure it was centered on one of the supporting posts that held the wires up and at an angle off the top of the fence.

There seemed to be no hesitation in Tresmond. As the other men watched from the ground, excited but not sure how he easily he could pull it off, Tres showed little doubt.

With a single step back and pause to measure up his move he sprang into action. Stepping forward he took hold of the supporting post and bent his knees. In one fluid motion he sprang up, pulling himself over by the post. His legs flew up in an arc, as smooth as if done by a gymnast. Before the other men could even register what they saw, Tres was landing on the other side of the fence.

A chorus of cheers rose up spontaneously from the men. Even Tres couldn't keep the hint of a smile that danced across his face.

"A ten! I give it a ten!" Gary gushed.

"I'd say an eight point five," Vic countered. "The landing was a little rough and he didn't keep his legs straight all the way through the flip."

"Well let's see you try it," Gary goaded. "Think you can do better?"

"I don't want to take away from what Tres just did," Vic said by way of excuse. "Why don't we let this be his moment."

Tres jogged over to the gate. On that side there was a post with a panel box identical to the one on the outside. Tresmond pulled open the cover.

"Is it a number panel or just a single button?" Danny asked, approaching the gate.

"Number panel," Tresmond pointed out.

"Damn," Danny cursed. "I guess we will be going over too."

"I got a better idea," Tresmond suggested.

He punched a few buttons on the panel and the lock disengaged with a pop. The gate slid open smoothly.

"How did you know the code?" Malachi asked as the group sauntered in.

"Don't tell me," Danny groaned, already guessing what it is. "Please don't tell me they . . ."

Tres reached into the panel box and pulled out an index card. On the card, written in black marker was 2557#.

"You've got to be kidding me," Danny fumed, throwing his hands up. "People are impossible, I swear. If it wasn't for people security would be easy."

"Let's be thankful for human error," Sid said as he passed through the open gate. "All the same, we can't rule out that our enemy already knows we are here."

"How would they know," Giovanni asked.

"They have their ways," Sid answered cryptically. "Believe me, they have their ways."

Once inside, the men took stock of their surroundings. Just as before the place was deathly quiet. Ahead, the road opened up to the front parking lot. Black asphalt with the yellow lines of individual spaces painted on them stretched as far as they could see. It looked like the space could accommodate well over a thousand cars. Up ahead they could see what looked like the main office building. Gathering clouds reflected in the tinted windows that covered all three stories.

"Guess we go this way," Vic said, beginning the long walk to the main building.

The other men filed in behind him without asking. Their footsteps echoed over the black asphalt that still looked freshly poured. Even the tar smell that rose up from its surface reminded them that it hadn't been there long.

Malachi felt more unsettled with every step they took. He felt exposed in the empty and vast parking lot. That surreal sensation of being watched surrounded him on all sides. He felt that just beyond the fence, inside the looming office building, even in the hills behind them. Someone watched their every move.

"Do we try the front door?" Giovanni asked as they neared the central office building.

No one moved in the building ahead. Like the rest of the property, there were no signs of life or movement anywhere that they could see.

"Let's scout the area first," Vic suggested. "Circle around back to the main building."

Behind the man office stood three larger buildings. These were long and domed, topped with bright white metal. Two stood side by side, running parallel to each other. The third was behind these first two, stretched out long ways to seemingly cap the others.

As they walked the property the men all grow more uneasy. The silence was deafening, almost oppressive. Everything about the place indicated it should be busy and full of life. Instead, it was empty and abandoned, a lifeless mockery of something that should be thriving.

"What is this?" Zach asked as they traversed the long side of the building.

"Sound studio," Danny offered. "It's where they would shoot their movies or shows."

"Are they always this big?"

"Oh yeah, these are actually small for a sound studio. But the fact that they have three of them is pretty impressive. I would expect a lot more material would have been churned out of this studio than what they've actually done."

"This place has a fake feel to me," Giovanni suggested.

"What makes you say that?" Sid asked, coming up beside him.

"I don't know," Giovanni shrugged. "It just looks . . .staged. The whole thing. I feel like if hit these walls hard enough they'll fall over."

For emphasis he banged on the wall of the sound studio. A deep and cavernous echo sounded that rumbled through the building. The strength of the sound made the other men jump, startled after the weight of the quiet.

"See what I mean?" Giovanni said with a shrug. "Sounds hollow."

"Indeed, it may be," Sid agreed. "It may all be for show."

"But this had to of cost millions to do," Danny objected. "Why would you put that kind of money into a sham like this? Especially if no one was going to see it."

"For one, money is no object to our enemy," Sid told them. "Nor does it mean as much to them as it does to us. For another thing, this place was built to be seen. To be seen by us."

That thought disturbed Malachi even more than the quiet. That anyone would go to this kind of trouble and effort to carry out a plan meant they would go even further to protect it. To think all that effort was directed at him and his little group of men almost made his knees buckle. Who were they to stand up to a power like that? They were just a Bible study. This was something definitely over their heads.

They tried the few doors they came across along length of the building. Everyone was locked. No sounds responded to their infrequent calls. After circling halfway around the lot, they decided to go back down the center, between the main two.

A wide, empty asphalt space divided these two front lots. Typically, one would expect them to be full of actors in costume hurrying to their places, scenery being toted by the set construction crews, or directors and executives hurrying between the studios on golf carts driven by underpaid assistants.

"Whatever was going on here, it's not anymore," Giovanni noted as they rounded the corner of the sound studio and into the alley. "This place is empty."

As soon as the words were out of his mouth, they all stopped short.

"Spoke too soon," Gary said.

They were not alone.

Chapter 17 - Shadow Men

The men stopped as one. Their uneasiness was replaced by a sudden wariness. Bodies tensed for conflict as adrenaline seeped into their bloodstreams. Malachi felt his own limbs coil in readiness. He couldn't tell if he was excited or scared.

Halfway down the alley, standing between them and the main building, were a group of men dressed all in black. They seemed to mirror the Swordsmen almost exactly. There were seven, lined in a row, silent and waiting. An eighth stood in front of the others, like Sid was standing in front of them.

The two groups silently regarded each other. Not a word was spoken nor movement made. From that distance Malachi could not make out any of their features too clearly. Only that they were men and dressed in black and he could tell they were as ready to fight as he and the others.

"Who are they?" Gary finally asked, his voice sounding dry and cracked.

"This is our welcoming party," Sid told them. "I guess they know we are here after all."

Malachi thought he could hear a tremor of fear in Sid's voice. This made him more frightened than anything else so far. Whatever Sid was scared of had to be terrifying indeed.

"Gentlemen, follow me," Sid instructed as he began to move forward. "But do not walk past me unless a fight begins."

As if by cue the two groups of men began walking towards each other. The silent alley echoed with the sound of their steps. The overcast light lent its own ominous feel to the moment while a wind blew in from behind them.

"If it comes to a fight, which it probably will," Sid warned as they continued forward. "Be on your alert, for these men are just as fast and capable as you are. They are called shadow men. They have certain powers, special abilities."

"Kind of like our gifts?" Giovanni asked.

"No, they're different. I don't have time to explain it now, but just be prepared," Sid answered.

"Prepared for what exactly?"

"Anything."

As they drew closer Malachi could make out more details of the shadow. They were all dressed the same. The black pants and shirts they wore gave off a sheen as if they were made of leather. Their boots, also black, were combat style, heavy and laced up high. Even the gloves they wore were black, with raised knobs on the knuckle, which could only serve one obvious purpose.

The shadow men approaching them walked with a confidence Malachi wished he portrayed. But as they got closer whatever confidence he felt began to fade. His mind raced back, trying to think when was the last time he had actually been in a fight. Not the sparring practice with the other men, but an actual fight. The only thing he could remember was a bathroom scuffle with Larry Helter in third grade. And that one was broken up by the janitor before any serious blows were exchanged. Not that third grade fights ever mean serious blows.

Desperately wishing he had more experience to draw on Malachi walked with the other men and tried to mask his fear. He looked to the eighth man approaching them, the one who appeared to be the leader. Like the others, he too was dressed in all black. But instead of the rigid, armor-looking outfit, this one was wearing dress pants and shirt. The black trench coat he wore fluttered in the wind.

Looking closer Malachi was amazed at the man's almost unnatural good looks. An olive toned complexion covered a face that was long but nearly flawless. Dark hair was combed close to his head. He carried a black cane, much like the one Sid used. Instead of being topped with a silver knob this one had a crystal that glowed with a soft, violet color. The handsome features held an arrogant look that Malachi associated with many beautiful people. Especially those who knew it.

Despite the good looks Malachi detected something awkward about the man. It wasn't something that he could pinpoint, no distinct feature that he could say made him look strange. It was more a general feeling. The man, no matter how arrogant or beautiful he appeared, looked uncomfortable in his own skin, like he didn't belong there.

"What the hell are they wearing?" Vic asked as they neared the approaching men.

"Looks like some kind of body armor to me," Gary observed. "Watch out for those gloves too. Some kind of reinforced knuckle on them."

"Hate to think what kind of party they throw," Vic said with exaggerated disgust.

The two groups of approaching men stopped with only a few feet between them. They silently appraised each other. Eyes that had been trained for combat searched the other assessing potential weakness and strength. Malachi found himself noticing things he had never seen before. The blonde-haired man across from him had a hitch in his step that Malachi knew was because his left leg was slightly longer than his right. The stocky one breathed shallow, possibly because of nerves. Another had a twitchy right hand. Was that just a tic? He saw all of these things and more in a glance. As another part of his gift was awakening in him, he assessed without thinking about it, the posture, gait, stance and tension of each of his potential opponents.

"Love the outfit boys," Vic said, breaking the silence. "Hope everybody remembers the safe word."

One of the shadow men, the one with a pale face and a scar running from his scalp to chin, snarled in response.

"Sid Bickley," said the man in the trench coat, the clear leader of the group. "Of all the men I thought might show up today, I was sure you would be the last."

"I wish I could say it was good to see you," Sid replied. "But the mere sight of you turns my stomach, Rip."

The man in the trench coat smiled and chuckled.

"I turn your stomach?" Rip asked. "Have you looked at yourself lately old man? You look like a shaving accident away from death."

"I've never felt better," Sid replied, throwing out his arms. "Never felt stronger."

Rip shook his head and pointed at Sid with his cane.

"You know, it must drive you crazy to see me this good looking," he said. "Especially considering how old and decrepit you've become. How does it feel Sid? Not the ladies' man anymore, are you?"

"Doesn't matter what skin you wear, Rip. You'll always be ugly, and you know it."

The smile fell from Rip's face. He ran a perfectly manicured hand through his oiled hair.

"You've gotten delusional in your age," Rip snarled. "Do you know how many girls throw themselves at me? You know how many women beg for me to pleasure them? Any idea, Sid? You never had it so good."

"It's all just tricks," Sid replied. "If you were to show them what you really look like they would run in terror and you know it. You trick women into bed, Rip. In fact, you're not much different than a frat boy with a bottle of Rufies."

Malachi could see Rip squeeze the cane in his hand. A vein popped out on his head with the effort as his lips drew tight into a severe line. It was obvious the two men had history, and not a good one. And for some reason, Sid was taunting the man.

"You made a mistake coming here," Rip said, spitting the words out. "I don't care how many new little slaves you have with you; it's over Sid."

"I think you'll find we're not that easy," Sid retorted.

"My men will devour yours, then you will die a slow and painful death to complete your failure," Rip threatened. "Because that's what you are, Sid, a failure."

Malachi could see that these words stung Sid more than any other. He even took a half step back, as if physically injured by the insult.

"What? With these leather daddies here?" Vic snorted. "You gotta be kidding me, Rip. I think you should put the ball gag back in their mouth and let us go our way."

Vic locked eyes with the man across from him, the one with the scar. Malachi could see the barely restrained rage on his features. The tension built as Malachi's heart thumped in his chest. He felt the release of adrenaline in his veins as his whole body tensed up for what he knew was coming.

Vic puckered his lips and made a kiss at the scarred one.

For just a moment there was heavy and silent tension. The whole world stood still. Even the air stopped moving.

The man with the scar exploded into action. A booted foot came towards Vic's head. The kick was swift and right on target.

With a cry of surprise Vic pulled back and put up a block just in time. Scar followed the kick with another sweeping roundhouse. Vic ducked and pulled up just in time to block the three rapid punches that came his way.

"Whoa! Shouldn't we get to know each other first?" Vic taunted as he backed away from the attack.

The Swordsmen looked across at the men dressed in black. They regarded their colleague now engaged in battle, and burst into action.

The man with the blonde hair fell upon Malachi. Alright, Blondie, Malachi thought. Let's see what you've got.

199

Malachi backed up, easily blocking the first punches thrown his way. A kick came towards him that made him duck and back pedal further. Blondie came in closer to grapple, taking hold of Malachi's arm. He twisted and tried to throw him over his back. Malachi quickly twisted his leg around Blondie's interfering with effort. Using his left hand, he pushed the other man away from him, freeing his arm.

Blondie turned and smiled at Malachi. Screaming out the man charged again, aiming for the head, then trunk. A knee came up that Malachi barely blocked in time.

Jumping back Malachi readied for the next attack. Blondie pulled back and walked around him, circling his victim.

From the corner of his eyes Malachi could see the battle raging all around them. Each of the Swordsmen were engaged in battle. Sid and Rip stood silently facing each other. Their hands were outstretched and each seemed engaged in deep concentration.

We have to decide this quickly, Malachi thought to himself. The man he was fighting looked and acted much more experienced than Malachi was. The longer this fight drew out he felt it had to be to their enemies' advantage.

It's gotta happen sometime, Malachi said to himself and fell into the attack.

His first punches were easily blocked by Blondie. Not wasting any time, the shadow man returned the blows with a combination of his own. Malachi desperately parried, barely keeping the punches at bay.

At booted foot came up that he didn't have time to block. It connected heavily with his chest and sent Malachi sprawling to the ground.

He hit the pavement with a thud, expecting his whole body to cry out in pain. Surprisingly, he felt very little. A tweak in his chest and back were all the discomfort that came to him.

Blondie smirked and circled again, not pressing the advantage. He's toying with me, Malachi thought.

Out of the corner of his eye he saw a strange interplay of darkness and light. Knowing he shouldn't take his eyes off his opponent Malachi still couldn't resist a peak. Glancing quickly over at Sid and Rip he forgot for a moment he was even in a fight.

A thick, black cloud gathered under Rip. It roiled like an angry thunderstorm. Violet forks of lightning crackled through it. It looked just like the storm cloud that had gathered over the mansion just yesterday.

With outstretched arms Rip seemed to be commanding the black cloud. It billowed and grew as he stretched out his arms, almost covering the dark man completely. Thick tendrils grew out of the cloud, like twisting arms that wove through each other.

Malachi felt a dread emanating from that cloud. It was the embodiment of fear itself. Hopelessness, dread, despair, apathy; all of these were mixed in with a cold terror that Malachi could feel stirring in the cloud. He felt his own limbs grow cold as the cloud grew. Whatever dark power Rip was handling, it was all the horror of the dark, and all the realization of every nightmare within it. He felt his heart sink just looking at it.

He looked to Sid and his heart felt warm again. From beneath him a bright, golden light began to shine. It looked like flames of fire, but white hot and fully alive.

The fire grew beneath Sid, as bright as Rip's cloud was dark. The flames coalesced into tendrils, spinning around each other in thick arms, almost like serpents. It looked like a dance for a moment as the bands grew and twisted and covered Sid in its intense light.

Malachi looked at the fire Sid had summoned and he saw in it the antithesis of everything that he felt out of the dark. Or rather, he knew somehow, that the dark cloud was simply the opposite of everything the light stood for.

In the light he felt warmth and peace, joy, hope and an intense, burning love. Here was everything good in life, the fire of life itself. Everything worth fighting for and defending, everything worth living for and dying for.

At the same time both Rip and Sid threw their arms forward. The fire and shadow obeyed and rushed towards each other. They collided in an explosion of light and dark. A grey fog spread out from the cloud, covering the alley and everyone who was in it.

Malachi felt a cold wind rush upon him as the black mist enveloped him. He heard Rip laugh as the darkness spread. It covered all the Swordsmen and the shadow men, and draped itself over their combat. Wisps of the white fire flew between the dark mist. Small, thin flames extinguished the shadows wherever they touched. Malachi was certain that the outcome of their fight would depend wholly upon what happened between these two men. For whatever power they may have acquired, it could do little to stand against that dark and fearful cloud that destroyed all hope.

Out of the corner of his eye Malachi saw Blondie run in for another attack. Cursing himself for his lack of attention, Malachi rolled away just as a booted foot came down where he had been lying.

In one quick motion he put his arms under himself and lifted himself back to his feet. Blondie came crashing in with another kick.

Malachi knocked the kick aside. He swung a punch at Blondie's head. It was ducked just as Malachi's fist swing around and returned with a fierce uppercut. Malachi threw up a forearm to stop the blow from landing.

Blondie backed away again. Dark mist with flames of light danced around him.

I wonder what else he's got up his sleeve, Malachi wondered as he prepared for another attack. I wonder what other power they have that Sid was talking about.

It was Tres who figured it out first.

Tresmond was happy.

It had been weeks since he had felt the sensation. A few times it threatened to creep up on him. But every time he felt the first fluttering of joy, he was quick to push it down. After all, he had no right to be happy. His world had been destroyed. His son was dead. It would be a long time before he could be happy again.

Except he was. In the moment, in the fight, he felt an exhilaration of pure joy. For now, he didn't have to think about his grief.

The pale, but muscled man lunged towards him, making Tres defend himself and put everything else out of his mind. He didn't think about the fact that his son was dead. He didn't think about how his wife wouldn't talk to him because she believed he was still alive, and since Tres didn't share her delusion, she wanted nothing to do with him. For the time being, at least, these things were the furthest from his mind.

Mostly he was happy because he was fighting. A part of himself believed that this is what he was made to do, and we always feel joy when we do what we are made to do. But he also rejoiced that these were the men who were responsible for his son's death, and he was fighting them. He hadn't been able to save his son. At the least he could avenge his death.

Tres was fighting for his son. He was fighting for justice, against the tyranny of a dark world that exploited and trampled the poor and defenseless. This was a holy fight. And he felt all the ecstatic power that belongs to those who engage in a righteous cause.

It didn't take long for Tres to figure out he had an advantage over the pale man. His opponent was better trained and had more experience than Tres, but he was not near as fast.

A few, fast test punches came raining in on him at the outset. He knocked these away quickly and pressed his own attack.

A quick combination took the pale man by surprise and he fell back quickly. Tres spun around with a roundhouse kick that was ducked then knelt down in one fluid motion to deliver a solid punch to the head.

Pale man defended just in time. He pulled away as his crossed arms blocked the punch but lost his balance and landed on his back.

Tres saw his opportunity. He dove forward to use his momentum to deliver a punch from above.

Pale man rolled out of the way just as Tres' fist hit the pavement. He hardly felt the pain. Grunting in frustration he jumped up and pressed the attack again.

Tres and the Pale Man exchanged flurry after flurry. Punch combinations, swinging kicks, flying knees and elbows came at each other.

The pale man blocked everything Tres threw at him, though each defense was a bit slower than the last. Tres could see his opponent slowing down. He mixed in acrobatics to throw him off balance. He dodged with a flip then flipped back over Pale Man and attacked when he landed.

Pale Man grunted with the effort of blocking that attack and fell back further. He was slowing down with every new attack and Tres could sense he was wearing him down.

Tres spun around swinging his leg out low. Pale Man made the expected move, jumping over the swinging legs. Tres lifted up as Pale Man was coming down, his arms out at his sides.

Undefended, Tres saw his chance. He punched out at the undefended middle and waited to contact the soft tissue of his belly.

Pale Man disappeared in a puff of black smoke.

Tres' punch passed through the traces of a black, swirling cloud. He looked at his fist, bewildered. The black smoke quickly dissipated, leaving no trace of the man he had been fighting seconds ago.

He had no time to consider this unexpected development. Out of the corner of his eye he saw the smoke coalescing on his left side. A figure materialized out of the smoke.

Tres tried to pull up his defenses but knew he wouldn't be in time. Bracing for the blow he felt the punch contact the side of his face, just below his left eye. His head exploded in pain. Something more than a fist had struck him. He thought about Gary's warning. Something certainly reinforced those knuckles.

Tres rolled away and got his defenses up just as Pale Man pressed the attack again. Renewed by his shot his opponent came on fast. Quick combinations of punches were followed by a flying knee that Tres had to bend over backwards to avoid.

Seizing the opportunity, he turned the back bend into a flip. He sent his leg out to kick Pale Man as he flipped over.

Another puff of black smoke and the kick met only air. Tres finished his flip just as the smoke coalesced again, this time on his right. He braced for the punch that only glanced this time. The reinforced knuckles struck the top of his head, sending out another spark of pain.

Tres pulled up. Blood trickled out from under his eye. The joy he felt at the fight had morphed into a growing panic. How could he fight an opponent that could disappear in smoke? And then rematerialize at will somewhere else?

He wondered if there was any other unexpected power the shadow man was hiding. As he pressed in for the attack again a dark cloud passed over them both.

Zach discovered this ability just after Tres did.

He was locked in a back-and-forth battle against one of the shadow men, this one shorter than the others but well-muscled and fast. Zach fended off the first attacks and countered with one of his own.

Fists and feet flew at each other. Up, then down, then spinning for a counter. The battle raged over the alley. It became a deadly dance with seven different fights weaving in and out of each other.

Zach felt himself losing awareness of anything except the fight in front of him. Somehow, he also remained aware of all the other fights as well. He knew Tres and Vic were gaining the upper hand and Danny was struggling to keep up with the attack and that Malachi and the others were all evenly matched.

As soon as the dark mist fell over them Zach felt a chill settle over his bones. His limbs felt heavy, weighted down with some invisible malaise.

A tendril of white flame struck him and a burst of energy coursed through him, momentarily fending off the dark.

With a new surge of energy Zach grabbed the next punch that came towards him. Using the momentum of his attacker he pulled the shadow man close, bringing up his knee to contact with his stomach.

The wrist he held fast suddenly evaporated and his knee hit nothing but air. He only had time to look at his empty hand when darkness coalesced on the edge of his vision.

A heavy kick contacted with his side and Zach fell to the ground. He looked up just in time to see his attacker coming in again.

Rolling to the side Zach pushed himself up and put up his defenses just in time to block the barrage of fast punches coming his way. A kick came towards his head, then at his knee. He blocked both and countered at the exposed attacker.

His fist passed through a cloud of black smoke.

How am I supposed to fight this, he asked himself as he braced for the attack that was coming.

He felt the shadow man re-form right behind him. Before he could turn, a strong arm wrapped around his neck from behind, cutting off his air. The grip around his neck tightened and he felt his head lift back.

Grabbing the arm around his neck Zach braced to throw him off. A sharp pain exploded in his back. He could feel the blade as it sliced through his clothes and punch through his skin.

He gasped as the cold steel cut through skin. Panic surged in him along with fear. The dark mist fell over him, draining all hope from him as his attacker tightened his grip and drove the blade in.

"Never bet against the dark," the shadow man whispered.

Zach felt the cold close over him.

I didn't have enough time, Sid desperately thought as he summoned the white fire. They aren't ready for this.

Out of the corner of his eyes he saw the mad fight begin between his men and the shadow men. They held their own well now, but any minute they would encounter the enemy's special power. The shadow men would begin smoke shifting, and his swordsmen had no idea what was coming.

He hadn't had time to tell them about the shadow men and their powers, or how to combat it. There was so much to teach them and he simply couldn't get to it all. Nor could he warn them about the battle he and Rip were about to engage in. He didn't have time to warn them that Rip would send out a consuming darkness, a black mist that would fill them with despair and fear, and it would suck their energy right out of them. He couldn't tell them that his fire would counteract the dark and that the light was stronger if they just held on.

He didn't have time to tell them these and much more. But that time was past and they would discover for themselves.

Sending up a prayer for help and strength Sid steeled himself for the battle ahead. He could see Rip's dark clouds rising up out of the ground. Its fierce electricity crackled in bolts of lightning, illuminating the dark clouds in flashes of violet.

Despair began to touch Sid as he saw the cloud forming. He had felt its effects and knew exactly what it was capable of. Every hope and shred of joy would be sucked out of a person who fell under that cloud. Nothing but fear and despair were in there, and they could consume even the stoutest heart. When one fell under its influence, he felt there was no hope or purpose to life, and that the best thing he could do was either run away in terror or simply lay down and die. Confusion would take over the mind as despair ate at the heart. One could not think or even imagine anything other than this dark fear and agony.

Thoughts of regret dissipated as soon as Sid felt the white fire surge in him. The counter to Rip's darkness, Sid summoned a burst of white in flames of fire that burned around him. Pure exhilaration and joy burst through him as he felt the fire rise. Strength coursed through his veins. He felt the power and virility of any ten men rising up in his muscles and sinew.

The laugh came out of him without restraint. This was hope and love and faith and joy. Everything good and beautiful was here. Light and life were the heart of this fire.

Lifting up his arms Sid formed the fire into thick tendrils. They wove together, moving like serpents, knotting themselves into a dome that covered Sid. He watched the clouds grow from Rip and he felt how puny and weak they were. Compared to this white fire they were nothing.

The fire grew and the tendrils snaked out further. He wove them together until they formed one thick trunk of white fire. Thrusting his arms out he shot them towards Rip.

While Sid wove his fire, Rip had been doing the same with his darkness. When Sid attacked, he threw out his black cloud. The two forces collided, sending out a dark, grey mist over the fighting men. Floating through this mist were wisps of white fire. They swam through the grey fog, seeking out the hearts that would receive them.

Sid was shocked at the power of Rip's cloud. When it collided with his fire it shook him with its force, almost pushing him back. He's gotten stronger, Sid thought to himself. Much stronger. Or maybe it's me. Maybe I've gotten much weaker.

Snakes of the dark cloud began climbing up the tendrils of white fire. Sid summoned a surge of power and sent them away. He heard Rip laughing. That was too easy for him.

"You shouldn't have come out here, old man," Rip said in torment. "You're too old for this, Sid. You're rusty. I can feel it."

Sid tried to shake away the taunt, but he knew Rip was right. He was terribly out of practice in this kind of fight. In fact, that last time he had engaged in this kind of battle . . .

No, he cried out to himself. He was not going to think about that. He refused to visit that shame and failure.

It was the dark, he knew. The dark was doing that to him. How it had already gotten through his defenses he couldn't imagine. That shouldn't have been possible. Not yet.

It's me, Sid thought. I brought it with me. I have too much self-doubt to fight this battle. I brought darkness into this fight.

No, not self-doubt a voice reminded him. You're doubting the one who gave you this power.

When I am weak, then I am strong, Sid reminded himself. He pushed again with his power, trying to force the darkness back. More of the swimming tendrils of light went out into the mist, searching out the good hearts to strengthen them.

Rip's cloud didn't budge. The dark man smiled at Sid through the surging battle of black cloud and white fire. Shadows danced over his features, casting him in a sinister light. He licked his lips and pushed his arms out further. Sid felt his light waver. The cloud came closer, pushing back the light.

I've failed you, Sid whispered to men who were long dead, and to the men who were fighting for their lives in the roiling mist. I should never have brought you out here. What have I done?

The darkness pushed again, closer. The light fell back. Sid tried to muster a counter but the wall of shadowy cloud wouldn't budge.

I've got to hold on, he told himself. For the sake of these boys. God help me, let me at least get them out of here before they are consumed by the dark.

A dreadful cold ran up his limbs. Sid could feel it in his blood, making his muscles tremble. He felt the chill settle upon his heart. Spidery, black veins crawled up the tendrils of light.

The white fire dimmed.

The mist got darker as Gary struggled against the shadow man. He felt a chill seep through his bones and reach out towards the deepest part of his soul. We're losing the fight, he thought.

Several times he had felt this sense of cold despair, only to have it lifted by the wisps of white flame that swam through the mist. Each time he was hit by one he felt a warmth and strength suffuse through his being, filling him with a surge of energy.

He couldn't help but notice that those wisps became fewer, and some had even faded to sparks. Still, when one found him that little spark was enough. He felt the lift he needed as the cold in his bones was pushed out. At the same time, he didn't know how much longer they would last. He needed to defeat this enemy in front of him and do something to help Sid.

For the better part of the fight Gary was on defense. The shadow man who had engaged him was small and fast (though everyone was small to Gary) and seemed to be everywhere all at once. Quickly, Gary had decided he would not out-speed his opponent. If he tried to fight that way he would certainly lose.

What Gary did know was that he was stronger. If he bided his time and waited, he could get a hold of the wiry man. Once he grabbed hold of him, it was over.

The shadow man came at him again and again with a barrage of kicks and punches. Gary backed away, defending, watching. He waited for his chance, timing the moves and attacks of his opponents.

Just as the mist darkened, Gary noticed a pattern emerge from the shadow man. After a quick combination of punches, he would lean in and deliver a stronger one. It wasn't enough to push Gary back, but he certainly noticed that the man put more into than his others. It was the perfect opportunity.

Gary backed away from a high kick that would have connected with his head. The shadow man spun the opposite direction and kicked out again. This one Gary knocked away.

The shadow man leaned in with a combination of quick punches. Gary held his breath, watching, knowing it would come.

The shadow man finished the combination with one hard thrust he leaned into. Gary almost laughed as he watched him commit himself too far. Anticipating the action, he lashed out with a big hand and closed it over the smaller man's wrist.

"Gotcha," he said with a grin.

He pulled back, to lift the small man off the ground and slam him back down. He hoped it would be enough to knock him cold.

Gary almost fell back when he pulled and there was no wrist in his hand. He looked at his closed fist, wondering how the man could have possibly gotten out of it. Opening his hand, he saw the last wisps of black smoke dissipate in the dark air.

Before he could even wonder about this, he felt the presence of the shadow man behind him. A sharp pain went through his leg as a booted foot made contact with the back of his knee.

Crying out in pain Gary fell to the ground. The cold of the dark mist settled into bones. This isn't fair, he thought as despair crept up his limbs and clawed at the wall of his heart.

Zach felt the stab in his lower back and waited for the cold steel to slice its way all the way in. The arm that held him was strong and cruel, and the shadow man used the hold to jab the knife in further.

I guess this is it, Zach thought to himself. He was surprised the knife didn't hurt more than the sharp sting. He was expecting something more terrible, more painful. Maybe I am just in shock, can't feel the pain yet. The same cold despair that the other Swordsmen were feeling was concentrating in Zach now. He would fail, die here in some unknown studio lot, killed amidst this grey, swirling fog. The idea that there was no point in fighting anymore seemed the most logical thing he had heard in a long time.

I should really just lay down and die, he thought. There's no point to this anymore. If the knife didn't damage any essential organs, then he would surely bleed out soon. What was the point of struggling? He was just prolonging the inevitable.

A wisp of white fire swam in the dark, grey mist. Carried by an invisible wind that swirled around them it rode up and down on the currents, straight towards Zach. It moved as if called to him, drawn by great need.

The white fire struck Zach in his chest. It penetrated him in a burst of golden light. Fire and heat exploded through his body.

No, he cried out in his mind. Not like this. If I am to die, I will go down fighting with my last breath.

With a cry of defiance Zach jerked his head backward. He felt it crush cartilage, then drive into the hard bone of the nose. The shadow man cried out but didn't let go.

Zach jabbed backwards with his elbow, feeling the grip around his neck weaken enough for him to push it off. He thrust back with another sharp elbow.

Whipping around Zach fell upon the stunned opponent. The knife clattered to the ground as the shadow man grabbed his nose that was pouring blood. He barely put up his defenses to Zach's pummeling attack.

Zach quickly landed another shot, a kick to the ribs. The shadow man grunted and fell back. Pressing the attack again Zach rained blows on him, some connecting but most blocked.

The shadow man made a desperate lunge, swinging a wide punch that Zach easily ducked. Seizing the opportunity Zach launched himself up, swinging an uppercut with all his strength behind it. His fist connected with chin, lifting up the shadow man as he sprawled back and landed hard in the ground.

Breathing hard in exertion Zach looked down at the unconscious man. He nudged him with a foot. The body didn't respond. A trickle of blood was flowing out from behind his head and Zach wondered if he had cracked his skull. He thought for a moment about checking on the man but another cold chill brought him back to more pressing needs.

Looking up he saw the battle raging against them. All of his fellow Swordsmen were in a desperate battle. Even Tres seemed to be weakening. The shadow men were getting stronger, faster, as the grey mist got darker and the wisps of light shrunk to tiny sparks.

He looked over to Sid and saw the old man in a hopeless battle of his own. The dark clouds that grew out from Rip had almost completely surrounded him. An oval of light still surrounded Sid but it was besieged by the encroaching dark. Thick tendrils of white fire circled around him, trying to keep the thick clouds at bay. But even these had webs of dark creeping up them. Wisps of white fire flowing out from Sid died in the darkening mist.

The thought hammered in Zach's head that if Sid failed then they all would fail. He knew this to be certain just as he could feel the cold settling into his bones again. Thoughts of despair and hopelessness began to creep into his mind again. He had to act.

Zach had no idea what to do, but he knew who would. Instinctively moving Zach ran to where Malachi was in his own fierce battle. The shadow man he was fighting disappeared in a puff of smoke and rematerialized behind him. Malachi barely ducked the swinging fist, but fell down with a knee in his back.

The shadow man had his back to Zach. As Malachi fended off the attacks from the ground Zach hurried over, not bothering to muffle his steps. The raging wind around them made hearing any other sounds all but impossible.

Aiming a punch for the back of his head Zach contacted clean. The shadow man cried out and fell forward, clutching his head. Malachi sprang up while Zach fell on the shadow man.

Together they attacked, pushing the shadow man back. Despite being pressed from two sides the shadow man didn't try his disappearing trick. Zach wondered about this as his fist contacted ribs. He felt the armored suit absorb most of it, but the shadow man grunted. Up high Malachi landed a fist across his cheek.

The shadow man fell back again. Zach swept in, knocking out his legs. Their opponent grunted as he scrambled to keep his balance. Malachi stepped forward swinging out his leg in a wide kick. The shadow man's head snapped back as Malachi's foot landed solidly on the cheek bone.

The grey mist got darker as the two men stood over the unmoving body of the shadow man.

"Is he dead?" Malachi asked.

Zach could hear a note of concern in Malachi's voice. Even being engaged in a desperate fight he didn't want to be responsible for another person's death.

"We don't have time to find out," Zach yelled over the growing howl of wind. "Sid's getting his ass kicked. We got to help him."

He pointed over to the older man besieged by dark clouds. They had managed to get even closer now, almost covering Sid in its shadow. A worn and beaten look was on Sid's face as he vainly struggled against the dark.

"What do we do?" Malachi asked.

"You go help him," Zach said. "I'll go help out the others."

The mist had grown darker, almost as black as the clouds summoned by Rip. Malachi couldn't see any of the golden threads floating through the mist anymore. Just tiny sparks remained of Sid's white fire that kept the darkness from taking over completely.

With the fall of darkness, a wind rose up that howled in the alley. It was all dark, grey and screaming wind. Malachi had to shield his eyes from the fierceness of the storm that had risen up. Looking around he could see figures still fighting, still holding on despite the dark that was overwhelming. He could tell the Swordsmen were slowing down. Their sluggish movements hardly able to keep up with the shadow men despite their numerical advantage. Only Tres seemed to be untouched by the shadow. Malachi could make his figure out like a distant shadow in the mist, still spinning and attacking unabated. Fueled by another energy that the darkness couldn't touch, the grieving father fought on.

The cold and despair settled into Malachi with a chill that almost took his breath. An almost irresistible idea welled up in him. Give up, it said. This is pointless. You can't win. Just look at the dark, at how powerful it is. There is no beating this, no defeating it. You're tired. Very tired. Just lay down and rest.

Give up.

Give up.

Give up.

Gritting his teeth Malachi forced himself through the roiling storm. With his arm up to shield his face he made his way to Sid. A glow of pure light still surrounded him. Snakes of white fire twisted around his beleaguered form, forming a shield against the encroaching shadows.

Sid's face was gaunt and drawn in agony. His eyes stared out in the gathering gloom, barely holding on to his last shred of hope. Arms trembled with waning effort.

"Sid!" Malachi yelled over the howl of wind.

The old man started, surprised to see Malachi right next to him. As recognition dawned on his face he shook his head.

"I should never have taken you to this place," Sid lamented. "You weren't ready. I'm sorry Malachi. Can you forgive me?"

"There'll be time for that later," Malachi said, reaching out to place a hand on the older man's shoulder. He almost pulled it back. His skin was ice cold.

"We need to beat this guy!"

Sid shook his head. His eyes watered as they pooled with tears.

"I'm not strong enough," he confessed. "I don't know why I thought I could beat him. He's so much stronger than I remember."

Malachi looked across the alley covered in the shadow of a darkening gloom. Rip smiled as the billows continued to swell from the ground beneath him. They pulsed with violet streaks of angry, forked lightning.

"There's got to be something we can do!" Malachi yelled as the howling wind rose higher.

"You need to run," Sid told him. "Get the other swordsmen and run. Get out of here and hide. Hide for these beings are too powerful. Their evil has vanquished us. We have failed. Run and get your family safe. I am done here."

Malachi couldn't believe what he was hearing from the old man. Never did he imagine he would give in to such despair. He looked around the winding fire and saw veins of dark crawling up their surface.

"It's just the dark talking," Malachi encouraged. "You can do this, Sid. I know you can. We need you, Sid."

It may have been his imagination, but Malachi thought the fire brightened just a bit at his words.

"I'm not strong enough," Sid cried out, shaking his head. "I'm too old and weak."

"I don't believe that for a second," Malachi argued. "Light is always stronger than the dark and you know it."

This time the pulse in power was unmistakable. The light had gotten stronger.

"This isn't your power you are wielding," Malachi continued, feeling inspired. He wasn't even sure what he was saying was one-hundred percent true. He felt they were true. He felt these were the words Sid needed to hear.

"You are only the vessel," Malachi went on. "This is the power of the light. This is the grace of God. It is stronger than evil. It is stronger than the dark."

"I . . . I don't," Sid tried to speak but couldn't find the words. The light around him grew stronger.

"He's so strong," he lamented.

"One candle," Malachi yelled to him, holding a single finger in front of his face. "One candle is all it takes. In a sea of darkness, in a world of night; one candle can vanquish the dark. One tiny flame can put to rout the most miserable shadows. And it doesn't need power. It doesn't need might."

He clapped the older man on his shoulders and looked him dead in the eyes.

"All it has to do is shine!"

This time the light surged in new awakening. Malachi felt the results immediately. A new burst of power pulsed within him. This one was even more powerful than before. Every nerve in his body exploded in sense and strength. He felt at that moment he could sprint a hundred miles with a van on top of his shoulders.

Pulling his hands away he noticed they were wreathed in the same white fire that Sid had summoned. Amazed, he passed his hands before his eyes. It was as if his hands were on fire. Pure, white flame danced along the edges of his hands and to the fingertips. But there was no burning sensation, only a thrum of latent power.

Looking across the alley an idea struck him. Even with the new surge of light, the shadow dominated this battle. Sid may be saved for the moment, but somewhere in those roiling, black clouds and howling wind his friends were fighting for their lives. Even the violet lightning had begun to flash in the alley.

A smile of victory was plastered on Rip's face. There was no joy in the smile. It was arrogance and pride and gloating over an enemy. Something his uncle Ray used to threaten him with came to Malachi's mind.

I'll knock that smile right off your face.

Malachi clenched a flame-drenched fist and ran across the alley, straight at Rip. Sid cried out a warning behind him, but Malachi couldn't hear it over the scream of the wind. Rip was concentrating on his magic and didn't see the danger until it was too close.

Pulling back with all his might Malachi delivered a punch to the center of Rip's face.

The fiery fist made contact throwing back the perfectly sculpted face. Rip cried out in surprise as he fell backward. His feet left the ground and he flailed for a purchase that wasn't there. White light exploded and Malachi felt a rush of heat.

All at once the darkness in the alley faded back to a grey mist. Wisps of light swam out in the mists, searching for the hearts that called out to them. They landed on the Swordsmen, filling them with a surge of new power. Malachi saw them take up the fight again with sudden and new strength.

"You little bastard!" he heard Rip yell out to him.

Malachi watched as Rip picked himself up off the ground. He scowled at this unexpected enemy. A crack ran diagonally down the center of his face. It was like Rip had been wearing a mask and the punch broke it. A scarlet mist leaked out of the crack. Looking at it made Malachi shudder.

At least I wiped the smile off of his face, he thought to himself. Rip was grimacing in pain and rage. Teeth were clenched in barely restrained fury.

With a scream of anger Rip summoned a thick, black cloud. Thrusting his arms out he sent it barreling towards Malachi.

With no time to react Malachi held up his hands, hoping the fire on his fists was enough to protect him. He only had a second to wonder what would happen if it didn't. That black cloud was enough on its own to drain every ounce of hope he possessed.

Just as Malachi threw up his hands, another force struck behind him. Snakes of white fire, twisting and weaving, flew around him and past him. A tunnel of swirling fire formed around Malachi just as the darkness was upon him.

In a flash the dark vanished. He could only see the golden glow of white fire. The weave of flame shot past Malachi and straight at Rip. The cracked face looked up, wide in surprise at the pillar of woven fire bearing down on him.

Rip disappeared in a cloud of black smoke. The weave of fire passed through, banishing the last, tiny wisps. Out of the corner of his eye Malachi could see all the shadow men do the same.

All at once the white fire died. The grey mist evaporated. Sunlight muted by the grey clouds came back into the alley. Malachi looked around and everything had been as if the shadow men were never there. He and the Swordsmen were looking around in confusion. Sid had fallen to one knee, his hand upon the black pavement.

That was a close one, Malachi thought to himself as he sighed in relief. But chalk up one for the Swordsmen.

Chapter 18 - Servers

"Well, that was fun," Vic said. He tried to sound cheerful but the tension in his voice was obvious to everyone.

The men looked around the empty alley. Just moments ago, it had been filled with a soul-draining mist and shadow men. In an instant it was cloudy daylight and quiet again. Their steps echoed off the asphalt as they turned, looking for any signs the enemy had been there at all.

For Giovanni the experience had been surreal from the very beginning. He had never been in a fight, as far as he could remember. When the shadow man bore down on him it was enough for him just to keep up his defenses. When the grey mist fell over him, he was sure it was all some horrible dream.

Now, standing in the overcast light between two towering sound studios, he was tempted to believe it was all a dream. There wasn't the slightest trace of the mist, or the men, or the guy in the trench coat that could summon black clouds. If it wasn't for the aching spot in his head where a punch had nearly knocked him out cold, he probably would convince himself it had been a dream.

"So, what the Hell was all that?" Danny asked, turning to the other men.

As soon as the mist had cleared Sid had fallen to one knee. Gary hurried over to his side to help him out as the other men gathered around.

"Were those the Fae?" Gary asked as Sid straightened up and leaned upon his cane.

"No," he answered weakly. "Those were men, all of them."

"I thought you said you were fighting the Fae," Tres spoke up, surprise in his voice.

Sid nodded, taking in a deep breath. He grimaced in unseen pain as Gary put out a hand to steady him. Sid nodded his thanks and straightened up under his own power.

"We are fighting the Fae," Sid confirmed. "As well as their human allies."

Giovanni shook his head in disbelief. If what Sid had told them about the Fae was all true, it was incomprehensible that any human would want to work for them, much less fight for them.

"Why would any person do that?" Danny asked, voicing the disbelief they all felt. "If they're trying to steal our souls, or feed off of us, whatever it is. Why would any person help that happen?"

"The same reason men have served tyrants and evil since the dawn of time," Sid answered. "For ambition. For power. Because they also are sadistic and love the evil in their hearts."

The words dug into Giovanni with a certain dread. To know that evil men lived in the world was bad enough. That often those men rose to positions of power and influence was the reason, he believed, for the problems that always infested life. But to think those same evil men could ally themselves with a power like the Fae was enough to make their quest seem hopeless.

"Whatever their reasons, it is the human allies that execute most of the work of the Fae," Sid explained. "Unfortunately, over the past fifty years that number has grown exponentially. When I first began as a Keeper, there were few and rare human allies with the Fae. Now, they are more numerous than I like to think. Because of this they have been able to infiltrate almost every institution in the world, on every level. At least in the civilized world."

"What was that thing the shadow men did?" Vic asked. "That teleportation?"

"The swordsmen have always called it smoke jumping," Sid told them. "It is one of their more deadly abilities. As you have seen, they can de-materialize and reform at will. The distance is only a few feet as far as I have observed, so they can't come at you with that over long distances."

"How do we fight this?" Gary asked.

"Punch them in the head," Zach answered.

Sid nodded. "Something like that."

"Yeah, but how can we punch them in the head if they keep . . . smoke jumping?" Vic pressed.

"I guess you have to get lucky," Sid told them. A groan rose up from the men.

"I don't mean that to be glib, but that's the way it is. If you can stun or hurt them, especially with a shot to the head then they can't concentrate enough to jump."

"Okay, what about the other powers?" Gary asked. "You said this was one of their more deadly abilities. What else do they have?"

"As you have seen they also have supernatural speed and strength as you do, along with the ability to resist damage and heal quickly. If they are tied to a warlock then they can be teleported out of danger along with the . . ."

Sid put a hand to his head as he swayed on his feet. Gary was quickly at his side, holding him up.

"I'm sorry, but the battle has tired me out," Sid told them.

"Do we need to go back?" Malachi asked as the men gathered around closer in concern.

"I just need to sit for a moment."

"Alright, get out of the way," Gary directed as he walked Sid over to the side of the alley.

Supporting the older man by the arm Gary took him to an abandoned golf cart. He sat down and took a deep breath, his eyes closed in concentration.

"I just need a moment," he said again.

Giovanni watched him in concern. Sid's skin had gone noticeably paler than it already was and he thought he could see a tremor in the hand he held up to his brow. Seeing what he had just accomplished Giovanni couldn't imagine the level of concentration and power it took to do something like that. And at his age - if he was being honest about that - it had to be almost deadly.

"The shadow men," Sid continued when he had taken his moment. "When the battle is lost their warlock, called their master, can transport them to a pre-determined spot.

"Other than that, I can only tell you not to engage them in an actual, real shadow. By that I mean a shadow cast at night. For in a night shadow, they become one with it. Within they can be anywhere and everywhere all at once."

"And I guess they call that shadow boxing?" Vic quipped. He only got head shakes for his effort.

"What about that guy?" Danny asked. "The one in the trench coat that summoned those clouds."

Sid waved the question away. "We have much still to do here today," he said. "And I am not certain we have enough time. Rip is a conversation that may take a while. Suffice it to say you do not engage him alone."

Gary reached down and helped Sid to his feet again. The old man was a bit unsteady at first but found his balance again. Giovanni thought he still looked pale. But he could also tell he was determined to stand on his own for now.

"Let's see what's in this building ahead," he instructed as he gingerly began to move forward.

The others began to follow behind. Giovanni paused, something catching his eye to his right. Walking over to where their battle had just taken place, he found a knife lying abandoned on the black asphalt.

Reaching down Giovanni picked it up and turned it over. It was a wicked looking blade, long and sharp with a serrated edge on the back side. The black handle was grooved for a better grip, and just holding it Giovanni could tell it was an effective weapon.

Figuring it must have been dropped in the fight, Giovanni started to toss it aside. He stopped and turned it over, noticing something strange about the blade. The tip had been broken off, probably a good inch of blade. And just where it had been broken was the unmistakable trace of blood.

"That was a stupid thing you did," Sid told Malachi as they walked down the alley, towards the main building. The other men were ahead of them, and Sid spoke in a low voice so they wouldn't be heard.

"It worked, didn't it?" Malachi said with a shrug.

Sid chuckled and shook his head. "Yes, it worked, though I don't know how it did. But if it had gone wrong, it would have gone terribly wrong."

"I guess we got lucky this time."

Sid grabbed Malachi's arm and pulled him to stop. He leaned in, his intense, blue eyes boring into Malachi.

"If Rip would have hit you with the full force of that cloud you can't imagine the effect it would have had on your mind."

"Would it be like the mist?" Malachi asked. Hearing the intensity in Sid's voice made him more than a little frightened at what could have happened.

"The mist was a weakened form of that cloud," Sid told him with a shake if his head. "As you probably noticed it drains hope from a person, fills them with dread."

"So, the full power of the cloud would just make me what?" Malachi asked. "Really, really depressed."

Sid looked down, averting Malachi's eyes for a moment. Breathing deep he thought on his words before looking back up again.

"If the full force of that cloud had struck you, then you would have been lost in a world of pure hopelessness."

"I would have come out of it eventually," Malachi said, though he wasn't as confident as he wanted to sound. "Once the cloud went away."

"The mind cannot operate without hope," Sid told him. "You would have been turned in on yourself, lost to us. Wandering in your own mind as despair kept you in the dark."

"What? Like a coma or something?"

"Something like that," Sid agreed. "But much worse. For you would be a prisoner in your own mind, tortured and lost. To the rest of the world, you would be unreachable. Alive, with eyes wide open, fixed on some unseen terror. You would lay like that until your body just gave up. Many good men have been lost to the shadow that never found their way out again. Even with help from us."

An involuntary shudder ran up Malachi's spine at the mere thought. He had never experienced anything close to what Sid described. Just touching the mist, feeling its effect in his spirit in that muted form, made him understand what Sid meant. For a moment he could imagine exactly what would have happened if he had been consumed by the black cloud. - lost in a grey world without light or hope, prey to all the fears that can haunt a soul.

"Good thing you were there," Malachi said as he smiled weakly.

Sid shook his head.

"I shouldn't have been able to do what I did," he said. "That display of white fire was of a level I have never been able to summon. Not even in my most powerful days."

"Then how did you do it?" Malachi asked.

Thinking for a moment Sid shook his head. He reached out and clapped Malachi on the shoulder.

"I have no idea," he confessed. "Maybe there is more to you than I assumed."

He looked over at the other Swordsmen as they approached the office building.

"C'mon, let's catch up with the others."

The two men walked in silence as they approached the three-story building that stood in the front of the complex. All of them had assumed this was the main office, the base of whatever operations were going on at the studio.

"It looks pretty empty," Vic said, his face pressed against the glass. "If this office here was ever used then it has been cleaned out completely."

"Let's see if we can get inside," Sid suggested.

Gary pulled at the glass doors. They were locked.

"Should we try another one?" he suggested.

Walking around the building they tried all the doors. As expected, each was securely locked.

"I think at this point we should just let ourselves in," Vic said, pulling on the front doors. They rattled with the motion but didn't give.

"If we broke in there would definitely be an alarm," Danny warned.

"They already know we're here," Vic argued.

"Yeah, but this alarm could alert the police," Danny said, pointing inside. "We fought off a couple of shadow men, not sure we want to do the same with county."

"There won't be any police," Sid told them. "If so, I can handle them."

"How can you be so sure?" Danny asked.

"Because there is likely nothing in there for us to find," he said, gesturing to the silent office building. "They already did what they wanted to with the shadow men, likely to test us out. If there was something they didn't want us to see they would have sent a lot more than they did."

The men looked at each other, uncertain. What Sid had told them was likely right. Still, a lifetime of being taught to be law abiding citizens was hard to break.

Gary shrugged his shoulders and walked over to one of the ashtrays sitting by the doors. It was the type made of tiny, beige rocks in concrete. He pulled it up without effort and heaved it towards the glass doors.

The ashtray shattered into four big chunks and fell to ground. The glass of the door shuddered and bent strangely in its holding but did not break completely.

"Too far to turn back now," Gary said and followed it up with a kick to the glass pane.

The safety glass bent over, still one piece. A thousand cracks ran up the length of the pane. Gary pulled at it and released it fully from its fixing and tossed it aside.

"Someone want to watch out for the popo," he suggested.

That someone ended up being Giovanni. He waited outside, strolling the front of the building, looking out for the telltale blue flashing lights that would mean they were caught. The others stepped through the now open door and into the office building.

"Something isn't right here," Malachi said as they entered the dark and abandoned office space.

"Probably a lot of somethings," Vic agreed.

Inside, the silence was nearly deafening. Footfalls echoed off linoleum so loud they sounded like explosions. Even the passage of air had fallen silent. They all stood still for a moment and Malachi thought he could hear a faint humming in the distance.

Gary toggled a nearby light switch. White, fluorescent light flared to life, bathing the rooms in a harsh glow.

"At least we know the power is still on," Danny observed.

"Cut them off," Sid commanded.

Gary toggled the panel again and the bright light extinguished.

They walked through the abandoned building, feeling more uneasy by the moment. Nowhere could they find any evidence of a functional workplace. There were no desks, or papers. No leftover chairs scattered about in random places. There were no wires snaking out of the floor where work spaces would have been.

"It's completely empty," Zach said, pointing out the obvious.

"You think they knew we were coming?" Danny asked.

No one answered that question. Malachi figured it was because no one had that answer. All they knew was that this bright office building and the new studios in the lot out back were completely abandoned.

"Even if they knew, there's no way they could have cleared out this fast," Danny said, answering his own question.

"An office this size would take days to shut down," Malachi agreed. "Maybe hours if you had a massive crew. No way they could have done it today."

They continued through the space, looking for anything that would indicate a human presence at one point. One wing was entirely filled with cubicles. The grid pattern of makeshift spaces sprawled and twisted like a labyrinth over a carpeted floor.

All the cubicles were as empty as the rest of the office. They had been picked clean and deserted completely. No pictures or random papers left behind or even the odd power cord that was forgotten. There weren't even any desks inside the individual units.

"They were never here," Gary said, echoing in the vast space.

"What was that?" Danny asked.

"They were never here," Gary repeated.

Stepping inside an empty cubicle he knelt down and ran a finger over the carpet. Looking down at his hand he shook his head.

"Yeah, no one has been in this office," he said. "Never been used."

"How do you know?" Malachi asked, coming to stand behind Gary, trying to see what he had seen.

"No dust," Gary answered holding up a clean finger. "If there had been desks here at one point the dust would have gathered around it, like it always does. There is no dust in any of these cubicles. There were never any desks here."

"Maybe they cleaned it," Danny suggested.

"Or maybe they never used this part of the office," Zach said.

"No," Gary shook his head. "I don't think they ever used it. Think about it. Even if they knew we were coming, they only had a few hours to clean this place out. No way they could have done it that fast. I think they never used it."

"That makes even less sense," Danny said. He gestured around to the vast space around them. "They just built this for what? A front of some kind? You know how expensive this would be? How much time and money they would have to sink into a place like this?"

Gary shrugged. "I'm just saying it looks like it was never used."

"As I said before," Sid interjected. "Time and money mean nothing to the Fae. They have been plotting and scheming for hundreds of years now. They work with a lot less urgency and a lot more patience than we do."

They wandered over to the front entrance of the building. Through the glass they could see Giovanni faithfully watching out for any signs of the police. Somewhere in the distance Malachi thought he could hear the humming again.

"Is that it?" Tres asked. "We got nothing to find here?"

Malachi could hear the frustration in his voice. Above everyone else Tres wanted to find something that would help him avenge his son.

"Let's finish looking," Sid told them. "Maybe there is something on the other floors that could help us."

Once they found the stairwell the men decided to split up. Malachi, Danny and Gary decided to see what lay in the basement. Victor, Zach and Tres would check out the upper floors. Sid volunteered to watch the stairwell door since they couldn't find anything to prop it open with.

As they walked down the stairs the air grew noticeably colder. The hum Malachi had heard rose to a distinct and unmistakable rhythm. It swelled and filled the stairwell until the air vibrated around them.

"Must be the server room," Danny said to their questioning looks.

"Why would they have servers in an abandoned office?" Gary asked.

Danny shrugged. "Maybe they're coming back for them. Moving servers isn't easy. Not like picking up a file cabinet or desk."

"I guess that kills your theory," Malachi suggested to Gary. "If they have servers then they had to have used this office at some point."

Gary offered a shrug of his own as they reached the bottom of the stairwell. Passing through the heavy, steel door they stood in a carpeted hallway. The cold struck them like a wave. Malachi felt a chill pass through him, thinking he was stepping into a refrigerator.

"Why is it so cold?" he asked. Looking up it seemed Gary was unaffected by the drop in temperature.

"Gotta keep the servers from overheating," Danny answered. "It won't be as cold in the actual server room. But this is some strong AC. They must have a lot of servers."

True to his prediction, the actual server room was warmer. They stepped through a frosted glass door and into a vast assemblage of processing towers. An eerie blue light filled the room, reflecting off the polished floors, casting a strange glow over the men.

"What in the name of all that is holy," Danny breathed as he looked out over the vast sea of processors.

Malachi had been in a server room once before. An errand to one of their IT guys sent him down to where the hospital servers were stored. Besides the blue light everywhere, it looked much like this room, but not nearly as large.

"This place is huge," Danny told them as he started walking among the metal racks.

"It is pretty big," Gary said, looking around.

It was when they brought the size to his attention that Malachi began to notice how big the room was. As far as he could see, in front and on both sides, racks of servers surrounded him. Towers stood as silent watchers, flashing lights and indicators that Malachi could not make any sense of. The hum of the machines working vibrated the air, filling his chest with their incessant rhythm.

"What were they doing here?" Danny asked no one in particular. He continued to walk among the racks, his mouth open in amazement.

"I guess they handled a lot of data," Gary pointed out. His voice died in the hum of machines.

"Not this much," Danny said. "Do you see how many servers they have here? This is incredibly huge. I can't even see the end of it. No way a studio would need this many servers. I doubt Google has this many in one place."

As Danny explained an uneasiness began to settle over Malachi. The sensation of being watched grew more intense. He even looked around for cameras, fully expecting them to be there. To his surprise he couldn't see any.

"What would they need all these for?" Gary asked. He had to yell this time to be heard over the ambient noise.

"The matrix," Danny joked. "I don't know. There's nothing I can think of that takes this much power. Not all in one place like this."

"Why did they leave it behind?" Malachi asked.

His uneasiness grew as soon as he asked the question. If whatever was going on here needed this many servers it must have been important. Too important to leave behind.

"This was the reason for everything," Danny said. To Malachi it sounded like he was talking from very far away.

"It had to be," he went on. "This is the whole reason they built the place. It was to house these servers."

"It's bigger than the building," Gary pointed out.

Malachi turned to look down the aisle of servers and saw immediately what Gary meant. He didn't have the best sense of spatial relations, but he could tell in just one glance that this room was bigger than the building above their heads. And it was bigger by a lot. He even wondered if it went as far as the front gate.

"Is there any way we can figure out what they were for?" Malachi asked.

"If you want to hack into it," Danny answered.

"You're the IT guy," Gary pointed out.

"Yes, IT, not a hacker. Different skill set all together."

Danny stopped and looked at one of the towers. Like the rest it was double stacked, its metal frame towering above him. He reached a hand out and felt over the surface of the machine. His eyes took on a distant and faraway look. It was one Malachi had never seen on his face before.

"I have a laptop in the van," he said. "I guess I could hook up to it and see what happens."

Without another word he turned and walked out of the server room. Malachi and Gary looked at each other. Gary had obviously seen the strange expression on Danny's face. With no more answers than Malachi, he shrugged and turned to explore the room further.

"What do you think these could all be for?" Malachi asked, his voice dying in the incessant hum that suffocated the room.

"Your guess is as good as mine," Gary answered, sounding far away. "But whatever it is it gives me the creeps."

Malachi nodded, not even thinking that Gary couldn't see the gesture. Uneasy was the word that came to his mind. There was something strange, even sinister, about all these servers left on and working, despite the reasons Danny had suggested.

And so many of them, Malachi thought. The room they were in could easily have fit three football fields inside it. Maybe I'm exaggerating, he told himself. Or maybe not exaggerating enough.

An image popped into his head as he explored further into the towers. It was from a story he had heard long ago, something from Greek mythology. He was in eight grade and they were studying the Greeks. Someone was put in a labyrinth. And in the middle of it was a minotaur, some half-man, half-bull monstrosity that prowled around with a wicked axe to slice up any would-be heroes.

Daedalus, Malachi asked himself. No, that was the guy who built the labyrinth.

Theseus, he remembered. That was his name. Theseus and the Minotaur. The endless rows of servers in their steel towers, with paths laid out between them made Malachi think of that labyrinth. It was like he was inside those twisting passageways, looking for a way out. As he searched there was the haunting fear of knowing a beast hunted him from the shadows, stalking, smelling the air, silently pursuing. Except, unlike Theseus, Malachi didn't have a ball of twine to keep him from getting lost.

That uneasy pit in his stomach blossomed into full fear. Something was wrong, terribly wrong. He couldn't figure out what it was or see what had him worried, but the warning bells in his head would not be denied.

Just as he opened his mouth to say something to Gary, they heard the door open again. Malachi made his way to the sound and found Danny kneeling down in front of one of the servers. His laptop was opened and he was pulling at the access panel that protected the server.

"They've got locks over the ports," he pointed and said. "I should have checked before I walked all the way to the van. We may be able to find one that is unlocked. Not sure how else we can . . ."

Before he could finish the thought, Gary had reached over and ripped the panel away. He tossed the little door unceremoniously over his shoulder and then presented the now open server to Danny.

"I doubt I will be able to find anything at all," Danny said as he plugged in and began to type onto his keyboard. "I'm no hacker and I am sure their security is well beyond my ability."

The laptop screen came alive a prompt asking for a password.

"When we were hit at the bank I decided to polish up on my hacking," he explained as he opened a program Malachi didn't recognize. "I downloaded a few things I thought might help me learn a little more about it, you know, test them out a bit. Maybe some of them will come in handy now. I doubt it, but it's worth a try."

Malachi watched as a dizzying array of letters and numbers rolled up the screen. It was complete gibberish to him, but to gauge Danny's reaction, it meant something.

"How about that," Danny exclaimed in genuine surprise. "I actually got in."

Windows began flashing up on the screen. Some had animations that looked like the cartoon. Others had the rolling programming language. Others still displayed the cartoon characters in incomplete form, mere outlines in green.

Watching him work Malachi grew more uneasy by the second. Something nagged at him, pulled at the pit of his stomach. He looked around, expecting at any moment to see the shadow men returned and coming for them. But they were alone in the server room. Too alone.

"What in the world?" Danny breathed, his voice lowering to a whisper.

Malachi looked over his shoulder, even as he knew he would likely have no idea what he was looking at. Just as predicted all he could see was a rolling screen of ones and zeroes. But just as he decided it was meaningless he thought he could discern a shape in the numbers. Looking closer he saw they were shaped like people, and there was a bookcase, and a table. Once he identified those features his mind began to put it all together. He was looking at a what appeared to be a classroom of some sort, all drawn out in ones and zeroes that flowed down the screen like water.

Danny kept typing at the keyboard. The image on the screen turned on its side and revealed deeper levels of code. It was the same basic shape, but repeated in layer after layer. There were at least six that Malachi could make out.

"This is incredible," Danny exclaimed as he worked through the program. "Whatever this is it is the most complex program I have ever seen."

"What is it?" Gary asked, just as perplexed as Malachi.

"Like I said, I don't know," Danny answered. "It's some sort of layered program. It looks like the image for the show. But there's something else there. A lot of something else. It's like the animation is just camouflage. All it's doing is hiding this thing under the surface."

"Can you tell what it's supposed to do?" Malachi asked. He could feel his heart thumping in his chest. The sense of fear was growing to a sense of doom.

"No way," Danny said. "This thing is AI level programming. Hell, it may even be AI."

The last level of ones and zeroes turned again and filled up the screen. Danny continued searching as the numbers flew by. Malachi found himself thinking of *The Matrix,* and the dancing code that made up that strange universe. There was no way, he thought, that Danny could even begin to understand what he was seeing.

As he watched Malachi saw the levels of code begin to change shape. They had flattened out as they rolled up the screen, and now he could see them begin coalesce as they flittered by. The rolling numbers warped around the center as if forming a circle. Then they warped again, twice in the center where eyes would be, then below that to form a mouth. The sense of panic in Malachi could no longer be resisted.

"We need to get out of here," he said.

Just as he spoke those words the image came into view. Shaped in the green light of ones and zeroes it twisted into the distinct features of a face. It seemed to look right at them, to look through them. There was something malevolent in that face, in those glaring eyes. Written in whatever strange language that birthed it, Malachi could read its evil intentions clearly.

The image put its lips together to speak. One word came out of its mouth.

"Boo!"

The sound echoed through the server room. The roll of ones and zeroes disappeared from the screen, replaced by the animated kids of Tooney Town. Cartoon kids ran across the screen while the theme song from the show blasted all around them.

> *Tooney Town, Tooney Town*
> *That is where the fun is found*
> *Up and down*
> *Round and round*
> *We all have fun at Tooney Town*

The ceiling above them gave a shudder, dropping fibered tiles all around them. The metal frames that held them in place followed, crashing down. A hideous groan rose up from somewhere above them and Malachi could hear the sound of gears grinding together.

"Yeah, let's go," Gary said, grabbing Danny by the arm.

Two steps to the door and they froze again in place. Thick, metal panes slid up from the floor. They boomed as they slammed into place, sealing their escape.

"Well, I guess we're not getting out that way," Danny said.

Gary wasn't as easily convinced. He hammered on the steel surface, then tried to dig his fingers into the edges to pull it apart. Both of these efforts proved vain.

"This door ain't budging," he said. "We'll have to find another way out."

The room continued to shake as they scrambled for answers. The sound of gears grinding fell on top of the theme song that played over and over. Malachi looked up and his panic fell away into cold dread.

"Guys, guys," he said desperately, motioning to the ceiling.

The other men looked up and saw what brought the sound of panic into Malachi's voice. The ceiling shook and trembled. Where the tiles had fallen away, they saw jagged and spinning blades of steel. They roared as they turned, eager to churn up anything in its path. In a shudder the ceiling dropped down, moving closer to the ground.

"Holy crap," Gary cried out. He turned and pounded on the door again.

"Hey! Hey!" he screamed at the unyielding metal door. "Help! Anybody! Help! Sid! Help!"

Danny joined him at the door. He dropped his laptop to the floor and began pounding uselessly beside Gary, shouting out a plea that Malachi knew no one would hear.

In the midst of this panic Malachi felt a strange calm come over him. The sense of foreboding fear, even the cold grip of doom fell away in an instant. He felt calm and assured. His mind cleared up and his thoughts came racing in, one after another.

"Gary! Gary!" he yelled at the big man.

He reached over and stopped his hand. Gary turned to him, his eyes wide in panic. For a moment, Malachi thought he might strike out at him. But his hand stayed.

"Gary, you try and slow this thing down," he instructed, pointing up to the spinning saw blades in the ceiling that bore down from above.

"What do you want me to do?" he asked.

Malachi pointed to the server towers. "Try to stack some of these up," he said. "Maybe we can slow it for a bit. Or even jam it up."

"Doubt it," Danny said. "This thing was probably made to crush the room."

"You try to stop this," Malachi said, ignoring Danny's comment. "See if you can get back into the system and shut it down."

"It just kicked me out," Danny said, gesturing helplessly at the servers.

"Do it," Malachi commanded. "I'm going to see if there's another way out."

Danny nodded and picked up his laptop. He plugged back into the server and scenes of cartoon kids dancing across his screen popped up again.

"See," he said, pointing at it.

"Find a way in," Malachi said, then turned to look for another exit.

Racing away Malachi followed the aisle between wall and the servers. As he ran, he knew he would never have time to run the entire perimeter, but hoped something was close.

The wall turned to his right, opening the room wider. Servers stretched as far as the eye could see. Row upon row of the silent and humming processors churned away whatever malicious program they were designed to carry. The theme song to Tooney Town continued to echo through the cavernous space.

> *Tooney Town, Tooney Town*
> *That is where the fun is found*
> *Up and down*
> *Round and round*
> *We all have fun at Tooney Town*

He raced on, following the wall as it turned again to the left. For a moment he thought of himself as one of those cartoon characters, running through a world that had neither beginning nor ending, with the same scenery zipping by over and over again. His efforts were all in vain, this thought told him. He was wasting his last seconds of life.

Up ahead Malachi could see the frames of another, smaller doorway ahead. He raced ahead but hope dimmed as soon as he got to it. A steel plate had slid over it, sealing the room in.

"Damn," he muttered, turning back to where Danny and Gary worked. There would be little point in looking further. Any and all exits were sealed.

As Malachi came running back, he saw Gary ripping another tower out of the ground. It gave away without hardly a snag at resistance. Even in his hurry Malachi couldn't help but admire the man's strength, and wondered at how powerful he had actually become.

Already there were a dozen of the stacks of towers piled on top of each other. One look and Malachi could tell they wouldn't delay their doom for long. The ceiling had dropped half its height and was grinding inevitably closer.

"That's enough," Malachi said breathlessly as he joined the other two men. "Danny, how are we looking."

Danny shook his head as he continued working his keyboard. A glance at the monitor told Malachi nothing he wanted to know. Two panels were pulled up, one was Danny's hacker program, the other the opening page of the server.

"I got nothing," Danny said, the tension strung high in his voice. "It's a brick wall. No, it's a steel wall. Nothing I have can even make it budge."

"Keep at it," Malachi instructed.

The ceiling shuddered and dropped down further. Malachi looked up at the churning blades lowering towards him. He could see the teeth of the spinning blades and could almost feel their hunger. How long had they waited up there, he wondered. How long had they waited for someone like us to wander in here?

"What now?" Gary asked. His face had gone pale as he looked up with Malachi. The ceiling was just a few feet from their stacked towers.

"Let's see if you can get through this wall," Malachi said, gesturing to austere, white wall of sheet rock that ran the length of the room.

"I'm on it," Gary said with a grim nod.

The song from Tooney Town still blared over the speakers, backed up by the whine of spinning blades. The room was noticeably smaller, almost claustrophobic. Malachi cursed whatever sick and twisted mind had devised this slow torture. Why not just kill us outright?

A feeling of doom fell along with the lowering ceiling. Malachi felt all their options dwindling. Behind him he heard Gary busting up the wall. Broken bits of gypsum flew out of his hammering fists. It was a desperate plan, but Malachi knew they had to try it.

"Wall's no good," he heard Gary say.

He knew it was coming but still felt his heart drop. Walking over to Gary he stared at the broken-up section of wall. A gleaming, steel panel peaked out from the jagged hole.

"Pull up another metal frame," Malachi instructed. "See if you can bust a hole through it."

Gary shook his head. "There's no way we can bust through that!" he screamed out over the sounds that had grown deafening. "Not if we had all day! Which we don't!"

"We have to go down fighting!" Malachi yelled back. He put a hand on Gary's shoulder and put all of his conviction into what he said.

Surprisingly, Gary nodded and turned to his work. Ripping out another of the towers he hoisted the metal frame over his head. He hurled the frame against the wall, busting out a larger portion of the sheet rock.

As Malachi turned from him, he knew that task was fruitless. He heard metal strike metal with a ring and could tell the wall wouldn't give. But he meant what he said. They would go down fighting.

The ceiling lowered down, inches now from their stack of towers. Malachi couldn't help but look at the gears grinding closer, their razor teeth spinning further down, clean and hungry. He shook his head and forced himself to turn away. He would go down fighting too.

"Danny, what's the status?!" he asked. He had to yell to be heard over the cacophony of sounds.

Danny shook his head again. "Got one more thing to try!" he yelled back.

Malachi breathed deep and reached out a hand to touch Danny's shoulder. He felt something pass from him into the other man. He didn't know what it was but something inside of him told him it was important. It also told him it needed words too.

Sparks flew from the metal towers as the spinning blades struck them. Malachi winced and had to push back the urge to look up at them.

"You can do this," he told Danny, trying to keep his voice steady and confident while he raised it to be heard. "Do you hear me? You can do this!"

A noticeable change fell over Danny's face. His lips had been drawn tight and Malachi could see the pressure and effort gathered there. All at once, as soon as Malachi spoke, the tension fell away. His features drooped and fell slack. His eyes glazed over and even his mouth parted. He looked like one mesmerized.

Malachi felt a stab of panic, wondering if Danny had shut down completely under the pressure. Or maybe the program had done to him what it had done to all of those children. It looked like nothing was coming in and nothing was going out.

Except for his hands.

Peering down he saw Danny's hands in flurry of motion. They raced over the keys, almost in a blur, faster than Malachi thought hands could move. Windows popped up on his monitor, one after the other, scrolling furiously line after line of code.

Malachi was always confused at this level of programming. But this was something altogether different. There was no way any human mind could process information that fast. Somehow, Danny was doing just that.

Malachi flinched as he heard the screech of metal being crushed. The ceiling moved down over their makeshift pillars. Sparks flew as the metal blades ripped into them while the pressure contorted them out of shape. He could feel the wind from the spinning blades.

"C'mon Danny," he encouraged again, his hand tightening on his shoulder.

Danny didn't seem to notice. He hands flew over the keys as more windows popped up and closed, all happening too fast for Malachi to comprehend.

The ceiling fell lower, just over their heads now. The makeshift barriers were all being slowly crushed. By the looks of it they hadn't delayed the progress of the machine at all. The spinning blades whined over their heads. The hydraulics screamed out their own awful tune. Malachi could still hear the *Tooney Town* theme song playing faintly in the background.

Ducking his head he tried to pull Danny lower with him. Sparks flew from the spinning blades as they contacted more of the metal tower frames. Lights flickered and exploded, sending electric bursts into the air.

Malachi felt his hope fade as the room darkened. Behind him, Gary cried out, sensing the end approach. As he fell to his knees he looked up at Danny, seemingly oblivious to the danger he was in. The crush of the ceiling was almost to his head. Malachi could see his hair moving from the wind of the spinning blades that were inches from slicing into his skull.

"Danny!" he yelled weakly.

In the strange, twilight dark he could see his friend's face. The dim, blue light cast a strange glow over his slack features. Then, a smile creased his face.

"Gotcha," he said, slamming a finger on the "enter" key.

All at once the whining stopped, the groan of the hydraulics fell silent, and the taunting theme song died mid-chorus. A silent pause, then Malachi heard the machine hum in reverse.

The ceiling drifted up, pulling up the litter of crushed towers that stuck to the now still blades. Malachi fell to his hands, relief washing over him. Gary grabbed him up in a crushing bear hug.

"Ahh, we did it," he nearly yelped, his voice taking in a high pitch.

"Danny, did it," Malachi corrected.

He stood up on wobbly legs. Adrenaline still coursed through him, making all his limbs tremble. Behind him the steel doors slid open again. He reached out to congratulate Danny for his work.

"I couldn't stop it," Danny turned to them and said, his face taut with anxiety.

Malachi shook his head. "No, you did . . ." he began.

Danny shook his head and pointed down. "The failsafe," he said, indicating fiercely beneath him. "I couldn't stop the failsafe!"

Everything seemed to happen all at once.

From the open door he heard Sid yell out their names. Danny pushed them towards the door, panic written clearly across his face. A rumble sounded from deep within the bowels of the earth beneath them. The room began to shake.

"Run!" Danny yelled.

Without waiting for explanation Malachi turned to flee the room. They ran into Sid, his face creased with concern, a hundred questions on the tip of his tongue.

"We got to get out!" Danny yelled to him.

Gary turned the older man around and pushed him towards the stairs. Sid responded with a surprising burst of agility and speed. Grabbing the rails he hobbled up the stairs faster than Malachi thought possible.

They burst out into the lobby as ceiling panels started to fall. The floor lifted and shook, knocking them to their feet. The rumble came on louder, shaking the whole structure.

"It's an earthquake!" he heard Tres cry out as the others raced around the corner towards them.

"Failsafe!" Danny corrected as he struggled to his feet. He gestured for the others to run for the door.

"Self-destruct!" he yelled in answer to their confused looks.

The reality of what was happening dawned on the others as Malachi picked himself up. They turned and raced towards the door. The floor heaved again but this time Malachi and the others were ready for it and kept steadily towards the exit.

The walls leaned in, sending plumes of dust and broken glass to the floor. Malachi saw the windows shattering beneath the crumbling weight. The whole structure bowed and fell in.

Gary was the first through the door. Putting his hands up he burst through whatever glass was left and knocked the frame aside. The others followed quickly, pouring out of the door as the walls began to collapse.

A groan went up from the abandoned building as metal struts collapsed beneath the awful weight. Malachi turned to see it begin to fall inward. It bent upon itself, slow and awkward at first, like an old man taking a bow. It paused, as if trying to hold itself up. Then, it a bursting cloud of dust it collapsed. The sound of a last, fatal crash shaking the ground.

Malachi bent over to catch his breath. Sweat dripped from his face and trickled down into his eyes. He felt his heart slamming in his chest. Disbelief and shock mingled all at once, making his head spin.

"Can you believe that just happened?" he asked as a laugh escaped. He heard the others laughing too, overcome with relief.

"C'mon, it's not done" Danny said, still gripped in panic. He ran back to the group and tried to move them on.

"What?" Malachi asked, not grasping the sense of urgency that still consumed his friend.

"You remember how big that room was?" Danny asked.

An image popped up in Malachi's head of the vast server room they had just escaped from. Its depths disappeared into a dark gloom. It had been big, bigger than the building itself. If a self-destruct had been triggered, it would be for the entire structure.

As if to answer Malachi's realization, the ground rumbled beneath them again. He looked up at the smoking ruin of the office building. It lurched like a living thing. The pile of shattered concrete slabs and twisted beams began to slide. The center caved in, sucking the ruins into the ground below.

"Run!" Malachi yelled out.

The ground shook beneath their feet as it began to slope. Malachi resisted the urge to look back, fearful of what desperate terror would be fast approaching.

This time, Sid fell behind as the others ran across the vast parking lot. Malachi forced himself to slow down and allowed the Keeper to catch up. Out of the corner of his eye he could see what he had not wanted to witness. The ground was falling away behind them, eaten up by the vast and hungry pit that approached.

"Go," Sid waved as he struggled to run, motioning Malachi to go ahead without him.

Behind Sid, Malachi could see the pit fast approaching. Asphalt buckled and cracked, then disappeared into the growing hole. Long fissures snaked out from the expanding pit, chasing Malachi and the others, faster than they could run. A crack ran between them, making the ground shudder.

"Gary!" Malachi yelled as he tried to pull Sid faster.

Gary turned and fell back, joining their pace. Sid tried to push him away.

"Leave me!" he huffed.

"Not today," Gary answered.

Ducking behind Sid he lowered his shoulder as if he were about to tackle the older man. In one motion he put his shoulder into Sid and wrapped his right arm around his waist. Straightening up he lifted Sid off the ground and onto his shoulder.

"C'mon," he yelled, breaking into a run faster than a man his size ought to be able.

Malachi stole a look over his shoulder. The edge of the pit was closer, and growing in speed. The open maw if the earth roared, a living thing that wanted to swallow its prey. Ground fell away, chasing the men faster and faster.

"Let me dowwwwwn!" Sid protested as he bounced on Gary's shoulder.

A dread certainty told Malachi they wouldn't be able to make it. The gate was still a hundred yards away and the falling ground was gaining. He groaned and pushed his tired legs faster, pumping them with all his might.

Salvation appeared as Malachi ran on. Up ahead he saw the van charge towards the gate, busting through without slowing down. Malachi felt exaltation lift in him along with a surge of hope.

Beneath him the ground pulled back, sloping upwards as it was eaten under his feet. Cracks spread out in webs of broken asphalt. The ground tilted as his legs churned harder and harder.

The van sped towards the running men. Just a few yards away Gerard whipped it around and the back door flew open. The men piled in, diving inside. Gary threw Sid inside and jumped in behind. Only Malachi was still left behind.

"Hurry!" Gary yelled from the back as the van inched forward. He leaned out, stretching his hand out to Malachi.

The ground surged beneath Malachi. He high stepped as the pavement fell away under his feet. Churning as hard as he could Malachi struggled through dust clouding up. The ground buckled and he almost fell over. A slab of concrete disappeared under him just as his foot pushed off of it. The hole roared beneath him.

Malachi screamed and dove forward. Gary leaned out the van, catching his arm. Smoke plumed from the van's wheels as it caught traction and burst forward.

Malachi felt he was being ripped in two. Gravity and momentum pulled him back as the van sped forward. For certain he would have slid right back out had not Gary's firm grip held him fast. He felt himself jerked inside the van as he fell hard onto the floor.

The back door slammed shut and the van sped away. Behind them they heard the angry roar of the valley being swallowed up. A plume of smoke billowed from the gaping pit, belched up from the bowels of the earth. The van streaked up the winding road, carrying its cargo to safety as the world behind them crumbled away into nothing.

Chapter 19 - The Ghost in the Machine

Forty-five minutes later the Swordsmen stumbled into the library at the mansion and collapsed into their chairs. They all expected a shower and a long rest after their harrowing battles from that afternoon. Sid, however, insisted on an immediate debriefing.

"First things first," he said as he joined the men around the long table. "Is anyone injured? Anything we need to attend to?"

The men all shook their heads. Some complained of minor bruises or bumps. Almost all were tired and claimed they could sleep for a week.

Zach raised his hand and winced at the effort.

"I think I might have been stabbed," he announced nonchalantly.

"Stabbed?" Malachi repeated, rising in alarm. "Why didn't you tell us you were stabbed?"

The men all gathered around in concern as Zach tried to explain. Sid waved them back and stood in front of him.

"Why didn't you tell us sooner?" Malachi chided.

"I wasn't really sure at first," Zach said by way of defense. "I felt something pinch in my back, but it wasn't too bad. After the fight I guess I forgot about it. It's starting to get sore, though."

"It may be worse than you think," Sid told him. "The blades of the shadow men are often coated in toxins. Show me where you were stabbed."

Zach stood and tried to remove his shirt. He winced again in pain and had to stop. Gary stepped over and helped him take the layers off.

"Lie down," Sid instructed as they cleared the table.

Once on his stomach they could all see the wound. A two-inch cut, just below the ribs, still seeped blood. The wound was angry and red, with splotches of deep purple radiating out along his back.

"Damn, that looks nasty," Vic whistled.

"Is it that bad?" Zach asked, trying to turn over. Panic had started to enter his voice.

"The cut isn't bad," Gary clarified. "Doesn't look too deep. I worry infection may be setting in."

"Poison," Sid told them. "Can you clean the wound? I am going to get some help."

Vic and Gary bent to work. Since both of them worked in the fire department they were experienced first responders. Giovanni brought in a first aid kit and the two began to clean the wound.

"There's something in here still," Gary said as he wiped the injury with alcohol.

Zach winced but stayed as still as he could. Gary leaned over and parted the cut while Vic shined his phone's flashlight on it.

"I see it," he said, handing the phone to Giovanni. "Someone hand me the tweezers."

Crowding over the table Vic worked the tweezers into the wound. Zach gasped and instinctively moved away. Gary warned him to stillness as Vic tried again.

"There she is," he announced, holding a small piece of gleaming metal in the tips of the tweezers.

Gary finished cleaning the wound as Sid came back into the room.

"A doctor will be here shortly," he announced. "Did you dress the wound?"

Vic nodded and handed over the offending piece of metal. Sid peered at it and nodded.

"I think he may need a hospital," Gary suggested. "This infection, or whatever it is, already looks bad."

"The doctor I have summoned here is no ordinary doctor," he told them. "As this is no ordinary poison. But rest assured, Eric will fix him up without a problem.

"But in the future, Mr. Metts, if you could tell us when you are stabbed so that we can fix you up then, that would be advisable."

"I didn't think it was that bad," Zach said, trying to shrug off the concern.

Vic laughed, shaking his head. "Didn't think it was that bad? How much worse does it have to be? You were stabbed, Zach."

"Yeah, I guess I was lucky."

"Luck has nothing to do with it," Giovanni said.

With a clatter he dropped the knife he had found onto the table. It was a wicked looking blade, sharp a sleek with a serrated back edge. Vic picked it up to get a better look at the broken tip. He gave a low whistle.

"You're more than lucky," he said, admiring the knife. "This is a KA-BAR. High carbon steel. Military grade. No way this thing should have snapped off in you."

"No kidding," Tres agreed, taking the knife from Victor. "This thing should have been six inches deep in you, rearranging your kidneys. This is more than luck."

"Guess the good Lord was looking out for me," Zach agreed.

"You may be more right than you know," Sid chimed in.

Taking the blade from Tres he looked it over carefully. He narrowed his eyes in concentration, looking from Zach then back to the broken knife. Dropping it back to the table he nodded in Zach's direction.

"One of the unique gifts that some swordsmen have exhibited is one they call steelskin," Sid told them. "It seems, Mr. Metts, that this one is yours too."

"Steelskin," Gary repeated in admiration. "Pretty nice."

"What does that mean?" Vic asked. "Is he supposed to be invulnerable or something?"

Sid shook his head. "As you can see, it does not render him completely invulnerable. But more so than even all of you. This knife, for instance; it was made to counter the heightened defenses that all of you possess. But Mr. Metts here, having even more than all of you, was able to take an attack even with this enhanced blade. You're resistant to many forms of attack. Your skin and bone can turn blows that would harm, or even kill ordinary men. But you're not invulnerable."

"This is getting unfair," Vic said, throwing up his hands. "Gary here is the Hulk. Tres is Spider Man. Now Zach is Wolverine."

"Without the claws," Giovanni pointed out.

"Even without the claws," Vic complained. "When am I going to get my superpower."

"You already have the power to annoy anyone you meet," Gary ribbed.

"Very funny," Vic answered. "I think you used that joke already."

"And it's greater than the power of ten, regular annoying people," Gary pressed on.

"More powerful than a dad joke," Giovanni chimed in.

"Faster than a TikTok trend," Gary responded.

"Can leap over bad puns in a single bound," Danny quipped.

"How do you leap over a pun?" Vic asked as the others laughed. "Seriously, though, when do the rest of us discover our gifts? How long does this usually take?"

"There is no set time," Sid said with a shrug. "Your gifts usually reveal themselves through combat or the execution of missions. It happens quite naturally. Sometimes, you can even miss it until another person points it out, as in the case of Mr. Metts. Or it may be something you've done for a long time but suddenly became better at, as in the case with Mr. Taylor."

Danny looked up sharply at the mention of his name.

"Wait, what? What gift are you talking about?"

"Have you always been this capable with technology?" Sid asked.

Danny shrugged and thought for a moment. "I've been Ok, but nothing to brag about."

"What you did in the server rooms, hacking into the software then stopping the trap from coming down, is that something you already knew how to do?" Sid asked.

"Well . . ." Danny began, then found he couldn't finish the thought.

"Do you even know what you did?"

Danny shook his head. "It's all kind of a blur to be honest with you."

"You did go kind of blank there for a minute," Malachi said. "Your eyes glazed over and it was like you had just . . . I don't know, phased out."

"Yeah, I don't know what happened," Danny confessed. Malachi thought he could detect a trace of fear in his voice.

"It was your gift taking over," Sid told him. "Don't worry, in time you will learn to have more control over it, even command it when necessary.

"The same goes for all of you when you discover your gifts. And you will discover them in time. Until then, let us proceed with the task at hand. Mr. Taylor, were you able to find out anything at all from your investigation of the servers?"

Danny shrugged and threw his laptop onto the table. It landed with a bang, and Malachi thought he could hear something inside of it break.

"I learned this thing is worthless now," he told them. "Whatever it came into contact with in that server fried everything in there - completely. And this was a work computer."

"We will compensate your employer," Sid assured him. "And provide you with a new laptop. But was there anything else you discovered?"

Danny started to speak, then closed his mouth. He shook his head, as if unwilling, or unsure of what to say. The image of the digital face rose up in Malachi's memory, the thing made of code but shaped like a human head. The malice that it projected at them was more than something a machine could produce. There was something diabolical in it. Malachi shuddered at the memory.

"I don't know what it was," Danny finally said. "It was . . . well the code was complicated to say the least. But it was something I had never seen before. It wasn't just complicated. It was different."

"Different how?" Tres asked. The grieving father leaned forward, intensely interested in what was being said.

"It was like . . . I don't know," Danny continued to struggle. "This is going to sound strange, and I don't even know if I have the language to explain it. Nor can I tell you how I figured this out. You're going to think I'm crazy."

"Just tell us what you believe," Sid assured him. "What does your gut tell you?"

Danny thought for a minute. He stared down at his hands and shrugged.

"Like I said, this is going to sound crazy," he warned. "But it looked like the code was somehow imitating human thought patterns."

"What? Like AI?" Victor asked.

"Yes and no," Danny answered. "It was AI, for sure. But not what you're thinking. At least the program wasn't. The program wasn't designed to think. It was mimicking the neural patterns of the brain, but not in the thinking way. It was designed to be - at least I think it was - designed to be an interface of some sorts. Kind of like the brain is."

"I haven't the slightest clue as to what you're talking about," Vic confessed.

"That's just it," Danny complained. "Neither do I. I just have some half-baked idea in my head and I have no idea where it came from."

Before anyone could respond Gerard stepped into the room and announced that Dr. Canta had arrived. The butler guided Zach out of the room while the rest stayed behind. Danny took the time to try and untangle his thoughts.

"OK, think of it like this," he said. Jumping up he approached the chalkboard.

"Bear in mind that I have no evidence or proof whatsoever concerning what I am about to say next," he warned them. "This is all theory. In fact, I was thinking about this all the way back and this is what came to my mind. I'm not advocating this as truth in any sense at all. This is just a working theory based on what limited experience I have had with this.

OK? No one take me to the woodshed about it because I know it is going to sound strange."

"Just get it out," Vic said with growing annoyance. "We'll let you know if you're crazy."

Danny sighed and shook his head. The internal struggle played out on his features as he lifted the chalk and rolled it in his hands. Finally, he began drawing.

Starting out with a square, Danny drew three cylinders one top. He made curls like smoke rising out of the cylinders.

"Let's say someone has a factory," he began.

"What kind of factory?" Vic asked.

"You want to make this last longer?" Gary chided as he elbowed Victor.

"It's a factory," Danny repeated. "And this factory is automated. Mostly run by computer."

Drawing a line from the factory Danny connected it to a crude drawing of a computer. Another line came out of the computer and ended at the profile of a human face. Danny even added hair to the top of the head.

"Who is the heck is that?" Vic interjected again.

The other men couldn't help but laugh as Vic brought attention to the odd detail in the sketch. This time, Gary didn't stop him, but joined in as well.

"Why did you give him a mullet?" he asked.

"Is that Uncle Randy?" Vic pressed on irresistibly.

"No, it's just a . . ." Danny said in frustration, trying to erase the hair with his hand. "It's just a person. He is the factory owner."

"We'll call him Randy," Vic insisted.

"Fine, it's Randy. Whatever you want to call him," Danny said in frustration. "It's the factory owner. He is the one that operates the factory."

"Listen up," Malachi finally had to interject, knowing this kind of thing could easily spiral out of control.

"Okay," Danny said, gathering himself to start again. "Like I said, you've got a factory that is automated by a computer. And you have the operator that runs a computer. Most of the operations are done automatically, but the human operator has to interact with the machine from time to time. Make some adjustments. That sort of thing.

"Now let's say this operator is in an upper room, an office somewhere and he actually can't see the factory with his eyes. He can only see through the computer. You've got cameras set up and that sort of thing. He gets information regarding the machines through the computer, and he gives commands to the machine also through the computer. You following so far?"

Heads bobbed in the affirmative.

"Okay, here's where I will give it a stretch," he warned them. "What if this is the way human beings actually work? What if our bodies are the factory? Our brains are the computer? And the soul is the operator in his tower?"

"I think I have heard this before," Giovanni interrupted. "It's been a very common analogy that our consciousness is the little man inside our heads, running the body like a machine. Like the operator you've described."

"Yes, but that idea was rejected a while ago by most thinkers," Danny pointed out. "The common problem with this analogy is the obvious: If our head has a little person inside running things, what's inside his head? What's running the little man? You see the problem?"

"How is yours any different?"

"It's not really," Danny confessed. "I am bringing back a rejected model. We have to say we don't know what's inside of the little guy in our head. We don't know who is running him. This is the soul, the immaterial, immortal part of us. Who or what he is will have to be a mystery for now. But that's not the theory I'm talking about.

"Let's just say that this is true, for the point of discussion. In this instance, our brain is simply the interface between the soul and body. It's just like the computer in this example. There are parts that the computer runs. But mainly the computer is a tool that allows the operator to speak to the machine."

"So, our brain is just a go-between?" Giovanni asked. "A middle man? It allows us to run the machine of our bodies?"

"Exactly," Danny said. "That's the job of the brain, to be a go between from soul to body. So, when someone suffers from dementia or brain injury, it's not the soul that's having problems, but the computer we call a brain. But since this is the interface between the soul and the rest of the world, including other people, it's hard for us to tell the difference."

"What does thus have to do with the servers we came across today?"

Gary asked. "Or the Sleeping Sickness?"

"OK, this is where it might get strange," Danny warned. "I'm assuming here that the brain makes it possible for soul to interact with body, the computer to our machine. That program I saw in the servers today, I started wondering: what if they found some way to imitate that same process? What if they were able to create a program that imitated the brain enough, that it could interact with the soul? What if that program was designed to . . . I don't know, talk to spirits?"

These last words were met with a stunned silence from the group. Malachi felt the enormity of the idea slam into him like an unexpected wave. A computer that could interact with the spiritual world?

"Are you saying the machine is haunted?" Malachi asked out loud.

"Yeah, is this like supernatural AI?" Giovanni followed up without waiting for an answer.

"Look, I don't know if this is what they did or even how they could do it. I don't know what it means or what this kind of technology is fully capable of. What I do know is that I saw something evil in that machine. There was a demon in that machine. Malachi, you saw it too. What do you think?"

Malachi's head was spinning. He truly didn't know what to think. But the image of the digital head, that grotesque and distorted imitation of life, wouldn't leave his mind. Malachi couldn't say for sure what that thing was. All he knew was that it was evil.

"I don't know what it was," Malachi expressed out loud. "But your theory is as good as any I could think of. But I've never heard of anything like that. I never thought programming could do that."

"Again, there's a lot I don't now here," Danny confessed. "I can't say if the code they wrote enabled the demon to get into the machine, or maybe the demon possessed it first and that made the new code possible. I don't know. All I know is that there was something living inside of that program. And guys . . ."

He trailed off, as if unable or unwilling to continue.

"This is the truth," he stated solemnly. "That program, that code - that was imbedded in the animation of the show."

This time, the stunned silence was followed by an outburst from all the men there. A hundred questions came hammering in all at once. If Malachi had been hit by a wave before, this one was a tsunami.

"Wait! Wait!" Tres stood up, demanding silence. "Are you saying that a demon was in that show? Is that what you're saying? That a demon got to my boy through that show?"

Malachi could see him trembling with barely controlled rage. The conflict was written clearly on his face. There was a crack in his voice as his lips struggled to form the words. Malachi's heart broke for him, watching the pain of a grieving father learn that the fate of his son may have been far worse than imagined.

"Tres, I don't know what this all means," Danny answered. "I really don't."

"But you're saying that this show, this animation had a demon inside of it and that is what got my son."

"I'm not sure," Danny said, shaking his head.

"Then what are you saying?" Tres asked.

Danny paused, looking to Sid for reassurance. The older man gave none that Malachi could see.

"What I am saying is that this code was imbedded in the animation of Tooney Town," he clarified. "It was in the show, the website, the games, everything. And in that code was something dark and evil. That I am sure of. How they did it, I don't know. What that means, I don't know. But it seems like what Sid was telling all along was right. Whoever is behind this seems to have written code that . . . I don't know opens a portal or something. It's like a program that was written to be possessed. And whatever possessed it was pure evil. What's been hurting these kids is not natural. At least not anything we know about. And I'm pretty damn certain this show had something to do with it."

"What are they doing with this?" Tres turned his question to Sid. "What did they . . . did they possess my son?"

Sid looked up at Danny's drawing. He didn't say anything for a while. He tapped his can on the floor and turned to the men.

"This is something new to me as well," he told them. "You have to remember I come from a different age. As much as I hate to admit it, the world has moved past me. A long time ago it did."

"You've got some idea, though," Malachi said. He could see it written clearly on his face.

"I don't understand all this," he said, gesturing to the drawings on the board. "But I do understand the Fae. And all this, though in different form, looks like something they have done countless times before."

That last statement hung in the hair, expectant and full of meaning.

247

"And that is?" Vic prompted.

"Find newer, better ways of doing what they've always been doing," Sid answered. "Control us and feed off of us. Different methods. But the end game is always the same for them.

"I don't know what they're trying this time or how this program helps them at all. But it's for the same end. We don't have to understand it all in order to stop it. We just have to understand enough to put an end to it."

Chapter 20 - Cloaker

After the stir over Danny's revelation died down Sid told everyone to get cleaned up and something to eat, then convene back in the study.

"We'll attack this with a fresh mind," he told them. "I'll call you down once I've checked on Mr. Metts."

They all went back to their quarters both eager and exhausted. Gerard told them food was available to anyone in the kitchen and would be out for the next several hours. Gary and Tres immediately went downstairs while the others cleaned up first and showered.

"We better get down there if we want something to eat," Malachi told Giovanni as he dried off in the stall next to him. "Gerard told us to eat as much as you want, and you know Gary takes that as a personal challenge."

The men shared a laugh, remembering epic tales of the big man's ability to put down food. True to form, the kitchen island that had been covered in food now looked like a ravaged battle site. Only the heels of a large loaf of bread were left among the scattered crumbs. The same work was done with the sausages. A few bits of cheese were left along with all of the olives and raw vegetables. An empty pie tin indicated a desert once filled it. Malachi couldn't guess what it was by the few remnants left.

"Mmmm, Key Lime," Giovanni said after licking his finger. He had managed to gather a few wayward crumbs that were left behind.

Before they could lament their lost opportunity the swinging doors to the kitchen swung open and Gerard came through pushing a cart. A smell wafted from it that sent Giovanni's mouthwatering.

"I see you've already finished off the appetizers," Gerard noted in his steady and careful words. Giovanni noticed again the slight British accent the butler spoke with.

"That would be Gary's handiwork," Malachi said, shaking his head.

"Well, I certainly hope he didn't fill himself up. This roast turned out particularly nice today."

Placing a silver serving dish on the island he took off the cover to reveal a steaming roast. Giovanni couldn't help but groan in appreciation as he saw the perfect medium rare of the sliced beef. It sat in a pool of rich aus jus and filled the room with its savory aroma.

Another tray revealed loaded baked potatoes, while a third presented steamed vegetables coated in butter. Gerard ended the presentation with a white cake covered in a whipped cream icing.

"What did we do to deserve this?" Malachi asked as a smile of appreciation crossed his face.

"Are you kidding, we earned this one," Giovanni said. "After today we racked up some major credits, wouldn't you say?"

"Indeed, you did, boys," Gerard agreed. "And let the others know as well. If they still have an appetite."

"Oh, you don't know Gary," Malachi said. "That man always has an appetite."

The two men fell heartily to their meal. Some of the other Swordsmen joined them and fell in to the feast as well. Eventually, word got upstairs that there was more food and Gary came back down for seconds.

When it was all finished, Malachi and Giovanni were the last ones still in the kitchen. Both were pleasantly full, but neither felt easy about leaving the mess behind.

"Should we at least pick up a little bit?" Giovanni asked, looking around. Gerard had not shown himself again after presenting the bulk of the meal.

"He told us just to leave it," Malachi said with a shrug. "Doesn't seem right, though. For over fifty years I've been conditioned to clean up after a meal, and now I can't leave a dinner table without at least putting a glass by the sink."

Giovanni smiled and nodded in agreement. "Yeah, I can feel my grandmother's disappointment already that I haven't washed a dish yet. But I also don't want to mess with someone else's kitchen."

"How about we split the difference, then," Malachi suggested.

The two men stacked and scraped all the plates and tried to arrange them as neatly as they could. The island was still a mess but they had allayed their conscience as best they could.

"I feel a nap calling me," Malachi announced as they surveyed their brief work.

"I think I might walk around a bit," Giovanni said. "I'm still coming down from the day."

After Malachi went upstairs Giovanni let himself out a side door that led to a greenhouse. He still had yet to master the layout of the mansion; despite the time he had spent there. Rooms seemed to pop up unexpectedly, and he found a greater depth to the house than he initially expected. Its vastness confused him and he couldn't help but wonder if there was a supernatural dimension to it that couldn't fully be explained.

Walking around the scattered remains of clay pots and bags of soil, Giovanni found a door that let him outside. The hot, summer evening washed over him as he stood in a small courtyard. The sun was setting over the trees in the distance. A dried-out fountain in front of him, full of leaves from countless autumns marked either the beginning, or end of a garden maze. Hedges still cut and well-kept formed a path behind the fountain, and for a moment Giovanni considered trying his hand at its depths.

Instead, he took a gate out of the courtyard and onto the green lawn. Not sure where he was going or what he even wanted to do, Giovanni let his legs carry them where they willed. He looked over at the woods, at the decrepit gateway that he and the other Swordsmen had stepped through just a few days ago. It felt like a lifetime had passed already since then. Or that it was another person who had walked through that night.

Giovanni quickly decided that was an accurate assessment of what had happened. It had been in another life when he walked through that gate. It had been another person.

Things were so different now. He was so different now. He couldn't rightly be called that same, timid music teacher that followed his brothers through that gateway. He couldn't even say that it was part of the same life. Everything was different now. The world had gotten a lot bigger, and a lot scarier since then.

Letting his mind and feet wander, Giovanni didn't notice where he was going at first. As he walked towards the south end of the house, he saw a terrace rising up to the second floor. The French doors that accessed it from the house were still open and two men were sitting at a table together.

One of the men was Sid. But Giovanni didn't recognize the other man at all. His back was to Giovanni at the moment, though he could tell that it was a handsome and well-built man that sat across from Sid. Thinking it was the doctor that was helping Zach, Giovanni made his way to the terrace to yell up and ask how his friend was doing.

As he got closer, Giovanni noticed something about the man that made him freeze in his tracks. He couldn't say what it was for sure.

Looking up Giovanni tried to make sense of this sudden feeling. He studied the man's features, from the blonde hair to the light-colored summer suit he was wearing. With his back to him Giovanni could make out little more than that, but still there was something there. The way the man held himself, his gestures, the slight incline of the head; there was something there that Giovanni felt was familiar to him. It was something regal. Kingly, was the word that came to his mind.

This is one of the Fae, Giovanni thought to himself as his blood ran cold. He couldn't tell how he came to this certainty, but he knew it, and there wasn't a shred of doubt in him. Sid was up there on his terrace talking to one of the Fae.

A thousand questions began hammering through his head. Why would Sid be talking to one of the Fae? Was he somehow in league with them? He distinctly remembered Sid telling them that some of the Fae were allies. But how could he tell?

Deciding now to get as close as he could to them without being seen Giovanni made his way towards the terrace as quiet as he could make himself. He was sure they hadn't spotted him yet, so he quickly walked over to the wall of the terrace, out of sight of the men above. He strained his ears but could not make out the words they were saying. They were muffled and distant.

He took a step closer to the outside staircase of the terrace, but that actually made the voices fainter. You'll have to walk up some of the stairs, he told himself.

As soon as he said this another certainty came over him, this one just as inexplicable and without a train of logic. He suddenly thought that if he concentrated hard enough on being quiet and unseen, that neither Sid nor the Fae he was talking with would be able to know he was there. It sounded ridiculous, but he partly believed it. Perhaps, he thought, if I just walk partway up the staircase, there against the wall of the terrace, they won't know I'm there. As long as I am really quiet and keep below the wall, there is no way they can see me.

As soon as he had decided this, he felt something fall over him. It was not anything he could see, but it felt like a blanket had been draped over him. He could almost feel it being dropped down over his shoulders and head.

He took a few tentative steps up, straining his ears. The voices still sounded too unclear to make out their words. They didn't sound alarmed either so Giovanni stepped closer.

As he walked up, he couldn't hear his own steps. The silence around him was complete. Leaning in, almost so his side was touching the terrace wall, he took a few more steps. The voices became clearer. He could make out a few words.

Giovanni looked up and saw that he could take three, maybe four more steps until his head would clear the terrace wall and he could be seen. He took those next few, stopping just where his head was beneath the top of the wall. Snippets of words came in clear.

"Well beyond my scope," he heard the Fae exclaim, louder than his other words. "I told you this from the beginning."

Whatever Sid said in response was too low to hear.

Giovanni felt alarm run through him at those words. Was he talking about Zach? Had this doctor been unable to heal him?

Turning his head, he tried to strain his ears even further. Only bits of the conversation fell clearly in his ears. Words came to him, unconnected from the larger context.

"Wait . . . not enough . . . fortunate for now . . . no way . . . cannot see another option," came the words from the Fae.

". . . have to try . . . right about our options . . . duty and obligation . . . no chance at all," came Sid's uneven responses.

Giovanni cursed silently and tried to move closer. Willing himself to be quiet he ducked down and moved up another step. The blanket felt thicker about him, deeper. The assurance that he could be neither seen nor heard fell upon him stronger now. He was nearly convinced of it.

As close as he dared to go and Giovanni still could not hear. He would have to get closer, but that would mean exposing himself.

Another idea came to Giovanni as he strained to listen. He would move up the stairs, quiet and casual, hoping the men wouldn't see him immediately and say something he could hear. That way, he could claim that he was just walking up the terrace and they didn't happen to notice him.

It sounded stupid in his head as he thought it, but he also knew he was going to hear nothing where he was. Their voices were too low, and the outside air dissipated their words too quickly.

As quietly as he could without looking completely obvious, Giovanni moved up the staircase. He felt the blanket fall about him heavier, assuring him he could not be seen. His head cleared the wall and he continued to walk up. Neither Sid nor the Fae noticed him. He couldn't stop without looking like he was obviously eavesdropping, so he climbed the stairs until he stood on the landing. The voices of their conversation fell clearly upon him now.

The Fae, who was as handsome as he threatened to be, was shaking his head at Sid. He wore a white shirt beneath the beige sport coat. Despite the late afternoon heat Giovanni couldn't see a single drop of sweat on him. As he stepped closer, he noticed the Fae's bare feet sticking out of his slacks.

"Sid, I have no access to any of the patients," the Fae was telling the Keeper. "None. Zero. Ever since this became an official pandemic the Department of Health has their own doctors that oversee one-hundred percent of their care. One-hundred percent. Not just doctors. Nurses, the aids. Hell, even the janitorial staff that cleans their rooms are Health Department. None of my people are allowed to go near the kids. I'm sorry, there's no way I can even get close to them."

Sid's back was to Giovanni so he could not see his expression. The older man did shake his head and Giovanni felt the disappointment, and maybe a touch of desperation emanating from him.

"Do you know any of these government doctors?" Sid asked.

The Fae shook his head and threw up his hands. "I don't know them and no one else does either. Not a single doctor in my hospital has even heard of these doctors. They said they're from DC, but we know that isn't true."

"But we know this is the Family at work," Sid more stated than asked.

"Without a doubt," the Fae answered. "I just can't figure out why."

"Has the why ever changed?" Sid asked.

"No," came the answer. "But they usually don't kill off their victims this quickly. At least not until they've had a chance to feed."

"Maybe they have," Sid suggested. "One of my men found an advanced program embedded in the show I told you about. Believes there may even be a presence inside it. Maybe they've found a way to siphon off the fire all at once."

The Fae shuddered visibly, looking horrified at the suggestion. At the same time Giovanni saw another expression on his face. It was brief, fleeting, almost impossible to see. But he was watching and saw it flash across the handsome features. Something eager and feral pulsed in the Fae. It was primal, a deep and unmoving hunger. He seemed enticed, even excited about what Sid had suggested.

"Impossible," the Fae said as the look passed as quickly as it had come. He placed a finger on his lip as he thought.

"No," he said after he had considered longer. "The first victims that came in, the ones I had been able to see; none of them had anything taken from them. If any fire had been siphoned off it was unnoticeable."

"Are you sure you were able to see clearly?" Sid leaned forward and asked.

A smile broke out over the handsome features of the Fae. "Oh, it was the first thing I looked for, old friend," he answered. "Trust me, the soulfire was perfectly intact. Completely undisturbed."

The Fae settled back in his chair and let his eyes drift over the terrace. Giovanni stiffened, watching as the eyes settled over him. He willed the blanket to fall over him, thicker, heavier.

The Fae stopped as his eyes met Giovanni's. He waited, expecting to hear the questions and the outrage about eavesdropping. Amazingly, the eyes passed over him without a word. They instead looked all around the terrace, as if searching.

"What is it?" Sid asked, turning around.

The Keeper's eyes also settled right where Giovanni stood but gave no notice that they saw him at all.

"I felt something nearby," the Fae said. He turned around to look and even craned his head up to look at the darkening sky. "Someone, or something is watching us."

"The house is safe," Sid assured him.

"Is it as safe as it always has been?" the Fae questioned.

"The protection of this property doesn't depend on my power. It is a safe place. Always will be."

Satisfied with the answer the Fae nodded but still looked around him one more time.

"If the soulfire was intact then the Family must have some other angle they are working on," Sid picked up the conversation again.

"If you have any theories, I am all ears," the Fae answered.

"This last girl, Alicia Wyatt, have you heard anything about her progress?"

The Fae shook his head. "Like I said, all government staff working with the Sleeping Sickness patients. We won't hear a thing until she dies."

Sid grunted in frustration. "No telling what they're doing with them in the meantime."

"It's frustrating, I know," the Fae said. He leaned forward and sipped from a teacup in front of him. "They even use coroners from the Health Department."

Sid jerked up straight. "Wait, they use their own coroners? So, no one sees the bodies after they die except their own people."

The Fae nodded.

"Then there is no confirmation that these children are even dead?" Sid suggested. "They could still be alive?"

"No, we have confirmation," the Fae answered, putting down his cup. "The parents view the body. I've been in the room with them when they do. Believe me, they're dead."

"But medically you've not confirmed it," Sid pressed leaning forward. "You've not laid your hands on a body?"

"Well . . . no."

"And none of the parents actually received a body," Sid went on becoming animated. "Mr. Bettis only received the cremated remains of his son. Said it was a precaution. Oh, it all makes sense now. Eric, don't you see?"

"Wait. You don't think?"

"Yes," Sid exclaimed emphatically. He slammed his hands down on the table, making the teacups rattle.

"I suspected it early on, when Mrs. Bettis insisted she knew her son was still alive. Sometimes a mother just knows. I didn't want to say anything to Mr. Bettis for obvious reasons. But it's the only thing that makes sense. Eric, these children are still alive."

Giovanni gasped at these last words. Being the only one who had no idea where Sid was going with his line of thought, when it was finally said aloud, it stunned him to disbelief.

At the sound of his outburst both men jumped from the table. When they looked at him this time, both men could see him.

The Fae had a dark look come over him as he moved forward. Giovanni took a step back and instinctively raised up his hands.

"House is safe, huh?" the Fae sneered. "I'll take care of this one."

"NO!" Sid commanded, holding an arm out to stop the approach. "This is one of mine."

"One of yours?" the Fae asked, gesturing in disgust. "Then why is he is spying on us?"

"I'm sorry," Giovanni plead. "I didn't know I was spying. I really didn't. I was just trying to walk up here quietly. I don't know why you didn't see me. I swear."

The Fae narrowed his eyes at him suspiciously. Sid was more indulgent. A knowing smile played over his face.

"They are new," he explained. "Still discovering their talents. Though this one, Mr. Santos, you're going to have to be careful with."

"I hate cloakers," the Fae said, turning away and taking his seat again.

Giovanni didn't know everything they were talking about, but he had a pretty good guess.

"So, none of you could see me?" he asked, not sure if he really believed it.

"Not until you gave yourself away," Sid told him. As he took his seat, he gestured for Giovanni to join them.

"As you may have noticed, Dr. Canta here felt your presence. If he had decided to look closer, chances are he would have found you."

Giovanni took a seat beside Sid as the reality of what they said began to wash over him. Once again, he found his worldview being shaken to his core. But this time, it came with its own excitement.

"Are you serious?" he had to ask again. "I was invisible?"

Sid nodded with a smile of his own. Even the Fae, Dr. Canta, was unable to hide his amusement. Infected with Giovanni's excitement, his scowl turned into a chuckle.

"They really are discovering their powers," the doctor observed.

"Yes, but not yet learning their limits," Sid observed.

"I don't even know how this is possible," Giovanni wondered aloud. "I mean, I felt like I was hidden, like I was being cloaked, like a blanket was being draped over me. But I could still see myself."

He shook his head in bewilderment. "This is all too unbelievable. It shouldn't be even possible . . . How can one even . . . ."

"It's not what you think," the doctor told him. "You didn't really become invisible. You just became un-seeable."

"What does that mean?"

"Nothing changed about your physical composition," Sid took up the explanation. "Your body didn't become see through or anything. You were just able to hide yourself from us. Make it so we couldn't see you."

Giovanni shook his head again, not sure if he was any closer to understanding.

"Yeah, but if I wasn't invisible in the literal sense, then why couldn't your eyes see me anymore?" he asked.

"The same reason you can't see much of what goes on all around you," the Fae answered, gesturing to the air around him.

Now, Giovanni was seriously confused. He looked at the empty air that the doctor had indicated, wondering what he could be missing.

Sid waved the idea away. "Forget that for now," he said. "Think of it like this. Whenever you see something, it is light that enters into your eye, but the brain is what takes that light and interprets it into what we call seeing. Ultimately, it is the mind that sees, not the eyes. Or at least it is as much in the mind as in the eyes."

Giovanni nodded, beginning to understand. "Yeah, I guess that's why people can hallucinate."

"Exactly," Sid agreed. "The mind is projecting images that some people can confuse with the world around them."

"Actually," the Fae interjected. "Many of those so-called hallucinations are just as real as the physical world you inhabit."

"Eric, he's not ready for that," Sid said, once again, waving away what the Fae's words. "Forget that for now. Just think about the mind and its role in seeing. When you cloak yourself, you are able to hide, not from the light or the eyes, but the mind."

"But how?" Giovanni asked, shaking his head.

"It is your gift," Sid explained. "There is something you are able to project that hides from other minds."

The wonder of it all came crashing over Giovanni. Until that moment he wasn't sure he had comprehended this new world that they had entered in. Rather, he hadn't understood the world he had apparently been living in his whole life. Words from Shakespeare came echoing in his head.

"There are more things in heaven and earth, Horatio, than are dreamt of in your philosophy," he quoted.

"Well put," Sid agreed. The Fae raised his glass in toast and drank.

"I was serious about being careful," Sid added. "You are not impervious to detection. The eyes can still see you, after all. And if you were to make too much noise or lose your concentration then you will appear again. Also, if someone suspects you are there and they look for you, they will find you."

"So, I can't do it to a person more than once," Giovanni asked.

"The suspicion has to be fairly strong," the Fae answered. "I suspected someone was there but it wasn't enough to see you. Next time, I'll suspect you, though. I will know it is possible for you to cloak yourself, so I'll know what I'm looking for."

Giovanni nodded as a heavy silence fell over them. The tea cup clinked against the saucer as Doctor Canta sipped at it again. Giovanni wanted to get away and think to himself for a moment about all that had just happened to him, but felt that there was something still unsaid between them. Sid looked at him with an urgent expression, almost like someone who needed to confess.

"What is it?" Giovanni finally asked.

Sid looked uncomfortable as he shifted in his seat. He glanced over at the Fae who simply shrugged with indifference.

"When you were listening to what we were saying," he began. "About the children."

Giovanni's eyes went wide as he remembered the conversation he had been eavesdropping on. It had only been a few minutes since he had overheard, but he felt like so much had already happened in the meantime.

"The kids," Giovanni exclaimed, almost jumping from his seat. "They're still alive?"

"I don't know for sure," Sid cautioned, reaching out towards Giovanni. "I suspect they are still alive. To me it's the only thing that makes sense."

"But the funeral..." Giovanni wondered aloud. "Who did we bury?"

"You buried an urn with ashes," the Fae pointed out.

"He's right," Sid agreed. "None of the family were able to go near the bodies by order of the Health Department. And all the children were cremated. Also by order the Health Department. Not a single death has been confirmed."

Giovanni shook his head. "But that doesn't prove they're alive."

"I know it doesn't" Sid agreed. "I only suspect they are. It's the only thing that makes sense. The Fae wouldn't benefit from just killing children, which has been bothering me from the start. Why would they kill them?"

"You can't feed off the dead," the doctor inserted. He produced a silver case and pulled out a hand rolled cigarette.

Giovanni looked over at the Fae when he spoke. A puff of smoke covered him as he lit his cigarette. If Sid was right then these were the very beings that were preying upon humanity. True, this one may be an ally, but that could be a blurry line. Giovanni tried to look past the handsome, otherworldly features for some trace of that feral quality he had seen moments ago. All evidence of it was covered by the chiseled, almost too perfect features.

"Don't worry, I'm one of the good guys," the doctor said when he noticed Giovanni's scrutiny.

"Couldn't this be some kind of experiment gone wrong?" Giovanni asked.

"It still could be," Sid confessed. "The Fae experiment with us quite a bit. But never have they been this public about it. They prefer to stay unnoticed, in the shadows."

"The dark shadows," the doctor echoed.

He puffed out a smoke ring that twisted and reshaped itself into a galloping horse. Giovanni watched the shape in amazement. He felt drawn in by it, pulled to look at it and nothing else. Everything around him became small and distant. The evening began to fade from his eyes as he fixated on the horse. It called to him, beckoned with an insistence he found hard to resist. The smokey figure trotted over the air, rearing back its head proudly before dissipating on the evening breeze.

"But, Mr. Santos, this is very important," Sid told him, shaking him out of his reverie. "You must not say anything to the others about this. Especially Mr. Bettis."

Giovanni shook his head, clearing the clouds from them. He looked up at the doctor in surprise, wondering what had just happened to him. The Fae wore a thin, knowing smile.

"Tres?" he asked. "Why wouldn't we tell him? This will mean everything to him."

"And what do you think he will do?" Sid asked. "If we tell him there is a possibility that his son is still alive?"

Giovanni shrugged though he knew full well what Tres would do. Sid had a point.

"He will move heaven and earth to get him back," Giovanni said.

"Exactly," Sid nodded. "He will go running off with no idea where to go. That, or he'll insist we all do something immediately. And he'll eventually convince the others because they feel bad for him. And then again, what if I'm wrong, and we get his hopes up just to have them dashed. It will be like losing his son all over again."

Giovanni nodded glumly. Everything Sid said was right. Tres had been laser focused on revenge. And while that was understandable it also made him a bit unpredictable. Giovanni had been thinking for a long time he was barely restrained as it was, so much so that it frightened him sometimes. If he found out now there was even the possibility that his son was alive there would be no holding him back.

"Our best chance of getting his son and all of those children back is to plan this carefully," Sid told him. "We will only have one shot at this. We have to make it count."

"Alright, so I keep my mouth shut," Giovanni agreed. "What's the plan then? What do we do next?"

Sid let out a long sigh. For a moment he looked every bit the many years he claimed to be.

"We have to find out where they are taking the kids." the old man said. "Right now, we don't have the slightest clue where that may be."

"How do we find out?" Giovanni asked.

Sid looked up at him and smiled. "That will be difficult to figure out. But with this new talent of yours it's given me some pretty good ideas."

Chapter 21 - Sharp Shooter

"Alpha team, ready to enter," Vic whispered into his comms.

Across the doorway, Gary gave him a nod. He looked around one more time, carefully scanning the area for enemies.

Empty oil barrels scattered across the porch of the dilapidated building. Old wires had been pulled out of the wall. The backseat of an abandoned car molded beside him as a makeshift porch bench. He had no idea what he would find inside.

"No visibility inside," Gary observed, nodding to the pitch-black darkness just inside the doorway.

"Switch to night vision," Vic commanded, pulling down the night vision goggles.

Immediately, the dark lit up with a strange, green illumination.

Vic's mind went back to another life as he and Gary prepared to enter the building. Long ago he had decided he was done creeping around with guns in the dark, not knowing what kind of danger waited for him on the other side of dark doorways. He had vowed never to go back to it. Too many bad dreams waited for him there.

But here he was, crouching outside a door, weapon at the ready, about to enter into a dark building that may or may not be abandoned. Life makes hypocrites of us all, he thought, and had to smile to himself despite the bitterness of the irony.

On a signal, just a barely perceptible nod, the two whirled and entered the open doorway.

The sound of guns popping exploded as soon as the pair whirled inside the door. Through the green night vision Victor could see the projectiles flying through the air towards them.

"Cover, cover," Victor yelled, crouching low and heading towards a set of three oil drums pushed together.

"Are you hit?" Victor asked as Gary knelt beside him. Both of the men hunkered down behind the barrels. The sound of projectiles hitting the metal drum echoed through the dark room.

"I'm clean," Gary answered. "Did you see anyone?"

Vic held up two fingers and pointed up and then to the side to indicate positions at twelve and ten o'clock. The sound of fire had died down for the moment.

"Let me see if I can flush them out," Gary said.

The big man whipped up and lifted his gun. The sound of rapid fire echoed through the room. As Gary fired Vic peaked up over the top of the drum. As soon as Gary stopped and ducked back down, he saw the figures emerge from their cover and return fire.

"Two more up top," Victor said as the drum reverberated with the sounds of projectiles.

"How do we get up there?"

"Stairwell at two o'clock goes up to the balcony," Vic answered, looking to his right. "Two shooters up there behind pallets or something."

"So, what we do?" Gary asked.

"Let me see if I can take one them out, then we'll flush the other."

The sounds of pinging drums died down and Vic eased to one side of the barrel. He led with the muzzle of his gun, held at the ready, peaking out just enough to get a visual, but not enough to offer a significant target.

Through the night vision goggles he saw the top of a head peak out. The twelve o'clock man, kneeling behind crates beneath the balcony. It was just the top of the helmet, but Victor knew he could hit it.

Taking a deep breath and holding it in, he squeezed the trigger. One pop sounded, sending the projectile speeding out. Immediately, he heard the satisfying crack of a direct hit. Through the goggles he could see a smear illuminated on top of the helmeted head.

"Go," Vic whispered.

Gary popped up and began firing. Pops sounded as they flew across the empty space toward the crates. The other man waiting behind them popped up, spooked at his comrade's unexpected hit. He ran for another set of crates to his right.

Vic was ready. Three quick shots came out in succession. Each one hit, in exactly the same spot. Dead center in the chest.

"I'm hit," Gary yelled out falling back down.

Vic saw the men on the balcony above them, both standing up and raining down fire. As he ducked down, he squeezed off two more shots. One scored another hit. The other sailed high as the other target ducked back under cover just in time.

"You ok?" Vic asked as he crouched down beneath the drum.

"Guy up top got me," he answered, touching the smear across his chest, glowing in the green light of the night vision goggles.

Pings echoed as the assailant on the balcony rained fire down again. Victor looked to the stairs leading up top. They were a good twenty feet away from him, too long a dash to make in the open. On top of that the stairs didn't even have a rail, much less even the barest cover.

"We got three of them," Victor pointed out. "Fourth is up there behind the pallets. Haven't seen the fifth."

"And you know who that is," Gary reminded him.

"I know," Vic nodded. "And I've been looking for him too. Squirrely bastard won't get by me this time."

The sound of the drums being hit died down for a moment. Vic peered out again. He ducked back just in time as return fire lit up again.

"He's sitting behind these pallets," Vic complained. "Got the barrel sticking though one of the slats."

"Perfect cover," Gary pointed out. "No way you can squeeze one through there at this distance."

"Aren't you supposed to be dead?" Vic asked in irritation.

"Just wounded," Gary answered with a shrug. "Or maybe I'm giving you that last bit of encouragement with my dying breath."

"I guess you run for the stairs," Gary suggested after he thought for a moment.

Vic shook his head. "I'm going to ping that little runt from here. Won't even know what hit him."

"Now way," Gary said, shaking his head. "You think you're going to squeeze a shot through the slats of a pallet."

"It'll fit."

"Remember what you're working with here," Gary said. "At this angle too. Not even straight on. No way you can get it through there."

"Just enough room," Vic said, nodding.

"Twenty bucks says you can't hit it," Gary challenged.

Vic thought for a moment, then nodded. "Twenty it is. But you got to help me."

"But I'm dead," Gary reminded him.

"Exactly," Vic agreed. Lying down on his side he held his rifle at the ready, just on the edge of the oil drum.

"Sorry to do this to you," Vic said, pushing on Gary with his foot.

"What are you doing?" Gary hissed. He was sitting with his back to the oil drum and pushed back against Victor's prodding.

"You can't do anything, remember."

"Cut it out, Vic."

"I need a distraction," Vic said, pushing him over further.

"You can't do this, I'm out," Gary protested.

"You're dead," Vic reminded him. "But I can still use your body."

"Vic, cut it out," Gary hissed. "He's going to light me up."

"Shhh," Vic said, pushing him over on his side. "Thanks buddy."

As soon as Gary fell over his head stuck out from the side of the oil drum. The assailant up top didn't lose a moment, raining fire down on the exposed man.

"Bastard," Gary cursed through clenched teeth as glowing spots burst out over his helmet.

As soon as he heard fire Vic leaned out over the other side of the drums. With his elbow propped on the concrete floor he leveled the gun upwards, towards where the shots were coming from. Through the goggles he could make out the pale, green form moving behind the pallet. Vic assumed two were leaning against each other, making the space between the slats even smaller.

Making his breath steady Vic concentrated on the small slit of space between the planks of wood. Gary had been right about the space. He would have just enough to sneak his shot through. It would have to be perfect.

The rest of the world seemed to shrink away as he focused. He felt the target draw near him, almost close enough to touch. A connection was formed between himself and that narrow space. Vic could sense it being attached to the barrel of his gun, like a string tied from one end to the other. His shot would travel across this connection. It couldn't miss.

Vic squeezed the trigger and exhaled. A grunt of pain came out from behind the pallet. Though he couldn't see what happened he could tell from the sound that he had hit.

"That's twenty bucks, big guy," Vic turned and said to Gary's prone figure.

"No way you hit that," Gary hissed.

"All thanks to you," Vic gloated. "And we thank you for your sacrifice."

"And we thank you for yours," a familiar voice sounded from right over Vic.

He didn't have time to even blink when the sound of the shot popped over him. He grunted as he felt the round explode into his chest sending a blotch of paint over his clothes. Blots of glowing paint splashed up on his mask.

"Lights!" he heard someone call out in warning.

Vic ripped off the goggles just in time. Bright lights flared to life, bathing the abandoned building in a harsh glow. Giovanni stood over him with a grin.

"I was watching for you," Vic complained. "I swear I was."

"I was hiding behind there," Giovanni said, pointing to another oil drum against the wall. "Waited until you were distracted, then cloaked myself and stepped out."

"How close did you get?"

"I could have unbuttoned your shirt when you kicked Gary over."

Vic cursed under his breath as Giovanni stretched out a hand to help him up. Vic looked him up and down and shook his head.

"I really don't think this is fair," he complained. "You being able to turn invisible and all. These special power things really suck for the rest of us."

"I really don't think it's fair you being able to shoot a paint ball between the slats of a pallet," Zach said as he came down the stairs.

Doctor Canta had worked a minor miracle on Zach just days earlier. It had taken only a day and afternoon for him to recover from the poison knife that had stabbed him. Now, he was as hale and healthy as before.

"Hey, that was from hard work and concentration," Vic insisted.

"Lucky is what it was," Gary joined in. "And I owe you for kicking me over."

"You owe me twenty bucks is what you owe me."

Gary growled in response, tearing off his helmet to look at the paint splatters that covered it.

"Good work, swordsmen," Master Sergeant Diggs said as he came down another set of stairs from the observation deck.

It had been three days since their encounter with the shadow men and the warlock Rip Starr. Three days and the men had been involved in intense training with the Master Sergeant again. There was a plan, Sid insisted, but the men were not yet ready to execute it.

This brought them all out to the compound that Diggs had set up for that very purpose. Executing tactics and working as a team was the mission for now. He kept dividing them into teams with different objectives and different levels of handicap. This one had been set up for a small tactical team against an unknown number of hostiles. Diggs had set up the room, then watched from his observation post.

"Good work, but not good enough," the Master Sergeant followed up.

"C'mon, it was five on two," Vic complained. "And if it wasn't for the invisible boy here, we would have taken them down."

"But that's just what you have to prepare for," Diggs warned them as the other men gathered around. "Vic, you're great against a conventional enemy. And you proved that again here. But we aren't fighting a conventional enemy. Nor does he have conventional weapons."

"What do you suppose we do, then?" Gary asked. "We can't prepare for every kind of power that might be out there."

"One man always has to be looking out for special abilities," the Master Sergeant instructed. "It won't always be someone who can cloak himself, but there will always be some power on display you have to prepare for. You have to be ready. It doesn't matter how small your team is, one of you has to be on the lookout for unusual abilities."

"That would have left only one of us to fight against the other four," Vic complained.

"Yes," Diggs nodded. "That's true. It may have taken a little bit longer. It may have made the odds difficult. But it wouldn't have made it impossible. If you aren't ready for a special ability then your odds may as well go down to zero."

"Who needs odds when you can make lucky shots," Zach took up his complaint again.

This time it was echoed by the other three men who had been hit by Victor's shots. Each one complained it was unlikely and lucky that they had been hit at all.

Malachi showed the top of his helmet, which he claimed was barely poking out. Danny displayed the huge paint splatter in his chest. Three hits he said, all in the same place as he was moving out of cover. Tres said he was hit as Vic was ducking down, and not even looking at where he was aiming.

"Gentleman, gentleman," Vic responded, imitating Sid's aristocratic accent. "No need to get jealous just because I am extraordinary marksmen."

"You're lucky is what you are," Gary grunted.

Vic chuckled at the grumbling of the men. Diggs stared at him intently, a question forming inside.

"What did you grade in marksmanship?" he asked.

Vic shrugged. "I qualified."

"Did you make sharpshooter?"

"I qualified," Vic reiterated.

Diggs walked over to where Victor had been hunkered down during the fight. He laid down on his side, imitating Vic's position, pointing up at the pallets Zach had been covered behind.

"You hit the paintball through the pallets?" he asked.

"Two pallets," Zach clarified.

"If you hadn't noticed there are spaces between the slats," Vic pointed out.

"Yes, and I bet they are just wide enough to fit a paint ball through," Diggs said. "Especially with two of them stacked against each other."

"I even had to work the barrel between them," Zach said, incredulity still rich in his voice. "It was tight, too."

"Qualified for marksmanship?" Diggs asked again. "How many targets did you hit?"

"Could have been twenty-four," Vic answered with a shrug.

Diggs shook his head and stood up. He turned and made for the door, gesturing for the men to follow.

"We got to see something."

Moments later the men gathered outside the training building. Diggs had set up a makeshift shooting range out of an old saw horse and a collection of the many empty beer and soda cans that littered the area. He walked Vic ten yards away from the targets and handed him the 1911 he had chosen as his firearm.

"Seriously?" Vic asked, gauging the short distance. "Ten yards? This is child's play."

"Let's start here," Diggs insisted. He backed up and covered his ears.

With a shrug Vic lifted the .45 and squeezed off four casual shots. Each one contacted with an aluminum can, sending it spinning away.

Diggs nodded and backed him up another ten yards. Just as casually, Vic popped four more of the targets. He did the same at thirty, but looked to concentrate a little bit more.

"Let's try fifty now," Diggs suggested as Danny ran to set up more targets.

The other men became intensely interested as Vic lined up for his shot. This was a considerable distance and not one any of the other men felt they could be accurate.

Vic tensed up more for this one. Bringing the pistol up he steadied himself before carefully squeezing off his shot. One of the cans went spinning off the sawhorse.

He squeezed again and another can flipped off the stand. Two more shots sent two more of the targets down.

The men applauded appreciatively. Diggs nodded in agreement and went to stand beside Victor, assessing the work he had done.

"Not bad at all," the Master Sergeant remarked. "Especially for someone who barely passed marksmanship."

"This may be good but it's not a special gift," Vic pointed out as he reloaded. "I know a lot of guys who can hit a can from fifty yards."

"True," Diggs agreed. "Let's see what else you can do."

The Master Sergeant held up a Coke can. He pointed to the "o" in "Cola".

"I want you to hit the "O" on this can," he instructed.

"I can't even see that from fifty yards," Danny butted in.

"And I want you to hit the dash on this one," Diggs said holding up another can and indicating the small dash between the words, "Coca" and "Cola"."

A chorus of laughter went up from the men at the suggestion. Vic nodded and smiled, feeling the challenge rise up inside of him. Danny ran down to the sawhorse and set up the two cans. At Digg's instruction he placed them only six inches apart.

"C'mon, at least turn the "O" to me," Victor shouted as he realized the can was turned the wrong way.

Danny ran back to the sawhorse and turned it so the target faced the shooter. He ran back to the group and covered his ears, waiting.

Victor sighed and rolled his shoulders. He stared down the target for a long minute, as if trying to bore through it with his eyes. Slowly, he lifted up the gun.

For a moment it seemed as if he was not going to shoot at all. His chest rose and fell with deep breaths. He adjusted and readjusted the grip on the pistol, bringing his left hand underneath his right for steadiness.

Two shots fired, only a second apart. The two cans flew off the sawhorse. Danny looked over at Diggs, then ran off to retrieve the targets.

From their distance the men could see Danny stoop down and pick up the cans. He rolled them over in his hands and shook his head. No could tell if he was saying he was amazed or disappointed.

"Well, what is it?" Gary yelled out impatiently. "Did he hit or not."

Danny waited until he was right in front of the men to show them. With a dramatic flourish he held up the cans. One had a clean hole right through the "O". The other was punctured in the upper part where a small dash separated the two words.

A cheer went up from the men as they congratulated Victor on his shot. Hands patted him on the shoulder as heads shook in amazement.

Diggs didn't engage in the celebration or even congratulate Vic on his shot. The two men stared at each other, something unspoken passing between them. There was an understanding that their business was not yet finished.

"The last batch of swordsmen I trained had a marksman among them," Diggs said, silencing the celebration. "It was a true gift, one that was far beyond what any ordinary person could do."

The Master Sergeant held up another can and walked to the sawhorses. After placing the target, he walked casually back to Victor and stood in front of him.

"I was told the marksman could feel the target he was shooting for," Diggs told him. "There was a connection between his gun and his target. He could feel his weapon attached to what he was shooting. That was why he couldn't miss. That's what made it a true gift."

The Master Sergeant walked to stand behind Victor. The other men had gone silent, intently watching the exchange. Diggs leaned close to Vic.

"Aim at the target but don't shoot," he instructed.

As told Vic raised his weapon and leveled it at the can fifty yards away.

"Focus on the target," Diggs said. "Try to feel it. Connect that can to the barrel of your gun. Let it pull on the muzzle."

The woods fell silent as Vic trained his weapon on the target. He held his hands steady, not firing or moving. His breath fell in silent rhythm, concentrating, feeling.

"Can you feel attached to the target?" Diggs asked.

Vic nodded. "It's like a cord is tied from the muzzle to the can," he said, his voice sounding distant and drowsy.

"Good," Diggs told him. "Now let your arm fall to your side. Can you still feel the connection."

Victor let his arm drop. He nodded.

"Good," the Master Sergeant said again. "Hold on to that."

Diggs produced a red bandana. It was the kind with the white swirls and paisleys drawn on it.

"Keep holding on to it," he instructed as he tied the bandana around Victor's head and over his eyes, completely obscuring his vision.

"Can you still feel it?" Diggs asked again.

Vic nodded, his arm at his side. The quiet thickened as some of the men held their breath and waited. Time stopped for a moment, all sounds and thoughts suspending.

"Fire when ready," the Master Sergeant instructed.

Without hesitation Vic raised the gun and fired. One loud report echoed through the forest. An empty casing flew from the chamber, spinning over Victor's head.

Fifty yards away, the can flipped end over end off the sawhorse.

A silence, almost reverential, greeted the accomplishment. Some of the men nodded to themselves, seeing all they needed to see. A lone tendril of smoke wafted from the barrel of the gun, still raised towards the target.

Vic took off the blindfold and looked at Diggs with a gravity that wasn't native to the usually jocular man. The Master Sergeant pushed the still-raised arm down and took the blindfold from Victor.

"What were you aiming for?" he asked.

"The six," he answered.

Diggs furrowed his brow. "What six?"

Without waiting for an answer, he went to retrieve the fallen target. Fifty yards away they could see him looking at the can, his face expressionless. He waited until he rejoined the group before holding the can up for everyone's inspection.

At the top of the can, in small letters, was written, "Since 1886." It was an innocuous phrase. Hardly anyone who drank Coke ever noticed it, except maybe in times when they turned the can over in their hands and happened to notice the date written at the top.

With this can you couldn't really read the date. The tiny six had a bullet sized hole punched in it.

"Looks like you found your gift," Diggs said, putting the can into Victor's hands.

"No more whining about everyone else having a cool gift," Gary said, elbowing Vic in the side. "Alright, Green Arrow."

"It's for guns, not bow and arrows," Vic corrected.

"Actually, the marksman's gift is for almost any projectile that you take time to master," Diggs told them. "Knives, axes, even bow and arrow."

"Green Arrow is very low on the hierarchy," Vic complained. "He didn't even make the Super Friends. That's got him below Aquaman. Aquaman!"

"Still complaining," Gary said, shaking his head as the other men chuckled. "Gets the gift of perfect aim and he still complains."

"It's not a flawless gift," Diggs interjected. "There are limits and weaknesses to it."

"Like what kind?"

"For one, you have to be able to concentrate if you want to lock on to a target," Diggs explained. "Otherwise, your aim will just be exceptional, just not perfect like it was here. For another, it's hard to lock on to people in this way."

"What makes people so hard to lock onto?" Vic asked.

"A can is an inanimate object. It has no will of its own. It can't want or desire not to be hit. Naturally, a person doesn't want to get hit. People have wills. So, if they know you're shooting at them then they can usually push away whatever it is that fixes on them."

"It doesn't work with people then?" Danny asked, obvious relief in his voice.

"It can and it does," Diggs clarified. "If a person doesn't know you're about to shoot them it works just fine. If they do know, however, their minds will automatically push yours away from locking in on them. They don't even know they're doing it, only that they don't want to get shot."

Vic nodded, looking down at his gun with a renewed admiration. For the next half hour, the men thought of all sorts of challenges for Victor's newly discovered gift. They had him shoot with his back to the target, standing behind a tree with his back to the target, blindfolded and spun around, blindfolded with his back to the target. One time they had him lock onto the target, then they hid it behind the other side of the building. Vic was blindfolded and had to hunt the target. This task proved difficult, but Victor was able to eventually hit the hidden can that was buried in pine straw.

It was right after Vic hit a can that was obscured behind an old piece of plywood, that Diggs received a call. He listened for a moment then urged the men to gather around him.

"Sid's on his way," he told them. "We're heading to the hospital. Alicia Wyatt just died from Sleeping Sickness."

Chapter 22 - The Last Death

Thirty minutes later the men were all loaded in the van and headed back towards the city. Gerard was driving, but at Sid's instruction had come tearing down the dirt road in a cloud of dust and squealing brakes. After commanding the men to hurry inside Sid had them tear off again at speeds Malachi found downright irresponsible.

"I assume Diggs informed you of the new developments we had this morning," Sid turned and said.

"He said Alicia Wyatt died," Malachi answered, holding on to the back of the seat as the van took a curve at perilous speeds. "But that doesn't explain why we have to all get killed in a van ride."

Sid shook his head and maneuvered himself out of the front. He made Vic scoot over and make room for him on the crowded bench.

"We believe this may be the last person who will contract the Sleeping Sickness," Sid informed them as the van hit a bump and jolted all of them. "If they were transmitting from the site we destroyed the other day then that means they won't be able to cause anymore of the sickness. Alicia is the last one."

"But that's a good thing," Danny pointed out. "It means we stopped it. We won."

Sid shook his head and looked up at Giovanni. In that brief glance Malachi thought he saw something, a warning unspoken, something only the two of them knew. Then it was gone.

"We don't know if we've stopped anything," Sid told them. "Because we still don't know what the end game is here."

"I thought it was just to feed," Vic said. "That was always the end game."

"Yes, but we still don't know how they're doing that," Sid answered. "And until we know that we don't know if we have stopped them at all. Besides, they can simply build another facility. Or maybe they already have another one, to start this all over again."

"So why are we tearing off to the hospital?" Malachi asked. The van skidded onto the paved road and raced off towards the city. "What's there that can help us?"

"Alicia Wyatt," Sid answered. He said nothing more as if that explained everything.

"And what is Alicia Wyatt going to tell us?" Vic asked when no answer was forthcoming from the old man. "If she'd dead she can't tell us much."

Sid glanced over at Giovanni. It was a brief and subtle look, but Malachi could sense something when their eyes locked. The two men knew something that they were keeping from the rest of the group.

"They're being very secretive about the bodies of the children who die from Sleeping Sickness," Sid informed them. "Even the parents aren't allowed to touch the body."

"That's true," Tres interjected. "We could only look at Owen through a window. Wouldn't even let us touch our boy one last time."

"Aren't they worried about infection?" Danny asked. "Isn't that just a precaution?"

"Except we know this isn't that kind of infection," Sid reminded him. "The men in charge at the hospital know that there isn't an infection that will get anyone sick. Still, only CDC doctors and officials are allowed anywhere near the bodies."

"Why don't they want anyone near the bodies?" Gary asked.

"That's the question that we need to answer," Sid told them as the van merged onto the highway. "What are they hiding about these bodies? Something they're worried even the parents would notice if they got too close. That's the question that we need answered. And Alicia Wyatt may be our last chance."

"Yeah, but you just said no one but CDC officials are allowed anywhere near the body," Malachi pointed out. "How do you expect to get a look at her?"

Sid looked at Giovanni again. This time the look was obvious and pointed.

"I guess they won't be able to know we're there," he said. "Isn't that right, Mr. Santos?"

Giovanni groaned and fell back against the van wall.

When the van pulled into Reedland Memorial it was stopped by a crowd that blocked the front entrance. News vans with network logos emblazoned on the side, worried citizens and curious onlookers had clogged the front lot. Orange striped traffic barricades manned by policemen stopped the crowd short, cutting off access to the hospital.

"I guess word has gotten out," Gary remarked at the sea of people that surged in front of them.

"They would have locked the hospital down," Malachi said. "No one without an ID is getting in."

"You've got an ID," Victor pointed out.

"Yeah, but mine's for the medical park over there," he answered, pointing to one of the three buildings outside the hospital, connected to the main building by walkways of tinted glass. "My ID won't get us in the main building if it's locked down.

"Get us in yours and we'll take the walkway over," Vic suggested.

Malachi shook his head. "There's a locked door on the other side of the walkway. Usually not locked, but right now I bet it is. And like I said, my ID ain't getting us in right now."

"Just get us onto the walkway," Sid told them. "I'll take care of the rest."

The van pulled out and headed towards the medical park buildings on the periphery of the campus. Here, the parking lot was near deserted.

"Mr. Santos, Mr. Green, come with me," Sid instructed. "Everyone else wait here."

True to his word Malachi was able to get them into his building. The place was as deserted as the parking lot suggested and the three men moved about without any seeing anyone. It took crossing two of the elevated crosswalks to make it to the main hospital. As Malachi predicted, the heavy, steel door at the other end was shut and wouldn't open to Malachi's ID card. He waved it in front of the access panel but it silently responded with a red light of denial.

"What do we do now?" Giovanni asked.

"We wait," Sid answered.

It was quiet inside the passageway. Malachi walked over to the tinted window. From his vantage point they could see the crowd gathered out front. They all pressed in towards the main entrance, trying to get as close as they could. Reporters waited for a break in the story or a chance to question those in authority. Protesters milled about, their signs blaming red dye or 5G for the sicknesses. A few curious onlookers crowded in, the type to always want to be where there was any chance of excitement.

How oblivious they are, Malachi thought to himself as he watched the silent crowd from a distance. They have no idea what is really going on. Here they are, gathered outside of the hospital thinking this is somehow where they will get answers. They have no idea what is really going on. Their world is so small.

"Wonder what it is they are looking for?" Sid asked as he came to stand beside Malachi. He gestured towards the gathering crowd.

"Answers, I guess," Malachi answered.

Sid shook his head. "I've seen them like this countless times. For some it's like a shark that smells blood in the water. Others are afraid. Some just . . ." the thought trailed off.

"I don't know, it's like a compulsion," he finished.

"Funny, I was just thinking how oblivious they are," Malachi shared. "They have no idea what is really going on, how deep this problem goes, how deep the world goes. And they go about, content in their little world full of little ideas and little problems. It's like a kid who thinks his playroom is the whole world. And he has no idea there's a mansion on the other side of the door."

"And that was you just two weeks ago," Sid chuckled and said. "And don't think that I am unaware that there is still a part of you that is envious of them, that really wants to go back to your safe and predictable world."

The words stung Malachi as soon as they were spoken. Sid was right, of course. Part of him was even angry at this crowd, milling about in their oblivion.

"I'm pretty good at what I do," Malachi said. "Maybe like them, in my little playroom I am competent and secure and confident in who I am. It's predictable. It's controllable. And I've got a pretty good handle on things. Is that so bad to want?"

"Even if it means it is all an illusion?" Sid asked.

Malachi shook his head. The words stung again.

"Here, in this new world, this world of magic and Fae and demons in machines; here I'm helpless. I'm like a kid again. The adults are doing their thing and dragging us along with them. And we've got no choice but to get drug along. Even if it means putting me in danger. I can't do anything at all about it. I've lost any semblance of control."

Sid put a comforting hand on Malachi's shoulder. Until that moment, Malachi didn't realize how bad this all was really bothering him. He had told himself he had gotten used to it, but really, he had just put on the brave face of a child. Like that kid who had to go to his grandmother's house with a wicked uncle Ray who always made him feel afraid, who threatened to smother him when his mother wasn't paying attention. And no one did anything at all about it.

"That semblance of control," Sid began. "That one you love so much and meant so much to you. It was all an illusion, Malachi. This world didn't change with your realization. You just came to understand what it was really all about. True, you may be like a helpless child again, but this idea that you were an adult and in any way in charge of the world was a farce. You never were. You just thought you were.

"And that kid. The one who was at the mercy of all the adults. He figured out a way to survive. He was a smart kid, resourceful and clever. He may have been at the mercy of a cruel and oblivious adult world, but he became a successful, and might I also add, good man. That kid did it once. He can do it again."

Malachi shrugged his shoulders, still feeling sorry for himself.

"Would be a lot easier if I had a gift like the others," he said. "A little bit more in control."

"Don't worry," Sid told him, patting his shoulder. "It's there. When you need it, it will come."

Both men jumped as the steel door leading to the hospital banged open. A hospital security guard peered out the door. He looked at the men before settling on Sid.

"You Sid Bickley?" he asked.

"I am," Sid answered.

"You and your friends come with me," he said. "Dr. Canta wants to see you."

"I had forgotten all about your hospital connections," Malachi said as they made their way through the hospital corridors. "You're friends with the god of medicine himself."

Sid stopped and whirled on Malachi. His face was grave and intense.

"You must never say that," he hissed. "Do you understand me?"

Malachi rocked back on his heels, shocked at the vehemence at which Sid spoke.

"Yeah, yeah, no problem," he said, holding his hands up to soothe whatever foul temper had suddenly taken hold of the old man.

"No, it is imperative you never use that name," he continued. "Especially in front of him. You don't realize the damage it could cause."

"I got it. I got it," Malachi said defensively. "No god of medicine."

"Perhaps it will make sense when you see him," Sid told him and turned to continue on.

"I've seen him before," Malachi called out. "Several times."

"Not like this, you haven't" Sid answered over his shoulder.

Malachi hurried after them, forced to wonder what these cryptic words meant. They were ushered by the guard past the administrative sections of the hospital, and up to where the doctors had their offices. It was an area that Malachi had never been in before. He wasn't a patient of any of these doctors, nor did his business ever take him there.

The difference between these halls and the rest of the hospital wasn't lost on Malachi. Here, the halls were wider, the air cleaner and brighter. The sounds of patients crying out for nurses and the smells of the sick were absent here. The clouds of worry and anxiety didn't hover in these corridors. It was like the hospital ended on the floor below, and didn't pick up again until the next stop on the elevator. Here was a refuge from all of those worldly matters.

The guard ushered them into an open office, one whose generous window view revealed the city below. The familiar figure of Doctor Canta rose to greet them.

Except he wasn't familiar at all.

It was still the same handsome figure that Malachi had seen before, passing in the corridors or up on stage at important hospital functions. It was the same athletic body, muscles outlined beneath his dress shirt, the same finely chiseled features that nurses swooned over, and the same golden tan, blue eyes and blonde hair. It all looked the same, but one glance told Malachi this was not the same Doctor Canta that he had known.

"You're a Fae," Malachi exclaimed before he even had time to process the words.

How he hadn't noticed it before he couldn't even begin to explain. It was so obvious, looking at him. It jumped out like an open wound on someone's face. The handsome features, the otherworldly talent he had with medicine; it all made sense. That his man was something other than human, something belonging to another realm was written all over him.

Dr. Canta looked to the guard behind them.

"Thank you, Lyle," he said. "You can leave us now,"

Once the door was shut the doctor shrugged.

"It's kind of rude to out somebody," he said.

Malachi shook his head, apologizing.

"I guess it just surprised me," he said. "I've seen you dozens of times, but I never realized it before. But it's so obvious."

"Obvious to you because your eyes are open," Sid told him. "And yes, he is a Fae, one of the Good Folk. He's here to help us.

"What can you tell us about Miss Wyatt?"

"The parents are here to see her one last time," the doctor told them. "Of course, they aren't allowed to go near her so we've put her in one of our operating rooms with a viewing station."

"So, we've got to get down to the third floor," Malachi said. "How close can you get us?"

"Thankfully, they haven't been able to shut down the whole floor, but almost," Canta informed them. "I can get you just down the hall from where they've locked everything down. But they've taken over our entire westside pre-op. The doors stay shut and locked and guarded by MPs."

"I guess I'll have to wait until someone goes in," Giovanni suggested.

"Which means we need to get down there fast."

The group made their way to the third floor of the hospital. Any worries of being questioned were quickly dismissed as Malachi took note of the general mood of the hospital. There was a palpable tension in the hallways. Doctors and nurses hurried by, their face to the floor. No one gave Malachi the smiles and greetings he was used to. Even those he knew gave him nothing more than a perfunctory glance before hurrying about their way.

"Is it always this tense in here?" Giovanni asked as they hurried through the corridors.

"Not at all," Malachi shook his head. "People are scared."

"Except they don't know why," Sid added.

"It's been this way ever since the CDC arrived," Canta told them. "Or whoever these people are. Everyone knows something isn't right. They can feel it. But no one knows exactly what it is or what they can do about it."

Doctor Canta ushered the group into a consultation room. Once inside he pulled the door closed.

"The westside pre-op station is just around the corner," he told them. "This is as far as we can get without being questioned."

"I guess it's up to you, now," Sid looked to Giovanni and said. "Believe in your gift."

Malachi could see the tension clearly marked on Giovanni's face as he nodded and mentally readied himself. If it was anything like what Malachi himself was feeling, he knew it would be intense. His stomach was tied up in knots of tension, and though he wasn't quite ready to admit it yet, a little bit of excitement was there was well.

"There's something else you need to know," Canta told them, his handsome face going grave. "There's another reason why there is so much tension at the hospital."

"Sautorus," Sid replied, his face as grim as Canta's.

"Who's Sautorus," Malachi asked, not liking the look the two men shared.

"He's one of the dark fae," Sid answered them. "A very powerful one. I saw the him a few weeks ago when this just started."

"I've felt him here a few times but haven't seen him," Canta said gloomily. "Just pray you don't run across him either."

"What happens if I do?" Giovanni asked, going a bit pale.

"Trust your gift," Sid assured him. "If you see him, and you'll know him if you do, cloak yourself as deeply as you can, and trust your gift."

Sid went to stand in front of Giovanni. He grabbed him by his shoulders and looked intently into his eyes.

"That is imperative above everything else," he said. "Trust in your gift. Do not doubt it. Trust it and it will serve you well."

"What about the cameras?" Giovanni asked. "Won't they see me?"

Sid smiled and shook his head. "Oh no, cameras are the easiest things to fool," he said.

"Really? I would have thought cameras are pretty hard to fool."

"Not at all," Canta interjected. "When you cloak yourself, you're telling other minds that you aren't there. Minds can push back a little bit. Machines can't."

"Cameras will see whatever you want them to see," Sid added. "Even if it's not there."

"Wait, what?" Giovanni asked, now thoroughly confused.

"Forget that," Sid told him, waving the conversation away. "We'll talk about that later. For now, just trust your gift. Be as quiet as you can, but try to see as much as you can. Don't try to do too much and come back to us as soon as you can. No heroics. Understand?"

Giovanni nodded and fished in his pockets. Pulling out his cell phone he held it up to them.

"I guess I should silence this," he said, turning the device over to put the silent mode on.

"I think you should just give it to us," Sid suggested, holding out his hand.

"Right." Giovanni reached out to hand it over.

Malachi didn't know why he spoke up then. Or why he said what he said next. Watching Giovanni hand his phone over to Sid he was overcome with a pounding certainty that he shouldn't do it.

"No!" Malachi said with much more force than he intended.

Three heads turned to him in unasked questions. Malachi shook his own in response.

"Keep it," he said. "Don't ask me why. But keep it. Make sure all the notifications are silenced. And share your location with me."

Giovanni looked to Sid for confirmation. The old man shrugged his shoulders and nodded.

"Alright, I guess this is it," Giovanni said after he made the necessary adjustments and pocketed his phone.

"Are you armed?" Sid asked.

Giovanni nodded, reaching around to pat the small of his back where the Glock was concealed.

Malachi reached out and put a hand on his shoulders.

"You can do this," he said with every but of conviction he could muster.

Giovanni nodded and the other men turned around. There was silence in the room until Malachi heard the door quietly opening then pushing shut again. They waited a second more before turning back to the closed door.

Sid bowed his head and breathed a quick prayer.

"He will cover you with his pinions and under his wings you will find refuge."

Chapter 23 - Observing Alicia

It felt strange to Giovanni to be walking down a hall full of people and not to be seen by any of them. The fact that people were keeping their heads down helped, but he knew even then he would be invisible to their sight. He felt the cloak over him like a heavy blanket. It wasn't something he could see with his eyes, but if he concentrated, he could see it with his mind.

Walking as quietly as he could Giovanni made his way to the closed double doors at the end of the hall. Two MPs watched over the entrance. Hard, steely eyes peeked out from the rim of their helmets. Giovanni walked near them without challenge, then stood to the side and waited.

Almost immediately a group turned the corner and walked towards the door. Two hospital officials with two more doctors and a hospital chaplain flanked a young couple holding onto one another. The woman had her head down, a tissue dabbing at the corner of her eyes. The man looked ahead, his eyes glassy and distant.

The MP's stood aside without a word. One of the hospital officials waved a key card in front of the access panel and the doors silently swung in. Giovanni found plenty of room to tail the group before the doors pulled shut again.

Behind the doors it reminded Giovanni of a movie he had seen once about a viral outbreak. Plastic was draped all over the bays as doctors and nurses decked out in full contact precaution were milling about. Inside the individual rooms, where there should be patients prepping for surgery, the plastic walls were sealed with zippers that ran across the perimeter. Behind them Giovanni could see the distorted light from computers that other technicians worked over.

This is all for show, Giovanni thought to himself as he moved silently among them. It was an intuition he couldn't deny. The eyes peaking from behind the plastic shields didn't belong to doctors or nurses. The technicians working in their plastic bubbles weren't working on anything real. The full precaution get ups were all unnecessary. This was an act for the two parents that were coming to view their dead child.

Giovanni was tempted to stay behind and see what would happen when the parents left. Up ahead the group was moving through another door and he had to hurry through before it closed behind him. They passed through another hallway and ushered the family into a smaller room. A thick glass window looked out into an operating room. Surgical lighting hung down from the ceiling, ready to illuminate the doctors as they opened up the human body and performed their modern-day miracles. There was no surgery this day, only the white room that stood empty and sterile.

"Dr. Jenkins will get your daughter now if you're ready," the chaplain told them once the couple was inside.

The woman nodded into her husband's arm. One of the doctors with a hospital administrator nodded in return and quietly slipped from the room. Giovanni hesitated for a moment, then decided to follow the doctors.

He was already a few steps behind when he made up his mind. In the hallway ahead a door was falling closed where the two had retreated. Giovanni hurried, but still had to put out his foot to keep the door from hitting him. The two figures up ahead had their backs turned to him and didn't seem to notice. He eased inside the narrow room and let the door closed behind him.

They were inside what Giovanni took to be the scrubbing room. Large sinks lined the wall that could be operated by foot pedals. The men ahead navigated between the sinks and the pods that held sterile equipment and gauze.

Sitting in the narrow room was a hospital bed covered by a white sheet. A vaguely human form rose out of it, outlined in the peaks and valleys of a body at rest. Dr. Jenkins snapped on a pair of gloves and grabbed a hold of the head end of the gurney.

"Let's get this over with," he said. "This whole thing creeps me out."

The other man nodded and took hold of the other end and they pushed the gurney out into the operating room. Giovanni came and stood in the open door. He could see through the window into the viewing room. Husband and wife still clung to each other in empty desperation. The chaplain leaned in and spoke to them, their words unheard through the thick pane of glass.

At a nod from the chaplain Dr. Jenkins stepped forward and peeled back the upper portion of sheet. The face of a young girl came into the light. Her features were soft and pale, devoid of any living color at all. No breath moved her lips or stirred the prone figure. One look, and Giovanni could tell the girl was dead.

The parents behind the glass came to the same conclusion. Even from behind the thick pane Giovanni could hear the wail of grief that went up from the mother at seeing her daughter lifeless and still. She threw her hands against the glass, desperately trying to reach out and touch her. Her face contorted in agony as her husband tried to take hold of her. She shook him off and pounded on the glass, each strike echoed by a cry of anguish.

Giovanni felt his own heart break for them. It broke for his friend Tres, who had been in this very place two weeks ago. There was no doubt, seeing the parents now, that they were being rent in two. How they even managed to remain standing was a marvel to him, and a testament to some of the everyday courage and strength that goes unacknowledged.

Watching the parents he felt a deep well of disappointment rise in him. Sid was wrong. These kids are dead. As dead as a body could be. Giovanni could see that. This girl wasn't ever moving again.

He realized how wise it had been of Sid to hide his suspicions from Tres. His own hopes felt shattered and broken, seeing this girl still and lifeless. He couldn't imagine the disappointment Tres would feel had he been given this hope, only to have it torn mercilessly from him.

After what seemed like an eternity the chaplain nodded again and the body was covered. The still wailing woman was ushered out of the room by her husband and the team that surrounded them. The silence they left behind was almost as loud as their grief.

Giovanni waited, watching the two men in the OR. As soon as the viewing room was empty, they wheeled the body back out.

"Where too now?" the doctor said as they pushed Alicia Wyatt back into the narrow hallway.

"Morgue," the other man answered.

Giovanni followed as Alicia was pushed into an elevator. An uncomfortable moment ensued with him inside. With the gurney and two men in the elevator, there was little room to be out of the way. Giovanni stood in front of the door, holding his breath as the men looked right through him.

"Trust the gift." Sid's words echoed in his head.

Once in the basement the doors slid open and Giovanni stepped aside. He followed the gurney down the cold hallway and into a sparsely furnished room. On the far wall was a mortuary cooler made of six metal drawers to temporarily hold the deceased of Reedland Memorial.

"We putting her in the cooler?" the doctor asked.

"Nope," the other answered.

"I'm done then," the doctor said, pulling off his gloves as he left the room.

Giovanni thought to follow the men but decided instead to stay with Alicia. That she was dead was beyond doubt. But perhaps he could find out what they wanted with these children for, once whatever nefarious purpose of theirs was finished.

The minutes stretched out long and eerie. More than once, Giovanni glanced at the steel drawers of the mortuary cooler and then back to the stiff body on the gurney. He became dreadfully aware that he was alone in this room with at least one, and perhaps up to six more, dead bodies. He had never considered himself particularly squeamish or sensitive to things like this. Then again, he had never had this much proximity to corpses.

The hallway door banged open, startling Giovanni with the sudden intrusion of noise. He felt himself jump and the cloak that hid him from the minds of others wavered. The feeling of the thick blanket around him slipped from him and for a moment he couldn't grab hold of it again. Footsteps echoed on the linoleum floor, followed by voices speaking to one another.

Forcing himself to focus Giovanni pulled the invisible cloak around himself again. It fell back over him just as three figures stepped into the morgue. Giovanni had to steel himself again as he recognized all of them.

Two of the men were dressed in green scrubs. One of them carried a cloth bag. At first glance they looked every bit like the many nurses and aids that filled the hospital hallways. But there was no doubting who they really were. The last time Giovanni had seen them he was fighting them in the alley at the studio.

The third man hadn't changed his dress at all. He still wore the flowing black trench coat and carried the cane topped with crystal. The warlock. What had Sid called him? Rip?

There was something different about the warlock, a glaring blemish on the otherwise perfect face. A long and jagged scar now ran diagonally across his face. It started at the dark hairline and forked all the way across the middle of his face to the chin.

A memory came flaring in Giovanni's mind of the man's face when

Malachi gave him that scar. He had been embroiled in a fight for his life, but couldn't help but see that the face looked like it was going to split in two. That ghastly crimson smoke had wafted from the cracked wound.

The warlock stopped as he entered the room, his brows furrowed in concentration. Slowly, he turned, searching every corner of the room. Eyes full of malice, peering out from either side of the jagged scar settled right in the place where Giovanni was hiding.

Giovanni looked away from the searching eyes. The knot of tension inside his gut pulsed with new anxiety, pushing against his concentration. The cloak began to thin around him, threatening to expose him.

Trust the gift.

Sid's words echoed in his mind again. Forcing himself to calm Giovanni pulled the cloak tighter about him, thickening the shell that hid him. He quieted all of his thoughts, his feelings. He pulled in a slow breath and held it in.

The searching eyes of the warlock passed over him and continued to look through the room. The shadow men with him didn't stir or seem alarmed at this behavior. They stood still and unmoving, waiting for whatever orders may be given next.

Slowly letting his breath out again Giovanni watched quietly as Rip ordered one of the men to pull back the sheet. Pulling at the top he exposed the neck and shoulders of the dead girl. Once again, the still and unmoving figure of Alicia Wyatt touched the open air.

Walking to the other side of the bed Rip looked the dead figure up and down. His eyes traced over her, looking for something only he could know. His cane tapped at the floor, echoing in the quiet space.

The warlock reached a hand out towards the body. It stopped, just inches from her face, the fingers splayed out wide.

"Breathe," the warlock commanded.

Alicia's eyes shot open and she drew in a sudden and shuddering breath.

A shock of surprise shot through Giovanni, causing him to tense up. He threw a hand to his mouth to hide his own shuddering breath. Instinctively, he pulled the invisible cloak tighter around him.

She was alive.

Damn it, Giovanni cursed. Sid was right. Alicia was alive. And if she was alive, then it was possible that all the other children were alive too.

It was possible, even probable, that Owen Bettis still lived.

"Get up," the warlock commanded the now awakened girl.

Alicia stood up mechanically. The sheet fell away, exposing a naked body as she waited by the side of the bed, staring straight ahead. Rip's eyes roved hungrily over the figure. Giovanni could feel his stomach turned as he recognized the lust that flashed in the warlock's eyes.

"Get dressed," he finally commanded as the cloth bag was thrown at her feet.

Without a word the girl obeyed. Giovanni studied her face as she dressed. Her eyes were open but otherwise her face looked as lifeless as it had when she lay prone on the gurney. Her face was rigid and displayed no emotion. Her movements mechanical and deliberate. Blue eyes stared out unfocused, as if she were watching something miles away, somewhere beyond the walls of the hospital.

"Go to sleep now," the warlock commanded once Alicia was dressed.

The girl climbed back onto the gurney without a word of protest. Lying on her back she closed her eyes again. One of the shadow men pulled the blanket over her and pushed the gurney towards the door.

The others followed and soon Giovanni was alone in the room again. He breathed deep in relief but still did not drop the cloaking that hid him. Rip was just outside the door and he feared the warlock would return at any moment.

His head swam with all that had just happened. Sid was right in his suspicions. Something was being done with the children but they still didn't know what. The Sleeping Sickness was not a disease that killed the children, but somehow rendered them lifeless enough that no one could tell the difference.

Then again, anyone who was expert enough to expose the facade wasn't allowed near the bodies. Careful plans had been laid to keep the plot—whatever it was—from being exposed. Authorities at the highest level had to be complicit in all this. The level of conspiracy was staggering.

As these thoughts barreled through Giovanni's head, he knew none of it mattered. He had seen enough to prove their suspicions, but they still didn't know what was being done with the children. Even more importantly, they had no idea where they were being taken after the faked deaths.

Fear rippled through Giovanni as he arrived at a conclusion that scared him to death. If they were going to stop the Fae in whatever mad plot they had hatched, Giovanni would have to find out where they were taking the children. If Alicia was going to be the last to contract this sickness, this would be their last chance to find out where they were.

Giovanni was going to have to follow Alicia wherever they took her.

Trust the gift, Sid's voice echoed in his head again.

Giovanni breathed deep and pulled the cloak tighter about him. He felt in the small of his back for his pistol, hoping he wouldn't have to use it. Finally, realizing he didn't have a moment to waste, he stepped out into the hallway, following the men who were taking Alicia away.

Chapter 24 - Losing Giovanni

Malachi waited impatiently in the consultation room. It had been almost an hour since they had turned their backs and let Giovanni walk out. For Malachi, those minutes drew out long and laborious.

The other men, Sid and Doctor Canta, seemed unbothered by the wait. Both of them sat quietly, lost in their own thoughts while Malachi paced the little room. Every ten minutes he checked his phone, confirming Giovanni's location. Each time the round dot with Giovanni's profile picture in it remained unmoved.

Or mostly unmoved. A few minutes earlier he had checked the location and had found it had moved to the parking lot. He refreshed the page and it moved back to the hospital proper. Malachi thought to say something but shrugged it off as another one of the nuances of technology that he hardly understood.

For the hundredth time Malachi wondered what was taking his friend so long. Giovanni was one of the newer members of the group, only joining last year. As such, he hadn't the time to get to know him as well as the others. Giovanni didn't seem the type to go rogue and do something crazy. But then again, the man was quiet and Malachi had to admit he had no idea what he was usually thinking.

He fished his phone out again. The location showed the parking lot. An uneasy feeling began to grow in the pit of Malachi's stomach. What if it was moving because Giovanni had been caught. Or maybe it wasn't moving at all, but for some reason the signal had him in the parking lot.

Malachi refreshed the phone again. His unease blossomed from the pit of his stomach and radiated all the way down his arms to the tips of his fingers.

"Guys," he said, showing them the phone. "Giovanni's not in the building anymore."

By the time Malachi and Sid made it back to the van, the signal was moving quickly through town.

"What the hell is he thinking?" Gary cursed, closing the back doors as Gerard sped away.

"Either he has been detected or he decided to follow wherever they are taking Ms. Wyatt's body," Sid suggested.

The idea that Giovanni could have been captured spread a gloom across the van. The men looked at each other, part for answers, and part to confirm that they were all thinking the same thing. Whatever had happened to Giovanni they were going to go get him.

"The likely scenario is that he is still cloaked and decided to follow the body," Sid reassured them.

"How can you be so sure?" Victor asked.

"I can't," Sid shrugged. "But the fact that he is still transmitting his location suggests that he hasn't been detected. If he were captured, they would have searched him and disabled his phone."

"So, he did this on purpose, then," Zach confirmed. "But why?"

Sid held up his hands in a helpless gesture, indicating he didn't know. But there was something that Malachi could see on his face that said otherwise. It was the same look that he shared with Giovanni, some hint of a secret about Alicia. It annoyed Malachi to know he was hiding something, but decided not to press it just yet.

"There was something he saw or heard that made him believe this was important," Sid told them. "I can't imagine what that might be."

He's lying, Malachi thought to himself. Sid knew exactly what Giovanni saw. He knew but he wasn't telling anyone.

"He's just arrived at the airport," Danny told them as he watched Giovanni's location move across the screen of his laptop.

"Crap, he wouldn't get a plane, would he?" Gary asked the group, his eyes wide in concern.

"Depends on how important he thinks this is," Vic answered with a shrug.

It took ten more minutes for them to get in sight of the airport. By the time they neared the terminal Danny announced that Giovanni was on the move again.

"Moving fast, too," he said. "Got to be taking off."

Danny looked at his screen then craned his head to try and see something out of the front windshield. He pointed off to the right.

"And we should be seeing the craft any minute now."

As if on cue a massive cargo plane roared into view. The van shook with the reverberation as the plane blocked out the sun and seemed to dominate the sky. The men looked up at the grey behemoth, marveling that something that large could even lift off the ground.

"That's a C-17," Zach whistled as the plane rumbled overhead.

"It's huge," Gary exclaimed. "A whole lot of plane for the body of one little girl."

"I suspect there is more on board than our friend and one small body," Sid suggested as he watched the plane ascend higher into the sky. "Let's just hope that it gives Giovanni ample places to hide."

"Why does he need to hide?" Vic asked. "The man's invisible."

"Yes, but it takes effort to maintain," Sid explained. "He needs rest. Especially if he needs to cloak himself for long periods of time."

The sound of the rumbling plane retreated into the distance. With it they felt their friend being pulled further and further away, forced to face some unknown danger alone. It didn't feel right to any of the men, and each was eager to rectify the situation.

"So what now?" Gary asked as the giant plane grew smaller and smaller against the pale, blue sky.

"Now is the time to prepare," Sid told them, thumping his cane on the floor of the van. "Trust your fellow swordsmen and get ready to help him. As soon as that plane stops, we have to be ready to act. Let's get you all equipped and ready to go."

The van rumbled with its own momentum as the men all nodded their agreement. Malachi felt that increasingly familiar feeling grow in the pit of his stomach. A little bit of nerves and a lot of excitement. It was time to go on a mission.

Chapter 25 - The Island

Just as Sid predicted, Giovanni felt himself getting tired. The cloak around him felt heavy and cumbersome. Instead of like a blanket that was covering and protecting him, it began to feel like a weight.

For the moment, he was hidden, and didn't fear any detection at all. He had wedged himself between a wall of dormant servers and the hull of the plane. But just beyond that wall were two shadow men that he knew wished him nothing good. And he was thousands of feet in the air headed to only heaven knew where.

Giovanni questioned himself again and the wisdom of his strategy. That he was going to find out what they were doing with the kids was undoubtedly a good thing. But the real question for him was what he was going to do when they got there. Wherever "there" ended up being.

Following the body had been much easier than Giovanni anticipated. Both the shadow men escorting the body were paying attention to what was happening around them, staying alert as guards should. After going up the elevator from the basement they left the hospital through a loading area. Alicia was pushed into the back of a box truck and her gurney secured to the floor. It was only her and the two shadow men in the sprawling and otherwise, empty cargo truck. Giovanni had plenty of room to stay away from the others, stepping into a dark corner and waiting.

When the truck stopped the back door slid open and brought in the harsh glare of the outside sun. Giovanni squinted, waiting for his eyes to get used to the light. As soon as they adjusted, he recognized the smooth and broad surface of the tarmac. They were flying Alicia out.

As he stepped into the sunlight Giovanni first thought to make his way inside to the airport. He had, after all, gained valuable information in his little recon mission. He knew the children were alive. And he also knew they were taking them away somewhere on a plane.

But what would he tell Tres? When his friend demanded to know where they were keeping his son? What would Giovanni say?

Pulling the cloak tighter about him Giovanni followed Alicia as the shadow men wheeled her towards the biggest plane Giovanni had ever seen in his life. The engines were already on and rumbling, and the back ramp was lowered.

All of this to transport a four-year-old girl, he wondered. But as he approached, he quickly saw this was far from the case. The plane was almost full already. The cargo bay had been packed with computer servers, similar to the ones they had found at the movie studio. Alicia's body was rolled through a small aisle between them and to the front of the plane. There she was strapped down again and her escorts took their seats on two black trunks.

I guess I got to find my seat, Giovanni said to himself as he moved up the ramp and into the rumbling plane. Sidling between the stacks of servers he found a place for himself hidden away from the shadow men. He sat down on what looked like another equipment trunk and pulled his legs up, settling in for what would be an incredibly uncomfortable ride.

His wait wasn't long. No sooner had he situated himself than the ramp was moved up into place and the plane shut up. It lurched as it taxied forward and got ready for takeoff.

The plane shook a lot more than Giovanni thought it would. As it reached take off speed, he could feel himself being rattled as the massive plane moved forward faster and faster. His stomach dropped when the nose pulled up and he could feel the ground pulling him below, as if the earth itself was reaching and trying to hold him onto the ground.

Even the earth relented her native grip. The plane slipped into the sky and smoothed out as it climbed higher. Giovanni pulled his legs closer, trying to preserve a warmth he figured would soon be in short supply. He pulled his cloaking around him tighter, though this offered no warmth.

All was quiet in the plane except for the incessant hum of the engines. The shadow men said nothing and made no attempt to engage each other, at least as far as he could hear. It didn't take long for the rigors of the day to begin to work their exhaustion into him. His eyelids felt heavy and his bones ached to be warm. He didn't think sleep was the best idea, but checked his immediate surroundings, just to make sure he couldn't be seen if he did doze off. Satisfied he couldn't be seen easily, nestled as he was behind a wall of servers, Giovanni leaned back against the wall of the plane. He wouldn't sleep, he told himself, just close his eyes for a moment. That was all he needed to take off the edge of exhaustion. Just a minute or two.

Giovanni bolted awake with a jerk.

The plane shuddered and rocked, jostling the servers into each other.

Below him he could hear the tires squeal as the brakes engaged. His momentum pushed him forward as the plane began a hard slow down.

"What was that?" he heard one of the shadow men ask from the other side of the servers.

Damn, Giovanni cursed to himself. He must have instinctively cried out when the plane touched ground.

The other shadow man responded too low for Giovanni to make out.

"You didn't hear anything," the first one said.

Another muffled response that Giovanni took for ambivalence.

From the other side of his hiding place, he heard one of the men get up. Giovanni held his breath as he heard footsteps come closer. He hoped his cloak would hold him.

Giovanni almost yelled out again when he noticed his cloak was gone. Figuring it had fallen away in his sleep he quickly drew it about him again. Immediately, he could feel the difference as that soundless and unseen covering fell over him. It wrapped itself securely in place just as a shadowed figure peaked over the servers where Giovanni waited. He felt eyes move over him and then continue to drift past.

"I guess it was nothing," he heard the shadow man say as the plane slowed to a stop.

A few moments later sunlight came streaming in as the ramp lowered. Giovanni peaked through the servers and saw Rip starting up the ramp, his cane echoing off the metal surface as he made his way up. The two shadow men stood up to face him.

"Sautorus is here," Rip said matter-of-factly.

The name dropped heavily, like the blade of a guillotine. Though the words were delivered with as much nonchalance as possible, Giovanni could tell they inspired fear in both the one who spoke and those who heard.

"Any reason why?" one of the shadow men asked.

Rip shrugged. "Who knows? All I heard was that he wanted to look at the patient before we took her off the plane."

As if on cue a shadow darkened the ramp entrance. It fell long and dark over Rip and the shadow men, casting itself an even deeper shadow than usual. Giovanni felt his own stab of fear and backed up, pulling his cloak tighter about him. Something about that shadow promised an ominous presence behind it.

A tall figure climbed up the ramp and came to stand in front of Rip.

Giovanni immediately recognized the features of one of the Fae. He had those otherworldly handsome features just like Doctor Canta, but very different as well. Instead of blonde hair and bronzed skin, this creature had pale features and raven black hair. He was tall and broad shouldered with massive hands that looked like they could crush rocks. The Fae wore a black suit, and curiously, no shoes on his feet.

"Is this my little girl?" he asked in a vaguely British accent. The words rolled off of his tongue like oil over water.

Giovanni shuddered as he heard Sautorus speak. There was something diabolical in that voice, something corrupt and beyond repair. As he looked, he could tell this wasn't what the Fae really looked like. He felt the whole appearance was a disguise hiding a reptilian figure beneath the veneer of human skin. Here was something rotten and putrid, though the outside was full of charm and good looks. It was a lie. And whatever it was that Giovanni felt, it made him bitterly regret his choice to follow Alicia Wyatt.

"As I told you, the girl is in fine condition," Rip said as Sautorus came to stand beside the prone figure. The warlock sounded petulant.

"There is no need for you to see to her arrival personally," he concluded.

"The servers were attacked before her transformation was complete," Sautorus noted as he stretched a hand out towards the girl.

Giovanni felt something in him twitch at seeing the Fae reach towards her. That filthy hand of his shouldn't touch the girl, he thought. He wanted to reach out and rip the hand from the wrist and toss it away.

Sautorus jerked his head to the side. He locked eyes with Giovanni, and for a moment he was convinced he had been found out.

Giovanni gritted his teeth to keep from gasping in sudden surprise. He pulled the cloak about him tighter, draping it thickly over himself.

The eyes still bore into him. They were black, almost devoid of any whites, and they stared without the slightest shred of mercy. He could feel them drilling into him, trying to penetrate the shelter that kept him hidden. Giovanni waited, holding his breath in tense anticipation. Any second he expected the call of alarm to go up from that awful voice.

Trust the gift, he heard in his head. Giovanni forced himself to calm and faced the black eyes boring into him.

Sautorus turned slowly back to the sleeping Alicia. His hand hovered over her, just inches away from the white sheet. Giovanni released the breath he had been holding as relief washed over him.

"We need to make sure she is ready before we mix her with the other children," Sautorus continued.

"My Lord," Rip stepped forward and pled. "I assure you the girl is ready. I checked on her myself."

"The Family has lost confidence in you, Rip," Sautorus said as his hands hovered over Alicia's body. "After you let Sid Bickley get the best of you again. Do you know how much money you cost us?"

Rip flushed at the mention of Sid and his defeat at the studio. Giovanni could see him grip his cane in an attempt at self-control. The scar that ran down the length of his face darkened a shade deeper than the rest of him.

"It was a minor setback," he said through gritted teeth.

"Minor?" Sautorus said as he pulled his hand away.

He reached forward and grabbed Rip's head in his hands. The warlock, shocked at the sudden movement dropped his cane. Sautorus turned his head to the light, inspecting the angry scar that split his face.

"Looks like more than minor damage here," he observed. "They almost split your face in half."

Rip pulled himself away and tried to compose himself.

"It's true, they surprised me," he said to defend himself. "Sid had recruited some new swordsmen. That's all. One of them wielded white fire and took me by surprise. It won't happen again."

"Swordsmen?" Sautorus asked in mounting anger. He stepped towards Rip, forcing the warlock to fall back.

"You didn't tell me you had allowed him to recruit new swordsmen."

"It's nothing," Rip said dismissively. "They're green recruits. Hardly know what they're doing."

"Seems like you are losing control of the situation. The Family will not be pleased."

"I haven't lost control, my lord," Rip said, trying to stand up taller the looming Fae.

"It was my understanding that Sid was finished," Sautorus cursed. "Why is he recruiting new swordsmen? Why is he even still alive?"

"This is just a last, desperate gasp," Rip assured him, shrinking by the second. "I assure you; it's nothing."

"Swordsmen ride once again with the Keepers of the Flame," Sautorus reiterated. "And one of them wields white fire. And you say it's nothing?"

Sautorus wheeled around and stepped away from Rip. The warlock relaxed visibly, even shrinking a bit now that the threat no longer loomed over him.

"The situation has obviously grown out of your control," the Fae observed. "The Family has lost confidence in you. I will be taking over this project."

"My lord," Rip stepped forward to plead. "I can do this. It's all but done. There are just a few, last touches to put on the project."

"And when the swordsmen return?" Sautorus whipped around to ask. "When they come here to shut us down? What will you do then?"

"I will be ready for them," Rip promised. "Me and my men will not be taken by surprise like we were last time. Besides, they have no idea where we are. They can't find this place."

"It is your arrogance that will ruin you and this project," Sautorus observed. "We will not let you do that. You will transfer your men to me and return to the palace. Daniels has other plans for you."

"My lord," Rip began to argue.

His words fell on the empty air. Sautorus turned and left the plane, leaving the warlock to plead with himself. The two shadow men looked at one another, then with one passing glance at Rip, followed Sautorus off the plane.

Giovanni sunk back among the shadows of the servers and thought to himself. He was, now, wherever the children had been taken. But what now? His location was still on, presumably letting the men know where he was, but he had no idea how long it would take for them to find him. Until then . . .

That thought trailed off as workers boarded the plane. Armed with dollies they began to pick up the servers and move them down the ramp.

Whatever he would do, he saw he couldn't stay there. He followed as a group of men who rolled the servers down the open ramp. Outside, the afternoon sun blazed fierce and hot. A quick look around showed him he was surrounded with what looked to be a jungle. Wherever he was, he was far from home.

Careful to keep his cloak about him Giovanni slipped away from the hub of activity. A pair of open and idling trucks waited as the servers were being loaded on. Giovanni looked to the thick jungle that surrounded him and back to the trucks. Probably the smartest thing to do would be to hide out in the jungle. But would that be the best?

Knowing the right answer without even having to think about it Giovanni sighed to himself and quietly slipped among the workmen unloading the plane.

Chapter 26 - For the Children

An hour after Giovanni took off on the C-17 the Swordsmen loaded a plane of their own. They had supplied themselves for every possibility they could think of: weapons, tactical gear, combat clothing for every possible climate, and loaded it all onto a private plane. Then they waited.

The plane belonged to Sid, or to the Keepers, he insisted. Zach was enamored with it from the moment they stepped inside its luxury environment.

"Hey guys, you know what this is?" he asked as he ran his hands over the white, leather seats. "This is the Gulfstream G650."

"I take it that's good," Gary said, arranging himself in one of the seats and leaning back. "Oh yeah, I could get used to this."

"Yeah, it's good," Zach continued to gush. "It's got twin Rolls Royce BR725 turbofans pushing this baby up into the sky at Mach .9."

".925 if we need it to," Sid corrected as he joined the others, taking the seat that faced Gary. "That's why we decided on this one. That and the fact it has a 6,500-pound payload so we can take everything we might possibly need."

"You mean there are others?" Zach asked, his awe turning into outright adoration.

Sid smiled as he leaned back. "Oh, this is the tip of the iceberg, Mr. Metts. We may be small in number right now but we are well outfitted."

"Any champagne on this flight?" Vic asked, looking around.

"Unfortunately, no," Sid answered. "Nor is there a stewardess. We decided to take extra ammunition instead.

"Did everyone bring their passports?"

All the men, now boarded, confirmed their documents were all in order.

"Hey, if we end up landing on foreign soil, how do we plan to get these weapons off with us?" Gary asked as concerned etched his features.

"That will be the least of our problems," Sid assured him. "I will take care of that. Now, try to get some rest. We don't know when we will get it next. And I have the feeling that once we start moving, we won't stop."

"What we do now?" Malachi asked.

Sid leaned his seat back and closed his eyes. "Now, we wait," he said. "As soon as Mr. Santos stops moving, we follow."

It was several hours on the plane before that happened. Once arranged, all the men tried to follow Sid's example and sleep. Before long, the cabin of the plane was filled with the sounds of men sleeping. All except Malachi.

For his part, he couldn't find it in himself to relax. Giovanni was out there somewhere, in danger of his life probably, and here he sat doing nothing. Although he knew there was nothing he could do, at least not yet, part of him felt responsible for the situation to begin with. He was the one who had allowed Sid into their group, had allowed him to talk everyone into this crazy quest. And while a part of him knew it was for the best, another part was already feeling extremely guilty for what Giovanni was going through. And if anything happened to his friend, Malachi knew he would never be able to forgive himself.

As the hours rolled on, even Malachi felt himself give over to sleep. This was all out of his control, he tried to tell himself. And as hard as that was to believe, that anything could really be outside of his control, he believed it enough to doze off.

Before he knew it the alarm Danny had set on his computer buzzed to life. Danny jumped up, rubbing the sleep from his eyes. He shook off whatever dreams still clung to him and looked down at his laptop.

"He's stopped," Danny announced to the rousing cabin. "The Azores."

"Which island?" Sid asked as he stood over the computer tech.

"Let me just zoom in here," Danny answered. He leaned in, squinting, then shook his head.

"This doesn't make any sense," he said.

"What doesn't?" Malachi asked, standing beside Sid. The rest of the men came to crowd around to get a look for themselves.

"There's no island there," Danny said. 'Wherever he is, it's . . . nowhere. It has the plane sitting in the water."

To prove his point Danny lifted the laptop for the others to see. True to his word the icon with Giovanni's face on it rested on blue ocean. According to the map he was in the middle of the ocean.

"Did he crash?" Zach asked in alarm.

Danny shook his head. "No, the phone would have been able to detect that. Especially a plane crash. No, this is . . . I don't know what this is."

"Maybe an aircraft carrier," Vic suggested. "Do these people have those kinds of resources?"

"Impossible. A C-17 can't land on an aircraft carrier," Zach quickly pointed out. "Not only is it too big but a carrier doesn't have close to the runway space a C-17 would need."

"Well, it landed somehow," Danny said, exasperated.

"Set a course for Ponta Delgada," Sid instructed Gerard who was waiting in the cockpit with another pilot.

"Keep looking for the island," he instructed Danny. "Something is there. We just have to find it."

"Well, it's not on the map," Danny pointed out, gesturing to the swath of blue that filled his screen. "And I'm pretty sure we've mapped every square inch of ocean in the world today."

"Someone asked if these people had the resources to commandeer an aircraft carrier," Sid began as he took his seat and strapped in. "The answer is yes; they do have those resources. And they also have the resources to make an island disappear off the internet. And off of every public map in the world."

"They can't make an island disappear," Danny protested.

"Exactly," Sid agreed. "Which means it can still be found. We're heading to the Azores right now. From there we'll charter a yacht to take us out to that place in the ocean, wherever and whatever it is. I would prefer to know what I'm getting into Mr. Taylor. You have until then to find out what you can."

Instead of being discouraged by these words, Malachi could have sworn that Danny was excited. A strange smile crossed his face as the plane began to taxi for takeoff. His eyes took on that distant and glazed cast. Malachi could tell he was about to get lost in that rare talent that had awoken in him. Whoever thought they could keep that island hidden was about to face off against a man working in the power of his gift.

It only took an hour for the gift to win. Just as the plane was cruising over the Atlantic, Danny pumped his fists in the air and let out a cry of triumph.

"I told you couldn't hide an island," he gloated. "Think you can hide it from me? Well, you can't you tricky little bastards."

"You showed them," Vic joked. "Now tell us where Gio is."

"Well, Sid, you were right," Danny began. "It was wiped off of every document I could get my hands on. Every map, every mention of this island was nada. They even took it off every official maritime map of the area, which is really messed up. Ships these days mostly run on cruise control right now, and they depend on these maps to, you know, not run into things."

"So how did you find it?" Malachi asked as he leaned over. The other men had gathered around Danny again.

"Well, like I said, you can't make an island disappear," he continued. "So, I just had to hack into a government satellite and take a look-see for myself."

Malachi felt his stomach drop at the mention of the hack.

"You hacked into a government site?" Malachi asked, aghast at the very suggestion.

"It wasn't even that hard," Danny answered with a shrug. "Kind of obvious, if you think about it. Don't know how I didn't notice it before, but there was a simple algorithm imbedded into every . . ."

"Just tell us what you found," Vic interrupted, gesturing to the laptop.

Danny frowned but abandoned his explanation. Clicking the keys he pulled up a satellite image of a small island surrounded by a sapphire blue sea.

"Welcome to Santo Fogo," he said, allowing the image to fill up the screen.

"Is this real time?" Sid asked as he leaned in for a look.

"More or less."

The island on the screen was C shaped. The northern top, or curve of the island, was bulky and made up the largest part of the islands land mass, like the letter C had a large growth on its hump. As the island curved out east, then south, and finally west, it tapered off to a point that eventually faded into the sea. A large bay filled up the center and the two points of the C were so close they almost touched, allowing only a small river of ocean water into the bay.

"What's that up there?" Victor asked, pointing to a grey mass of structures in the northern bulk of the island.

"Looks like some kind of building," Danny said as he zoomed in further.

With the closer resolution they could make out a stone wall that bordered the southern end of the structure. Behind the wall grew a rectangular building with wings on each side, connected by a thin hallway. The back of the building opened out into a courtyard that was bordered by another, thicker wall. The northern end had no wall. It was an open field that was guarded on the north by cliffs towering over the ocean below.

"Looks like our target, boys," Sid remarked as he perused the image.

"There's the plane," Gary pointed to the eastern edge of the island. A large cargo plane sat at the end of a long strip of exposed land.

"I guess we could land there if we needed to," Zach suggested.

"Yeah, why don't we call ahead and let them know we're coming," Vic shot back. "Maybe see if they can give us some help unloading our weapons before we attack their compound."

"Don't be ugly," Gary said, poking Victor.

"I guess not," Zach said sheepishly.

"What's that over there?" Tres spoke up for the first time, pointing to a circular, red roof standing off on its own. It overlooked the open field on the northern end.

"Looks like a tower, I guess," Danny said, zooming in further and scanning the area.

"What about in the open field?" Tres asked. "Is that exercise equipment?"

Danny moved over the wide, green space, focusing on the strange structures Tres had pointed out. As Malachi looked at them a sense of familiarity washed over him but he couldn't put his finger on what they were. One looked like two wooden triangles connected by a wooden beam. A green board stuck out from a platform. Next to it was a bordered area of sand. Next to that was a twisted metal contraption and a set of equally spaced bars.

"No, that's a training ground," Vic pointed out. "Some sort of army camp, I would guess."

Malachi could hear Sid sighing heavily behind him. The old man reached forward and placed a hand on Tres' shoulder. His expression was serious and full of dreadful portent.

"Mr. Bettis," he said. "I want you to try and remain calm."

Tres looked up at the old man, a worried expression blooming over his face. He shook his head, not comprehending what was being said. Malachi felt his own concern growing. It felt like that moment between the lightning and the thunder. The flash had already gone off. Now he was waiting for the sky to erupt.

"It's important that whatever we discover, we remain level headed about our mission," Sid continued.

Sudden realization dawned on Malachi as he looked down at the satellite image of the island. The structures in the field finally made sense. Sid was right. An explosion was coming.

"Crap in a hat," Danny cursed as he finally understood what he was looking at.

"That's a playground."

A quiet as thick as the grave fell over the cabin as each man understood what was being said. Tres rocked back on his heels as if he had just been punched in the face. His eyes grew to big circles and his mouth fell open. Soundless words tried to form.

"You . . ." he finally managed to spit out, leveling a gaze of anger and hatred at Sid. "You knew . . .you knew my boy was alive."

"Mr. Bettis . . ." Sid tried to answer.

Before anyone could intervene, Tres hurled himself at Sid. Grabbing the old man by the lapels of his jacket he slammed him against the plane's forward compartment. With gritted teeth he pushed his face inches from Sid's.

"You knew my boy was alive!" he screamed at him. "This whole time!"

"I suspected," Sid answered in a pained voice. He made no attempt to dislodge the hands that held him fast.

The other men jumped into action. Vic landed on one side and tried to pry the hands away that held the old man fast. Gary reached in and took hold of Tres' arms.

"Settle down, Tres," the big man instructed.

"I trusted you!" Tres yelled. Tears began to spill down his face. Weeks of pent-up grief and rage spilling over.

"I trusted you and you lied to me!"

"I did not lie," Sid answered.

"You knew he was alive!" Tres accused.

"I suspected, Mr. Bettis," Sid answered with more force. "Suspected. I didn't know. Not for sure. And I still don't know."

"What's that playground for, then?" Tres asked, shaking Sid by the lapels. "Huh? If not for kids, then who is it for?"

"Some children are alive for sure," Sid agreed. "But I don't know who. Did all survive? Just some? I don't know. We won't know until we get boots on the ground."

"You knew," Tres growled, but his conviction was dying. "Why didn't you tell me?"

"Yeah," Gary agreed. "I think this is something you could have shared with us all."

"Agreed," Danny said. His sentiment was echoed by the nodding heads of the other men.

"I couldn't tell you because of the way you're reacting now," Sid told them. "What would you have done if I did tell you? Huh? Would you have waited? Or would you have charged off half-cocked into heaven knows what mess down there?"

"We're going to that island, now," Tres demanded, shaking Sid for good measure. "I don't care what's down there. We're going now."

"We're going to land in Ponta Delgada," Sid told him with a voice that grew in authority. "From there we will plan our point of attack. That is the only chance we have of success. And if you want to be a part of this mission then I must be convinced of your willingness to abide by the plan. Otherwise, you will be left behind."

"Just try to stop me," Tres growled.

"I will stop you," Sid answered, leveling a gaze at Tresmond that emanated power.

Malachi felt it from where he watched. There was more to the old man that he had yet expected. Sid had been holding out on them. The authority was undeniable, perhaps even supernatural.

"Now, unhand me, Mr. Bettis," Sid commanded in that same tone of authority.

Surprisingly, Tres dropped the hold he had on Sid. He crumpled to the ground and began to weep. His body wracked with shuddering sobs.

"My boy!" he wept, gripping the sides of his head. "My boy! Oh, my boy!"

None of the men moved to try and comfort the grieving father. There was something sacred in his tears, and in the violence of his grief. It was something that should not be interfered with. It had to run its course, to be let out in the fullness of its agony.

"How long have you known?" Tres asked once the tears slowed down. He stood up and wiped his face.

"I still don't know for sure if your son is alive," Sid reiterated. "I only suspected it was a possibility."

"How long did you know?" he demanded again.

Sid sighed and straightened the lapels of his jacket.

"I suspected from the very beginning that the children were not dying of the disease," he told them. "It simply didn't make sense for the Fae to kill them. But this was just speculation. It wasn't until the funeral, when I talked with your wife, that I felt certain the children were still alive."

Tres' face contorted with fresh grief. He fell into a chair and dropped his head into his hands.

"She knew," he said in a broken voice. "Grace knew. This whole time, she knew. And I didn't believe her."

"Don't beat yourself up over it," Sid said as he stood over him.

"How could I not?" he asked in a broken voice. "If she knew, then I should have known. I'm his father."

"Exactly," Sid agreed as he sat across from Tres and took hold of his hand.

"You did not grow him in your body nor did you nurse him at your breast. These are things a mother does. They forge a connection between mother and child that a father simply does not possess. Sometimes, a mother knows these kinds of things because they can feel their children through that connection. It's not your fault, Mr. Bettis. You simply didn't have the same information she had."

"I should have believed her," he said, shaking his head.

"You believed what your mind told you was real," Sid assured him. "And those mother feelings aren't always right. Lots of mothers say that when they are just wishing their children are alive. Or they're feeling their spirits hovering near even when they are, in fact, dead and just haven't moved on yet. There's nothing at all wrong with believing what your eyes see and what your mind tells you is the truth. We're not meant to be totally credulous. But we must always keep our minds open to new possibilities. And to new wonders.

"You know now, Mr. Bettis. But I need you to keep that same wit about you. If your boy is still alive, we will get him back. We will do everything in our power and even lay down our lives if need be. But we will be smart and careful about it. Can I rely on you, Mr. Bettis?"

Tres looked up at Sid, his face, though wet with tears, was clear and determined. He wiped the tears from his face again and stuck out a hand. Sid took it and they shook solemnly.

"Let's go save my boy."

Chapter 27 - Recon

Giovanni waited until night. It wasn't that he didn't trust his gift. He knew his cloaking was complete, and had even deceived the powers of the Fae Sautorus, if only barely. It just felt like pushing his luck to walk around in broad daylight in the middle of dozens of hostiles.

The memory of those dark eyes searching for him had a lot to do with him hiding out as well. When Sautorus felt him in the plane, when he had searched him out, and that gaze settled on him - Giovanni shuddered at the memory. He hated to think what would have happened if he had been detected. There was no mercy in that face.

So, Giovanni waited in the truck he had smuggled himself aboard. He had squeezed himself among the servers as it was being loaded. Through the tarp covering the back he could peak out quick glances.

The truck bounced up a winding road through dense foliage. At one turn Giovanni could see the ocean, confirming his suspicions that they were close to the sea. Where this could possibly be Giovanni couldn't guess. The plane ride wasn't terribly long so he figured they couldn't be too far. The smell of the ocean was strong and the air was humid and thick. The best he could figure was an island somewhere in the Atlantic.

After a precipitous turn Giovanni peaked out to see grey walls looming over him. They reminded him of a castle. Built of grey stone, the wall was topped in a battlement watched over by armed guards. A steel gate slid open to let the truck through and they drove into a wide courtyard. The truck turned and parked against the walled end of the courtyard.

Once the truck was empty Giovanni dared a peak out. The sun still shone brightly in the wide area, and Giovanni made sure to stay in the shadows under the tarp. What he saw confirmed the first quick view he received on the way in.

The truck sat in a semi-circular courtyard. To his right the wall curved around, guarding what he took to be the south end of the complex. To his left was a larger building built of the same grey stone as the wall. Two steel doors guarded the building. He could see it was accessed by a panel to the right of the doors. Guards coming in and out punched in a code that caused the steel panels to slide open. It seemed to him a strange mix of medieval and science fiction, old school construction, almost nostalgic in its makeup, blended with a touch of modern technology.

Over where Giovanni hid in the trucks waited four others just like it. Parked in between the trucks were dark colored jeeps, outfitted with heavy caliber guns mounted on top. On the other side of the courtyard was a two-bay garage and a fuel depot. Two mechanics sat outside, lazily watching the guards and other servants hurry about the courtyard.

All of this was watched over by a single guardhouse. One armed guard stood watch here. At different times he opened up the sliding front gates, operated by a single button inside the small hut. Giovanni couldn't tell how the guard knew when to open the gate. The building was made almost entirely of glass, except for the bottom three feet and the metal roof. But he could see inside enough to tell there were no monitors inside.

Noticing this, Giovanni looked around the top of the courtyard walls. There were no signs of cameras or any other electronic monitoring devices. On a hunch he looked at his phone and could quickly tell there was nothing resembling internet access on the island. Wherever they were, they had definitely gone off the grid.

Though he desperately wanted to explore more, Giovanni waited to make his move. Just as the sun began to dip below the horizon, when the sky was lit with a cascade of colors, he saw his opportunity. The doors of the main building, the one that he had already begun to think of as the castle, slid open. Six guards, armed with automatic weapons stepped out into the courtyard. Their arrival was greeted with a stir among the waiting guards, and some greetings of relief. It was the changing of the guards.

"High alert," said one of the guards to the new shift.

"Seriously?" one of the new ones asked as he lit a cigarette and shook his head. He looked like he wanted to be on anything but high alert.

The first one shrugged. "Word from the boss man himself. Worried about something."

"Can't imagine what," the replacing guard said in a puff of smoke. "Hadn't seen shit out here in eighteen months."

"High alert," the first guard repeated, quickly losing patience with his replacement.

Giovanni slid from the truck as the new guards took their places and the old shift gathered in front of the castle door. He pulled his cloak tighter about himself and peered at the guard punching numbers into the access panel. 7745#. The doors slid open and the guards filed in with

Giovanni unseen among them. Slipping inside Giovanni found himself in a room that he immediately recognized as a checkpoint.

The space was wide and austere. Made of the same grey stone as the rest of the castle it held only an assortment of metal shelving on either sides of the door with spare weapons, Kevlar vests, tactical helmets and boxes of ammunition scattered among them. On the far side of the room two guards looked out from behind bullet proof glass. The muzzle of a machine gun protruded from a loophole below the observation window. Another sliding, steel door waited on the far side of the room. There was no access panel beside this door. If one wanted entry into the inner castle, it would have to be through the guards behind the glass.

After holding up their IDs to inspection, the guards behind the glass opened the entryway. Giovanni filed in behind the guards into a hallway. Another window of bullet proof glass waited in the hallway beyond the doors, another machine gun from a loophole beneath it stood ready and waiting.

From there the guards were able to access the doors with their own code. Giovanni followed as they turned to the right through another door into a wide room that looked like a training area. Some of the guards were involved in combat instruction while a few others were firing their weapons in an indoor range.

None of the guards he followed paused for these, but kept moving towards another doorway and long hall that led to the east wing of the castle. Passing through these doors the smell of food wafted through, making Giovanni's stomach rumble in hunger. He realized that he hadn't eaten for almost twenty-four hours. While the peril of his situation was able to abate his hunger for a while, he felt that nature would not be denied for much longer.

The guards he was following all took their seats at a long wooden table where others were already eating. Giovanni slipped into the kitchens beyond, and then into a connecting pantry. He didn't dare try to take some of the prepared food. Instead, he contented himself with the only food he could find that was readily available, a few apples and a bag of potato chips which he scarfed down in the dark pantry. Twice he had to stop while cooks came in for supplies. Thankfully, the pantry was big enough for Giovanni to stay safely out of the way.

Already feeling stronger for the food, Giovanni decided to undergo a thorough exploration of the castle. The floor above him, he quickly discovered, served as the barracks for the guards. Peering into the rooms he tried to get a count of how many armed guards there actually were. The rooms held rows of bunk beds, some made, others in disarray. Giovanni had no way of telling how many were used and gave up trying to assess that way.

In the floor above were more living quarters. These were small and barren, but obviously lived in. The people moving through these halls seemed to be the workers and servants. Mechanics, cooks, cleaning staff and yard maintenance were the majority. At the far end of the hall were rooms that looked suspiciously different.

It took a moment for Giovanni to figure out what these were. They were as small as the others, but lavishly decorated. Hanging lights or candles covered them in soft and warm lighting. The beds were a little larger and incense smoke wafted through. The walls were usually decorated in tapestries or hanging, multi-colored cloth. The women (and they were all women) who occupied them were all quite striking in their beauty, and each of them were dressed up as if they were about to go out on an eagerly anticipated date.

It wasn't until the first grinning soldier approached that Giovanni finally put the pieces together. The young, blonde woman smiled back and embraced him eagerly. Giovanni felt himself blush despite his invisibility to them. The woman was a prostitute.

Giovanni couldn't decide what he found more shocking, his own naivete or the fact that the couple didn't even bother to close the door. Feeling the heat continue to suffuse into his face he hurried from that hallway to explore the other parts of the castle.

All told it took Giovanni well into the night, but he felt he had a pretty good idea of what the castle held. Back in the main building, on the other side from the training grounds he found a set of labs that he quickly discovered was for work on the children housed here.

In fact, the first child he saw there was a boy, about eight years old sitting upright in a chair while a researcher in a white lab coat positioned a monitor in front of his eyes. Images flashed on the screen alternating from the pastoral to the macabre: a meadow, a blooming flower, raindrops on a green leaf; then a body being opened up for autopsy.

While these images flashed on the screen the researcher watched the child intently, taking notes. Sometimes he would move a flashlight before the boy's eyes, intent on something Giovanni could not discern.

The boy didn't seem to notice any of this. His stare was rigid and fixed. His eyes wide and unfocused. It was not the slack and inert stare that he had seen with Alicia. This had a sort of intensity to it but was not fully conscious either. It was like the boy was in the throes of a waking nightmare, oblivious to the world around him but seeing some awful visage invisible to the rest of the world.

Giovanni moved on from this, disturbed by whatever experiment was happening to the boy. He found the rest of the labs deserted. Their machines stood silent in the dark. One room looked like a surgical bay, and Giovanni shuddered to think what might go on there.

A stairwell in a corner room took him to the lower floors. Here he found the power and pump rooms. The buzz and hum of their activity made the whole floor vibrate, and the air seemed alive with unseen energy. He peered into these rooms but found nothing of interest. Still, he logged their location in his memory, believing it could be helpful later on.

Just before he mounted the stairs again Giovanni stopped and turned back. Something didn't seem right. He stood outside the power room, wondering what was off. A sticker with a lightning bolt boldly warned all intruders of the dangers of electric shock behind that door. He looked up the short hallways and back to the stairwell.

Suddenly, it became obvious. The hallway was too short. The two rooms on that floor, the electric room and the pump room were the same length, making this whole area too small. The main building was much larger, which meant there was more to this floor than these two rooms.

Making his way back upstairs, Giovanni crossed over the main hallway and back into the training room. This area was deserted now, with the smell of sweat and exertion still lingering in the air. On the far side he found another stairwell going down. This one ended in another sealed, steel door. Giovanni hesitated before the key pad, unaware of what might lie on the other side.

Just as he decided to leave this door alone, the steel panels hummed and separated. A guard with his gun shouldered stepped through and almost plowed into Giovanni. As quietly as he could Giovanni threw himself against the wall as the guard passed. The door hissed again, sliding closed. Giovanni had just enough time to realize he didn't want to go down there.

A dark hallway stretched past the door, with steel doors on each side.

The doors all had smaller panels in the center; the kind found in prisons, where the guards could access small openings to pass food and drink through. These were the dungeons. Or whatever passed for the prison here. The scent of fear and neglect wafted through the corridor as the doors hissed closed. Mixed with these aromas was the stench of unwashed human bodies and the dank mildew of forgotten and untended corridors.

That one glance told Giovanni all he wanted to know or see. He turned to hurry back upstairs before noticing the stairway continued down. What could be in the underbelly of this place made Giovanni hesitate, but curiosity eventually got the best of him.

The stairs wound down longer than Giovanni had anticipated. The grey, stone walls gave way to roughhewn rock. The light dimmed with only sporadic bulbs illuminating the narrow way. Even the smooth steps became rougher, as if they had been hastily carved out of the rock.

Heat began to emanate from some unknown source the further Giovanni went down. The corridor thinned out and the spiral of the staircase grew tighter and tighter, until Giovanni felt he was simply spinning in a circle. All the while the heat increased until it was stifling and the air grew thick, making it difficult to breathe. Sweat began to pour out of him while a dull, red glow began to suffuse through the old stairwell.

The stairs finally ended in a ragged archway that looked like it was made when some giant hand punched through the rock and left the opening unfinished. Giovanni had to duck when he stepped through and found himself on a landing that overlooked a vast cavern.

Looking out over the space the first thing he noticed was the roiling pool of magma in the center of the chamber. Bubbles of red, molten rock rippled over the surface, bursting in ruptures of flame. Heat waves shimmered in the air, making it almost unbearable in the stifling cavern. Giovanni shielded his face instinctively though it did nothing to mitigate the overpowering heat. Sweat continued to drench him.

As his eyes adjusted to the orange-red light he heard the sound of clanging nearby. Giovanni walked to the edge of the landing and saw figures moving about next to the pool of lava. He counted six or seven of them, mere silhouettes washed out by the shimmers of heat. A hand operated crane stretched out over the pool of lava. Near the pool. figures pounded away at molten shapes, sparks flying off the hammer blows.

Whoever they were, and how they could bear the heat was beyond him.

Curiosity beat out his discomfort and Giovanni took the rough steps down to the chamber below. Waves of heat pushed him back and with a grimace he plowed forward, trying to shield the heat with his hands. Sweat poured out of him in rivers, stinging his eyes and soaking his clothes so they stuck to him.

As soon as he got close enough for a better look, Giovanni recoiled in surprise. He stared as his hands dropped to his side, forgetting the heat for a moment. Never had he seen such curious and strange creatures in his life.

They were human-like creatures, but unlike any human he had ever heard of. Their skin was brownish-grey, wrapped around thin and wiry muscles. Their limbs were long and gangly, the hands ending in pointed and stretched out fingers. Their heads were completely bald and a heavily browed face was dominated by long and hooked noses. The only clothes they wore were leather jerkins that covered their chests inn front, and tied around their waists and hung down like a kilt to the calves. None of them wore anything on their feet.

Giovanni was fascinated and frightened all at the same time. As he approached closer, he saw some of them pounding away on the anvils. Long, molten-hot blades of steel or some other metal lay upon the anvils, held by one the strange creatures. Another pounded at them with large hammers, flattening the blade further, sending up sparks with each blow. A pile of these long, flat pieces cooled next to the blacksmiths. They had been hammered so thin they reminded Giovanni of feathers.

One of the blacksmiths finished with his work and his assistant added it to the pile, then hurried to the crane by the pool of lava. The blacksmith looked up and fixed his hooded eyes on Giovanni.

"What is it you want, son of man?" the thing asked in a gravelly voice.

Giovanni stopped in his tracks, stunned and panicked. "You can see me?" he asked.

"Gillen has eyes, doesn't he?" the creature asked in return.

With horror Giovanni realized in all the heat and bewilderment he had let his cloak fall away. He cursed himself for lack of concentration, but could do nothing about it now. None of the other creatures seemed to notice or care that he was there

"Who are you?" Giovanni asked.

"I am Gillen" the creature answered, his stare growing hostile. "He is one of the master's gnomes."

Giovanni nodded as if this were perfectly reasonable, to be talking to a gnome in the bowels of the earth next to a bubbling pool of lava.

"Are you going to report that you saw me?" Giovanni asked. He felt hostility from the gnome, but it seemed to be defensive.

Gillen waved away the suggestion. "Gillen is the master's blacksmith, not his guard.

"What is it you want?" the creature asked again.

Giovanni struggled for words. The gnome obviously didn't have any mean intentions, but wanted to know all the same the reason for Giovanni being there.

"I am just curious," he said. "I wonder . . . what is ii you're building."

"These are for the master," the gnome replied.

Giovanni didn't need to hear who the master was, but the felt he had to ask anyway.

"Who is the master?"

"Sautorus, the right hand of the Deceiver."

For a second the chamber grew cold. Hearing Sautorus' title sent a chill through Giovanni, even making the sweat pouring out of him feel like ice water on his skin.

"What is this for?" Giovanni asked, nodding to the pile of blade like creations.

"These are for the tower," Gillen answered.

"What tower?"

"It is for the tower of Shinar."

Giovanni had no idea what the gnome meant by that cryptic saying. Something tugged at his memory, something he felt he should know. But for the life of him he couldn't pull it out of the depths of his mind.

The other gnome returned to the anvil with a glowing hot bar of steel, held by a thick pair of tongs. The thin muscles of the creature strained but held the bar and placed it on the anvil. Gillen turned away from Giovanni and began his work again.

A new chorus of ringing steel echoed through the chamber. Gillen pounded rhythmically on the molten steel. Whatever interest he had in Giovanni was gone.

Looking around the chamber one last time, Giovanni noticed a pair of tunnels carved into the far wall. He stepped over to Gillen and pointed them out.

"Do you know where those go?" he asked.

Gillen looked up from his work, clearly annoyed. "The one on the right goes to Gillen's home," he said. "You are not welcome there."

"And the other?"

"You can't smell it?" Gillen asked. "It goes to the ocean. And there is a staircase there."

Giovanni nodded then pointed to the left tunnel. "Will you let me go down that tunnel to the ocean?"

"What does Gillen care where you go?" he answered, turning back to the anvil and his work.

Seeing that he had gotten all out of Gillen that he could, and that any more inquiries would annoy the gnome even more, Giovanni stepped across the cavern. He hesitated at the mouth of the tunnel. A cool breeze invited him further, and true to Gillen's words, he could smell the salt of the ocean.

He looked back across the pool of lava. The gnomes had fallen to their work again without the slightest concern for Giovanni and what he did. Satisfied, he turned into the dark tunnel.

Only a few feet in and Giovanni had to turn on his phone light. He had wanted desperately to conserve the battery, but the pitch blackness of the tunnel left him no choice. There was no way he could fumble through this total dark.

The tunnel looked like a natural formation, something carved out by a river, or more likely volcanic activity. The rounded walls and ceilings were made of a rippled brown stone. Stalactites dropped down at odd and inconvenient places. At one turn Giovanni had to squeeze between two of these natural pillars that had grown up next to each other.

Water trickled down the walls, making the stone slick. The slant of the passageway, tilting slightly down, made a natural stream of this water, and it ran down the center of the tunnel.

Thankfully, there were no forks or turn offs, and the tunnel was not long. Giovanni felt that he had gone maybe a hundred yards when the ocean breeze became unmistakable, and the crash of waves fell gratefully on his ears. Dim light ahead indicated that the end was in sight.

The little stream at the bottom of the tunnel spilled out onto a rocky coast. Giovanni stepped out and felt a spray of salt water hit him as waves crashed against the rocks. A full moon had just begun to rise, and in the blue light he could see among the rocks, worn smooth by the ocean tides, a path that wound to his left. The path steered out towards the ocean and ended at a thin strip of beach that pointed out into the ocean like a finger.

It would be the perfect place to land, Giovanni thought to himself. Whatever the Swordsmen were planning, this would be the ideal spot to launch an attack. They could land on that little spit of beach and come up through the tunnels. If he found where the children were, it might even be possible to sneak them out without anyone knowing. Of course, they had no way of knowing about the tunnel and Giovanni had no way of getting that information to them.

Frustrated, he turned to head back down the tunnel. Something caught his eyes in the moonlight that caused him to stop. It looked like something was carved into the cliff. He stepped closer and could see it clearly—a staircase chiseled out of the cliff side.

The steps were narrow and slick, coated in green algae and water from the incoming tide. Giovanni took a few tentative steps bracing himself on the outcropping rocks, then found better footing as the steps dried off a few feet up. They continued up in steep ascent.

As the cliffs rose up the staircase plunged into another dark tunnel. Giovanni flicked on his light again and worried about his fading battery life. But this trip proved not much longer than the first, though his legs burned by the time he reached the top. It ended at a wooden trapdoor. It pushed open easily when he put his shoulder into it. The hum of machinery filled the air as he stepped up into a concrete closet.

Giovanni carefully eased the door back down behind him. The little room he found himself in had nothing in it except the trapdoor. Another door with a frosted panel letting in a dull, yellow light proved the only other exit. Giovanni made sure to cloak himself again before easing this open.

The hum of machinery grew louder as Giovanni carefully pushed the door open. Inside the yellow light he saw green pipes and tanks snaking around each other indicating another pump room. A rusted hand rail covered the perimeter of an open pool in the middle of the machinery.

Next to the pumps he found a room full of pipes connected to dials with valves beneath them. Figuring it must be some sort of control room for the pumps he continued out and up another staircase. The hum of the machinery grew distant and faint as he climbed these stairs which opened up into a dark and quiet hallway.

As soon as he stepped out into the hall Giovanni could tell this was some sort of living area. The passageway was dark but had a lived-in feel to it. Quietly making his way down the linoleum floors he found a vast kitchen attached a dining space. He made special note of the small chairs and the tables about half normal height.

The other end of the hall ended in a playroom. Small tables were set up among play stations: a tiny, plastic kitchen, boxes of toys, a corner with small book cases and reading mats.

Giovanni had found the children's space. It was a dormitory. And he knew that if he followed the staircase in the playroom, he would find the sleeping children.

He pulled the cloak heavier about him and crept up the stairs. The silence in the dormitory was almost deafening, and he felt his quiet footfalls were like gunshots in the still night. The linoleum under his feet creaked more than once, and Giovanni half expected guards to come running out with guns at the ready.

But there were no alerts or alarms. Giovanni made it to the top of the stairs and it ended in another hallway. Two main doors exited off this hall and each of these pushed open without resistance.

Giovanni held his breath as he peaked in. Inside was quiet and still. Rows upon rows of bunk beds filled the room, leaving only a narrow, open space in the middle. Each bed held the body of a sleeping child.

Though he tried to count from the doorway, he couldn't be sure if he was near right or not. But according to his quick assessment there were close to eighty children in the compound. That would account for every child that died because of Sleeping Sickness, and perhaps even a few more that they didn't know about.

Easing back into the hallway Giovanni let out the breath he had been holding. It took a moment to understand what he had just seen. Even though he had seen Alicia, who was declared dead, up and breathing again, he still reeled from the shock. Every child declared dead from the Sleeping Sickness was still alive. It was all a lie. Every bit of it.

Giovanni slid to the floor, his head in his hands. His breath came in shallow, ragged gasps. He tried to shake it off, to tell himself that he had known all along, that this is exactly what Sid told him was going on, but something wouldn't listen. It was one thing to know these things, another altogether to see them with your own eyes.

Everything is a lie, Giovanni thought. With this one thought he realized the true source of his shock. It wasn't the plot that had him rattled, or even the discovery of the children. What had him shaken to his core was the realization that his entire life, that everything he thought he knew about the world and their existence, was a lie. It was as if he had been living in another place and time, and was just now realizing it.

"God help me," he whispered, feeling the ground beneath him start to crumble away. It was all a lie. All of it.

"Can I have some water?" a little voice asked him.

Giovanni jumped at the sound, panic shocking him out of his self-absorbed thoughts. He looked up to see a boy, no more than six years old, dressed in blue pajamas about two sizes too big for him. For a moment he thought he had let his cloaking down for the second time that night. But he could still feel the sensation of the thick air around him.

"Can you see me?" he asked the boy as he took to his feet again.

As soon as the words were out of his mouth, he realized how stupid they were. Of course, the boy could see him. What he really wanted to know was how.

"Yes," the boy answered with flat affect.

"Can I have some water?" he repeated. "I'm thirsty."

"Yeah, sure," Giovanni answered.

He leaned in to take a better look at the boy. His blond hair was ruffled from sleep. Blue eyes stared out blankly, like he was under the geas of hypnotism or some enchanter's spell. His features were still and emotionless. Giovanni waved his hand in front of the boy's eyes, but got no better response.

"Can I have some water?" the boy asked again. "I'm thirsty."

"Of course," Giovanni answered. "I guess . . . wait here."

"Okay," the boy agreed without emotion.

Giovanni padded down the stairs to the kitchen. Filling a glass of water, he brought it back up to the waiting boy. He had not moved from his spot, standing a silent and loyal vigil.

After handing the boy the water Giovanni watched him drink it down without pause and hand the glass back. He turned to go but Giovanni reached out to stop him.

"Hey wait a minute," he whispered, leaning in again. "My name's Giovanni. Um . . . what's . . . what's your name?"

"I am Drusus," he said without hesitation.

Then, he made a gesture with his head, the first genuine Giovanni saw from him. He turned it to the side as if he were thinking, or remembering.

"No," he said, a little bit louder. "My name is . . ."

The words trailed off and the boy shook his head. He began again and squeezed his eyes together.

"My name is," he repeated without finishing the sentence. "My name is . . . my name is . . . my name is . . ."

Giovanni had to resist the urge to finish it for him with, "the real Slim Shady." For some reason, that idea came into his head in Victor's voice. Any humor he felt at that idea was immediately smothered when he saw tears pooling in the boy's eyes.

"My name is . . . my name is . . . my name is . . ." he continued, bobbing his head up and down.

"Shhh, it's okay," Giovanni tried to soothe.

The boy was having none of it. His head bobbed with greater violence and he balled up his hands in two fists, pumping at the air.

"My name is . . . my name is . . ." he said, getting louder with each unfinished sentence. Tears began to flow down his face."

"You got to be quiet," Giovanni warned, trying to take hold of the child.

"My name is . . . my name is . . . my name is . . . MY NAME IS! MY NAME IS! MY NAME IS!"

The boy was yelling out his refrain. That lone voice, now reaching a fevered pitch, echoed and bounded in the quiet hallway.

"MY NAME IS! MY NAME IS! MY NAME IS! MY NAME IS!"

In full panic Giovanni cloaked himself and backed away from the boy. Just as he began to back down the stairs the doors to both dormitories opened and female, adult figures came shuffling out into the hall. Giovanni ducked down the stairs and quietly hoped whoever was in charge of these kids would assume he had some sort of breakdown.

Making sure his cloaking was tight about him again; Giovanni stole from the building and out in to the night air. He hurried as he looked around, eager to put as much space between himself and the dorm as possible.

He walked across a wide yard that was bordered by walls on three sides. Only a small fence protected the field from the cliffs below. Off to his right he recognized a variety of playground equipment. Swings, slides, monkey bars, a sandbox, waited in the hours of night for the children to return again and bring them to life.

On the far side of the field a stone staircase ran up the wall. Giovanni took these to the top, and only then did he turn around to see what might be happening behind him. The dormitory was still and dark. Not even a single light came on to indicate that something was amiss there. Thankful he had escaped that one, he turned to get his bearings.

For the moment Giovanni was standing on top of the wall. It was twenty feet thick and ran the perimeter of the large field containing the playground and the dormitory. From his vantage point he could see the whole field plus walk to any spot around the wall.

Walking to the other side he found that it opened into a courtyard. Stairs on this side led to some sort of garden. A fountain stood in the center of flowers and small shrubs. The manicured lawn and flower beds were divided by a stone walkway into four equal quadrants.

Giovanni looked at the doorway on the far end of the courtyard. It led into the main part of the castle, and together with the cliff stairway he found were the only ways to access the field and dormitory where the children were. Two ways in, he thought to himself. One of them hidden and the other one easily defensible.

Feeling it didn't bode well for any rescue missions he went back to the other side of the wall to look over the field. Scanning for any other point of entry he spied a small, postern door on the west end of the wall. Excited now, he hurried back down to the field and through this small entryway.

The narrow hallway he found himself in was cold and dark, lit only by single bulbs spaced almost too far apart to illuminate the passageway. A musty smell lingered in the cold air, and there was something unsettling Giovanni felt as he passed through. It was like the residue of something evil that had come before him and he could still feel the lingering there. Pulling the cloak tighter about himself he hurried down the dimly lit hallway.

After a few turns that Giovanni surmised took him west, the tunnel ended in another small door. Pressing his ear to the door he could hear nothing on the other side. With a slow turn of the handle, he eased the door open.

His caution turned out to be unnecessary. The door opened into a dark and quiet room. It looked to be some kind of foyer or waiting room. Antique sofas were arranged around the walls with coffee tables in front. On some of the tables stood toys that looked decidedly out of place in the otherwise formal room. Giovanni found something odd and disturbing about all of this, but couldn't quite put his finger on what exactly made him uneasy about it.

Listening at the next door he stepped through and into a large and formal dining room. A chandelier hung from the ceiling over a long table covered in white table clothes. China and crystal decorated each place setting in front of ornately carved chairs. By the abundance of silver that was set around each plate Giovanni assumed it was prepared for a long and multi-coursed dinner. He counted at least thirty places around the table.

For now, the room was dark and looked to be unused for some time. There was a stillness in the air that had not been disturbed for several days. The lack of dust told him it was at least cleaned regularly. But much about the place felt to still be new, like a toy that had not been played with yet.

Beyond the dining room Giovanni found the kitchens and another stocked pantry. Since these were empty and dark as well, he took advantage and stocked himself with food. He even considered firing up the ovens and cooking something for himself but thought this much too risky.

Beside the kitchen he found a game room. Like the waiting room he had been in earlier, this one also was equipped with toys as well as two billiard tables, dart boards and a shuffle board table. A smaller billiard table, one obviously kid-sized, stood off in a corner next to a small bowling lane. A bar stocked with every known imaginable type of spirit glistened on the far end of the room.

That same sense of wrongness struck Giovanni as he looked at the game room. There were distractions for every age, which should seem a good thing, but in this context distinctly bothered him. There was something about them, together here like they were, that felt off somehow.

Storing away these incomplete thoughts he took stock of the rest of the rooms. Upstairs he found two hallways filled with formal bedrooms. Like the dining and game room these were furnished opulently with a flair towards the antique. Four poster beds draped in veils stood among dark stained furniture. The bathrooms had claw foot tubs on ornately tiled floors. Each room opened up onto a balcony that looked out over the ocean. Finally getting his bearings from the view they offered Giovanni surmised he was in the west wing of the castle complex.

Like the dining room, Giovanni had the feeling that the bedrooms were unused or had yet to be used. There was a new smell about it, like a car that has yet to be driven off the lot. Also, like the other rooms he felt there was something off or stained about them, even though they had yet to be occupied.

Giovanni looked around one of the last he had entered on the third floor. It had a light blue color theme which touched the wallpaper, bathroom tiles, towels, even the profusion of pillows on the king-sized bed. Almost everything except the dark stain of the wood, the marble tops of the tables and the Persian rugs was the color of a summer sky. He turned to open one of the mahogany wardrobes when he finally put it all together.

Next to the wardrobe was another, just like it. Same wood, same design, same dark stain. The only difference was this one was smaller, child sized. It was a perfect replica of the large wardrobe but one that was obviously made for a smaller person. Made for a child.

Giovanni stepped back in horror as his mind finally made the connection. This room was designed for adults and children to stay in together. The kid games in the game room and the foyer, the tunnel that connected this wing with the playground, the little wardrobes; they were all designed for one purpose. Maybe the whole island was designed for this same purpose—to supply children to pedophiles.

Is this what this whole plot is about, Giovanni asked himself in horror. The disease? The faking of their deaths? Their transport here? Was this nothing more than to satisfy the sick and twisted sexual appetites of child molesters?

He stepped back and felt himself fall down on a stool next to the bed. Dimly, he connected this too. The little steps on the stool, made that way so smaller legs could climb up on the big bed. He jumped up from the stool, feeling tainted by its touch. He turned around, aghast, seeing nothing but the horror, feeling nothing but the evil of the place.

Giovanni stumbled from the room, needing to breathe cleaner, fresher air. The walls of that place began to close in on him. The heavy weight of their evil intent filled his lungs with putrescence that clung to him like oil.

It wasn't just evil, it was sick, he heard himself say. It was a sickness, a dread disease. For one of the first times in his life he saw with clear eyes, unfiltered by any propaganda or lies, that scourge of all humanity called sin.

We are lost he moaned as he stumbled back into the tunnel. His cloak had fallen away but he didn't care at that moment. The gun in his waistband called out to him, begged to be used. He wanted to be seen so he could empty a clip into the first person he saw, to cleanse this evil place of its taint.

Lost, he moaned as he stumbled on. We are lost.

Chapter 28 - Making a Plan

Tres paced the third floor of the rented villa. Full of coiled and anxious energy he stepped out through the arched pillars and onto the balcony. Malachi could see him through the sheer white curtain that fluttered in the breeze. He tried not to watch him, tried to ignore the harried pacing. But the more anxious Tresmond grew the more anxious Malachi became.

Tres hunched over the rail. Beyond the balcony the ocean reflected the colors of the setting sun and welcomed in the clean scents of the ocean. Malachi could see that Tresmond neither enjoyed nor even noticed these things. And he couldn't blame his friend at all for that. He had just learned his son was alive. He was alive and achingly close. At the same time, he was impossibly far away.

The door of the third floor opened and Sid stepped inside, his cane tapping on the tiled floor. Tres jumped from his watch and hurried to face him. His face was etched in the lingering question he was desperate to hear answered. The other Swordsmen gathered in, hearing Sid's return.

"We won't be able to move on the island until tomorrow night," he told them.

Tres threw up his hands in frustration. Malachi could feel the anger burst from him like an explosion of heat.

"Tomorrow night?" Tres cried out. "No! Why not now?! Tonight!"

"Our transportation won't be ready until tomorrow morning," Sid informed them.

"Then we leave in the morning," Tres demanded.

"We will need the cover of night if this operation is going to be successful," Sid countered.

Tres threw up his hands again and walked out onto the balcony. Two seconds later he stormed back in.

"Use your connections," he demanded. "Get another boat."

A heavy sigh came from the Keeper as he shook his head. "You may not know this Mr. Bettis, but renting a mega-yacht is not something that can be done in an hour. Our transport will be ready tomorrow morning. And that is with my connections. And a whole lot of money I might add."

"I will pay you whatever you need," Tres promised, leaning on the back of a sofa and staring down Sid. "Why do we need a yacht anyway? It's not like this is a pleasure cruise."

"There could be over seventy children on that island," Sid answered. "We need a vehicle that can safely get all of them away. Plus, we need to carry a substantial amount of equipment to be ready for anything. Not to mention we need some kind of cover while we're here. Not like we can go asking for military grade vessels here in the Azores where they are very few. We also need a reliable tender to get ashore, not to mention the technology and equipment for reliable recon and information. And finally, yachts are the most available big boats around here. This was the best and fastest I could do. Any other questions Mr. Bettis?"

With a groan Tres dropped onto the sofa and let his head fall in his hands. Despite the nervous energy that he emanated, Malachi could not help but feel sympathy for his friend. And by the looks of the other men gathered there they felt the same. Every one of them, to a man, was imagining how he would feel in that same situation. And every one of them knew he would move heaven and earth to get his kids back safely.

"What am I supposed to do until then?" Tres asked in desperation.

"We plan," Sid answered.

With a nod to Danny, he stepped back and took a seat beside Tres. Danny flipped on the TV mounted on the wall and keyed up his laptop. An image of the island popped up on the screen.

"This is the image of Santo Fogo provided by our good friends in the American government," he said of the C shaped island.

"From the satellite images it looks like there are four possible landing sites," he continued. "Sid tells me the vehicle we have secured comes with a Novurania LX 600 tender. This little boat should accommodate all of us and our equipment and get us to shore. The only question is where. Because of the rocky terrain and the cliffs on the island there are not many places where we can get to the island and access the interior.

"Like I said, we have four possible beaches. The first and most obvious is the one in the bay. This would be the easiest to get to. Unfortunately, there is a guard tower and station just inside the line of trees on the beach. It would be near impossible not to get noticed and announce our presence if we tried that."

"Let's put that at the bottom of the list," Vic suggested.

"Copy that," Danny agreed. "I think the same goes with this beach on the northeast section. It's only about a hundred yards from the airstrip, also home to guard station and tower."

"Next," Gary echoed.

"That leaves us with only two options," Danny said, zooming in on the north section of the island. The image showed a small area of sand that stretched out like a finger into the ocean.

"This one may be the best strategically," Danny told them. "The children seem to be held in the north section of the compound. We can see them moving around the open field here and I assume they live in this building in the northeast corner. A few guards monitor the top of the wall, but it is relatively accessible."

"This looks ideal to me," Victor spoke up. "We can quickly secure the kids and only engage the guards when they counter. Gives us a great place to set up defensive positions while we get away."

"What's the drawback?" Gary asked.

"As usual, you have read my mind," Danny said, moving the image to the area around the beach. "Doesn't seem to be any access from the beach to the rest of the island. This is a relatively unguarded area for a reason. The whole north end of the island is cliff except for this spit of beach. If we want to get up to the compound we got to climb."

"And if we want to get the kids out then we would have to find another way to leave," Malachi pointed out.

"Exactly," Danny agreed. "Which leaves us with this last place here on the south end of the island."

Danny moved the image again. Where the C shape of the island curved on the bottom he zoomed in on another stretch of white sand.

"The south end has a beach as well. No guard towers and there are a few options for getting to the interior of the island. This end isn't covered in cliffs, but does have some mountainous terrain to get through. There is a pass to the east but it opens out close to the guard station on the bay. But if we cross the mountains, we would still have to get around the bay, which means walking right by this guard station and tower."

"May as well drive right into the bay," Zach suggested.

"Negative," Vic said. "Driving into the bay they see us coming. If we land on the south end, we have a chance to take them out by surprise. Better if they don't see us coming."

"What kind of security is on the south end?" Gary asked.

"Good question again," Danny said with a thumbs up. "There is a light patrolling of the area."

The screened darkened and the image of the island faded to a dark green mass. On the south end was a blob that rippled in red and yellow.

"Here is an infrared image of the island at night. You see here a guard on the beach we want to target on a fairly regular basis. From what I can tell this is part of a pretty consistent patrol. The guard will leave the station on the bay, and crosses through a pass in the mountain and then arrives at the beach. Most of the time he looks around for a few minutes then returns back to the station. Once he returns it appears another guard exits the station and goes on the same route. This is pretty much day or night. The round trip takes about an hour. Thirty minutes one way."

"So, if we time it right, we could have an hour of open beach to land and get moving," Vic said.

"Not really," Danny cautioned. "The yacht's tender is going to make a good bit of noise. We probably want to wait for the guard to be through the pass until make our move. And we want the boat back on the yacht and the yacht itself out of sight by the time the next guard gets in sight of the ocean."

"That leaves us about thirty minutes, then," Vic corrected himself.

"That's what I would say. If we want to be on the safe side. We probably want to keep the yacht two miles off coast with the lights out until the guard reaches the pass."

"I guess we're landing on the south beach," Gary said.

"Looks like."

"Wait a minute," Malachi said stepping forward. He pointed to the large bay in the center of the island. "We still have to traverse this area here. Somehow get past the guard house and the watch tower."

"I think we're going to have to take those out," Vic said.

"Take them out?" Malachi asked.

Vic made his finger into a gun and imitated shooting at the screen.

"You don't think that's a little early to be letting our presence known to the island?" he asked. "That looks like a castle we're trying to attack. As soon as they know we're coming they will lock that place down pretty tight. Our chances of getting in will be almost zero."

"What choice do we have?" Gary asked. "We can try to sneak by the guard house, I guess."

"Too great a chance at being seen," Vic argued. "That beach is wide open."

"What about the jungle behind it?" Zach asked. "We could ambush the guard at the pass then try to go through all that thick cover behind the guard house. That would work, wouldn't it?"

Malachi shook his head. "We don't know how dense that area is."

"Mostly mountain, too," Danny pointed out.

"Plus, if we take out the guard that only gives us an hour to get into the compound before he's due back in. If a guard doesn't come back, I'm sure that will set off some kind of alarm."

"What do you suggest, then?" Vic asked. "I think our best shot is trying to take out that guard house with as much secrecy as possible."

"Gunshots aren't very secret," Danny said, barking out a laugh.

"I can silence my rifle. Take at least a few of them out."

"What about the rest?"

Vic made a slicing motion across his neck. "Close combat."

"Only takes one to set off an alarm," Malachi said.

"So, what do you suggest?" Gary asked again. "This is the best chance we've got."

Malachi looked at the screen. He could certainly see the point the others were making. With limited options they would have to engage the guards on the beach. At the same time, he knew that would be a risky maneuver, almost certain to alert the people in the compound they were trying to get into.

Still, he couldn't shake the idea that there was some other way to get in. He looked at the other beaches, the north and northeast ones, and they didn't feel right at all. Their landing point made sense, but not how they would get into the compound.

Though he couldn't tell why, he kept coming back to the bay. It was a wide-open space, but it was unguarded and lead straight to the compound. At the end of the bay, they would have to traverse some rocky terrain, but it was passable.

Of course, the bay was also covered in water. There was no way they could get across it unless they swam. And who knows how long that would take. Plus, their equipment would get soaked and they could still get spotted by the guards in the tower.

Malachi shook his head. He knew the bay was a stupid idea. Even though he felt it call out to him, drawing him irresistibly. It wasn't an audible voice, but nearly so. Cross the bay, it said. That is your way in.

Malachi opened his mouth to just air the idea, see what the others thought. Good sense came in just in time and he let the matter drop. Vic would have a field day with him.

"I guess not," Malachi shrugged. Despite the call of the idea within him he couldn't bring himself to voice something so ridiculous.

"What about you, Tres?" Victor asked, turning to the one who had the most stake in the mission.

Tres, usually a quiet person on the best of days, had withdrawn into silence as soon as he found out they wouldn't be leaving that day. His legs shook with nervous energy and he threw up his hands in resignation.

"I can't focus enough to think of anything right now," he said. "I don't care how we do it. Ya'll come up with a plan and I'll make it work."

"Okay then," Danny said, zooming in on the guard house and tower just off the beach in the bay. "How do we want to handle the . . . ?"

"What were you going to say?" Sid interrupted. He looked intently at Malachi, his blue eyes boring into him.

The ridiculous idea of the bay called out again, stronger this time. It jumped inside of him, hammering at the confines of his mind.

"It's nothing," he said, waving the suggestion away.

"No," Sid insisted. "You had an idea in your mind. What is it?"

"It's stupid," Malachi said. "Forget it. It wouldn't work."

Even as he dismissed the idea, he felt it stir in him with greater urgency. He could even feel a flutter inside of himself, an eagerness to tell it. It reminded him of those Christmas mornings, siting at the top of his stairs waiting for his parents to let him down and see what Santa had left. It was almost an irresistible energy. He felt the same energy now.

"I can tell you want to let it out," Sid smiled as he read Malachi's feelings out loud. "It may be more important than you think."

"Fine," Malachi said, buckling under the pressure. "This is stupid. I know it is, but . . . Well, I was thinking, or rather, had the thought . . . that we should go across the bay. There it is. I know we can't get across the bay, so let's move on."

Silence greeted the proposal as the men absorbed the idea. Vic nodded, though Malachi could tell he was biting back a few witty comebacks.

"Like swim?" Gary asked.

"I don't know," Malachi answered. "That's why I didn't want to say anything."

"What about those submersibles?" Zach asked. "You know, like in James Bond. Kind of like a handheld submarine motor."

"Do those even exist?" Vic asked.

"Doesn't matter," Danny interjected. "Bay's too shallow for something like that."

"Could we zipline across?" Gary asked.

"How would we even get the zipline across the bay?"

"Yeah, and I think they would see a bunch of guys ziplining over the bay."

"Look, I appreciate you trying to make this work," Malachi said. "But it won't work. Our best option will be to take out the guards on the beach."

"I will get you across the bay," Sid said. He announced it with a sense of finality.

"How?" Malachi asked. "How are you going to get us across the bay?"

"You let me worry about that," he said. He tapped his cane to the ground and stood up to walk over to the screen. "You get us on that beach and across to the south end of the bay."

Sid pointed with his cane to the side of the bay across from where the compound stood.

"Get us there and I will make sure you get across the bay undetected. Figure out what we do to get into the compound. We leave tomorrow afternoon."

He banged his cane on the floor again. It sounded like a gavel coming down.

Meeting adjourned.

The next afternoon, around four o'clock, a sleek yacht pulled out of the harbor in Ponta Delgada. It stood out among the smaller boats and even the larger pleasure craft of the rich vacationers from all over the world. Some looked at the craft and wondered who was the lucky man who owned it.

As soon as the yacht passed out the harbor and into the open sea, the tourists and gawkers forgot all about it. Just one more of the ultra-rich who made the world their playground. There would be others like it tomorrow, then probably the next day. It passed through their lives distant and unattainable, an object of envy to be wished at from afar.

Chapter 29 - Landfall

Twilight was falling as the yacht neared an island that was on no map or chart available to the public. The boat slowed down three miles from the island. Its motors silenced and it bobbed in the current, waiting for full dark to close in.

Inside, the group of men looked out of place amid the opulent dressings of the pleasure craft. Donned in black battle dress they stood out against the beige couches and plush, carpeted floors. A chandelier lit the space against the twilight sky, but the bright light was swallowed up by dark tactical gear.

The men dressed in silence, donning boots and gloves along with the black battle dress. Sid had offered them any armor that they wanted and some of the men took advantage of it. Danny and Malachi chose the vests with ceramic body armor while Victor, Zachary and Gary opted for Kevlar. Tres refused all of them, wanting to maintain every bit of agility and speed he could.

"We can dodge bullets," he reminded them.

"Not from automatic weapon fire," Danny pointed out.

Tres shrugged. "That little plate won't do much if we get hit that hard. Besides, I'd rather have the speed."

Sid did insist that each of the men don a protective sleeve on the forearms. This had a plate inserted within to withstand most blunt and bladed attacks.

"Every knight must carry a shield," he smiled and said.

The weapons were the same they had chosen when first given arms training. Each man was equipped with a rifle and pistol of choice along with ample reserve clips. Grenades and flashbangs were the only explosives they thought they had the weight to carry. Besides this, Sid gave each man a knife.

"You are all called Swordsmen," he told them. "But the modern warrior no longer carries a sword into battle. So, I will give you the next best thing."

He presented each of them with a fixed blade knife in leather sheath. Twelve inches of bright steel grew out of the wooden hilt. Letters in an undecipherable language were carved out over the length of the blade. Vic whistled as he spun the knife around, admiring its perfect balance.

"The finest blacksmiths you have never heard of forged these for you," Sid told them as they looked over their new weapons. Each man could tell there was something special about the knives, something more than personal.

"What are these carvings here?" Zach asked.

"Words in a long-dead language," Sid told them. "They imbue the blades with special properties."

"Magic?" Zach asked with suspicion.

Sid shook his head. "Not magic, just some durability and sharpness. Nothing too far out of the ordinary."

Satisfied with this explanation Zach nodded his head and sheathed the weapon. Fully equipped they stood before Sid who reviewed them like a general before battle. Of all the men, he was the only one that seemed to fit in the richly decorated yacht. As usual, he wore a suit. But in awareness of the task at hand, this one was all black, even the shirt and tie. The shoes he wore, though they looked formal, were equipped with comfortable and durable soles. A black hood came out of the formal jacket, something to keep his white hair from standing out against the night.

"In a moment we are going to move within view of the island," he began. "So, I'd like to address you before we have to kill the lights."

Pausing for a moment Sid looked down and gripped the silver knob of his cane. He seemed lost in some memory, or some old regret. He even looked to Malachi like he might change his mind about the mission completely. Overcoming whatever conflict raged inside of him, he nodded to himself and looked at the men.

"As you have come to learn, our enemy is a group of beings that are not human. But when we make our move against this compound you will likely see very few of them there. Maybe only one. I'm hoping none, but I doubt we will be that lucky."

"Who's in this compound then?" Tres asked.

"What we will confront are the human allies of the Fae," Sid told them. "These are the ones that carry out and execute the plans. The dark Fae are rarely hands on involved. Most of the grunt work is below them anyway."

"Kind of like Rip and those guys in the S and M outfits?" Vic asked.

Sid smiled and shook his head. "No, most of them are not like the warlocks or shadow men, though I have no doubt that we will confront both tonight. Most of the people on the island, will be regular people. They have skills the Fae can use and are willing to work on whatever plot that has been cooked up."

"Do they even know the extent of what is going on?" Danny asked.

"On some level they do not," Sid answered. "We have captured several high-ranking Family members and put them to extensive questioning before, and it is clear they don't know everything. But they know enough. They know they are traitors to the entire human race. And believe me, most of them have enjoyed every moment of it."

"Why are you telling us all this now?" Malachi spoke up. "How does this pertain to the mission at hand?

Sid smiled and pointed at Malachi. "Always on point," he said. "For one, you need to know what you will be up against. Mostly human servants and soldiers. Rip will probably be there with his shadow men. There may be a Fae, most likely one named Sautorus. He is a particularly powerful and ruthless son of a bitch, but he will be my problem. Most of your weapons will be ineffective against him anyway.

"But mainly, what I need to know from you, is whether or not you will be able to do what will be required of you."

"Meaning kill," Vic finished for him.

"Yes, Mr. Dodds, that is what I mean. I need to know, and know now; when the time comes and the necessity arises, which it most surely will, can you pull the trigger?"

"Yes," Tres stated flatly and without hesitation. The confidence and coolness with which he spoke sent a chill through Malachi.

Vic shrugged. "It's war. Don't like it but it's what it is."

Gary and Zach both nodded but with less confidence as Victor and Tres. Sid turned his gaze to Malachi and Danny.

"Is there no other way?" Danny asked. "I'd really hate to take someone else's life. Especially if there is a chance for redemption."

"There may be a chance for redemption, but not tonight," Sid explained.

Danny thought for a moment, obviously struggling within himself.

"I guess if we want to save the kids then we may have to . . . kill some people."

Sid nodded and turned his gaze to Malachi. The very thought of what he was proposing made Malachi sick to his stomach. He had never taken a human life before and hoped that he could go his entire life without having to.

But today he was faced with a situation that made straddling the fence impossible. Dozens of children had been taken for some nefarious purpose, and the people who held them would not give them up without a fight. There was no higher institution to appeal to or authority who could bring these guys down. It was up to them to get the job done. And to do it he would likely have to get his hands dirty.

"I don't like it," Malachi said. "But I can do what's necessary."

"The day you like it," Vic looked at him and said with gravity. "Is the day you lose your soul."

For a moment a window was open to Victor's soul, and he exposed a part of himself that was usually covered with the nonstop jokes. Malachi could see a deep pain there, a regret that cut to his soul. Malachi had known about his time in the military, the fights he had been involved in during tours in Iraq and Afghanistan. But he had never seen the toll it took on the man.

He could see it now. It was a burden that Vic carried with him all the time. He could even see that the humor and joking was in large part a way to keep that darkness at bay.

"Alright then," Sid continued, seeing the men were all on board. "Now with that out of the way I can finish telling you about what you will be facing there.

"As I've said you will have human soldiers as well as the shadow men to contend with. The warlock, Rip, will probably lead them as before. He will use the shadow that he cast the last time we fought and I will counter with the white fire. Sautorus will also likely make an appearance, but only when Rip has failed."

"That's nice of them," Vic chuckled. "To come at you one at a time."

"It has nothing to do with fairness. The Fae hate getting involved. It's a part of their nature. They are afraid of white fire and are vulnerable to blessings and bindings. You will only see Sautorus if he has to reveal himself or the odds have turned so much in his favor that victory is a guarantee."

"I take it all back then," Vic added.

"Other than that, the only other enemy you will likely see today is one of the Anakim."

"Anakim?" Danny asked, recognizing the name. "Isn't that a giant?"

"It is," Sid answered with a nod. "The Anakim are the last of the giants. And Sautorus is known to employ them."

"How giant we talking about here?" Malachi asked.

"Big, very big," Sid answered. He looked over at Gary.

"Bigger than Mr. Walsh here. I would say by about one and half times."

"Since when did I become the unit of measurement?" Gary lifted his hands and asked.

"You didn't know you were an official unit?" Vic joked. "It's in the handbook of Standard Weights and Measures."

"One Gary," Danny chimed in. "Is exactly six foot five and two hundred and eighty pounds."

"Two seventy-five," Gary shot back.

"Is one European Gary the same size as an American Gary?" Vic continued.

"What about a metric Gary?"

"OK, enough about our new standard of measure," Sid quieted them down. "The Anakim is serious business. Like I said, he's big. Close to eight feet tall and four hundred pounds of pure muscle. And don't let the size deceive you. He's also fast."

"Faster than a bullet?" Vic asked.

"Maybe not that fast, but it doesn't matter. The giants have thick skins and powerfully dense bones that make most guns ineffective against them. There are a few places where bladed weapons can get through but these are not easy to connect with. Under the armpits, at the neck where it meets the shoulder, inside the thighs, either side of the Achilles heel and the two hollows where the leg meets the torso. Pierce these places and you can draw blood. Not necessarily kill, but wound."

"So how do we kill them?" Gary asked.

Sid tapped at his forehead. "If you were to strike them hard enough on the forehead between the eyes then they will be killed."

"I like it," Danny said with admiration. "Very Biblical, makes sense."

"One between the eyes," Vic remarked. "No problem."

"It may not be as easy as you think," Sid warned them. "Whatever weaknesses you are aware of Sautorus is also aware of. Just be careful when you engage him. The giants are strong and fast and not easily hurt.

"Any other questions?"

When none were forthcoming, he asked the men to gather around him.

"This is a dangerous mission," he warned. "All of you have shown

336

incredible courage by coming this far. Be careful. Let your gifts lead you and trust in the abilities God has given you. Believe in Him. Bow your heads now."

The men joined hands as they lowered their heads. Sid walked around the circle and laid hands on each one of them as he prayed.

"Blessed and eternal Father, I thank you for each one of these men. I pray you fill them with a heart of courage today. Give them steady hands and hearts. May their aim be true and their souls be pure before you. Grant them your protection and peace, and may each one of them return from this mission today unharmed and unscathed. Grant us success this day, and go with us in the power of your Holy Spirit. We ask this in Jesus' name, Amen."

"Amen!"

"We will be moving into position in just a few moments. We will have to turn off the lights as we near. I recommend that as soon as we kill the lights all of you take a moment and make confession in your private prayers. It will be your last opportunity until we return."

The men nodded their consent and took their seats again. Malachi found a place apart from the others, on a cushioned seat against one of the wide windows looking out into the ocean. Only Tres didn't sit. He continued to prowl about the room like a caged animal. Pent up energy threatened to break out of him with every step. He seemed on the verge of explosion, and if they didn't start soon Malachi worried that would be exactly what happened.

After sitting down Malachi found his thoughts did not stay long with Tres. He heard the engine start up again and the boat lurched forward. Soon the lights would be shut off and they would begin. There would be no turning back.

What have I got myself into, Malachi asked himself. The moment threatened to fall down upon him with fatal force. He, Malachi Green, the mild-mannered business manager of a cardiac center was about to invade an unknown island guarded by sinister forces. He was about to go in with guns blazing, possibly kill or be killed, when most of his life experience with conflict consisted of women fighting over who would set the thermostat in the office.

He felt someone sit down beside him and looked up to notice Sid Bickley settle in on the seat. The older man held the cane in his hands and looked straight ahead, but Malachi could tell his attention was on him.

"You feel ok about the mission?" Sid asked.

Malachi nodded but didn't say anything. What could he say? If he weren't ready now then there was little he could do at this point. They were about to ride into chaos and he was sitting shotgun.

"Because I am feeling a heavy sense of dread coming from you," Sid pointed out. "Just want to make sure you feel ok."

"I'm supposed to feel ok about this?" Malachi asked back. "I always thought this was a situation one would rather avoid."

"True," Sid nodded. "But when the time comes, I would like you to have some confidence that you can succeed. To feel good about it in that way."

Once again Sid had hit to the center of his anxiety. In truth, Malachi didn't feel confident at all. Even with the abilities he had gotten from the night in the crypt, he felt it wasn't near enough to stand against what they had coming.

"I think we got a good team," Malachi said. "I believe in these guys. They're my brothers for real."

When Sid nodded Malachi felt he knew exactly what he meant. He knew that Sid didn't just hear what he said, but what was left unsaid.

"There's something I want you to have," the Keeper said.

Reaching beside him he held out an antique sword. It was still in the scabbard and the age was shown clearly over its features. Rust had decayed a few places and it was worn all over. Still, it looked well cared for and Sid handed it to him with reverence.

"What is this?" Malachi asked as it was placed in his lap.

"It's a sword," Sid answered glibly.

"I know that," Malachi chuckled as he picked up the weapon. It was heavier than it looked and also felt more durable than its old and worn features suggested.

"You are the Swordsmen," Sid continued. "I felt it only natural that you should carry a sword into battle."

"This doesn't look like it could do much," Malachi noted.

He pulled the sword from its sheath and noticed how it still rang out, as if it were a new blade hungry for action. But this sword was anything but new. The edges were bitten and chipped away. Cracks spider-webbed out in several places. When he inspected the blade where it was still intact, he could tell it held a decent edge. Still, he knew it would shatter into a thousand pieces if he were to hit anything with it at all.

"Don't judge by appearances," Sid warned. "This weapon has served swordsmen for a long time now. It has seen many battles and has cut down many a foe. Legend has it that it has even slain down a dragon or two."

"And you want me to take this with me?" Malachi asked. If he were honest, he would rather not be burdened down with another piece of equipment.

"For good fortune," Sid told him.

Malachi looked down at the sword and felt it was an honor greater than he was aware. Just knowing that it was carried into battle by countless legendary warriors, and that he was holding it, felt a privilege to Malachi. The things this weapon had seen and done. It would be a marvel to hear them all. He knew he should feel honored, but at that moment all he felt was terribly inadequate.

"Is this about your gift?" Sid asked, cutting right into the heart of the matter.

"You mean my lack of one," Malachi corrected.

"Don't be so certain Mr. Green. Some gifts are slow to come, but others are slow to be noticed."

"What is that supposed to mean?" Malachi asked.

"Look at your other swordsmen," he said, gesturing with the silver knob of his cane. "They have all showed a special talent, a gift that is helpful for combat. All except for Mr. Taylor. His gift is with computers, and probably extends to all machines. It's a different kind of gift, but a necessary one."

"But that is a gift," Malachi pointed out. "So far, I've got nothing."

"Yes, but would we have known about Mr. Taylor's gift if a situation hadn't arisen that required that particular gift?" Sid asked him. "Had you not been in that crisis it is doubtful Mr. Taylor would know about this gift at all. And then we would have a lot less information about our target than we do. So that kind of works out in our favor."

"I get it. I just haven't been in the right situation yet," Malachi said, replacing the sword in its sheath. "But in the meantime, what do I have to offer my brothers in the fight we have ahead of us? What? I'm a dead weight, Sid. Maybe not that bad because I can fight, thanks to that night we spent in the crypts. But if I don't have my place, my talent to offer, then maybe I don't belong."

There, it was out, Malachi thought. He wanted to weep at the admission. Not sure if it was from shame or relief, he couldn't tell. There was both in him at that moment. Long ago voices, from his uncle to that asshole in college, from the dozens of others that had been able to convince him he didn't really belong, all clamored to have their say in his head right then. And they all said the same thing: you're an imposter, you don't belong.

"Do you know why I chose to give you the sword?" Sid asked him. There was that tone of command again in Sid's voice. The one he had heard in the plane that talked down Tres.

Malachi shrugged. "Because I've got nothing else to offer?" he suggested, letting his insecurity go on full display.

"Wallowing in self-pity is not worthy of any Christian man, least of all one that God has chosen as a swordsmen," Sid chided.

"No, Mr. Green, I didn't give you that sword because I felt sorry for you or because you had nothing else to offer. I gave you that sword because you are the leader of these men. Whether you know it or not, or even like it. These men look up to you. It was you who called them and gathered them together. It was you who held them together and kept them together. And it took an incredible and necessary gift to be able to do that."

Malachi recalled all the emails and texts he had sent out to the group. It was a running gag among the men that if you joined the group then you would get inundated with communications from Malachi. Despite the jokes he knew that it was necessary to keep them together. You had to stay in touch, keep communication open. It wasn't easy and it wore him out sometimes, but he knew it was needed to keep the group together.

"Persistent electronic communication?" Malachi asked, not entirely serious.

"No, faith Malachi," Sid answered, his voice stern and serious. "It takes faith."

"All these guys have faith," Malachi said, trying to dismiss the idea. In truth, what Sid said made him uncomfortable for reasons he couldn't begin to guess.

"True, they all have faith," Sid agreed. "But that's not the same thing as the gift of faith. And I can see that in you."

"Is that going to help us win today?" Malachi asked, regretting the words as soon as they left his mouth. Not only were they self-deprecatory, they were borderline blasphemous.

"I think you know better," Sid told him. "It's a spiritual gift, faith. And one that is the most powerful of all the spiritual gifts. Remember what our Lord said, it is faith that makes all things possible."

Malachi nodded but said nothing. He didn't trust his own mouth at that moment. Knowing Sid was right but still unwilling to accept the truth of it, he stayed silent instead.

"It has a name, you know," Sid nodded at the sword and said.

"What is it?" Malachi asked as he held up the bitten and chipped blade. He tried to imagine what the sword looked like in the fullness of its glory.

"It is called Faithful," Sid answered. There was something that nagged at Malachi's memory when he spoke the name. Something he thought he should remember.

"Fitting, I think. There used to be a compliment to the sword as well," Sid continued. "It was part of a pair. The other sword was named True. It's been lost for a very long time now. That's a whole story in itself. But there was a legend that circulated among the swordsmen about the two blades. It was said that when the two swords were united again, then that would be the sign . . ."

Before Sid could finish the cabin went dark. It was the signal they all knew. They were coming in sight of the island.

A calm came over Malachi as soon as the lights went out. There was no time for reflection or rumination, or even doubt. It was time for action. Whatever inadequacies he may or may not have, it didn't matter now. There was a job to be done, and by the grace of God Malachi planned to get it done and see that every single one of his men made it home safe.

Malachi slipped the sword over his shoulder, adjusting the leather strap as best he could to make it ft beside the rifle that was slung there too. He could tell already that carrying the sword with him into this operation would be inconvenient at best. At the same time, he took reassurance knowing it was there.

"Men, believe in your gift." Sid announced as the engine died down. "Trust in your gift, and trust in your brother who fights at your side. More importantly, trust in the one who gave them both to you."

The men nodded silently. They made the final preparations and adjustments to their equipment. They checked rifles and secured side pieces. The time had come.

"The Lord is my strength and my shield," Malachi intoned, feeling the moment called for it.

"Whom shall I fear," the men answered back.
"The Lord is the stronghold of my life."
"Of whom shall I be afraid."

Chapter 30 - Crossing the Bay

As soon as Danny gave the signal, indicating that the guard had finished his patrol of the southern end of the island, the six Swordsmen, Sid Bickley, and the ever-present Gerard entered the yacht's tender. The boat was small for all the men and all their gear, but they managed to board silently and efficiently. Gerard manned the steering as the boat splashed down off the back rollers and bobbed in the ocean current. The motors rumbled to life as he steered them around and pointed towards the island.

Malachi felt himself pulled back as the engine gunned to full power and the tender shot forward. They sliced through the night, bobbing on the waves. Salt spray splashed on his face with each bounce of the boat.

Sooner than he wanted the dark shape appeared that Malachi knew was Santo Fogo, The Saint of Fire. At first it appeared as a darker spot on the horizon. As they sped closer it rose out of the water to take on ominous form, like a shadow looming over them. He couldn't tell if it was his imagination or some level of spiritual perception, but as the island grew taller before them, the dark, mountainous mass blotting out the sky, Malachi could feel the presence of oppressive evil growing stronger. The island wanted to swallow them whole, to devour them soul and body, and leave no trace that they had ever existed at all, except in the fading memories of the people who knew them.

These thoughts turned his mind inevitably to his wife. What would they tell Clara if he didn't return? He had told her business had called him away on a last-minute emergency. She trusted him, had no reason to doubt at all. That trust only made him feel all the more guilty.

But what if none of them returned, he thought. If they all died here, what would happen then? When he never came back home Clara would inquire at work about him and find out he never went on a business trip after all? What would she think then? That he ran away with some other woman? Would she look for him? Wonder the rest of her life what happened to him? The mere thought filled him with an ache in his heart.

Malachi shook these thoughts away. He couldn't afford to dwell on those things right now. Not only did he need focus, his brothers needed it from him as well. And whatever weakness he perceived in himself, he would not allow distraction to be one of them.

The boat didn't slow as it neared the shore. Malachi could make out the trees and the contours of the foliage ahead. They had only a few feet of beach until the jungle took over.

The tender hit the beach with a lurch but managed to ride up onto the sand. Tres leapt out of the bow, rifle at the ready. Vic and Gary filed out next, flanking the point man and scanning the area with their rifles.

Malachi leapt out of the boat, still amazed at how his new body felt. Just a few weeks ago he would have crept out and had to be careful of his knees when he swung over. But ever since he had risen out of the cemetery pool, he was a new man. Bounding out of boats onto the shore was an easy task, easier, in fact, that it ever had been.

"Clear," he heard Vic announce over the radio.

"Clear."

"Clear."

Sid was the last out of the boat. Malachi turned to watch him struggle through the sand and wondered if it wasn't a terrible idea to bring him along. But he was the one who would get them across the bay. Or at least he promised he would. Besides this, the Keeper had insisted that one of his kind always went into battle with the swordsmen. There were enemies, he insisted, that the usual weapons of war could not fight.

As soon as Sid was out of the boat Zach pushed the tender back into the water. Gerard, still at the wheel turned it around and zoomed back out into open water. It took all of thirty seconds and the beach was quiet again. This was it, Malachi thought. No way to turn back now.

The men quickly made their way to the cover of the trees. In their planning stages they agreed this route would give them the bast chance to get to the compound undetected. But they also knew it would take one person firing one shot to blow their cover and ruin the element of surprise.

The ground turned steep almost as soon as the trees began. Sweat beaded all over Malachi as they made their way through the jungle. The laurisilva forests towered all around him. As they climbed higher the trees gave way to more ferns and mossy overgrowth over bulging rocks. His breath grew deep and rapid, but the exertion brought him strength rather than tired him out.

To his surprise, Sid was more than able to keep up with the other men. As they plowed through the foliage and the sharp incline of ground, the Keeper used his cane to dig into the soft ground and pull himself through.

Even in the places where they had to almost climb on their hands and knees the older man did not lag behind far. Malachi had to marvel at his stamina and strength and wondered at what deep power kept him vital at such an advanced age.

"I couldn't have done that two weeks ago," Gary said through panting breaths when they reached the top.

The climb had taken them to the top of a ridge that ran the whole southern length of Santo Fogo. From their vantage point they could see almost the entire island laid out before them. Directly in front of them the land descended sharply to the bay. On their left the two pieces of land came close together to form the thin strait that allowed access to the ocean. On their right they could see the beach and the guard tower that guarded the entrance. Beyond that the lights of the landing strip shone out of the dark foliage.

Directly across the bay they could see their target for the first time with their own eyes. From the water the ground rose up sharply, higher than the vantage point they enjoyed at the moment, and ended at the imposing walls of the compound. A steel gate was the only access they knew. Atop the stone walls they could make out dim, shadowy figures of the patrolling guards. They were close, and each of the men could feel the place pulling them, drawing them closer, as if it were their destiny to breach that fortress.

But between them and their fate lay an expanse of water that to Malachi looked uncrossable.

"You're going to get us across that?" Vic asked, sharing Malachi's skepticism.

"I am," Sid answered, undeterred by the imposing waters of the bay. His breath was more labored and ragged than the other men by far.

"You know I didn't pack my bathing suit," Vic said, still unconvinced.

"Let's get down to the water," Sid instructed, not even bothering to try and convince the others.

The climb down was much easier, and the men swiftly made their way through the undergrowth to the edge of the bay. As they stepped out of the shadows of the trees Malachi had to skid to a stop. The land ended suddenly in a steep drop that fell into the water's edge. Loose pebbles and dirt kicked out from underneath his boots and splashed down into the bay below them.

Malachi looked over the edge into the water below as it lapped the rocky side. It was only a drop of about four feet, but there was no way to tell how deep the water was below them.

"End of the line," Vic remarked. Malachi could tell there was a growing impatience in his voice, unlike the usually cheerful man.

"What's the easiest way down the water?" Sid asked, looking out over the bay.

Vic snorted. "Just take another step and you'll be there."

"Do I detect a trace of doubt in you, Mr. Dodds?" Sid asked with a touch of amusement. There was even a smile on his face.

"More than a trace," Vic answered, gesturing to the water. "Unless you want us to pull a Peter on you here and walk on water, we're not getting across."

"Oh, you of little of faith," Sid answered. "Mr. Dodds, find me an easier path down to the water."

Vic threw his hands up in frustration, but turned to walk parallel to the edge in search of an easier landing. A few of the men followed him while others took the other direction. Within a few minutes they found a favorable spot.

The men gathered at a place where the drop off was less severe. One big step could take them to the water. A grouping of volcanic rocks even provided a step to the edge of the bay.

Sid looked around, surveying the spot they had chosen. The bay was relatively still. A few waves bobbed in the dark night and lapped against the rocks. To their right they could see the guard tower on the beach peeking out over the trees. Lights moved in the ground below and made its way to the south. Another guard was making his rounds to the other end of the island.

"I guess this will have to do," he said.

Arranging a spot on the edge of the drop-off the Keeper sat down and folded his legs. He took a deep breath and rested his hands on his knees. His cane was laid across his lap.

With his black hood pulled up over his head Malachi couldn't help but think of a wizard. Dressed all in black, blending in to the night around him with his head covered gave the appearance of a cloaked figure working arcane powers in the shadows. Malachi shuddered, sensing some unseen chill passing through him.

"Are you about to work some magic here?" Zach asked. Even with his changed attitude he couldn't help but take an instinctive step away from the meditative figure of the Keeper.

"Not magic," Sid answered. "I am calling forth a spiritual gift. Very biblical."

Silence for a moment. Then, "You do know about spiritual gifts, don't you?"

"I've heard of them," Zach answered, still suspicious.

"Some theologians believe the spiritual gifts have ceased," Danny pointed out. "That they were just there for the apostles and the founding of the Church."

"Funny, the Bible never mentions the ceasing of the spiritual gifts," Sid answered. "In fact, it says 'I will pour out my spirit on all flesh.' That doesn't sound like God has any intention of stopping those gifts."

Danny didn't have an answer. He gave a shrug that Sid could not see.

"Utterance of wisdom, utterance of knowledge, faith," Tres surprised everyone by speaking up. "Healing, miracles, prophecy, discernment of spirits, speaking in tongues and interpretation of tongues."

"Yes," Sid agreed, his voice sounded distant, distracted, as if his thoughts were a million miles away from them. "The nine gifts of the spirit. Actually, there are seven true gifts as some of those go together. But they can manifest in such unique ways that you could even say there are hundreds.

"But yes, those are the gifts I speak of. The Keepers, as appointed as we are, have been given a portion of all of these gifts, yet there is only one of them in which we excel. They are used to defend the people of God and advance the great work of the Kingdom."

"Speaking in tongues has always seemed like a pretty pointless gift to me," Vic said with a shrug. "Have you ever heard people doing it? It's crazy. It's like they've lost their mind."

"Would you think it's pointless if you had the ability to understand or speak in any language at all?" His voice was sounding drowsy now, trailing off into sleep.

"That doesn't sound so bad," Vic agreed.

"Or to understand the language of plants and animals and even the wind?"

"Ok, that is pretty cool. If you could do that."

"That is the gift of tongues," Sid told them. His body swayed beneath an unfelt breeze.

"So, what about you?" Malachi heard himself ask. His own voice sounded far away, separated even from himself by a great distance.

A smile creased Sid' lips.

"Miracles."

The Keeper threw his head back, staring wide to the night sky. His eyes had rolled up into his head, showing only the whites. His mouth dropped open as he exhaled a hissing breath.

As he watched there was a part of Malachi that told himself he should be alarmed, that something dreadful and haunting was about to happen. Zach felt it too, stepping back further and throwing out a hand out as if to ward off whatever power Sid was summoning.

It passed through them like a ripple in the fabric of reality. Radiating from Sid it stirred the air, the earth, the light, existence itself. A wind, Malachi thought. Some divine wind has moved among us.

Whatever it was it froze him to his spot in a feeling much like fear, but deeper than any fear he had ever felt before in his life. At the same time, he wasn't afraid for his life, or concerned that he would be harmed. This was a different kind of fear, for it was terrifying and wonderful all at the same time. It made him want to fall down on his face and jump up all at once, to scream out from the top of his lungs and to remain mute forever, to weep with every grief of the world and to laugh in inexpressible joy. And this was just a breath stirring the world around them, the barest touch of the divine hand.

While this happened Malachi could feel his own mind slipping into a dreamlike state. His conscious mind pulled back, further into the recesses of his mind. He saw and heard everything that went on around him, but it was distant, far away, like he was watching it happen to someone else.

As he felt himself being drawn inward, he looked out over the bay and saw wisps of smoke rising from the water. Tendrils of mist snaked out over the surface, gathering and thickening. All over the bay it was happening, covering the water in a shroud.

From out over the open ocean a thick fog started to roll in. Dense and grey it billowed towards the bay, cascading over the rippling water. Malachi watched it tumble over the tendrils of fog that had risen up until the entire bay was obscured in a thick, white cloud.

All sense of time departed with the strange sensation that fell over the men. Malachi watched all this happen with detachment. He knew it should interest him, should be of vast importance to what they were doing, but at that moment he couldn't exactly say why. He watched with a drowsy smile on his face and let the mellow joy wash over him like the fog that was washing over the bay.

"It is time," he heard a voice call to him.

He knew it as Sid's voice though there was something different about it. This didn't matter to him at all. What mattered was the call and that he would answer.

The entire bay was shrouded in fog. Where they stood only stray wisps reached up and grabbed at their feet, but over the water it looked thick enough to walk upon. Across the bay they could still see the compound looming up ahead, and the lights from the guard tower to their right dispersed through the fog in blinding coronas of light.

"Follow me," the voice said.

Malachi watched Sid get up and step towards the shrouded bay. He followed at his heels and heard the other men fall in line behind him.

"Be careful to walk only where I walk," they were instructed. "Beware the voices you will hear inside the mist. Pay them no regard and heed nothing they say. They cannot harm you as long as you follow me"

As they stepped down to the water a part of Malachi screamed out a warning. They were about to plunge into the bay. Another part of himself, the dream part of his mind that had taken over, felt this to be the most natural thing in the world.

Walking fully into the mist that waking part of his mind trembled with fear. At every step it braced for the shock of cold water that never came. This can't be happening, the voice said to him. You're going to plunge right through. But with every step he found secure footing.

The mist that swirled around was cold to the touch. It sent chills through Malachi's body and at the same time a cold sweat broke out over his flesh. It felt more substantial than regular fog, composed of something other than cloud and vapor.

Ahead he could see Sid's figure guiding them through. He hoped the men behind him followed as well but couldn't afford a single second to look behind and check. It was only the barest outline of a body he could make out, and it took every bit of his concentration just to keep the figure in focus.

"Malachi," he heard a familiar voice call out to him from the mist. "Malachi, why did you leave us?"

It was voice of his wife, trapped somewhere out in the dense fog.

"Malachi," it called out again, wailing in a pain that hurt to hear. "You lied to me, Malachi and left me all alone. These men came and took us away. Malachi, help us. Hellllp usssss."

"Ignore the voices," he heard Sid warn, his voice echoing through the fog. "They are voices of deceit."

"Malachi, hellllp ussss," the voice of his wife continued to wail.

"I'm sorry, Mom," he heard Zach wail behind him.

"Ignore them!" Sid commanded, harsher this time.

Zach burst into weeping. He tried to muffle the sounds but the sobs broke through and bounded off the water. Malachi couldn't help but feel sorry for the man. Whatever claws she had gotten into him as a young man must have been deep, and they were still attached to him without relent.

"Malachiiiii," his own ghosts continued to wail.

"It's just Zach's mom," he said, too quiet for anyone else to hear.

He knew the idea was ridiculous. The voices in the mist were no more Zach's mother than they were his wife. It was an idea his dreaming mind came up with and it made perfect sense right then. He wasn't going to listen to those voices because it was just Zach's mother out there calling to him, deceiving him, trying to get her claws into Malachi and the rest of them just as she had with her son.

Just as he convinced himself of this the voices faded and he was walking through a silent mist again. Sid turned and Malachi followed, just before the fog was able to close over him and obscure him completely. He walked like this for what felt like days, or maybe even months. Time lost all sense and orientation. It seemed like they wandered back over ground they had already walked before sometimes. Other times they walked in circles, or turning back one way then another.

All through the strange journey Malachi remained detached, in a dreamlike state. He observed everything his body did from a distance, as if he were the observer and not the actor. Grey mist passed over him and he only dimly felt the cool and humid touch. His body moved by automatic command. All the urgency of their quest became as muted as his consciousness, a problem from another life, to be dealt with by other people in another time.

Then, it was all over. Malachi saw Sid step up in front of him, then his own feet felt a rising stone beneath him and he was lifted up. Another step up then he felt Sid's strong hands over his own pulling him out of the mist.

Malachi looked up and the night was clear around him. Above him the ground rose up sharply, with the slope covered in the growth of native trees. Beyond that, he could see the top of the compound walls rising up against the night sky.

As Sid helped the rest of the men onto the shore Malachi saw them all shake the disorientation from their minds. Like him, they had been walking in a stupor across the fog and mist. Like him, they were finding themselves awake at last.

"What was that?" Danny asked as he looked out over the bay. Already the fog was beginning to dissipate.

"Some things are better left unexplained," Sid answered with an amused look. "Wouldn't you agree Mr. Taylor?"

Danny opened his mouth as if to respond, then simply nodded in response. It was something that would have been impossible for him to do only two weeks ago. But he was always a fast learner. In this new world they lived in, there was much you had to simply accept. Perhaps that was the way the world had always been, but man had gotten so talented in reducing it to just those elements they could control, to those questions they could answer, for the sole purpose of being able to turn away from the unexplained, to ignore the unexplainable.

"However it happened, we're here," Gary pointed out, already moving on from the uncanny experience on the bay. "Let's get on with the job."

The group made their way through the growth under the shadow of the trees. The large ferns stirred as they climbed steadily up the steep ascent. The quiet of the night complete except for the brief sounds of their passage.

Vic called a halt when the trees broke into a thin clearing. Malachi looked and saw packed sand under his feet. The clearing twisted off in both directions.

"This is the service road," Vic whispered to them. "It leads right up to the front gate. If we read the satellite images right there should be a ridge at ten o'clock, about a hundred and fifty yards away. That's our first attack point."

The men nodded and started to follow Victor up the road. He stopped and whirled back around.

"Remember," he whispered. "The ridge has an unobstructed view of the top of the compound wall. We will get a clear view of the guards but that means they will have a clear view of us."

After this brief warning he turned and hurried down the dirt road. At the bend, where the round curved up and around, Vic plunged into the forest again. The other men followed, grateful to have the cover of the trees above.

The ground turned rocky as soon as they left the road. Tall trees gave way to shorter, twisted trunks and the ferns replaced with native and wide branching bushes. The moon had yet to rise, so only the light from the stars illuminated their trek. Even this felt exposed to Malachi as they climbed towards the ridge.

The group passed through a short clearing before the cover grew thick again. The ground rose up sharply, even to the point where Malachi had to use his hands to leverage himself up. As soon as he was over that rise the ground opened up and he found himself on a ridge overlooking the land below.

"This is it," Victor said in a whisper.

Malachi surveyed the open ridge where they would act out the first phase of their attack. It was higher than the ground around it and offered a good vantage point. It was mostly flat and free of any trees or foliage, granting an open view to the compound. At the same time the openness of the ridge exposed them.

"There it is," he heard Danny whisper beside him.

Malachi looked across the ravine to the looming compound that was their target. The ridge, though high, was still lower than the grounds the compound was built on. The walls rose up dark and imposing. From where he looked, he could see shadowy figures on top of the wall keeping watch.

"Stay back in cover," Vic warned.

Some of them had wandered out onto the ridge to get a better look. Malachi slipped back into the shadow of the trees and reminded himself that if he could see them, then they could see him.

"Alright, Tres, it's time for you . . ." Victor began, but stopped abruptly.

A figure had wandered onto the ridge. The rise had blocked out the noise until he appeared, pulling his way up to the open ground. Malachi couldn't make out much about him but could see the shadowy figure lean down and wipe dust from his knees. He straightened up, exposing the rifle that was slung over his shoulders.

The men froze inside the tree line. Still in the shadows they remained unseen. But that wouldn't last long.

Malachi's mind raced as he watched the guard lazily survey the ground around him, as if he were a tourist enjoying the nice view. He reached for the 9mm at his side but didn't dare draw it. They were in a terribly precarious situation. The wrong move would expose their location and alert the whole compound. The report of a gun, a scream, the sight of a scuffle on the ridge by the compound guards; any of these things would ruin their element of surprise.

The guard wandered over to the tree line where the men hid, still unaware of their presence. Malachi pulled in a breath and held it, his heart pounding in his ears. The guard turned towards the trees and looked up, stopping dead in his tracks as he looked up into Victor's face.

His eyes widened; the whites visible in the dark of night as he rocked back. A still moment of indecision fell over them. The guard, shocked to see men on the ridge was frozen in surprise. The Swordsmen, unsure of what to do, stayed rooted and stilled in their spot.

The moment drew out for what felt like an eternity. The guard, sensing his danger, pulled at the rifle slung over his back. His mouth opened as he drew in breath for a cry of warning.

Gary was the one to act. With speed that belied his great size he took one step into the clearing. A large hand flew up to the guard's mouth and with the other jerked him out of the clearing.

By the time Gary had pulled the guard into the shadows he had gotten him wrapped up. With one hand over his mouth, he held him fast with the other. The guard kicked and flailed, struggling vainly against Gary's strength. Still, Gary seemed to struggle to hold onto him.

"A little help," he whispered harshly.

The men had all stepped back and watched the fight unfold. Indecision gripped each of them. Like Malachi, most had never been in a situation like this before and were unsure of how to react. His mind raced in a thousand different directions, screaming at him to do something, but not able to figure out what.

The guard's hand went to his side. In the dim light Malachi could make out the fingers closing over a sidearm. His mind screamed out an alarm even as his feet stayed rooted in the ground.

It was Tres who made the move first. Just as the guard was pulling out his pistol Tres leapt over the short distance separating them. In a flash of movement, he whipped out the knife at his side. Metal gleamed in the briefest of seconds, then the blade was plunged into the throat of the struggling guard.

"What the hell?" Gary exclaimed, dropping the guard as Tres pulled out his blade.

The guard struggled for a moment, silently clutching at his throat before going still. Reality hit Malachi like a wave of ice-cold water. This man was dead. Tres had killed him.

"What did you do?" he heard someone exclaim.

Danny turned and retched as he held onto the trunk of a tree. The other men stared in stunned disbelief. They couldn't make out any features of the dead guard but that did not shield them from the reality of what had happened. A man was dead, and at their hand.

Malachi could feel a sick feeling washing over him. His legs wobbled and his head went light. He reached out to steady himself against one of the nearby trees until the moment passed.

"I'm sorry," Sid told them as he stepped forward. "But this had to happen. There was no other way. And there will be many more deaths before this night is over."

"I'm not," Tres said as he walked to the corpse and cleaned the blade on his clothes. "This is one of the monsters who took my kid. I'll do the same to every one of those bastards I come across."

Malachi couldn't blame him for the coldness in his voice. Still, he hated hearing it. As justified as Tres was in his anger and violence, Malachi feared it would take him over if it sat for too long inside him.

"That guy's dead, Malachi," Danny groaned as his heaving settled down.

Malachi placed a hand on his friend's shoulders, unsure of what he could say to help. He didn't think there were any words for seeing a person killed for the first time. Even Victor didn't seem to have the jokes he usually inserted in times like this.

"Clock's ticking, boys" he reminded them.

The command gave them all the chance to push the dead man out of their minds. It was a necessity really. They could be haunted by it later. For now, there was a job to be done.

The men returned to the tree line and looked at the imposing structure of the compound walls. Three silhouettes still manned their places. From what they stood, a good 200 yards away from the wall, it appeared as if the guards did not know what had just transpired.

"Zach, you're up," Victor instructed.

Zach unshouldered his pack and pulled out a length of coiled, steel wire. Searching for just the right tree he looked out over the ridge then asked for Gary to help.

"I'm gonna need a boost," he said.

Gary knelt down and let Zach climb up on his shoulders. When he straightened up again Zach wrapped the wire around one of the thicker trees and secured it with a clamp. Testing it with a hard pull he nodded and Gary knelt down to let him off.

"Alright, Tres it's all ready for you," he said, handing the coil off.

He ran over the instructions one last time for securing the wire below, then Tres crept out over the open section of ridge and disappeared from sight.

The men watched the wire as it bobbed and jerked. Somewhere below them Tres was creeping through the trees with the other end of wire in his hand. They had timed it out, estimating how fast he could cover the ground and still remain undetected. Malachi had to keep checking his watch. Whatever they had assumed it already felt like a lot longer to him.

After and agonizing wait Malachi saw the wire go taut. It vibrated as Tres was securing it below. Zach reached up and pulled on it once. Satisfied he nodded to Victor.

"All secure," Vic whispered over the comms.

Malachi's stomach roiled as he thought about the next phase of their plan. Here was where he thought it was most precarious. He peered out into the dark, straining his eyes for some glimpse of his friend.

According to their plans Tres was supposed to be scaling the outer wall of the compound. Malachi had at first thought it impossible he could even do that. Tres proved him quickly wrong as he scurried up the wall of their rental, showing him what he was capable of. The stucco walls didn't even offer any handholds, but that didn't slow him down the least.

Malachi watched him, mouth agape, as Tres managed to use the small irregularities in the surface of the stucco to leverage himself up. He may as well have been an insect, body flat against the wall, and moving as quickly as if he were using a ladder.

"You are the real spider man," Vic had observed, both amazed and amused at the display of talent.

Now, Tres was supposed to be scaling the compound walls. Malachi squinted, trying to see, even as he knew the effort would be in vain. It was much too dark to see anything. But somewhere in that darkness Tres was making his way up.

As they waited Vic prepared for his part. He unslung his rifle and attached a suppressor to the muzzle. Lying flat he aimed at the walls, peering through the scope. He moved first to the guard on his far right, then angled back to the middle guard. He did this two or three times, looking as if he couldn't decide who to shoot first.

"Locked in," Vic whispered over the comms.

Seconds after he said that Malachi saw a shadowed figure crawl over the battlement mere yards from the guard on the far left. Vic took a deep breath and steadied his aim.

Tresmond's shadowy figure hunched down and approached the guard. From the silhouetted figures he could tell the guard was looking the opposite direction. Tres' shadow paused, crouched and ready to spring. Malachi held his breath.

All at once the shadow sprang into action. He leapt at the guard, getting a forearm around the neck and lifting the head back. His other hand whipped around and sliced over the guard's throat. In one smooth action Tres pushed the body over the wall.

As soon as Tres made his move Vic fired. The thwump of the silenced rifle cut through the air. The middle guard jerked and fell over the wall.

Vic whipped the rifle to the side. Again, the silenced shot erupted from the gun. The last guard clutched at his chest and crumpled to the ground.

Before Malachi could exhale his held breath, it was all over. The wall had been cleared of all the guards.

"All clear," came Tres' voice over the comms.

"Move out," Vic commanded, pushing Gary in front of him as they moved out to the exposed ridge.

The men worked quickly and in silence. Gary latched a cable trolley to the wire and walked it to the edge of the ridge. He looked back and got a thumbs up from Victor. Grabbing the handles of the trolley he picked his feet up and zipped down the wire.

Vic came next, attaching his own cable trolley. He counted silently then sped down the wire. Sid followed Victor; the old man surprising all of them with his strength. As soon as he had plunged into the darkness it was Malachi's turn.

"How do we know we aren't going to run into the side of another tree?" Malachi asked, having second thoughts. The wire he was supposed to rappel down plunged into the dark of the trees below. He would be flying blind, his greatest fear come to life.

"I guess we don't," Danny said with a pat on his back. "A leap of faith, brother."

"Leap of faith," Malachi said himself as he lifted his feet off the ground and let gravity pull him down.

The descent was faster than Malachi expected. As soon as his feet left the ridge the cable trolley hurled down the wire. The dark air whipped past him as he plunged into the shadow of the trees. Leaves whipped his face and more than once a smaller branch grazed him, stirring up fears that he would collide at any minute with something larger.

I'm going too fast, he thought as he continued to hurtle through the night. The compound wall grew higher as he raced towards it. The descent leveled out and he could sense the ground was closer. He braced for the coming impact.

Strong hands grabbed him from out of the night. They slowed his descent just before his feet hit the ground. The sword fell off his shoulder onto his arm as his feet hit the ground.

"I gotcha," he heard Gary say as he remembered to unlatch the cable trolley.

Detached from the cable Malachi tried to get his bearings. He turned and saw nothing but shadows all around him. Behind him he could hear Danny arriving at the end of his ride down the ridge. He had to shake the disorientation from his head. Everything was moving too fast. The land around him was unfamiliar and shrouded in dark.

The plan, he reminded himself. Stick to the plan.

Making his way through the shadows of the trees Malachi moved towards the looming shadow of the compound wall. Twenty yards from his landing the forest ended and he stepped into the clear again. A rocky rise led up to the foot of the wall.

Sid was waiting for him outside the wall. A rope hung down from the heights above. The Keeper motioned him forward.

"You're doing great, Mr. Green," Sid encouraged as he handed the Malachi the end of the rope.

Malachi slung the sword back over his shoulder and took the rope from Sid. Strange, he thought to himself as he began to climb up the wall, that Sid never called them by their first name. Even stranger, he realized, that he should be thinking that at this moment.

Pushing aside the unbidden thoughts Malachi concentrated on his ascent. He climbed the rope with ease and his feet, planted on the stone wall nearly ran up the edge without effort. He thought back to the last time he had climbed up a rope. It had been ninth grade gym class, more years ago than he wanted to even think about. Then he had flailed and struggled and barely made it to the top as the jocks snickered below. When he got to the bottom again, he swore he would never again humiliate himself like that.

Now, as he raced up the wall with ease, he wished his old classmates could see him again. A smile creased his face as he took pleasure in that thought and an even greater pleasure in the effortless way his body responded to him.

Malachi slipped over the battlements when he reached the top. He dropped into the narrow wall among the other waiting men.

"Move back," Vic whispered, instructing him to make room for the others.

Moments later Danny slipped over the wall, followed by Zach. Sid would be waiting by the front gate when they had cleared the courtyard.

"Tres, you're a go," Vic cleared.

Up ahead Malachi saw Tres creep down the wall walk. As he disappeared around the curve of the wall Malachi peered over to assess the grounds below.

They had climbed up the western portion of the wall. In the courtyard directly below them Malachi saw transport trucks silent and waiting. Beyond them two guards stood on either sides of the open space, one near a door that accessed the interior of the compound, another smoked a cigarette by the rolling doors of a garage. Another guard sat in the guard station next to the main gate. He sat back with his head down, reading something Malachi couldn't see.

"Ready," Tres whispered over the comms.

The muzzle of Victor's rifle peaked out between the crenellations of the battlement. It aimed at one guard then the next before swinging back to the first one. A flash of fire erupted as the suppressed sound of rifle fire reported into the night.

The guard next to the door rocked his head back and fell down. A shadow dropped down from the wall above the gate. The guard next to the garage doors looked up, hearing the sound of the rifle. He heard but his mind had not yet comprehended the sound or what was happening. His cigarette was poised halfway to his mouth.

Another report of the rifle sounded before he could react. The guard fell backwards, his half-smoked cigarette falling from his fingers.

Gary threw the rope over the other side of the wall. One by one they scrambled over. Malachi landed between two transport trucks, their shadows obscuring the rest of the courtyard. He pulled at his rifle, trying to get it at the ready. It snagged on the sword he carried beside it.

Malachi grunted in frustration as he tried to untangle the two weapons he had slung over his back. Perfect, he thought to himself. Not only do I have no real talent to offer this mission, I'm stuck back here struggling to even draw my weapon.

After finally untangling the two Malachi unslung the AR and put it to his shoulder. He moved out of the shadow of the trucks, the muzzle of his rifle scanning for immanent dangers.

Just as he had feared, by the time he had emerged from the trucks the courtyard had been cleared. The other men gathered by the guard station. Another guard was lying there, sprawled on the ground. Tres was wiping the blood from his knife onto the dead man's clothes.

Malachi slid over to the group, hoping they wouldn't notice his late arrival. That hope was immediately dashed when Vic smiled back at him as he drew near. He could feel what was coming.

"Oh, look who decided to come along," he said grinning. "Making sure all the truck tires were fully inflated?"

Malachi felt his face go hot at Vic's jab. He thought to explain but knew it would only make things worse.

"All good," Malachi answered. He turned to scan the rest of courtyard before Vic could say anything else.

"Alright, what's next?" Zach asked.

"Let's see what Danny can hack into," Vic answered, jerking a thumb towards the guard station.

Inside, Danny had opened his laptop and was looking over the control panel. He looked around the sparse hut and shook his head, holding up his hands in helplessness.

"Nothing to hack into," he said. "Got a comms station that looks like it feeds into a source outside the gate and a few other places in the compound. Big red button here. Probably opens the front gate. Nothing else. Isolated station without a connection to the rest of the compound. We're running old school here."

"So how do we get into the rest of the compound?" Vic asked.

Danny shrugged, stepping out of the cramped guard station. He pointed across the courtyard to the steel doors that accessed the interior of the compound.

"I guess I can try to hotwire that panel over there," he said. "It probably opens that door. After that, your guess is as good as mine."

"How about we let Sid in?" Gary suggested, bringing them back to the plans they had made. "Maybe he has an idea."

"Or maybe I could help," a familiar voice said from behind them.

Despite recognizing the voice Malachi felt a rush of fear at the unexpected sound. Shouldering his rifle he turned. He sensed the others putting their weapons at the ready.

"Whoa, whoa," Giovanni said as he held up his hands. A grin spread across his face.

"I've been gone for a few days and you've already kicked me out of the club?"

Chapter 31 - Storming the Castle

Overwhelming relief washed over Malachi as he looked up at Giovanni smiling back at him. He hadn't realized how anxious he was about his friend until that moment. Feeling tears of gratitude welling up in his eyes Malachi wrapped him up in a hug.

"Gio! Alive and well!" Vic exclaimed as the rest of the men gathered around.

"Don't ever do that again," Malachi warned, wiping the tears from his eyes.

"Can't promise anything," Giovanni grinned.

Danny opened the front gates as the rest of the men congratulated Giovanni and tried to catch up with him. Sid strolled into the courtyard and the men parted, making way for the Keeper to see Giovanni safe among them again.

"Mr. Santos," Sid greeted with a nod of his head. "Your maneuver was ill advised even though the result was favorable. I do not recommend doing anything of that sort again."

"Yeah, dumb idea to stow away in an enemy plane," Vic remarked. "But since you already did, what can you tell us about this place?"

Giovanni went into a rundown of the compound. He briefly told of how he got there, then explained the layout and how the place was manned.

"I'd say there are about fifty guards scattered over the whole island," he explained. "Most of them are here but there is a good number at the airstrip."

"What about the kids?" Tres asked, stepping forward and taking hold of Giovanni by the arm. "Have you seen Owen?"

Giovanni shook his head. "I know where the kids are," he said, pointing back behind him. "There's a dorm in the back, on the north side. I got close to one kid, but he could see me. Even cloaked. I haven't risked getting near them since then."

"I'm sure he's back there," Danny said.

"So how do we get in?" Tres asked, getting fully back into mission mode.

Giovanni turned and they all looked across the courtyard at the steel doors sealing them off from the rest of the compound.

"Beyond that door is a check point," Giovanni explained. "I can get you through that door but it only leads to a more or less empty room. To get though the next door the guards have to let you in. And they're sitting behind a few inches of bullet proof glass with a fully automatic M40 mounted through a loophole. They can spray the room with lead in seconds."

"Any other access points?" Vic asked.

Giovanni shook his head. "Through that door is the only way to get to the interior of the castle."

"Castle?" Vic exclaimed. His brow furrowed in disgust as he shook his head.

"Yeah, that's what I've named the place, the castle," Giovanni answered.

"We've been calling it a compound."

"Well, it's clearly a castle," Giovanni insisted. "It looks just like one. It even has the little gaps in the wall at the top, whatever they are."

"Crenellations," Danny interjected.

"Yeah, those. It's obviously a castle."

"I don't like calling it a castle," Vic said. "Castles are for good guys. Compounds are for, you know, cults and militias."

"What about Castle Greyskull?" Zach asked.

"What about it?"

"Didn't Skeletor live there," Zach pointed out. "He was a bad guy."

"Actually, I think Castle Greyskull was good," Gary said. "It just looks bad because of the skull and everything."

"Gentlemen," Sid interjected with obvious impatience. "Let us forego this conversation until a later date."

"Right," Giovanni agreed. "Still, the only way to get into the . . . the compound is through that access point there."

"Alright," Gary said with a shrug. "I guess we're getting through there. What's the plan?"

"You didn't have a plan in place already?" Giovanni asked with dramatic shock in his voice. "That doesn't sound like something Malachi would let happen."

"We had a plan," Malachi said defensively.

"I was supposed to access the doors from the guard's station here," Danny said. "Turns out it isn't connected to anything but the front door."

"Yeah, they're kind of old school here."

"I guess I could try to hotwire something from that panel," Danny suggested. "Though I couldn't say for sure if it will work."

"We may just have to force the doors open," Gary said. "Do it the old-fashioned way."

"With what?" Vic asked. "I know you're strong, but not that strong."

"You want to bet?" Gary took up the challenge.

"Why don't we just blow the doors?" Zach suggested. "Are they the same as these?"

Giovanni nodded. "Heavy steel. Two panels. All the mechanisms in the wall."

Unshouldering his pack Zach dug around and produced a green coil. It was a flat material that looked like rubber weather stripping. Zach grinned as he held it up for the others to see.

"Strip charge," he told them. "I was hoping to use this."

"Is that strong enough for these?" Vic asked, jerking a thumb in the direction of the two steel panels that were blocking their way in.

"I'm not going to blow a hole through it," Zach admitted. "But we just need to knock them off their tracks."

"I'm going to prepare for plan B," Gary said.

Strolling over to the rolling doors of the garage he lifted one up and looked through the workspace. It took him a moment to sort through the scattered tools to find what he was looking for. With a triumphant grin he held up a long crowbar.

"You're not forcing your way through steel doors," Vic chided him. "I don't care what you think."

"We'll see about that," Gary said, not goaded at all by Victor's skepticism.

"Fine, we have plan A and B," Sid interjected, eager to get the mission going again.

Vic nodded, his expression growing serious again. He unslung his rifle and checked the clip.

"Gary, you're behind me. Zach, behind the big guy," Victor instructed. "When Gio opens the door, I'm going to hit the guard station with a few rounds, see if I can break the glass. If not, at least it will be hard to see through when they unload on us. We've got to get to the opposite wall fast. Otherwise, we're just a sitting duck and those seven-point sixes will cut us in two."

Silently, the men all arranged themselves in formation. Giovanni knelt beside the access panel, ready to key in the code. Vic held his rifle at the ready. Behind him, the other men shouldered their weapons and tried to prepare themselves for whatever they might find on the other side of the door.

Malachi stood at the back of the line next to Sid. The nerves, which had abated for a moment while they regrouped in the courtyard flared to new life. Once this part of the operation began there was likely no stopping until it came to its conclusion. Whatever that conclusion may be.

A nod from Victor and Giovanni punched in the code. The light over the numbers flashed from red to green. The steel panels slid open with a whispered hum.

Chapter 32 - Storming the Compound

As soon as the steel panels parted Victor pushed the barrel of his rifle into the opening. Dim light filtered down from a single hanging bulb, illuminating a cold and sparse surrounding. A harsher, white light glowed from the window on the other side of the room. Three faces appeared on the other side of the bullet proof glass. Their expression at first was a mild annoyance, obviously not expecting anyone to pass through at that time of night.

Their expressions turned to shock and fear as the first blast came from Victor's rifle. A bloom formed on the glass, white and opaque like it was just a snowball that had hit it. Cracks webbed out from the impact as the men inside jumped back instinctively.

Working the bolt action as fast as he could Vic loaded another round. Another blast erupted from the muzzle followed by a third. Three hits frosted spots on the glass but it didn't shatter.

Just as the fourth round slid into the chamber red streaks of light flew from the mouth of the machine gun mounted under the glass.

"Return fire!" Vic yelled, charging for the opposite door.

As soon as the words were out of his mouth the room erupted in the staccato of automatic gun fire. Flashing blasts flared out of the mounted muzzle. Sparks flew up as the stone walls became riddled in holes and the metal shelves were ripped apart by the sweeping destruction.

Vic slammed against the metal doors in a dead run. Another body bumped against him, almost crushing him against the steel.

"Did you have to hit me with all your weight?" he groaned, pushing himself out from under Gary.

"Quite being a baby," Gary snapped back.

A flashing red light blinked from all four corners of the room. The blare of a klaxon alarm sounded barely over the eruptions of gunfire.

"I guess everyone knows we're here now," Vic said as he looked back, taking in a quick assessment.

Against the far wall they were safe from the machine gun fire which was coming out from a loophole beside them. The rest of the room was being devastated, torn up by the rapid and constant barrage from the M40. Red steaks danced around the room, just ahead of the shots, making it look like a laser show accompanied by gunfire. To his relief, no bodies lay on the floor or in the open doorway leading to the courtyard. But Zach wasn't with them either.

"Zach didn't make it in?" Victor only half asked.

Gary shook his head. Turning, he tried to yell over the gunfire.

"Everybody good!?"

A raised thumb poked out of the open door before quickly being withdrawn. The M40 continued to roar, spraying the room and open doorway with gunfire.

"Looks like it's just us," Vic remarked. "I guess it's plan B after all."

Gary smiled and brandished the crowbar. "Let me teach you something about opening doors," he said.

He felt along the middle of the steel door, finding the seam where the two panels came together. Probing at the small crack he pushed at it as if he wanted to pry it open with just his finger. Satisfied with whatever he found he hefted the crowbar in both hands, pointing the flat end at the doors.

"Here goes plan B," he said, slamming the edge towards the steel doors.

The crowbar bounced off the steel door, sending Gary recoiling back. Vic chuckled and looked at the unmarked door.

"Not even close," he said.

Gary grunted and launched himself at the door again. This time it made a small dent at the seam of the two doors. Another stab at the door and the dent grew wider, forming a two-inch-wide opening between the two panels.

With a roar Gary reared back and slammed the crowbar into the small opening. The steel bar sunk in between the panels. Gary smiled and nodded towards the lodged bar.

"Door ain't open yet," Vic pointed out.

Gripping the crowbar Gary grunted and pushed against it. His feet slipped on the stone floor and the door refused to yield. Repositioning his hands he pulled instead.

The bar bent under the pressure and at first the doors remained unyielding. A groan came from the steel panels as they shuddered under the pressure. A metallic pop sounded and they eased open an inch.

Redoubling his efforts Gary strained at the bar. The doors shook and screamed out as they were forced open further and further, one straining inch at a time.

Dropping the bar Gary grabbed at the doors. With a hand on each of the panels he began pushing them apart. Screaming out in protest, they inched further open.

His face red and veins bulging Gary began to cry out under the pressure. His arms trembled but held tight. A high pitch whine sounded from inside the track as metal rocked against metal somewhere within its mechanisms.

Gary stood, heaving the doors open. Like a modern-day Samson, straining at the pillars of the Philistine palace, he pushed with all of his might. A roar broke out of his lips as the doors finally gave. The panels fell apart, ripped from their tracks. With a crash they toppled to his feet.

Dropping his arms down Gary breathed deep with relief. Vic came up beside him with a smile and clapped his shoulders.

"I knew you could do it," he said.

Neither man had time to enjoy the victory. In the hallway beyond another panel of bullet proof glass waited, connected to the same guard room. Below this another mounted machine gun protruded from the wall.

It took a single beat for one of the guards to realize what had happened. He peered through the glass and made eye contact with Gary and Victor. They both looked at each other as they took the situation in, considering what it meant for them both.

With eyes widening in comprehension the guard reached for the trigger of the mounted gun. Gary had just enough time to grab hold of Vic when the red streaks began projecting from the muzzle. Machine gun fire erupted, barely missing the two men as they dove out of the doorway.

"Well, this has certainly improved our situation," Vic yelled out over the new burst of noise.

On one side the machine gun still rattled the room and held the other Swordsmen outside. Now, out of the door they just tore down came a fresh barrage of gunfire, trapping them between the two. The blasts continued to devastate the room, echoing reports in the small space as the alarm continued to blare its warning.

"We're running out of time," Vic warned. "The calvary will be here any second to swarm down on us."

Gary nodded, realizing how desperate their situation had become. Trapped between the two guns, their little space of wall was their only safety. Time was ticking down before the mission would become a complete disaster.

Looking around, Gary searched for something to help them. Whatever other tools were in the room were inaccessible now, if not chewed up by machine gun fire. Besides what they brought with them the only other thing in the room to help was the crowbar that lay discarded at his feet.

An idea popped into Gary's head as he regarded the crowbar. He picked up the heavy bar, still partway bent from the pressure and then down at the barrel of the machine gun beside him ripping out rounds into the room.

"Time for plan C," he said, flipping the bar in his hand.

"What's plan C?" Victor asked.

Without answering, Gary lifted the bar over his head and brought it down on the barrel of the gun. Sparks flew up with the contact and the barrel bent almost a full ninety degrees. The sharp sounds of the report went dull in an instant.

Cries rose up from inside the guard room as the gun exploded, sending a cascade of shrapnel cutting through the gunner. Both guns fell silent.

"Clear," Gary yelled out. He shrugged at Vic who was staring at him in disbelief.

The other Swordsmen came quickly pouring into the room, guns at the ready. Zach came up beside Gary and looked at the door torn from its track.

"I guess you didn't need me after all," he observed, disappointment in his voice.

The machine gun fire out of the hallway started up again, sending the men back against the wall.

Gary jerked a thumb towards the window where three blooms of gunfire webbed across the reinforced glass. "Plan C." he said. "Can you blast that open?" he asked.

Zach smiled and brandished the roll of explosives. "Piece of cake."

Hurrying to the window he stretched out a piece of the flat rubber looking substance over the glass in three strips. He set the charge and motioned the men to get flat against the wall.

"Fire in the hole!" he yelled out.

The window exploded in a shower of sparks and glass. No sooner had it shattered than Vic swept over to the exposed window, his Glock at the ready. Two shots sounded, one on top of the other.

"Guard room, clear," he announced.

Without holstering his pistol Vic catapulted into the guardroom. Gary followed and Malachi came up behind them, looking through the space where the bullet proof window had been. Inside, three guards lay dead. Two had bullet wounds to the head and the third had his face ravaged by shrapnel. Malachi looked away as Danny bumped into him.

"Coming through," Danny said, pulling himself into a jump through the window.

"Gio and Zach, you cover the hallway," Vic instructed. "Malachi, Tres, in here with us, we got company coming."

Malachi jumped in and joined the others. Inside the guard room Danny looked over the instrument panel, quickly familiarizing himself with its operations. A third window opened up to the interior of the compound. Beyond, he could see a vast room that Giovanni had told them was for training. From a corner staircase, men in black tactical gear came pouring in, answering the summons of the alarm that continued to blare. Each one carried an automatic rifle and held it with the easy familiarity of experts.

"These guys are ex-military," Vic said, watching the men pour in, expressing Malachi's very thoughts.

"No machine gun here," Gary observed, noting that direction wasn't armed as the other two were.

"Bummer," Vic mused, scanning the room beyond the thick pane of reinforced glass.

"Well, there is some good news," Danny remarked, looking over the vast array of out-dated equipment that made up the control panel. Buttons, dials and switches covered the large array. It looked almost deliberately antiquated.

"I don't have to hack into anything here," he continued. "I can control every door, window and lock from right here."

"Make sure the door to this place is locked tight," Vic said. "And any ingress into the hall outside or the room behind us."

"Copy that," Danny answered, flipping down several toggles. "And I may as well lock down this one labeled 'Armory' too."

"And shut this alarm off," Gary plead. "It's starting to get on my nerves."

Seconds later the blaring alarm went silent. In the sudden quiet Malachi joined the others looking through the reinforced window to the training room beyond.

Inside the training room the guards had begun rolling in large steel panels. All were over six feet tall and mounted on wheels. Some had windows near the top, but all carried side mounting for their weapons to be easily fired from behind cover. They grouped them together in three bunches, surrounding the guard room where the Swordsmen waited.

"Mobile defensive shields," Vic observed. "As soon as they get these into place, they're going to shoot out this window. What do we got, about fifteen men out there? Military grade automatic weapons, they'll have this down in a second. After that they'll pin us down with suppressive fire and roll those in closer, probably toss in grenades or tear gas."

"What's the plan?" Gary asked. He checked his rifle and readied it to return fire.

"We should probably throw them back," Vic answered with a chuckle.

"Very funny," Gary answered.

Stepping closer to the glass Gary peered through at the activity that had slowed in the training room. Three lines of defensive positions had been arranged in an arc around the guard station. Faces in tactical helmets stared silently back at him.

"I wonder what they're waiting for?" Gary asked out loud.

As if in answer gunfire erupted from the training room. Opaque, white spots bloomed all over the glass as it was struck by a barrage from the automatic weapons. Gary instinctively fell back from the window, throwing himself onto the floor.

"I guess they were waiting for an idiot to stick his face in the window," Vic laughed as they all took cover on the floor.

The reinforced glass continued to explode in white spots as machine gun fire riddled the pane. The staccato sound of bullets ripping through the air and pinging off the glass blended into a forbidding harmony. Huddled on the floor, the men could only watch until the window exploded under the pressure.

"Seriously, what's the plan?" Gary yelled out.

"Seriously, throw the grenades back," Vic yelled back. "Or we can lob some of our own, try to get them past the defensive position and break them up."

Malachi looked down at the bandolier slung across his chest. "I got three," he said. "And two smokes."

The window was almost covered in white concussion points. The sounds of gunfire spilled on top of each other.

"Smoke," Tres called out.

"What?"

"Gimme some smoke," Tres said. "Fill that room up with smoke and open the hallway door. Let me take care of the rest."

Tres unsheathed the long knife Sid had given them. Stopping to think for a moment he unshouldered the PSAK-47 and brandished instead the .380 automatic.

"Sure you don't want the rifle?" Gary asked, though he could tell the conviction carrying Tres at that moment admitted no doubt.

"It'll just slow me down," he answered with a shake of his head.

"You heard him," Vic confirmed. "As soon as that window busts out throw whatever smoke you got at 'em. Might as well toss a few frags in there too. Wait until you here the explosions."

Tres nodded and jumped through the blasted-out window and back into the room they had first entered. Malachi unhooked the grenades from his bandolier and passed them around the room. Each man took hold of one and waited with his back against the wall.

The armored glass exploded in a deluge of diamond shards, finally giving way under the pressure. The sounds of unmuted gunfire erupted into the guard room as thousands of sharp slivers burst out, cascading the room in deadly shrapnel.

"Smoke 'em if you got 'em," Vic yelled out as he pulled the pin on his grenade and lobbed it through the newly shattered window.

The other men followed suit, pulling their pins and hurling the grenades through. Startled cries and warnings echoed back at them. Seconds later came the first of the explosions. At least two distinct voices cried out in pain.

Malachi turned to the open window and watched as the growing cloud of smoke billowed through the opening. He could hear the coughing and confused orders beyond. Somewhere in that cloud Tres would begin stalking them, one by one. He lifted up a silent prayer that his friend would not only be safe from his enemies, but also from the darkness that was stalking his own heart.

Tresmond was one with the clouds of smoke. He had wrapped a bandana around his mouth and nose before slipping into the training area. Despite this the acrid smoke still stung his throat and eyes. Strangely, this did not bother him. He opened himself to it and let it fill him. Even as tears pooled in his eyes, he didn't resist the smoke.

I am the hunter, he told himself. I am the stalker in the smoke and darkness. I am the shadow of death unto my enemies.

When Owen was three years old, Tres had taken the family to see an old friend they all called Chinny back in high school. The guy had just landed a huge account as a drug rep and was desperate to show off his new wealth to everybody. Chinny insisted that Tres come over and see the new place, and take the family swimming.

Owen was in the pool, just splashing around the shallow end. He didn't know how to swim yet and Grace was keeping a close eye on him as Tres was being shown all the new toys, the state-of-the-art features of the new house. Chinny displayed them all like a proud father showing off his kids.

It happened in just an instant. Grace had to go inside and told Tres to keep an eye an Owen. He nodded but didn't fully register what his wife had said. Chinny was walking him through the outdoor sound system, carefully explaining every feature and exactly how much they cost.

Tres only remembered thinking how envious he was at that moment. He didn't like Chinny in high school, and marveled how such incredible fortune could have fallen at the feet of such a schmuck. It didn't seem fair that Tres was working his fingers raw and sometimes they barely kept their heads above water, and this guy just fell into sudden fortune without even trying that hard. He turned his head to briefly survey the pool. The surface was empty and still. Owen was nowhere in sight.

Immediate panic surged through Tres as he raced over to the pool. A thousand nightmare scenarios ran through his head. Every one worse than the one before.

He looked down by the edge to see the dark-haired head bobbing just beneath the surface. Arms flailed out, searching for purchase that lay just out of reach. Finger desperately scraped at the edge of the pool.

Tres reached in and pulled the struggling boy out of the water. Owen coughed and sputtered, retching out the pool water as he wiped tears from his eyes. Relief washed over Tres as he hugged the boy to himself, not caring one iota about any of the crap that Chinny had acquired for himself. It seemed like nothing but trash to him in that moment.

Of course, Grace was furious at him. She kept it together pretty well for the rest of the night at Chinny's. It wasn't until the trip home that she unloaded on him and let him know how pissed she actually was.

Tres took the abuse silently. He took no steps to defend himself, realizing how much he deserved every bit of her wrath. His strategy was to simply suffer in silence and let Grace unload on him until she felt better about what had happened. It was Owen who came to his defense.

"Don't be mad, Mommy," he mumbled sleepily from his car seat in the back. "Daddy will always save me."

Those few words silenced Grace for the rest of the ride home. Though still plenty mad at him she didn't want to shake the confidence the boy had in his father. She would vent the rest of her wrath later that night.

Tres felt the words strike him to his core. It was the greatest compliment he had ever received in his life. Such an innocent and pure expression of trust. Despite his brush with danger that Owen didn't fully realize, he had faith in his father. Instead of the incident sowing doubt in his heart, it had strengthened his trust. Dad would save him.

The minute Tres heard that Owen might still be alive, those words echoed in his head with deafening clarity. Daddy will always save me.

He knew he didn't deserve such trust. A part of him even warned that it was borderline idolatrous to even entertain that he could live up to it. He knew he couldn't. But he also knew that he would move heaven and earth trying. Somewhere, his son was still alive, God willing. And if he had it in his power to save him, he wouldn't let anything stop him. Not the guards. Not the Fae. Not even this Sautorus, whoever he was. Not the smoke or the fear.

Tresmond was vengeance, and he was death to all who would stand in his way.

Moving through the cover of smoke Tres approached the first group of guards. They sheltered behind their mobile defense shields, attention still fixed towards the window they had just shot out. He could only make out one clearly through the dense haze.

Tres struck fast and hard. He thrust the point of his knife into the neck at the collarbone. The soldier gargled and grabbed at his throat, helplessly trying to stop the blood that raced from the wound.

As the first guard slumped over Tres brought the blade across the throat of the second. He had no time to register his surprise as he keeled over. Bringing the knife back he stabbed at a third guard. This time the blade dug into the flesh between the ribs.

This guard cried out, alerting the one beside him. As he turned Tresmond lifted the .380, firing two shots into his throat. A fifth figure rose up, aiming at Tres.

Two more shots knocked this guard back, striking the Kevlar vest. Tres stabbed at the guard at his feet, finishing him off. He raced over to the fifth, still reeling from the impact. Before he could bring his rifle around, the edge of Tres' blade found the soft flesh of his throat. A gurgled cry escaped from the ripped trachea as he crumpled to the ground.

A dim part of Tres revolted at the carnage before him. Guilt grazed the back of his mind, warning him, begging him to stop. Louder still were the simple words of his son. Daddy will always save me.

With the first grouping finished off Tres stalked towards the next. Somewhere behind him he heard the sound of fans being engaged. A breeze began to softly stir against him. He had to hurry.

"What the Hell was that?" a confused and panicked voice called out from the smoke. "Morris? Morris?!"

Tres approached the second grouping. A guard knelt over another one who had fallen to the ground. Through the smoke Tres could see the traces of shrapnel that had ripped across his face. Another body lay beyond his, unmoving.

"Morris!" the kneeling figure cried out again.

Tres struck before he even looked up. The blade of his knife plunged into the unprotected back of the kneeling guard. He cried out in pain and fell over.

There was no else in this second grouping. Three bodies lay at his feet behind the mobile shields.

Tres felt the smoke quickly thinning around him. The ventilation system, operated by the two large fans on the far wall, was emptying out the thick haze. Just as he had finished off the second grouping, he could make out five figures of the third just ahead of him.

And they could see him too.

Three of the guards dropped to their knees, raising their rifles to the ready. Red streaks shot out of the rifle muzzles warning Tres of shots to come. Four penetrated right through his chest.

Reaching out beside him Tres grabbed one of the mobile shields. He swung it around, pulling it in front of him just as the first shots fired.

Automatic rounds pummeled the shield. His hands shook with the vibration as it pushed him back. He holstered the gun and dug in his feet, resisting the urge to let go.

Tres angled the shield and pushed forward, charging at the guards.

The gunfire cascaded off the steel, throwing up a shower of sparks.

With a grunt Tres rammed the shield into the kneeling guards. Two of them toppled over backwards. Grabbing the end, he swung it around it a wide arc, striking a third guard and sending him to the ground.

As two more guards moved in to engage, Tres felt all thought and deliberation slip from him. He moved by instinct, letting his body go. Unbridled, another will leapt up in him. Pure action. Pure movement. A leaf dancing on the spirals of the wind.

He felt his hand unholster the .380. Two shots fired into the face of the guard, beneath the protection of his helmet. Before those bullets even struck, he had thrown the knife at the other approaching guard. The blade buried itself into his neck.

With the momentum of that throw Tresmond flipped over the three guards he had struck with the shield. Vaulting over their prone forms he landed behind them. He reached back, grabbed his knife from the throat of the falling guard.

One of the prone figures stood, raising up his rifle to aim. Taking hold of the knife Tres ripped it free, knocking the rifle aside. Coming back around he leaned forward, raking the blade across the guard's throat.

His left hand crossed over, firing two shots into the side of another guard. The last one began to struggle to his feet. Swinging the blade back around Tres reversed the grip. Before the last guard could even find his feet, the knife was buried into the soft flesh above his sternum. The lifeless body slumped to the ground.

Breathing hard Tres looked down, almost daring one of them to try and get up. None of the bodies moved. Nodding to himself he started to sheath the knife away.

Two red streaks passed through his torso. Without thinking Tres leapt to the side just as bullets whizzed by. He felt the air stir from their passage. Leaping to the side he looked up. Two more guards stood by the far wall, their silhouettes rippling in front of two massive and twirling fan blades.

Tres reached out for the mobile shield, spinning it around. Just as he took hold of it the crack of a sniper rifle exploded in the air. One of the silhouettes fell back. Another report sounded, rocking back the head of the last guard.

Turning towards the blasted-out window Tres saw Victor leaning out, quickly chambering another round. The barrel scanned the room, searching for any remnant of enemy. Tres held up his hands.

"I think it's clear," he called out.

He couldn't help feeling a touch of disappointment that the fight was over. Blood still pounded in his ears. His limbs still shook, desperate for action. The cry of his conscience was still as his rage called out for more blood.

"Tres, you alright?" he heard someone ask beside him as a gentle hand touched his arm.

He looked up at Malachi, his face etched in concern. Not just concern, there was fear there too. Malachi was worried about him, maybe even scared of him.

Nodding, Tres sheathed his knife. He turned away from the accusing eyes, not ready to deal with their concern or their worry. There was still work to be done tonight. There was still a reckoning to be had. He would not rest until his son was rescued and his enemies stilled.

He heard Owen's voice echo in his head again. Daddy will always save me.

"Let's go," he heard himself say, stalking from the carnage of dead bodies and looks of concerns that followed him as he headed out of the room.

Chapter 33 - The Battle of the Courtyard

"The courtyard is right out that door," Giovanni told the group as they moved down the hallway, rifles at the ready.

"On the back end of the courtyard is a wall with a set of stairs leading to the top. On the other end is the playground. All the kids are kept in a dormitory on the far side."

"What's the guard situation?" Vic asked.

Giovanni shrugged. "Usually, three watching the playground. But since the alarm has gone off, who knows? At least ten more unaccounted for, not counting Sautorus. I'm guessing the backups down below will be making it this way."

"Hopefully they don't have a way of getting through the main gate," Danny said. "Would hate to have any behind us."

"We'll deal with that if and when it happens," Sid advised as he took up the rear of the column. Giovanni walked beside him, advising them from the back.

At the end of the hallway the sliding, steel doors had already been opened. They could see in the night air ahead and the courtyard beyond. Green manicured grass was cut through with paving stones that surrounded a marble fountain. The fountain was dry at the moment, and beyond that they could see the massive wall, casting a shadow across the entire courtyard.

A sense of being watched fell over the men as they entered the courtyard. Rifles scanned the quiet darkness. Serene scents of garden flowers and freshly turned soil gave off a deceptive calm. The men tensed as they filed through the doorway, searching for an enemy they knew to be nearby.

Red streaks flew through the darkness, stabbing towards them from above.

"Incoming!" Vic yelled in warning.

Carnage erupted from the courtyard walls. Automatic fire burst out, pummeling the ground below as dirt erupted from the grass and flakes of stone and marble showered the stunned men.

Vic lunged towards his left, leading the men away from the fire. He ran against the wall, towards a shallow set of stairs. Giovanni, still in the doorway jumped back, pulling Sid with him back into the hallway.

Gunfire roared and sliced through the air around the men as they ran. Vic leapt down the shallow staircase, each of the men following his lead. They thumped down on a small landing. Bullets tore through the windows of a potting shed behind them.

The shallow walkdown afforded cover for the moment. The men huddled against the wall, wincing as gunfire rained down around them. Malachi checked to see all the men except Giovanni and Sid were accounted for. Peering up as far as he dared, he didn't see any bodies lying on the courtyard either.

"Where's Gio and Sid?" Vic asked, taking his own assessment.

"I think they ducked back into the hallway," Zach answered, thumbing back towards the way they had come.

Vic nodded, for the moment satisfied. "Anyone get a look at how many we got up there?"

"At least four or five," Gary suggested. "That's just a guess."

"Well, that won't do at all," Vic said, shaking his head.

"Does it matter?" Tres asked. "We got to get all of them regardless."

"Slow down, we'll get there," he said, trying to ease him down.

Bullets rained down relentlessly. Malachi felt them zipping through the air. Shrapnel from breaking glass and torn stone fell as traces of red streaks warned them where the fire was coming. It was too much to keep up with all at once. Panic began to creep over his mind as it shook from the barrage of stimulus he couldn't make sense of.

"We're gonna have to hit 'em from different directions," Vic called out over the hail of gunfire.

"Zach, Gary, Danny; when I give the signal you need to give us covering fire. Don't worry about hitting anything, just get them to slow down a bit. Tres, you make for that fountain and try to take out some of those shooters on the east end. Malachi, you go with him and hit the opposite side."

"What about you?" Malachi asked.

"I'm gonna try to take out a few from the top of the stairs."

The men nodded their agreement and readied their rifles. Tres looked at his PSAK and looked like he was considering leaving it behind again.

"Rifles first," Vic warned, seeing the process on Tres' face.

Tres shrugged and checked the chamber. With a nod they signaled they were all ready. Malachi tried not to think about the lead he heard whizzing around, knowing he was about to run right out into it.

"Trust the gift and the giver," he said to himself.

Vic took a deep breath and gripped his rifle. "Cover!" he yelled.

The three men stood up on the deepest part of the stairwell, firing at all once. Shots echoed through the walkup, blasting out into the night.

Turning to Tres he meant to tell him it was time to run, but the other man was already streaking across the courtyard. Cursing, Malachi picked himself up and followed.

As soon as he stepped out of the walkup, he could feel the sudden vulnerability in the open. Eyes and guns were trained on him from on top of the wall, waiting for their opportunity. He pumped his legs as fast as they would go, marveling at the speed he possessed.

Halfway to the fountain a red streak passed in front of his face. He ducked down without slowing as he heard the report of the rifle and felt the bullet zip overhead. Two more warning streaks lasered down. He leapt over one and stopped short for the other to pass by harmlessly.

Just as he reached the edge of the fountain another streak came bolting by, just over the top of the marble. Malachi slid beneath the cover of the fountain as another bullet flew overhead, ricocheting of the stone paver behind him.

A rifle report sounded from behind him. Malachi recognized it immediately as Victor's. An unexpected cry came from on top of the wall, indicating a hit.

"One down," Tres said to him as he hunkered down beneath the outside wall of the fountain.

"What now?" Malachi asked.

The return fire from on top of the wall began again. Red streaks darted through the night. High powered rounds zipped through the air and exploded on the ground.

"We shoot back," Tres answered, turning away.

For the moment Malachi could only watch. His nerves tumbled in his stomach, making his breath come in gasps and threatening to give him over to total panic. He felt penned in by gunfire.

Tres popped up and returned fire. The PSAK barked as it spit out rounds. After four shots he threw himself down as the men on top shot back.

"I need some cover fire," he said as he sidled over to Malachi.

"When can I get up?" Malachi yelled, his stomach in knots.

"Go where the you don't see the red streaks," Tres instructed and slapped him on the chest.

Malachi nodded and breathed deep, trying to still his nerves. Blocking out the sounds of gunfire all around him he steadied himself. Red streaks continued to dance around him. They seemed to cover the entire fountain area except for one small window beside the fountain itself.

"Trust the gift and the giver," Malachi told himself again.

Timing the shots Malachi leapt up and stepped over the fountain wall. He pressed himself against the fountain and pulled the AR up to his shoulder. Marking the silhouettes he fired up, streaking the barrel across as he sprayed the wall.

The red streaks stopped as some of the men pulled back. He heard Tres fire beside him. Another cry came from the wall as a body tumbled over. Malachi marked another one down in his mind.

A red streak flashed across his eyes. He pulled completely behind the fountain as bullets ripped through the air where he had just been.

"Keep it up," Tres yelled.

Malachi let go of his fear and allowed his gift to carry him through the battle. He popped out the other side, firing four quick shots, ducking under cover before the enemy could fire back.

The PSAK erupted in a barrage of rapid fire. Tres had switched to fully automatic. Bursts exploded from the top of the wall as the stone was chewed up. One of the men rocked back, decimated by the 7.62 caliber rounds.

Malachi fired up at the wall. Bullets rained down back towards his as he ducked behind the fountain. He checked his magazine and threw it aside, loading in a fresh one.

Confidence built in Malachi with each shot he took. Timing his shots in between the red streaks he took hold of this advantage. Up high, ducking down, from one side of the fountain to the other he shot back at the men on the wall.

The fountain blew up chunks of marble as one of the shots hit right next to his face. Malachi grimaced as the shards cut into him. Putting a hand to his face small streaks of blood came back.

Blinking, Malachi and looked around, checking his vision. His left eye blurred, but was otherwise in working order. Anger now bubbled up beside the tension of the fight. Something inside him clicked in understanding. It was us or them.

Malachi moved to the opposite side of the fountain. The shots had slowed down considerably, offering longer windows of fire. Leaning against the fountain he raised his rifle, aimed at one of the shadowy figures crouching down atop the wall.

Squeezing the trigger he fired the rifle. One shot, and the shadow jerked and fell over. One moment, the man's silhouette stood out on top of the wall. The next, he was gone.

I guess that's it, Malachi told himself. I've shot somebody now. Maybe killed him.

The event felt strangely distant as the firefight continued to light up the courtyard. Even as he stopped to think about what had just happened, it didn't seem real to him. It was just a shadow, after all. Maybe it wasn't even his gun that had fired the fatal shot. There were lots of people shooting in the courtyard.

All these thoughts were interrupted with a pain that exploded in his side. Malachi cried out as it felt like fire ripping through him. He spun around from the force of the hit and landed on the floor of the fountain.

"Malachi!" Tres yelled out, jumping over to come beside him.

"I'm hit," Malachi groaned.

Tres pushed back his bloodied hands and looked down at the wound. In the dim light he could only see the black shirt glistening around a hole in the fabric. He felt around the other side and touched blood on his back.

"Went straight through," Tres noted. "Are you ok?"

Malachi grunted as he shook his head. "I'm shot, what do you think?"

"Actually," he said before Tres could answer. "I don't think it's that bad."

"I don't think it hit anything important," Tres said as he looked Malachi over again.

"You a doctor now?"

Tres laughed despite himself. "I'm a trainer," he said. "Next best thing."

Malachi grunted as Tresmond probed the wound further. A stab of pain radiated out from his side. A wave of nausea forced him to close his eyes.

"I think it just grazed your side," Tres said.

Malachi breathed deep as the nausea passed. The pain began to subside along with the shock of the wound. As the emotions ebbed thoughts about what had just had happened rattled around in his head.

"What's so funny?" Tres asked, seeing the smile play across

Malachi's face.

"The two things I worried most about happening all happened at the same time," he answered.

"And what was that?"

Malachi opened his eyes, looking at his friend, who for the moment seemed to forget his quest for revenge. The quiet and gentle-natured Tres was back. At the moment, he took more comfort in that than the subsiding pain in his wound. That meant his friend was still in there, no matter what he was feeling.

"That I would shoot someone or be shot myself," Malachi answered.

Before Tres could answer he stopped and looked around.

"It's quiet," he said, noting the sounds of gunfire had ceased.

Malachi leaned forward, eliciting a new bout of pain he was able to ignore. The courtyard had gone quiet. From the staircase the others were beginning to emerge.

"Everyone ok?" Vic called out as he crept out of his spot and surveyed the empty courtyard.

"Malachi's hit, but I think he's alright," Tres yelled back.

Victor began to hurry towards them as the other men emerged. He stopped short, his rifle going back to the far wall of the courtyard.

Malachi saw the motion and forced himself to turn around. A new set of silhouettes stood atop the wall, their dark forms standing out against the panoply of stars beyond. Something in their carriage was instantly familiar to Malachi. The way they held themselves, even in shadow, gave away who they were.

"Shadow men," Tres said, expressing Malachi's thoughts.

Another silhouette stood among the shadow men, this one taller than the others. A dark power emanated from this one, something deeper and more sinister than the others. He loomed over the entire courtyard in a dreadful presence. Just looking at him sent a chill of fear through Malachi. Sid had promised a powerful Fae was among them. This had to be the one.

"Hope everybody saved something," Vic warned. "Looks like the fight has just begun."

Chapter 34 - The Battle of the Courtyard, Part II

As soon as gunfire exploded in the courtyard Giovanni pushed Sid back. Shots rang out, echoing and falling over one another in the chaos of battle.

Giovanni looked down at the 9mm in his hand. Hearing the automatic fire rip through the night the Glock felt incredibly inadequate. For the moment he was more than eager not to enter into the fray.

"I guess we're stuck here for the time being," he turned to Sid and said.

The Keeper seemed unperturbed by the sounds of fighting in the courtyard. His blue eyes looked ahead, seeing something that Giovanni could not. He caught himself wishing he had the same sense of calm, then had to remind himself how old Sid actually was and the number of fights just like this he had been through.

"Is there another way into the courtyard besides this hallway?" Sid asked, nodding ahead.

Giovanni started to shake his head, then remembered the passageway he had found.

"There is another way," he said. "I found a passage from the western corridor that leads to the playground. We can access the back stairs of the wall."

"Show me," Sid commanded.

The two men turned and Giovanni led them down a side hallway. They passed the large windows opening on each side to the laboratories within. A connecting passageway led them to the west wing of the compound. As they entered, the foyer it was just as Giovanni remembered. Or rather, the foreboding sense that it was made for something dark and unspeakable still remained. Antique tables and couches, ornately decorated, stood quiet and unused. Children's toys scattered about them.

"I think this wing was made to house honored guests," Giovanni explained as they entered. "Pedophiles too. Maybe both."

"They are likely one and the same," Sid observed. "Not unusual for the Family and their allies."

"Do you think that's why the kids were taken?" Giovanni asked, not sure he wanted to know the answer.

Sid shook his head. "Not the main reason. But I'm sure it was part of it."

In the distance, they could hear the sounds of gunfire echoing through the night. A thousand unasked questions waited on the tip of Giovanni's tongue. Feeling Sid's urgency as well as his own he kept these to himself and led them to the other door.

Inside the tunnel the dark pathway twisted around to the contours of the compound. As they delved further through it the sounds of gunfire grew closer. Unable to see, Giovanni only had his imagination to tell him what was going on just beyond the walls. The firefight sounded fierce, with some rounds even vibrating the stone just to their right.

Giovanni held his Glock out in front of him as the cold and narrow tunnel took them further. The dim bulbs, spaced at wide intervals made it impossible to see in the distance. Even straining his eyes, it was impossible for him to tell what lay ahead. He could only hope that any enemy they might encounter was as equally handicapped as he was.

Giovanni stopped at a metal door. "The playground is beyond here," he said. "There's a staircase that will take you to the top of the wall that overlooks the courtyard."

Sid nodded and gestured for Giovanni to open the door. He eased the lever up and pushed with his shoulder, his Glock leveled and aimed at the tiny crack of an opening. The sounds of muffled gunfire exploded into sharp clarity. Flashes bursts from the top of the wall.

Giovanni kept easing the door open, scanning the empty playground. He hissed and fell back into the dark of the tunnel.

"What is it?" Sid whispered from behind him.

"Figures on the opposite wall," he said. "Just across from us."

Sid pushed Giovanni aside and eased the door open a bit more, careful to remain in the shadow of the tunnel. As the door crept open Giovanni could see the shadows clearly. Eight figures stood still and unmoving. One rose taller than the others and emanated an aura of unmistakable power.

"Can they see us?" Giovanni asked. He thought he recognized all of the figures on the opposite wall, even from their shadows. The knowledge filled him with a certain dread.

"They're watching the fight, not the yard," Sid told him.

As soon as it was said Giovanni could see it for himself. Their heads were still but turned to their left, watching the men fire down into the courtyard. They stood rigid and unmoving, passively watching to see how the drama in the courtyard would play out.

The flashes and bursts of gunfire slowed from the wall. One after another the guards fell over or were thrown back by return fire. As he watched the defenders thin Giovanni prayed that his friends were escaping unscathed.

With only three defenders left atop the wall, the remaining guards began to retreat. They moved back, still firing down at the courtyard below. The shadow men on the adjacent wall stirred as soon as the retreat began.

Giovanni watched as the shadowy figures moved slowly towards the courtyard. There was no panic or haste in their movement. They strolled atop the wall as if they had all the time in the world, or they were certain of the outcome ahead.

"We have to warn them," Giovanni hissed from inside the doorway.

Sid held up a hand.

"They won't be taken by surprise," he promised.

The shadow men neared the wall over the courtyard. One of the retreating guards had already fallen and the other two fled towards the approaching figures. Giovanni watched in horror as one of the guards was grabbed by a shadow man and forced to his knees. A flash of metal gleamed in the night as a hand moved across his neck. The guard shook and fell to the ground, clutching at his throat.

The other guard was seized and casually tossed over the wall. His body flipped end over end and hit with a sickening crack. His body writhed and flailed helplessly on the ground as he cried out in pain.

The shadow men spread out over the top of the wall. Standing with arms folded they looked down into the courtyard. They made no move at first. Then, as if by a silent signal they all stepped forward and leapt down the wall. Only the looming figure of Sautorus remained on top of the wall.

"I think now would be a good time to engage your cloaking ability, Mr. Santos," Sid warned as he stepped out of the doorway and into the playground.

"It won't work if you know I'm there," Giovanni said.

"I will forget you are there," Sid told him. "After these instructions I will say nothing to you, nor look back. But I need you to hear what I say now. I am going to confront Sautorus. I need you to help your brothers in the courtyard. Stay cloaked until you attack and you should get a jump on one of them. After you clear the shadow men, I need Mr. Green to come to my aid. This is very important, Mr. Santos. I can only hold off Sautorus for so long. Is that understood? Defeat the shadow men as fast as you can and send Mr. Green up to help me."

The fear in Sid's voice was unmistakable. Giovanni felt the night grow darker, the figure atop the wall loom more sinister. He nodded, even though he knew it couldn't be seen.

Giovanni stopped and watched Sid approach the wall. He walked straight and confident, his hood pulled up and the cane only barely touching the ground. But the tremor in his voice belied the fear behind the swagger.

At that moment Giovanni discovered a new found admiration for the Keeper. He had seemed almost immortal to him before, a mysterious figure possessed of mythic powers and great age. Now, he seemed all too human, but with an even more heroic courage to face something decidedly more powerful than himself.

Pulling the invisible cloak about himself Giovanni followed Sid at a distance, careful not to give himself away with his steps. He crossed the playground and up the back steps of the wall. When he reached the top, he could see the battle was already in full force below. Shadow men and Swordsmen clashed in hand-to-hand combat.

Sid stood atop the wall, opposite Sautorus, neither of them moving toward the other. Giovanni slipped behind them, stopping at the top of the stairs to look back at the looming confrontation.

"It's been a long time, Sid," Sautorus said, his voice deep and smooth. It pulled at Giovanni with some hidden intoxication.

"Not long enough," Sid answered, all the fear absent from his own voice now.

"When did we meet last?" Sautorus asked. "What was it, LA? The seventies?"

"It was Chicago," Sid corrected. "1968."

"Oh yes," Sautorus purred. "1968. What a good year that was. Wouldn't you agree?"

"Ancient history."

"Oh, but you wear the years, don't you?" the Fae taunted. "You're an old man, Sid. You should be retired now, sitting in a condo in Florida and complaining about young people."

"Who can retire with still so much work to do?"

"Your time is over," Sautorus said, spreading his arms wide.

Dark clouds billowed from out of the ground beneath Sautorus' feet. Violet streaks of lightning forked within, flashing out deep shadows.

Sid mimicked the move. Holding his arms as a golden glow suffused his features. For a moment they erased the years, casting Sid into the bloom of youth. From beneath him flames of white fire snaked out in pillars of twisting light.

"You're wrong, Sautorus," Sid cried out, his head thrown back in ecstasy as the white fire circled around him. "Today is my renaissance."

Arching his back Sid threw out tendrils of white fire. It exploded into the air all around them. Giovanni felt the fire pass through him and a sudden surge of strength bloomed in his bones. He felt unstoppable, strong enough to hurl a mountain into space. A smile crept irresistibly across his face as the fire flew into the courtyard, small columns of flame circling all of the Swordsmen.

Sautorus responded in kind, thrusting out his hands. A dark column of cloud shot straight at Sid. It collided with the white fire, twisting around the golden flames. A chill passed through Giovanni as grey mist radiated out, sapping a portion of the new strength he had just received.

Pausing for one more look back Giovanni whispered a quick prayer for Sid and bounded down the stairs to join the battle in the courtyard below.

"What are they waiting for?" Malachi asked. He tried to stand up straight but the wound in his side screamed out in pain.

On the wall of the courtyard the eight shadowed figures looked down on them without moving. Their presence marked the true beginning of the battle. Everything else that had come before it, Malachi realized, was but a precursor, a prelude. The true fight for this quest, for the lives of the children, would go through the shadow men and the other looming presence on the wall.

"Come back for another ass-kicking?" Vic called out to the silent figures above. "Alright, then. C'mon, let's get it over with."

The other men laughed despite the tension in the courtyard. Victor's taunt was just what they needed to break the hold of fear that had settled over them. And it was just the boost of confidence they needed. They had beat them before, and they could do it again.

387

An almost imperceptible nod came from the larger figure and the other men stepped off the wall. They landed on the ground below with casual ease, like they had just dropped off a high step. Each one produced a long, wicked knife from his belt, curved and twisted.

"We are down a man this time," Gary noted as the shadow men came forward.

Vic whipped out his .45 and aimed at the approaching men. "Let's just take care of it now," he said.

Three shots rang out in quick succession. Three of the shadow men exploded in a puff of dark smoke. Immediately, they coalesced again, forming back into the men they were, whole and unharmed.

"I guess it's knives this time," Vic said as he holstered his sidearm and produced a knife of his own.

The other Swordsmen unshouldered their rifles and reached for their blades readying themselves for the battle ahead. Malachi felt his side still throbbing. He tried not to think of the blood still leaking from his wound as he brandished his own knife.

"Can you fight?" Tres whispered to him as the shadow men drew closer.

"We're about to find out," he answered. He wasn't sure himself if he could, but at the moment, there was no other option.

"I'll take care of mine and come help you," Tres promised.

He brandished his blade, and instead of waiting, charged right for the approaching men. A flurry of motion exploded from him as he leapt forward swinging his knife down. The shadow man stepped back, knocking the blade aside. A second charged at him, forcing Tres to knock the attack aside with the shield plate on his forearm.

Malachi moved to go to his aid. Another of the shadow men charged at Malachi, forcing him back. Close in Malachi recognized the mane of bright blonde hair on his assailant.

Blondie, Malachi said to himself. As if drawn by some unknown force of synchronicity, he faced off with the same man he fought at the studio. Or maybe it was on purpose, the shadow man needing to redeem himself.

Whatever the reason, it was rage that drove him. Malachi backed away as the curved and twisted blade came raking in at him. Blondie's face was contorted in a snarl, driving in his weapon.

Malachi knocked the blows back with his own blade. Steel on steel rang out through the courtyard. Blondie attacked fast, the knife darting towards Malachi's head, then his side. He slashed and stabbed as Malachi backpedaled, his side screaming out in protest.

Kicks came in, mixed with the knife slashes. Malachi pushed the pain back as he tried to keep the blows at bay. The knife sliced through the air; a stab aimed at his throat. He leaned back, twisting his head to keep the exposed flesh away from the hungry and poisoned edge.

Off balance, Malachi threw his arms out to keep himself from falling over. The shadow man took advantage of the opening. Pulling the knife arm back he stepped forward and kicked out at Malachi's side.

The steel enforced toe made contact with the fresh wound. Malachi's side exploded in pain. His knees buckled and he felt his back hit the courtyard ground.

Blinking away the tears of pain threw his left arm up to ward off the renewed fury of the shadow man. The knife edge struck the armored plate in the forearm sleeve.

Malachi tried to pick himself up but was kicked back down. The shadow man reversed his grip, stabbing down violently at the prone figure. The blade thrust down again and again, searching for vulnerable flesh. Malachi blocked with his forearm plate.

With his free hand Malachi pulled himself along the ground, trying to gain separation from his attacker. Blondie came on relentlessly, smelling blood on the water. The fury of his attacked giving away to a violent madness.

Malachi tried to ward him away with a kick. The wound in his side flared to new pain, forcing his leg down.

I'm running out of time, Malachi thought desperately. He continued edging away, knowing the wall would find him soon. And then what?

Out of the corner of his eye he could see Tres fighting desperately for his life. Two shadow men were on him, their attacks coming in fast and deadly. All over the courtyard the melee raged. Each man consumed with an opponent every bit his match.

The energy drained from him as Malachi fought back desperately. His arm weighed a thousand pounds. It took every bit of effort in him to keep warding off the knife attacks.

The shadow man kicked away Malachi's arm. He felt it go limp and fall to the ground. Blondie grinned, seeing the exposed Malachi lay ripe before him.

Help me, Malachi prayed. He braced himself for the coming blow and tried to command whatever reserve strength he could. Blondie raised the knife high and leaned in for the kill.

White fire exploded from the top of the courtyard wall.

Malachi's eyes widened as tongues of pure, golden flame struck his body and suffused him with its power. All at once he felt strength enter his limbs and power into every fiber of muscle. The wound in his side closed up and the pain receded to a dull ache. His senses sharpened and his awareness flared with almost supernatural perception.

Blondie roared as he launched his attack. With the sudden surge of power Malachi pulled his legs in and kicked them out. Both feet contacted solidly onto the shadow man's chest. Blondie flew back, flailing through the air before hitting the ground.

Malachi flipped himself back onto his feet. He readied the knife and watched as Blondie struggled up. The shadow man gripped his chest, grimacing. He scowled at Malachi, frustration blooming across his features.

Malachi motioned his enemy forward, daring another attack. The shadow man snarled and charged forward. The two men fell upon each other again, blades flashing in the starlit night.

Giovanni watched the fights rage over the courtyard, trying to figure out where he was needed most. A grey mist drifted among the combatants, tinged with flames of white fire. The mix emanated from the battle above, as hope and despair, manifested as golden flame and dark cloud.

To his left, Tres was hard pressed by two shadow men. They attacked in a flurry of flashing knife blades. Speed born of supernatural power stabbed and sliced. Combinations of kicks and punches flew in between the bladed attacks. They became dark blurs in the night, limbs moving almost too fast for the eye to register.

Tres danced among them all like water flowing over rock. He spun and parried. He ducked and dodged. He moved with a feline grace, almost effortless in its display.

For every attack Tres had a counter. A roundhouse kick came swinging at his head. Tres ducked and dropped to both hands, kicking back up at his assailant's face. The shadow man disappeared in a burst of dark cloud.

The other attacker fell in with a quick stab. Tres smoothly finished the motion of the kick, coming upright again and blocking the knife with his forearm plate. He ducked as the first attacker materialized again behind him, swinging for his head. Tres rolled away and popped up just in time to fend off yet another stab.

Giovanni watched, mesmerized by the mastery his friend displayed. A part of him screamed out to help his friend, while another part simply wanted to watch the clinic that he was putting on.

All around him the other Swordsmen were engaged in their own battles. Knife blades flashed in the night. The sounds of steel on steel rang out among the thickening mist. Giovanni watched with indecision and awe.

A knife came slicing at Tres' head. He flipped back, kicking the knife out the shadow man's hand. The blade landed two feet from Giovanni. It's strange, twisted blade quivered in the soft earth.

The opportunity shook Giovanni from his indecision. He looked around for a weapon. Only finding the border stones of the flower beds, he reached down for one at his feet as the shadow man hurried over to retrieve his blade.

Pulling the cloak of concealment tighter around him he moved his arm slowly into position. Just as the shadow man reached down for his knife, he brought the stone down.

A sickening thunk sounded as stone contacted skull. The shadow man grunted and fell over. As soon as he struck the ground he disappeared in a puff of black smoke.

"That's one down," Giovanni said, turning back to survey the battle around him.

Tres, now only fighting one, pressed his advantage. With supernatural speed he flew at his opponent, this one a tall and pale man. Knife strokes blurred at him. Tres leapt and kicked out, driving him further back.

Strains of the fight were visible on the shadow man's face. His pale features twisted as he struggled to block the raining blows. Twice he dissipated in clouds of dark smoke. Both times Tres was ready, perfectly slipping the attacks as the pale man reformed. It was as if he knew exactly where his opponent would be.

Giovanni crept close to the unfolding combat, trying to choose his opening. It moved almost too fast for him to enter. A head shot, he thought. That was what interfered with their ability to shadow jump.

Circling around Giovanni let himself slip into the rhythms of combat. He let his mind go, allowed it to stop thinking about what he should do, and let the instincts take over. Almost instantly he felt himself pulled into it. He felt the currents usher him into its strange and twisting tides.

Two sweeping slices of his knife sent the pale man stepping back. He leapt to his right, bringing his back to face Giovanni.

Seizing his chance Giovanni stepped in, sending a fist to the back of the shadow man's head. Contact sent the man to his knees, gripping his head in pain.

Tres didn't hesitate, lunging in with a stab of his long knife. The pale man rolled away, the blade just missing. Tres countered with a slash, drawing the blade across the white skin of his opponent's face.

The shadow man cried out as the blade bit into him. Blood poured from the slash in his cheek. He instinctively threw up a hand to the wound as he tried to keep rolling away.

Reversing his hold on the blade Tres leapt towards the flailing enemy. He knocked the defensive arm away as he fell towards him. With all of his weight behind him he brought the knife down.

Bright steel stabbed into the tender flesh of the neck. The pale man's eyes went wide in shock, suddenly sensing his own death. Too late, he realized.

Tres drove the blade in as he fell on top of the shadow man. He snarled into the pale face, locking eyes with the man as he struggled in his death throes.

Giovanni stepped back in horror. This was not the Tres that he knew. Even in the throes of grief, with the desperation of trying to save his son, this wasn't him. The rage and hate belonged to someone else.

Tres ripped the blade out as he stood up. He turned to face Giovanni, his face still contorted in anger.

A grey fog had settled over the courtyard, covering the air like a death shroud. It gave the night a ghostly cast, like they had stepped into the realm of lost and wandering spirits. Tendrils of white flame danced through the fog, floating on unseen currents.

Through the haze Tres looked to be taken over by madness. He was a part of the dim and grey landscape. He was one of these tortured ghosts, doomed to wander the grey landscape forever.

One of the white flames floated through the haze towards Tres. It struck his chest, entering into him with a ripple of gold.

He sucked in a breath, as if struck by cold water. He opened his eyes wide and shook his head. The dark cloud of rage passed, returning the light to his eyes. Tres looked around, confused for a moment, then nodded at Giovanni.

"Let's help the others," he said, wiping off his blade on the grass.

Without waiting for any response Tres ran back towards the battle. Giovanni felt a trickle of fear for his friend, fearing wounds not caused by weapons. He sighed to himself, pushing the thought away. That would be a battle for another day. For now, their fight was against flesh and blood.

Chapter 35 - Sid Bickley's Nightmare

Sid Bickley smiled to himself even as he felt the strain of the battle, the column of white fire colliding with the cloud of dark. Sautorus was strong. Much stronger than he remembered. The darkness he threw at him was almost overwhelming. It hammered and raged at him, threatening to break his will completely. The black cloud roiled endlessly from beneath the Fae. Violet streaks of lightening shuddered the dark with vibrations of malevolent power.

In contrast, Sid's white fire could barely hold it back. He felt as if he were trying to push back a massive wave. With every moment he was forced further back, the dark slowly but inevitably gaining ground.

Still, Sid was able to smile because he knew if he just held on, they could defeat the powerful Fae that stood against them. From his vantage point on top of the wall he could see clearly into the courtyard below. The Swordsmen were winning the day.

Giovanni and Tres had just dispatched two of the shadow men, even killing one of them, which was quite difficult to do. The odds clearly in their favor now, it would only be a matter of time.

Sid held on, forcing himself to resist the barrage of dark power. It had been a long time since he had experienced a victory of this sort. Too long, really. The Keepers had endured defeat after defeat over the last eighty years, and in Sid's mind, were long overdue for a victory.

"You are weak!" Sautorus cried out over the roar of the dark clouds.

"It is not my strength," Sid answered, not letting himself be drawn in by the taunt. "But the one who is in me."

The white fire brightened, responding to Sid's faith. The dark fell back, ever so slightly, fading in the surge of light. Just a little longer, Sid told himself.

"You know, this is inevitable," Sautorus continued. "Your resistance only drags this out."

A dark tendril snaked out of the swirling cloud. It crept out like a black vine, inching across the column of white fire. A chill shuddered through Sid as he felt its evil intent. The cold, icy touch seemed to feed off of the warmth of the fire.

"The only thing inevitable is the victory of Christ," Sid yelled back.

Sid watched as the black vein inched closer. Slicing out with a bolt of white fire he stopped its approach. The dark tendril recoiled but didn't retract. It waited, hungry and eager to consume.

I can't let it get to me, Sid told himself as he eyed the creeping vine of darkness. He knew what lurked inside. He knew what awful memory it brought with its touch. Just a few more moments. That's all he needed. Give the boys a little bit more time and they could face Sautorus together.

"Looks like your little slaves are doing pretty good down there," Sautorus said, nodding down to the courtyard.

There were only two shadow men remaining. The last two of the Fae's soldiers were surrounded and desperately fending off attacks from every side. The Swordsmen had pushed them into the shallow staircase on the far end of the courtyard. Victor was rounding the back side of the walkdown, and leapt inside to fully surround them.

"You don't think this is the end, do you?" Sautorus asked when Sid did not respond. "You don't think this is all I brought to the battle?"

A presence drew near the two figures locked in battle. Sid could feel it loom over him, large and domineering. His magic faltered. The white fire dimmed and the shadow from Sautorus grew stronger, even darker than before.

A giant stepped into Sid's field of vision, just behind Sautorus. A massive figure, over eight feet tall with wide shoulders and a grotesquely muscled physique, he stared down at the battle of light and dark with a sneer. Sid looked up at him in horror, his hope growing cold. The distorted face was a perfect mask of hatred. It was the face of one who had only the desires of violence and a thirst for blood.

The giant wore all black: combat boots, fatigues, and a shirt with torn sleeves to display the massive muscles of the arms. The only armor he wore was a steel helmet. A narrow plate of the helmet fell down between the eyes, protecting the only vulnerable place on the giant's body. He stood now, not only massive and strong, but nearly unbeatable.

"Attal, kill the intruders," Sautorus commanded. "I don't want there to be anything recognizable left on a single body. Do you understand me? Destroy the swordsmen."

Attal the giant nodded and turned. He leapt off the wall, out of Sid's sight. The earth shook as the massive figure hit the ground.

Dear God help us, Sid prayed, eyes wide in terror. The light faded again, giving ground to the shadow. The black vein continued to climb again up the column of white fire, like a vine twisting up the trunk of a tree. It sought out Sid's mind, hungry to feed on the despair that was blossoming terror into his soul.

Sid fought back, desperately trying to push the black vein away. Blooms of white fire burned at it, flicked the new growth that crept towards him. The fire burned without effect. The dark and seething vein crawled on, nearer and nearer to the Keeper.

Desperation settled into Sid as he felt the vein creep closer. The white fire still blazed from him, flickering and weak, but still alive. Dark clouds roiled thickly, billowing fear and despair.

"Hold on boys!" he cried out as he felt the black vein touch his temple.

He gasped as cold fingers dug into his head. Eyes wide, he threw his head back, unable to resist the creeping tendril inside him now. His mind threw itself open, exposing the deepest and most vulnerable parts.

The world faded all around Sid as he felt himself being pulled away. Away from the war of light and shadow. Away from the battle just beginning to rage again in the courtyard below. Away from the time and place where he stood, pulling him deep into the recesses of memory.

Chicago.

August 1968.

It was night time as the limousine turned onto South Halsted. Despite the hour, the streets were packed with people. A steady stream walked in the same direction as the limo. Mostly young people, they were carrying signs and chanting slogans as they walked. Some yelled at the black limousine as it passed. More than once some unknown projectile thumped against the side of the car.

"Not sure a limo was a good idea," someone inside the car remarked.

Sid Bickley looked up at the man who spoke to him. They were seated across from each other. Both looked out at the steady stream of young people crowding the streets around them. The tension was thick in the air, almost as much as the sweltering summer heat that still lingered despite the night.

"It wouldn't do for wealthy Democratic donor Sid Bickley to show up in a taxi, would it?" Sid asked as he puffed on a cigarette. He tried to sound nonchalant, but the tension in his own voice was unmistakable.

"Taxis are on strike anyway," the man next to Sid remarked.

Marion, Sid thought to himself as he watched the memory unfold. That was Marion Healey next to him, a high school science teacher. Sitting across from him was Sonny Logan, the butcher, uncomfortable in the dark suit that Sid made him put on. Next to Sonny was Rip Starr.

Alarm rose in Sid as he watched Rip stare out of the window. He knew what was coming. He knew this would be the day that the Keepers were broken. They would be betrayed and broken, never to challenge the Fae again. Today, the war would be lost.

Sid tried to scream out in his mind as this memory played out before him, to warn the men in the limo what was about to happen. But not only were his screams to no avail to the others, it didn't even help him. He was just a silent watcher, an observer of this day of tragedies.

"Even if not, we're not showing up in a taxi," Sid reiterated, tapping the ashes of the cigarette. "Or any other way that would get us too close to . . . this."

He gestured out the window at the swell of humanity marching as one down the crowded Chicago street. The contempt in Sid's voice was palpable, undisguised. He even wondered himself if he played the role of the arrogant aristocrat a little bit too well.

As the older Sid watched his younger self, he couldn't help but admire the man that he once was. Although he was over a hundred years old then, he looked to be a man in his mid-fifties that was aging extremely well. A line of grey had appeared at the temples, accenting the dark hair that was slicked back over his head. A few lines had appeared at the corners of his eyes and his skin had darkened from its native pale hue. All these changes only heightened his handsome features, as was typical for many men who reached a prime later in life.

"This is the future of our nation," Sonny remarked against Sid's contempt. "You would do well to get to know them a little better."

"They'll grow out of it," Sid said confidently. "Once they have to become accountable for their own financial wellbeing, you'll see them lose a lot of the enthusiasm for revolution."

Sonny shook his head. Just as Sid looked the part of the aristocrat, Sonny resembled every bit the man of the people that he was. His square face and receding hairline, large hands, calloused with labor, and broad shoulders gave him the look of a man who worked for a living. He kept pulling at the suit, obviously uncomfortable in it.

"It may not even come to that," Sid continued. "Take that girl there, the one in the white linen shirt, almost see through. Well, see through enough to tell she has no brazier. This is all great fun now, because all her friends are a part of it too. But just wait until some of them start getting married. Her friends will no doubt find a smart husband for themselves. Maybe a house in the suburbs somewhere and a new car. Once that happens, bathing in lakes and sleeping in parks won't seem nearly as glamorous as it does now. Why, I imagine there is a part of her right now that is starting to regret her decision. She's wondering if she shouldn't . . ."

"Damn it, Sid! What are we doing here?" Marion interrupted, losing his patience.

Ah Marion, Sid heard his distant self say as the memory replayed. Marion was always the impatient one. His pinched and serious face, looking out through thick glasses that made him seem more intense than he actually was. Marion was an open book, serious and honest, but also with a deep and authentic joy that Sid always relied upon, and was sometimes jealous of. He was also the type that liked to get right to the point.

When Sid had called them all and said to meet him in Chicago, Marion demanded to know why. Sid didn't know who was watching, who was listening, and told Marion to wait, even though Sid knew this had to drive him mad. Now, his patience was at an end.

"Show him," Sid instructed, nodding to the fourth man in the back of the limo with them.

Rip Starr produced a manilla envelope and tossed it onto Marion's lap. Of all the men there that day, Rip was the one that filled Sid with the most regret and sadness. He was also the one that looked most different from how he did today.

The warlock they would face in the alley more than fifty years later wasn't there yet. The dark and handsome features were not yet Rip's. For now, he was the awkward and unseemly man that Sid remembered. The narrow chin looked even smaller beneath lips too large for his face. A nose that was too small for the wide nostrils turned up slightly. Large eyes looked out through horn rimmed glasses that always sat crooked on his ears. Topping the pale and freckled face were large waves of thick red hair that never seemed to look real. To say that Rip Starr was less than handsome would be a vast understatement.

But he was a friend. And as Sid watched from a distance, feeling everything he felt that day, he also waited for the betrayal that would destroy the Keepers. A wound was coming, he knew, a wound that he felt down to the present. Watching helplessly as these events unfolded, he knew also that it was a wound that still crippled him.

Marion opened the envelope and slid out six black and white photographs. He sorted through them with haste, hardly giving them a glance.

"What am I looking at here?" Marion asked in mounting frustration.

Sid snorted in disgust and tapped the top photograph. In it several men were on the stage at a packed convention center. One loomed larger than the rest, his height dominating the other men.

"You don't recognize him?" Sid asked.

"Of course I do," Marion retorted. "It's Sautorus."

"Do you recognize who he's with?"

Marion looked at the pictures longer this time. He thumbed through them and shook his head, handing the packet back to Rip.

"Those are all high-ranking bosses in the Democratic Party," Sid pointed out. "And this one here next to him is Richard Daley, the Mayor of Chicago."

"So the Fae are cozying up to politicians," Marion said with a shrug. "What's new?"

"Don't you see?" Sid asked, shaking the photographs. "This is different."

"It's nothing different," Sonny said, speaking up. "We've known this for a long time. They meddle with the Democrats, Republicans, the Socialists, everybody."

"Yes, meddled, but not to this level," Sid argued. "They've taken steps to run the party now. Don't you see? Sautorus is even stepping out in public. The Family has never been exposed like that before. They're making their move."

"What move?" Sonny asked.

"Whatever it is they've been building up to," Sid almost exploded. "Don't be thick, Sonny. You know this has been coming. You know they have been preparing, planning for something like this."

"We don't know anything of the sort," Marion argued.

"We really don't," Sonny echoed.

"We don't know specifics, but we know something is coming," Sid countered. "It's all been building up to this year. The assassination of Kennedy."

"Oh, don't start with the Kennedy assassination again," Marion huffed in frustration.

"We know who was behind that."

"But it's a dead end, Sid."

"Maybe not," Sid argued, stubbing his cigarette out He leaned forward as he laid out his case. "They're starting to show their hand. Look who they've killed this year. Dr. King, Bobby Kennedy. Then the Tet offensive. Now this. Something big is happening and Sautorus is behind it. You know it, Marion."

"But they haven't accomplished anything by those assassinations," Marion countered. "The Civil Rights movement goes on, even without Dr. King. The anti-war movement is as strong as ever without Kennedy, as you can see."

He gestured out the window where the crowds were growing thicker. Nearing the convention center the protesters began to spill out into the streets, chanting and hurling insults at the passing limousine.

Sid shook his head and sat back again in his seat. Staring out the window he looked to be at a loss for words. The Sid who was watching it all knew that wasn't the case. He knew what he wanted to say but was unsure if he was ready to yet.

"There are no more lions left in Rome," Sid said quietly, almost to himself.

"What was that?" Marion demanded.

"There are no more lions left in Rome," Sid said again, louder this time.

"What is that supposed to mean?"

"It was said by a Roman senator when he stood up to oppose the tyranny of Tiberius. And no one stood with him. Don't you see? Marion? Sonny? They're getting rid of all the lions. Any man who might have the backbone, the integrity to stand up to them, they're getting rid of. And once that happens, we'll be a nation of sheep. No more lions."

"But Sid," Marion answered, his voice softening in sympathy. "You've said it yourself, if people want this then we have to let them have it. They have to decide for themselves. If not, we're no worse than they are."

"Our job is to preserve that choice," Sid countered. "Isn't it? To keep them from being bullied and manipulated in such a way that their spirit dies within them? And they become worse than slaves?"

"This is just political maneuvering," Marion said, though his argument was weakening.

The limousine slowed down as it neared the International Amphitheater. A stone, arched gateway stretched over the entrance. "Hello Democrats. Welcome to Chicago," the sign read, stretching across the gate.

Crowds packed the streets outside the convention. Inside, they were choosing the Democratic candidate for president. Outside, protesters mobbed the streets.

The limousine turned in as the crowd pushed against the car. Bodies pressed against the glass of the windows, inches from the men inside. Hands banged on the glass, on the top. Some even shook the car as it tried to squeeze through.

Chants and slogans were being hurled at the limousine. Stop the War, signs were hoisted and waved, alongside with a sea of others: Mathematicians for Peace, Imperialism Saigon Prague, Bring the Troops Home. One sign even read, Pigasus for President.

"Our operatives inside the party tell us differently," Rip spoke up for the first time. "Sautorus is doing more than just influencing, he is bullying the party. And as these pictures show, he's coming out of the closet too. Marion. Sonny. You know that matters."

Police came in and pushed back the crowd. The limo eased slowly forward pushing aside the crowd as they entered through the stone gates.

"We need this," Sid plead. "You know we do. How many defeats have we suffered recently? How many? We're losing this war. We need a win."

Marion shook his head as a heavy sigh came out of him. He looked to Sonny who shrugged in indifference.

"What you suggest we do?" Marion asked.

"We chase Sautorus off," Sid told him. "We have to. We dislodge him. Hurt him bad enough he has to go away for a while."

"They'll just replace him with someone else," Marion pointed out. "Someone even worse. Like Danileoth."

"But it will give time for the party to recover," Sid argued. He sensed he only needed just one more push to get him over to his side. "Get their heads straight again."

Marion shook his head again as the limo finally made it past the crowd and into the Amphitheater parking.

"Do we have any swordsmen with us?" he asked.

Sid nodded with a smile. He knew the sound of concession when he heard it.

"Deion, Jackson and Riley are waiting for us inside the convention," Rip answered.

The watching Sid remembered what his younger self felt at that moment. He soared. As Marion and Sonny consented to the operation Sid felt a weight lift off of his heart. They were doing something, finally. They would strike back and begin to take back the war they had been dreadfully losing for years now. The future was open again. Hope was real.

Except the Sid who watched this knew it was all a lie. As he saw his younger self emerge from the limo, buttoning the dark jacket and sliding from the seat, he knew it would be the last time. Never again would Sid feel that hope, that sense of optimism that the future was really wide open. In mere moments, all hope would come crashing down, killed forever.

The group made their way across the lot to the International Amphitheater. A thick knot of armed guards saw them through. The concourse was full of people, some running up and down the passage. They shouldered their way through the throng and up the ramp that led to the arena.

A swelter of heat and the smell of panic greeted them as they stepped into the amphitheater. Sid rocked back on his heels, surprised by the sudden noise emerging from the sea of humanity. For a moment he doubted, overwhelmed by the scene that greeted him.

Below them, chaos ensued in the arena. Long signs indicating state delegations rose up beside campaign signs and war protest signs. Mobs of people pushed against other mobs. In one knot men in suits fought with each other while others tried to pull them apart. Another group of people were chanting, "Stop the War." On the raised seats beside the stage men were arguing heatedly. All the while a man on stage pounded a gavel on the podium and desperately tried to restore order.

"The hell is going on here?" Marion whispered, more to himself than anyone else.

"I'm going to go find the swordsmen," Rip said, rushing off into the chaos below.

Sid looked around for answers. Seeing a reporter a few seats down he made his way over and grabbed his sleeve.

"What's happening?" he demanded to know, pointing down at the chaotic scene

"The anti-war platform just got defeated," the reporter said as he scribbled down notes. "All the McGovern people are pissed off. They can see what's coming."

Sid looked at the scene unfolding in the amphitheater below. People screamed and pushed. Police in riot helmets were dragging some protesting members away by the arms. Men in suits were brawling, or shouting red-faced at one another. The political process had just descended into mayhem.

"What's coming?" Sid asked, not sure he wanted to know.

"Can't you tell?" the reporter asked back, pointing down at the chaotic scene. "Those sons of bitches are going to nominate Humphrey."

"Humphrey?" Sid asked, his confusion breaking the spell that the swarming crowd had cast over him. "Has he even won a single state?"

"Doesn't matter," the reporter said with an edge of anger. "The bosses have spoken. It's gonna be Humphrey, and the war is going to keep on. From what I hear, this came all the way from the top."

Sid felt himself grow cold. All the way from the top. It had Sautorus' prints all over it. Humphrey would be the nominee and the Vietnam War would go on. What their reasons for the conflict were Sid had not been able to discern. But if the Fae wanted Vietnam to continue, it would be their job to stop it.

"When you say it came from the top . . ." Sid let the question linger.

"The President himself." the reporter said. "Who else? The bastard says he doesn't want to run for reelection. Instead, he wants to control things from the inside."

With those words all of his suspicions were confirmed. Sid nodded and walked back over to the Keepers to tell them what he had just learned. They nodded, not surprised. Resolve replaced uncertainty.

Sid heard someone call his name and turned to see Rip running up towards him. Three swordsmen followed, dressed as bodyguards for state delegates. Deion. Jackson. Riley. Seeing them again, even in memory, stung the Sid who was watching this all unfold like a bad dream.

"Sautorus isn't here," Rip said as he reached the others. "I've been told he's at the Hilton right now with the bosses from the Party. There's two other Fae with him and several shadow men. Something is happening, and it's big."

403

Nods from the swordsmen confirmed everything Rip had said. Whatever was going on, the convention was just the tip of the iceberg.

"We got two cars out by the stockyards," Deion said before Sid had to ask. "We'll get you out through the back way."

Guided by the swordsmen they went back into the concourse and followed them to the service corridors below. Minutes later they were back outside in the sweltering August air. Behind the amphitheater the putrid aromas of the stockyards wafted over the hastily built fence.

Everything became a blur once they got outside. They piled into two cars and raced north. They twisted onto the South Loop and turned onto Michigan Avenue. As soon as the car made the left it came to a screeching halt.

Lining Michigan Avenue was a sea of protesters that choked the street completely. They filled the park next to them and spilled out, chanting and waving signs. A waiting line of cops stood on the other side, blocking the protest from moving any further.

"Get us around back," Sid instructed. "We're not going in the front door anyway."

Deion whipped around and took them up side streets. He pushed the pedal as hard as he dared, weaving through the protesters that were flowing into the park from inside the city. More and more kept pouring in, pulled by the gravity of those already there. Something big was happening and they all wanted to be a part of it.

That same feeling was taking over Sid and the Keepers. The swordsmen with them could feel it too. Something was going down that would force big changes onto the world. They stood on a pivot, a hinge of human history. And if they didn't stop the hands that were moving it, then everything would get pushed in the wrong direction.

Tires squealed as the cars stopped in the streets behind the Hilton. Just on the other side they could hear the protesters who had gathered thickly in front of the hotel. Leaving the cars in the streets, swordsmen and Keeper alike got out and ran towards the back entrance.

As they pushed through the service entrance the swordsmen surrounded the Keepers and ushered them through like bodyguards in a panic. Deion had his hand on Sid's arm, pushing him through the Hilton's kitchen. Cook and busboy looked up but no one challenged them. With the panic outside and the hurried way they rushed through everyone assumed they were politicians being ushered to safety.

In the stairwell they dropped the facade. Jackson consulted a notepad and pointed up.

"Seventh floor," he said. "At least that's where a bellhop took his luggage three days ago."

Sid nodded and without hesitation they darted up the stairs, taking two at each stride. By the time they reached the seventh floor they were winded but far from tired. Adrenaline coursed through Sid, making his hands itch for the fight to come.

At the seventh floor Jackson peaked out the door and turned back to the landing.

"About halfway down the hall we've got at least four shadow men guarding," he reported.

Marion took a look for himself and nodded. "Sid, what have you got for us?" he asked.

Before Sid could say a word Sonny stepped forward. "I've got this one," he said.

"You sure?" Marion asked. "This isn't exactly your area of expertise."

Sonny smiled and shook his head. "Oh, you men of little faith," he smirked. "The tongue is indeed a mighty weapon. Didn't you know that?"

Sonny was the glossal of the group. His gift being tongues and languages, it was the most unusual, but also the most underrated of all the gifts the Keepers operated in. Even his fellow Keepers kept underestimating what Sonny was capable of doing with his gift.

Stepping forward Sonny opened the door just enough to stick his head through. He looked into the hallway and turned back to the men on the landing.

"Can I get some mood lighting?" he asked Sid.

Sid nodded and closed his eyes. Breathing deeply, he reached out to the spirit that always hovered near him, one he knew always dwelt within him. Placing his hands on the wall he prayed and pulled himself deeper. Reaching in and reaching out all at once he felt the power inside him waken.

The lights flickered inside the stairwell before going dark completely. Emergency lights blinked on, bathing the landing in an eerie, red glow. Sonny nodded in thanks and opened the door again.

This time, Sonny stepped through, letting the door close behind him. From the landing Sid could hear the Keeper speaking in a harsh whisper.

They were words he couldn't understand, words that no human tongue knew nor any human ear could comprehend. But there was some part of him that did understand. There was a part of him that did know.

As Sid listened to the low and guttural sound coming from the other side of the door, he felt a presence stir inside of him. It was a voice, deep in the recesses of his own mind. It was the voice of an urgent and undeniable command.

He had a job to do, the voice told him. He had left it undone and would be in deep trouble if he didn't go and do it immediately. Urgency was of the utmost importance. This was critical. He had to drop everything he was doing and hurry downstairs to do this or everything would fail.

Even knowing this voice came from Sonny on the other side of the door, it was still difficult for Sid to resist. He felt the command pull at him, insistent and overwhelming. Fear began to ripple through him, growing with every moment he disobeyed.

"I've got to quit underestimating that guy," Marion said, echoing Sid's thoughts. A sheen of perspiration glistened on his forehead as he concentrated on resisting the command of the glossal.

The door to the hallway pushed open and Sonny stuck his head out. "Coast is clear."

"You got to get us earplugs next time," Sid remarked as they stepped into the darkened hallway.

Sonny smiled, holding the door open for the others to step through. The red exit signs cast the only light in the hallway. A few of the doors were opened with curious tenants wondering what had happened to the lights.

Sid and the others made their way to room 712. They stopped and looked at the door and then at one another, knowing but not knowing what lay on the other side.

"Any idea how many he's got with him?" Marion asked after they had stared at the door for a moment.

"There's still about three or four shadow men unaccounted for," Deion informed them. "Maybe two more Fae. That's all we know for sure."

"Do we kick or should I blast it down?" Sid asked, readying himself for the battle ahead.

Except the watching Sid knew he wouldn't be ready for the battle ahead. He couldn't be ready. What lay on the other side of the door was worse than he could ever anticipate. It was worse than he ever wanted to.

Before Sid could do anything the handle to room 712 turned on its own. The door creaked as it slowly fell open. A flickering, golden light cast an eerie glow inside the room. But the feeling of darkness within was even more palpable than in the hall outside.

Don't go in! Don't go in!

The watching Sid screamed to the younger version of himself. He screamed to Sonny and Marion, breaking inside as he watched them nod to each other. He screamed at Deion, Jackson and Riley, the three bravest men he knew. He screamed out as they pushed the door open the rest of the way and stepped in.

Always the loyal and true swordsmen, they stepped in first. Always the brave and unyielding men they took the first steps into the dark and unknown, ready to sacrifice themselves for the cause.

The watching Sid screamed out, because he was the only one that knew. His younger self followed the others, oblivious to his cries of warning. They all stepped through: Marion, Sonny and Rip. They stepped into the room illuminated by candlelight and full of a dark evil.

Sid yelled out warning to no avail. He would be the only one that knew. Inside, he broke with that dreadful knowledge. Of all the men that walked through that door, he would be the only one who walked out.

Chapter 36 - Battle of the Courtyard, Part III

The last of the shadow men disappeared in a cloud of dark smoke, drifting away on the breeze. With the last of them gone Malachi stopped to catch his breath. The wound in his side cried out in protest. He touched the tender area and grimaced. Though the light from Sid had begun to heal it, it still radiated pain.

"I think that's another win for us," Vic said as he picked up his rifle and shouldered it.

The men came together, checking to see if they all came out of the fight in one piece. On top of the wall, they could see the battle of light and dark. A swirl of black clouds emanated from the Fae, streaks of violent electricity crackling within the living shadows. Sid stood opposite, surrounded by swirls of white fire. A column of the golden energy emanated from his hands, colliding with the pillar of dark cloud from the Fae.

The men smiled, lifted by the energy that flowed out of the Keeper. Strength, hope and courage were born on those flames. Tongues of the fire floated through the courtyard, granting a burst of energy whenever it struck one of them.

"Malachi, you need to get up to the wall," Giovanni said as they watched the battle of light and shadow. "Sid needs you up there."

"Me? Why?" Malachi asked.

"Can't say for sure. Just that Sid said it was important you get up there as soon as you can. I think he needs help with that Fae."

Malachi nodded and started forward, still holding his side. He stopped short as he watched a massive figure step into view.

The figure stood atop the wall, just beside Sautorus. Dark shadows cast over his features by the interplay of light and dark.

"That must the giant I have been hearing so much about," Vic said in voice that tried to be light hearted. "Using a giant? C'mon, that is so fifth century BC."

The giant stepped off the wall and landed on the ground below. The earth shook as his feet made contact. He stood up to full height glaring at the Swordsmen from across the courtyard.

Malachi looked up at the towering figure, terrified and awed all at once. He stood at least eight feet tall by his estimate. Out of the cut off sleeves Malachi could see the grotesquely bulging muscles, almost misshapen in their proportion. Veins snaked beneath taut skin, threatening to burst out completely.

But it was the look on the giant's face that made Malachi's skin grow cold. He couldn't recall seeing such anger and hatred, such malice and murder written on one single face. Dark eyes glared out through protruding brows. As they looked, Malachi could see that they only looked for something to annihilate. This was a creature that was bred for one single purpose, that had just one mandate in life - kill and destroy.

Victor unslung the rifle and brought to his shoulder.

"I don't think bullets will kill it," Danny pointed out as the giant approached.

"We just have to slow it down," Vic said as he took his first shot. "Get Malachi up to that wall."

The giant flinched as the bullet made contact. He brushed the spot off on his chest where the shot had hit and started forward.

Two more shots fired out of the rifle. The giant didn't slow. His approach came on, steady and unwavering.

"Let's try your weak spot," Vic said as he aimed the rifle higher, striking the plate between the giants' eyes.

The massive creature recoiled as his head was thrown back. Another head shot threw him back again.

The giant stumbled and fell to one knee. He glared at Victor, pure hatred spitting from his eyes.

Not wasting the opportunity Vic poured the shots on. He fired as fast as he could, aiming for the protective plate between the giant's eyes. With each shot the giant was knocked back.

With a growl the giant leapt to his feet. Covering his forehead with his hand he charged forward, surprising everyone with his speed.

"Malachi! Get to the wall!" Vic yelled as he pedaled back, firing as he retreated.

The giant ripped the rifle from Victor's grip, swinging it at his head. Vic barely ducked the blow, rolling away as he unholstered the .45. The giant snapped the rifle in two and dropped it to his feet.

Rolling to his knees Vic leveled the pistol, unloading the magazine into the raging giant. The creature didn't seem to notice the shots, charging forward with undiminished fury.

A huge fist came careening toward the kneeling Vic. He tried to pull back, but too late. Malachi could only watch, knowing that fist could break his friend in two.

A blur of motion stepped between Victor and the fist. Gary stood, arms crossed, blocking the blow. Both his arms trembled, holding back one of the giant's.

"Are you the strongest they've got?" the giant sneered and pulled his other hand back.

With a roar Gary pushed back the first hand in time to block the second blow. He stumbled back under the sheer power of the shot. The giant darted in, throwing quick punches at Gary.

Gary backpedaled, trying to furiously block the shots aimed at him. With both hands he kept the shots at bay. The strain on his face showed it took every ounce of energy, even with both hands, to block the powerful blows.

"Malachi! Get out of here!" he managed to cry out as he was thrown back against the wall.

The fight had moved so fast Malachi had only been able to stand and watch. The fury and speed, the strength and power on display were more than he had ever seen. The combat paralyzed him with fear just to look at it. That there were powers like this walking among the children of man seemed an affront to nature. How they were expected to defy this was beyond any ability of his to reckon.

Gary's cry shook him out of his stupor. Malachi looked across the courtyard and saw the open path between him and the stairs leading to the top of the wall. He raced across, putting all of his speed in getting away from the giant.

As Malachi took off Tres darted to the side of the giant. His knife flashed in the night, stabbing at the outside of the giant's knee.

The blade bounced off as it hit the leathery hide of skin. Tres looked at the knife in bewilderment. The giant snarled at the distraction and swung a backhand at his assailant.

Tres had only a split second to respond. He bent over backwards as the massive hand passed over. He pushed the motion into a handspring, pushing himself safely away.

The giant turned back to Gary, hardly missing a beat. The massive fists rained down, pummeling the big man. Gary scrambled to block them as best he could with his back against the courtyard wall.

The other Swordsmen sprang into action. Danny and Giovanni unloaded their pistols into the hulking form. As soon as they were empty Vic took a leaping kick at the giant's knee. Zach charged in and slammed against the giant's back.

None of these attacks moved the massive form at all. It wasn't until he turned and noticed Malachi running across the courtyard that he relented.

With another snarl the giant turned and started towards Malachi. Gary reached out and grabbed a massive arm. The giant whirled and threw a punch back. Gary let go and slid to the ground as the punch landed against the wall. Stone cracked and dust flew as the fist punched a hole in the rock of the wall.

Just as Malachi neared the far stairs the giant took two steps and leapt into the air. With agility uncanny for his size, he jumped over the length of the courtyard. The earth shook as he touched down with a boom, mere feet from Malachi's running figure.

As soon as he landed the giant reached out and grabbed at Malachi. The wide span of fingers grasped the rifle and sword slung over his back. The giant pulled and threw Malachi back, sending him twisting through the air.

Malachi felt himself lifted off the ground and the world spun and tumbled as he was hurled through the air. The strap of the sword ripped off and the weapon fell away. He hit the grass of the courtyard in a heap, rolling to a stop. The wound ached in him again along with a dozen new bruises.

The giant stood on the opposite end of the courtyard; arms outstretched. He was sending a clear message. If any of the men wanted out, they would have to go through him.

The Swordsmen lined up on the other side, appraising their enemy. Above him, on the wall, they could see the white fire dim around Sid as the shadow made progress. Not only could they see it, they began to feel it as well. The air around them grew thick with the shadow. The grey mist dotted with wisps of gold became darker, the gold smaller and dimmer. With the growing darkness they felt a cold creep up inside of them. A desperation began to take hold, a hopelessness that threatened to destroy them from within.

"I guess we fight this giant," Gary said, pulling himself to his full height.

"Any ideas?" Danny asked.

"Huh," Gary answered with a grunt. "I was hoping you would have one."

"We have to do this together," Vic said. "Let's all grab a limb. Two on the legs. Gary, see what you can do with him."

The men nodded and spread out. They formed an arc and moved down the courtyard towards the waiting figure. The giant charged forward without hesitation, straight towards Gary. When the distance closed, he pulled his arm back for a crumbling blow.

Tres leapt out and grabbed the arm with both hands. The arm fell down, weighed by the figure who had attached himself to it. Gary charged in with his shoulder, putting all of his weight to collide with the giant's midsection.

The hulking figure grunted as he was thrown back. He reached up to claw Tres away when Vic leapt on the other arm, dragging it down to his side.

Roaring in frustration the giant tried to spin around. The other four men leapt forward, grabbing onto the massive legs and holding with all their might.

The giant struggled against his captors. Swordsmen held all of his limbs, covered him and weighed him down. He tried to move, but even his massive strength was mired by their combined might.

"You know what I found out about bullies?" Gary asked as he delivered a punch to the giant's gut.

The muscled frame of the behemoth shuddered and fell back under the blow. Gary reared back and slammed another fist into the ribs. He swung in with the opposite hand, making contact with the other side.

"Bullies love to give out the shots," Gary continued as he rained punches on the giant.

With each blow Gary reared back and threw himself forward. All of his might went into the punches. Every ounce of the magnified strength of his gift went into his fists. He threw himself forward straining with his legs and twisting as hard as he could. Each blow was enough to shatter the bones of an ordinary man into shrapnel.

"But they can't stand taking them."

Gary twisted and shot out a vicious uppercut, taking the giant under the chin. The goliath's head flew back. His feet buckled under the combined strain of punches and weight on his limbs.

Gary pressed on, not giving the giant a second to recover. He swung out with an arcing hook, making contact with the cheek. Again and again, he went for the head, rearing back and putting all of his might into each contact.

The giant recoiled under the rain of blows. Blood dripped from his mouth and ran down the granite-hard chin. His head flew back under another massive punch to the head.

Gary felt his fists scream out in pain. Each shot reverberated through his bones and down his spine. Soon, he thought, one of them had to break.

Aiming for the nose, Gary leaned in, driving his fist forward. Just as his hand was to make contact the giant dipped his head and pulled it to the side.

The blow glanced, just grazing the cheek. Gary pulled back and tried to right himself, containing his momentum.

The giant strained and jerked his torso. His head snapped forward. A bone rending crunch sounded in the courtyard as the armored forehead of the giant made contact with Gary's face.

Crying out, Gary rocked back and threw up his hands. He fell to his knees, blood spilling between his fingers.

The giant lashed out with mouth gaping open at Tres. He bit hard, teeth digging into the soft flesh of the shoulder. With a jerk of his head, he ripped the man off.

Tresmond's scream echoed Gary's cry. He let go of the giant's arm and tried to pry himself loose.

The giant jerked his head again, releasing Tres from the grip of his teeth. The titanic hands gripped Vic on the back of the neck, easily prying the man away. He held him at arm's length and pulled back with his fist balled up in rage.

Malachi watched their plan fall to ruins as he held onto one of the giant's legs. The giant pulled back to strike, and he knew the vulnerable Victor, struggling at the end of his muscled arm, would be crushed.

Without thinking Malachi leapt up and grabbed hold of the giant's shoulder and lifted himself up his back. Reaching for anything to hurt the massive creature he jabbed at the only vulnerable spot he could think of. Malachi's finger found the tender opening of the eyes and pushed with all his might.

The giant screamed out in frustration. He dropped Vic to the ground and grabbed at Malachi, roughly throwing him off. Malachi hit pavement this time, the contact jarring his teeth and shaking every bone on his body. He felt his side split open and begin to bleed again.

Vic scrambled over to Gary as the giant freed himself of all his entanglements. Lifting his friend, he tried to drag him away. Gary struggled to his feet, his legs buckling at first. Blood poured from his nose.

"I think he broke my nose," Gary cried out as he found his unsteady feet.

"It was too big anyway," Vic retorted, pulling him away from the giant.

Smelling blood, the giant advanced toward the retreating figures. Zach called out a warning. Vic whipped around just as the hulking mass bore down upon them.

Pushing Gary aside Vic dodged the shots coming in hard and fast. Amazed at the speed of the massive frame he backpedaled, knowing one contact would crumble him to the ground.

"C'mon, fat ass, try to catch me," Vic taunted, trying to draw the giant away.

The goliath was only too eager to comply. He leapt towards the dodging Victor, flashing out with strikes impossibly fast for his large frame. Vic ducked and dodged, moving away from Gary.

The other Swordsmen circled around. Zach ran up behind the giant and kicked out at the side of his knee. Danny followed with a leaping kick at his back. Giovanni struck the opposite leg.

None of the shots had a noticeable effect except to irritate the behemoth. With each shot he lashed out, always a beat too slow. Vic continued to taunt and feint, keeping the giant off balance and wondering where to focus.

Malachi picked himself off the ground and wondered why he felt so heavy. A deep ache permeated his every limb. His arms and legs weighed more than he remembered. Exhaustion racked his body. He could feel the wound in his side open and bleeding again.

Standing up he saw the battle going terribly wrong. Tres picked himself up, bleeding from his shoulder. Gary was struggling to his feet holding a nose that had been smashed against his face. The other four were circling the giant and raining down ineffective blows.

Worst of all the courtyard had grown dark and cold. The grey mist had thickened into an almost black miasma. It swirled around them in a quickening wind, a vortex centered around the battle at the top of the wall.

Sid was almost lost. A dim light still shone from him. Weak flames of white fire spouted out from under him, barely keeping him from being consumed by the black cloud. Pillars of thick darkness hammered at the Keeper, threatening to consume him at any moment.

Malachi would have to get up there, and fast, or all would be lost.

Hating to turn his back on his warring brothers Malachi ran for the stairs again. His legs pumped slow, like he ran through thick mud. The darkness buffeted at him, draining his strength with every step.

There's no way we can win, he heard himself say. He shook his head, pushing the thought away. Cold and desperate thoughts kept creeping towards his heart, scratched at the surface of his mind, demanding to be let in. They demanded that Malachi acknowledge there was no way they could win. All was lost. They should simply lie down and give up. Let destiny take over and have her way here. It was inevitable after all. He was a middle-aged man. What could he do, after all?

"The Lord is my strength and my shield," he said to himself, feeling a pulse of strength in the saying.

As Malachi stumbled forward the other Swordsmen continued to engage the giant from all angles. Leaping kicks came from every side, the attacker darting away before the creature could counter. The giant growled in frustration as his massive hands swiped at empty air. He spun around, searching in vain for any he could vent his wrath upon.

"C'mon," Vic himself growled. "You have to wear down soon."

Except Vic could tell he was the only one wearing down. The giant seemed driven by an inexhaustible energy while he felt pulled down by an invisible weight. His breath came in deep and ragged gasps. Looking around he could see the same wear on the men around him. It was the darkness, he knew. The thick and growing black storm that was swirling around them. It wore them down moment by moment.

Tres, finally finding his legs, leapt up on the giant. He pulled himself up, straddling the massive shoulders. Digging at the giants head he tried to claw the helmet away.

The giant roared out in frustration. He jerked forward and spun his arms around but couldn't reach Tres as he pulled away at the steel head guard. The other Swordsmen dove in, seizing the opportunity, kicking at

415

the legs and feet of the stumbling creature.

With another roar the giant charged forward. Pulling his arms in tight he held Tres in place as he raced towards the wall. He leaned down, like a bull charging. Tres clawed at the helmet, scrambling to hold on to the head that shook and evaded his grasp.

The giant hit the wall with a trembling shock. Leaning forward he put all of his weight behind the collision, hitting first with Tresmond.

The wall shook as stone and dust flew out from the impact. Deep cracks ran up the side of the wall, threatening to topple the structure completely.

Tres had no time to react. His eyes went wide in shock as he collided with the wall. Every ounce of air pushed out of him as he felt bones in his rubs crack under the pressure. With the strength in his arms giving way, he let go of the giant and crumpled to the ground. His mouth opened and closed, grasping for air.

"Tres!" Malachi cried out as he saw his friend fall to the ground struggling for air.

The giant whipped his head around. A malicious and evil glare cut through the darkened and swirling fog. He lurched towards Malachi.

Malachi turned to run, only feet from the stairs. The giant quickly closed the space between them, his massive fist upraised for a finishing blow.

Victor flew in and slid across the ground. He kicked his feet out, tangling his own with the giant's. The creature pitched forward and tumbled to the ground. His face bounced off the turf as the ground shook under the impact.

Seeing the opportunity the other men leapt on the giant's back, pinning him to the ground. Vic untangled himself from the flailing legs and grabbed at the helmet. He fell on the head to keep it still and took hold of the steel armor in both hands.

"Go!" he yelled at Malachi.

The giant bucked and writhed, almost throwing the men off. He rolled over onto his back, crushing Danny beneath him. Danny was forced to let go and tried to push the suffocating weight off of him. Flipping back over the giant gathered his legs beneath him and stood. He threw his arms out shaking off Giovanni and Zach. Reaching up he easily peeled Vic off and threw him aside.

Malachi was halfway up the stairs when the giant shook himself free.

He stumbled on, feeling each leg weigh as much as his entire body. The dark wind was howling now, buffeting him with near hurricane force winds. He fell against the wall as his legs gave way. Groaning, he picked himself up again to make his way up.

The giant stood up to full height, seemingly stronger than when he began. He reached down with both hands and picked up the groaning Danny. Lifting him high the giant hurled Danny towards the struggling Malachi, heaving him like a human catapult.

Danny flailed helplessly as he flew through the air. He slammed into Malachi, his head striking the stone wall. A gash opened on his head and blood poured out as he crumpled to the stone unconscious.

Malachi struggled as he rolled down the steps. His body slipped over the side and he crashed to the ground below. The earth rumbled as giant footsteps pounded towards him.

The giant stood over Malachi before he could find his feet. Menacing eyes glared down at him, almost glowing red in the dark wind. A huge fist reared back to deliver a crumbling blow.

Just as the fist came down a figure hurled in and knocked the arm away. The giant stumbled against the wall as Vic pushed the blow away. With a roar he reared back to hit his new assailant.

Vic ducked just in time as the huge fist sailed over his head. He tried to backpedal, out of range of the long arms.

This time, he was too slow. The giant reached out with his other hand and grabbed hold of Vic's shoulder in a crushing grip. Victor only had time to groan when the giant pulled him forward. At the same time, he raised a knee into the soft flesh of the stomach.

Vic folded onto the ground, holding his mid-section. All the air had been forced from his lungs and a dull pain roared through his body. The first responder part of his mind came alive, assessing all the tender organs within that may have been ruptured.

The giant lifted Vic by the neck, bringing him face to face. The massive hand squeezed down, cutting off the flow of both air and blood. Vic scrambled against the iron hands that refused to yield. He could feel consciousness slipping away from him.

A stone from the garden came flying in, striking the giant on the side of the head. Before he could react, another bounced off the steel helmet. The giant turned as Giovanni and Zach each reached down for another stone from the garden. He hurled Victor away and charged at the two men.

Both the men threw their rocks and split away. The giant went right towards Giovanni. He came down fast throwing a flurry of punches. Giovanni struggled to avoid them, his body feeling weak and slow. The dark wind was eating away at him as it had the others. Each move a bit behind the one before it. Each dodge of the fist a little more delayed.

Zach raced over to Malachi's side, helping him off the ground. Blood poured from the wound in his side. He barely could keep his feet beneath him.

"We got to get you up there," Zach said, slinging Malachi's arm over his shoulder.

"I got nothing left," Malachi groaned. "We've lost Zach. What can we do?"

"We don't have a choice," Zach said, jostling him a bit. "C'mon, let's get up those stairs."

Malachi felt a surge of strength from his friend. They didn't have a choice. That was the truth. If nothing else, they would fight to the end.

It was a strange assurance to have, even Malachi recognized that. Being pummeled by the dark wind which howled all around them, which drained all their hope and strength, it sounded like utter nonsense. It was pure folly. They would lose, the gale of dark fog told them. There was no point to go on.

Keep up the fight, the other voice said. Give God a chance to step in.

Against all odds Malachi felt strength in him again. He tried to push out the dark voice of despair and listen to that small, almost whisper, of hope.

Leaning against Zach he put one more foot in front of the other and moved towards the stairs again. On top of the wall the fight had grown even more desperate. The darkness closed in tighter about the struggling Sid. The light from him had grown dimmer and weaker.

A cry from inside the courtyard drew their attention. Malachi turned to see Giovanni lose his race to stay out of the giant's attack. A fast and powerful fist caught him on the side of the head. He stumbled and fell back.

The giant stepped in with another blow under the chin. Giovanni's head rocked back as he flew off his feet and landed on his back. Arms splayed wide on the ground. The prone figure didn't move. Malachi could only pray he wasn't dead.

The giant turned his attention back to Malachi. He could feel all the malice in that glare as the behemoth approached through the howl of dark wind. This would be it, he told himself. We're about out of tricks.

"Get up the stairs," Zach said, releasing Malachi and squaring up against the giant.

Malachi fell against the wall and had push himself off again. His arm trembled with the effort as a lightheadedness began to swirl through him. I'm losing blood, he thought. Got to do something fast.

Zach stood between him and the giant. As the creature approached, he gave no ground or sign that he would move. Malachi could only watch in horror as the giant neared and leaned in for a punch.

Throwing up both his arms Zach blocked the blow. He stood his ground, not giving an inch despite the massive shot that had just been delivered. The giant looked down at his own hand, as if not believing what had happened.

"Is that all you got?" Zach taunted, daring the giant to strike again.

The giant struck again. Again, Zach blocked the shot.

The giant sneered and leaned in, charging at this newer, frustrating enemy. The smaller man was thrown back by the force. Crashing into Malachi he sent them both to the ground.

Malachi grunted as he struggled to disentangle himself. Massive hands closed around his ankle and he felt himself pulled away. For the second time that night Malachi was thrown back across the courtyard.

As he soared through the air, flipping end over end, he cried out in despair. The world spun around him and didn't stop until he crashed to the ground. He felt the breath forced out of his lungs as his body cried out in pain, the searing wound in his side spasmed in agony.

Forcing himself to his feet again hope shriveled up inside him. He was back at the far side of the courtyard. The giant, who loomed over Zach now, stood between him and the stairs he needed to reach.

The dark fog grew even darker. The wind howled around him, knocking him to his feet. Swordsmen lay prone all over the courtyard. On top of the wall, the dim light of white fire around Sid faded with each second.

Chapter 37 - The Fall of the Keepers

August 1968

Sid was the last to step into room.

The memory unfolded before him in a surreal and almost distant way. Rip was just in front of him, but off to his left, just as he remembered. They walked through a short but narrow passageway that opened up into the suite.

The room was lit by candles that filled the room. Orange light flickered from at least a hundred little flames scattered all over. Strange and twisting shadows danced across the ceiling and up the wall. Three figures stood at the window, their backs to Sid and the others. All were dressed in black suits. None of them wore shoes.

"A beautiful sight to behold," said the one in the middle, towering over the others by at least a foot.

"Drink it in," Marion said with a challenge. "It won't last."

"Ah, that's where your wrong, Keeper," Sautorus said as all three of them turned around. "This is just the beginning."

Sid fanned out with the others, facing the Fae in a line. Rip took his place behind Marion, ready to pour his power into him. It would be more than enough, Sid remembered thinking. Including Sautorus there were three Fae. With Rip and the three other Keepers it would be more than enough.

A door to the right opened and four shadow men emerged. Deion saw them first and the swordsmen went to stand between them and the Keepers. The two groups faced each other but made no move to attack.

"I think you've meddled enough," Marion said to Sautorus. "It's time to let the people alone. Let them make their own choices."

The sounds of protest outside the hotel grew louder. Whatever was happening with the gathering in the park it was growing quickly out of control. Sautorus turned and looked out the window again.

"Are you sure you don't want to see this?" he asked, amused at whatever he was witnessing.

"I just want to see you gone," Marion answered. "And to stop interfering in the affairs of men."

Sautorus chuckled and crossed the room. He poured himself a drink, and after inhaling deeply of its scent he sipped.

"As usual you are showing up late, and to the wrong party," the Fae said.

He stepped over to a record player. Lifting the wooden lid, he reached inside and produced a vinyl disc and twirled it between his fingers.

"You see, you probably think this is about politics, don't you?" he asked.

Sautorus nodded at the Keeper's silence and placed the record on the turntable.

"This isn't about politics," the Fae continued. "Or presidents for that matter. We actually don't care who the president is. Don't get me wrong, we know who the president will be. And it won't be Hubert Humphrey. But that's not near as important as you think it is."

"You think we're stupid," Sid spoke up, not being able to resist the taunts of Sautorus. "You've been digging yourself and the Family deeper and deeper into politics. We know what you're up to."

Sautorus shook his head and placed the needle on the record. The baritone voice of Charles Trenet filled the hotel room with the French anthem "La Mer."

> La mer qu'on voit danser
> Le long des golfes clairs
> A des reflets d'argent, la mer
> Des reflets changeants sous la pluie

"Most everybody today prefers the Bobby Darin version," Sautorus said as he sipped and listened to the song. "But I find the Trenet original as an ode to the sea a more poetic and haunting piece of music. Not to mention, everything sounds better in French, wouldn't you say?"

Sautorus walked back over to the window and peered out again. The milling sounds of thousands of voices had grown louder and more panicked. Some of the shouts turned to screams. A bullhorn belted out orders to disperse. Breaking glass crashed somewhere down below.

"No, I think it's safe to say you have no idea what we're doing here," Sautorus continued as he stared out the window. "This is bigger than one election. This is bigger than America. Tonight is the night when we take control."

Something in Sautorus' voice dug at Sid's nerves. The Fae was taunting them, so sure of himself.

Unable to resist Sid walked over to the wide hotel window. Parting the sheer curtains, he looked down at the chaos that had erupted across the street.

Lincoln Park had exploded in violence. Young protesters clashed with police armed in riot gear. The haze of tear gas hung thick in the air, almost obscuring the scene below. Sid watched as a shirtless, young man with blood streaming down his face threw a bottle at the line of approaching cops.

Everywhere Sid looked there was pandemonium. Protesters scrambled away from the police, some forming pockets of resistance. Police beat at the protesters with billy clubs. Many were being dragged away towards waiting wagons. Projectiles were being lobbed at law enforcement. Screams of pain and protest, demand and order, drifted through the scene of unfolding chaos.

"You wanted to start a riot," Sid whispered, stunned at what he realized. "That's what this is about? Starting a riot?"

Sautorus furrowed his brow at Sid and shook his head slowly.

"Riots? No, this is about control, Sid Bickley. We can sow chaos anytime we want. Now, we can impose order. Anytime we want. The old order is finished. Do you hear me, Keeper of the Flame? It's done. A new day is coming upon the world. The Age of Aquarius, yes?"

The Fae laughed, earnestly amused at himself.

"No, not the Age of Aquarius I'm afraid. The flesh fails and we are the light of the new world," he said with eyes wide, embracing whatever mad vision was driving him. "Let the sunshine in."

A deeper realization dawned on Sid as he looked into the wide, fanatic eyes of the Fae. He was right, Sid could see that now. He was right. This wasn't about politics or presidents or riots on the streets. The Fae were destroying the old order of the world. And they had been doing it for decades. The world wars, the Great Depression, the Communists, NATO, the assassination of Kennedy, King, counter culture, pop culture, anarchists, the Pill, the military-industrial complex, globalization; it all unfolded before his eyes in an awful and horrendous clarity. They weren't just influencing and moving the world of man, they were reshaping it in their own image.

Worst of all, it was finished. The work had been complete. On this one night they had taken hold of the reins of the world. Politics, economy, culture, education; even religion was by and large under their control. The war was lost.

Sid backed away from the window, his feelings of horror written clearly across his face. Sautorus smiled deep and wicked. The other Fae stepped beside him, their handsome faces impassive and cruel.

Reaching within Sid summoned streams of white fire. They flowed out of him and around him, drowning out the dim candlelight.

Marion and Sonny stepped up beside him, forming a wall that faced off against the Fae. The other men summoned their own spires of white flame. Rip stood behind Marion, reaching out to touch his shoulders. His healing power would magnify Marion's already formidable white fire, making it impossible to resist.

The Fae summoned clouds of darkness. They swirled thick and ominous, streaked with violet charges of fork lightning.

The two forces collided in the candle lit of room 712 as Charles Trenet's "Le Mer" rose into a crescendo. Outside, the riots surged. Downtown, the Democratic Convention unfolded into chaos. In the other rooms in the Hilton people huddled in fear and uncertainty as they listened to the raging across the street in Lincoln Park. Soon to be Democratic nominee Hubert Humphrey watched the riots from his window and could smell the tear gas as the clouds drifted in the still and sweltering August night.

A sensation of dread settled over the city that night, and even the nation as a whole. Most would attribute it to the mayhem in the streets and cities of America, the volatile turn that politics had taken. Few would suspect the awful truth. Few would understand that the old world of free men, of virtue and wisdom, the world of beauty, truth and goodness, mystery and magic, faith and romance, was making its last stand against the rising new order of ancient idols reborn into the glow of the modern world.

Instantly, Sid could tell the power the Keeper's wielded was greater that night. The fury of his faith drove back the darkness, swallowing it up in coiling, golden flames. The Fae stepped back, quickly pressed against the window. On the other side of the room the swordsmen fought the servants of the shadow, quickly gaining an advantage as the glow of hopeful energy filled the room.

Rip touched Marion's shoulder. Sid waited for the expected burst of power. The glow would end up swallowing the room in bright light, making the struggle brief tonight.

What happened next would be replayed in Sid's mind over and over in the ensuing years. He didn't need for it to be played out again before him. He remembered every gesture, every expression, every interplay of light and dark.

Rip touched Marion's shoulder. But instead of the light increasing, it dimmed. The glow of white fire faltered. Golden flames that swirled in dominant power turned pale and grey.

Sid turned to Marion, confusion riddling his mind. It was wrong. What he was seeing was all wrong. Rip's healing power should have multiplied Marion's power. Instead, it seemed to be draining it.

"Rip," Marion called out as he tried to turn around. Suddenly weak, he fell to his knees.

Rip looked down at his hand as a wicked smile crossed his face. His eyes widened in awe, impressed by the new power he had just displayed.

"I never knew it could do that," he said as he continued to stare at his hand. "Did you, Sid? My healing power doesn't just give life. It can take it away. I can drain it."

"Rip! What have you done!?" Sonny cried out, realizing just before Sid what had happened.

"I have real power, don't you see?!" Rip responded in joyful triumph. "I don't have to hide behind anybody, playing support to the real warriors. I am my own man now."

"What are you talking about?!" Sid screamed at him. "What did you do to Marion?!"

Rip looked down at the Keeper who had collapsed at his feet. Marion had gone pale and trembled with a sudden cold. His face began to waste away, sinking into the hollows of his cheeks.

"Don't you see?!" Rip answered, showing not the least compassion for the dying man. "I am a god!"

"That's right!" Sautorus answered, having to yell over the howl of wind and flame. "You are a god! And today you have taken your place among divine creatures! Human no more, you will rule beside us in the new world!"

Just as Sid was comprehending the depth of Rip's betrayal, a rush of dark clouds billowed from the Fae. He watched in horror as it consumed Sonny. His faltering light could not stand against the rush of living shadow. His screams died away, muffled in the cloud that suffocated him.

"Don't take it personally!" Sautorus laughed as the clouds gathered to strike at Sid. "This is just progress!"

A pillar of darkness shot towards the Keeper. Sid summoned every bit of strength and faith into the protecting white fire. Even as he wove it around himself, he knew it wouldn't be enough.

Just as the pillar struck the edge of his light, another figure dove in. Damion stood between Sid and the dark cloud. Every bit of its malice and despair struck him, protecting the Keeper from its fury.

"Nooo!" Sid cried out, watching the darkness consume the swordsmen.

Damion opened his mouth to scream but no sound came out. He writhed in agony, his mouth opening and closing in silent terror. Collapsing to the ground as the shadows crawled over the convulsing figure, invading though his mouth, his eyes and ears.

Sid stared at the dying figure in shock and fury. Marion was dead. Sonny was dead. Deion lay dying at his feet. Across the room the other two swordsmen lie in puddles of their own blood, the shadow men wiping their blades clean.

His mind raced to comprehend it all. How could this have happened? And so fast? Rip had betrayed them and lead them to their deaths. And his was soon to follow.

The shadowy clouds pulled away from the now still figure of Deion, a swordsman of true valor and courage. But his sacrifice would be for naught. The darkness gathered to strike at Sid again, who stood only with a fading nimbus of white fire around him.

The Spirit came upon the Keeper. Unexpected and sudden. It blew in on an unfelt and unheard wind, into the mind of Sid as he waited for his death.

Fire, the Spirit said.

Sid cried out and opened himself up to the power. He reached out to the candles still burning around the hotel room. He seized every flame and pulled them together, weaving them into one, single, burning strand.

A great circle of fire, earthly and burning, formed and began to turn. It roared as it circled the room in licks of orange heat. Sid turned the great wheel of flame, sucking all the air from the room as heat burst from it.

The clouds of shadow disappeared under the sudden appearance of this new attack. Rip cried out, shielding himself with his arms and ran from the room. The Fae stepped away from the circling fire, their backs pressed further against the window.

425

Sid threw his arms out and pushed the spinning fire towards the shadow men. Only one was able to phase out in time. The others cried out on searing agony as they caught fire and fell to the ground.

Sid turned to face the Fae pinned against the window. Firelight reflected in his eyes with all the rage of the flames. The smile had fallen from Sautorus' face as he glared back. He shook his head and pointed at Sid.

"This doesn't change anything, Keeper!" he yelled over the roar of fire. "You're only delaying the inevitable! We're coming for you, Sid Bickley!"

Before Sid could lash out with the fire, Sautorus turned and kicked the window out. A rush of air filled the room and the three Fae stepped out into the night, riding away on the wind.

Sid collapsed in exhaustion and grief as the curtains caught fire. An alarm sounded and the sprinklers came on, dousing the room in water. The fire went out as Sid let it go, plunging the room into darkness.

Sid had fallen to his knees, the weight of his failure bearing down fully upon him. What have I done, he thought. Water streamed down his face, soaking the suit he wore. From the shattered window the sounds of the riot outside poured into the room. The smell of tear gas floated in with the noise.

That's what has become of our world, he thought to himself. The people in chaos. The authorities beating them into submission. What would become of the people now? Their lives had been taken from them, little by little, crisis by crisis, one small deception on top of the other.

And it's all my fault, Sid told himself. He stumbled to his feet, barely able to stand beneath the weight of his failure. He had been a Keeper in the century of their greatest folly. How long had they kept the people free from the tyranny of the Fae? Thousands of years. And it fell to his watch that they failed.

Sid stumbled from the hotel room. Out in the hallway the lights were still out. Dim emergency lights glowed from the floor, casting the hall in tall shadows.

A wave of exhaustion hit Sid and he fell against the far wall. He wanted to collapse against it, fall down and never get up again. Only a small voice inside him told him he had to keep moving.

Movement from the end of the hall shot a surge of energy in him. He struggled to push himself away from the wall and stumbled towards the hunched figure. The overhead lights flickered, illuminating the form at the end of the hall. Rip Starr glared at him, hate and malice filling his face.

"Looks like you're still God's favorite!" Rip yelled at Sid.

"What have done, Rip?" Sid yelled back, full of rage and confusion.

"Always the favorite," Rip continued to rant. "Don't you get tired of being so loved all the time?"

Sid felt a wave of dizziness hit him. He stumbled but pushed it away. Anger rose up, giving strength to his weary limbs.

"Why Rip?" he asked. Inside, he knew he didn't care about what Rip's reason might have been. He was a betrayer. That was all that mattered.

Rip answered with malicious and cruel laughter.

"You may be God's favorite but you're an idiot," he said. "We're losing. Can't you see that? Any fool can. You can sit up in your mansion smoking your expensive cigarettes and having your little dalliances. All the while you believe you're doing something great! But you're not!"

"Is that what this is about?" Sid asked. "Are you jealous of me?"

Rip sneered as his anger flared. He waved the suggestion away.

"It's not all about you, Sid," he spat. "This is about me. This is my time. The Fae have promised to give me what you never could."

"What could they give you that is worth your soul?" Sid countered. "You've given yourself to the darkness, Rip. Do you understand what you've done?"

"You Irish are always so dramatic," Rip answered derisively. "I'm just playing the game of life."

"You have betrayed God!" Sid yelled at him.

The door behind Rip opened and a beautiful woman with flowing blonde hair walked in and stood beside him. Standing a head taller than Rip she wore a tight, red dress that hugged her feminine curves. She reached out with manicured nails and stroked his head as she smiled down at him.

"Today, he is a god," she purred into his ear, but loud enough for Sid to hear.

Blue eyes turned towards him, mocking and vicious.

"Which is more than will ever be said of you."

Sid shook his head as he finally understood.

"So, that's what this is about. An Elioud whore seduced you and now you're going to sell your soul."

"Her name is Sierra," Rip said through gritted teeth.

The Elioud scowled at Sid, her striking features turning stormy. She leaned over and whispered something in Rip's ear.

"You're finished, Sid," Rip told him, shaking his head.

"The Keepers will continue," Sid promised. "And we will come after you."

"Who will come after me?" Rip laughed. "Jean and Asagne? As of last night, they were thrown into a North Vietnamese POW camp. It will be like they never existed. Paul and Julian? They'll be executed in Chile in a few days. Don't you see? We've been planning it this way for a long time now. There's no one left but you. But don't worry, you'll be joining them directly."

Sierra stepped back as Rip spread his arms wide. Dark clouds rose from the floor beneath him. Thick and black clouds, full of electricity that sparked beneath his command.

Sid summoned all the white fire he could muster. Anger and grief battled within him. He tried to put all of his rage into the fire, even as he knew that the white fire was never fueled by rage.

Trembling with the effort Sid steeled himself for the conflict. Before the white fire and cloud collided, he knew it wouldn't be enough. The pillar of black smoke pushed back the weakly shining golden flames that Sid produced. He shuddered as he felt a cold seep into his bones. The cloud wrapped around him, squeezing out the glow that protected him.

"How does it feel, Sid?" Rip taunted as the cloud grew darker.

Sid struggled to keep the fire around him. It paled again, growing dimmer. The noose made of roiling clouds coiled tighter and tighter.

The part of himself that watched it quaked in fear. This is me now, he thought to himself. The part of himself that stood on the wall, facing Sautorus, was surrounded and dying as Sid was dying those many years ago. Except then he had one more trick left.

Feeling the fire slip away Sid lashed out in a desperation. Forming one small but powerful coil of white fire he sent it out. Not towards Rip. This one flew straight at Sierra.

The Elioud saw the streak of white fire fly right towards her. She screamed and threw up a hand to ward it off. Rip turned at the cry and his clouds retreated.

The streak of white fire struck the Elioud in the arm. The scream of surprise turned to one of pain. She shrieked as her forearm caught fire, burning in golden flames.

"Sierra!" Rip cried, turning all of his attention to the woman beside him.

Sid turned and fled down the hallway. He could hear Rip behind him consoling the Elioud woman as he ran. He cursed both of them, then cursed himself for his weakness.

It is all lost, his heart broke and said. He ran out of the hotel and into the turmoil of the night. He ran into the riots, just one more body in the mass of confusion. Through the park he ran, trying to outrun the dread that had settled over him. Past the people, the noise and the chaos he ran on.

It was all lost.

All lost.

Lost.

Chapter 38 - To Slay a Giant

Zach held off the giant with heroic effort. He slipped and dodged the hammering blows from the massive fists. At every open chance he returned with shots of his own.

Across the courtyard Malachi couldn't tell if they had any effect. His breath came in gasping heaves as he lifted himself off the ground. Through darkness he could see Zach slip, then return a shot to the ribs. Duck and return a sweeping kick to the knees.

It was hard to tell through the haze, but the giant looked more annoyed than hurt. Most of his shots went wild. Every time he did contact, Zach shook it off.

One fast shot connected with the Swordsmen's face. Zach's head shot back and Malachi could tell he was dazed. But he shook it off and stepped back into the fight. Slipping another punch, he returned one to the giant's ribs.

The giant growled in frustration and grabbed for the Swordsmen. Zach rolled beneath the grasp. Popping up he hammered out a shot to the giant's kidneys, pushing all of his weight into it.

The giant grunted and shot out an elbow, catching Zach in the nose. He stumbled as his head rocked back. His foot slipped beneath him and he fell to one knee.

He's fading, Malachi thought. His gift enabled him to endure massive amounts of punishment without taking damage, but he was still human. If he can do it, I can, Malachi told himself.

Picking himself up again Malachi felt the world spin. The dark and howling fog seemed to penetrate his head, swirling and buffeting his brain. His legs gave out and he fell towards the ground again.

Strong hands took hold of his, pulling him to his feet again. Malachi looked up at the bloody face of Gary looking back at him. He gave him a shake, waking up his weary limbs.

"Big G," Malachi groaned with gratitude.

Gary's face was pale. Blood streaked down from his nose and over his mouth and chin. The nose itself was almost flattened against his face and had torn open at the break. Another gash opened under his eye and was still bleeding. Malachi wondered how the man could even be standing.

"Yeah, Big G's got you," Gary answered, pulling Malachi's arm over his shoulder. He began to walk him towards the far wall where Sid's light had faded even more.

"I don't think I can help anybody," Malachi said as he tried to hold himself up as best he could.

"We gotta try," Gary said. He breathed heavy as he helped Malachi walk. The strain on him was all he could take.

Through the dark and howling fog they could see Zach losing his fight with the giant. A heavy cross from the massive hand sent him stumbling backwards. He barely kept his feet, but the hulking creature could sense him weakening.

The giant charged forward, leaning his shoulder forward. Zach only had time to get his feet beneath him before leaping out of the way. He fell to the ground as the giant passed by.

With surprising dexterity, the giant stopped short and charged back at the prone figure. Zach scrambled to his feet as the towering mass closed in on him. He absorbed two hooking punches that slammed into his side. A third contacted the soft flesh of his stomach. Zach was lifted off his feet, his legs buckling as he slammed back to the earth again.

The giant reached out his massive left hand and grabbed the collar of Zach's shirt. He pulled at the smaller man, forcing him to his feet. The rock-like fist came hammering down at his face.

Zach knocked the first blow away as his feet scrambled for purchase of their own. The next made contact, buckling his legs again. Another smashing fist followed. Then another. Each one contacting flesh and bone, rocking the head back.

Malachi and Gary watched as Zach's legs gave way completely and his head rolled to the side. Still the giant punished him with crushing blows. Blood poured from his nose and cuts across his face. He would be dead in seconds.

"Help him, Gary!" Malachi cried out, unable to watch his friend perish if he could do anything at all to help.

Gary didn't hesitate, letting Malachi drop back to his knees. He charged in at the giant who continued pummeling at the limp figure in his fist.

With a cry of fury Gary leaned in, putting all of his strength, all his momentum, every ounce of power he still commanded into his fist. He lifted through with his legs and drove up. White knuckled rage slammed into the side of the giant's head.

The head of the behemoth rocked beneath the blow. The giant dropped Zach and stumbled away. He cried out, hurt for the first time that night.

Wasting no time Gary charged in again. The giant looked up to glare at him. A cut had opened underneath his eye, streaming out a black ochre of blood.

Gary smashed into the distorted face, knocking him back. Swinging hard with his left he hit again, following it with a right.

The giant fell back under the rain of blows. The black fog swirled and blasted around them as Gary drove the giant back. Blood spilled from his fist as the skin tore. He kept up the hammering blows.

"Leave . . . my . . . friends . . . alone!" Gary cried out, accentuating each word with another staggering punch.

The giant fell to one knee. His head dropped down. Gary knocked it up with an uppercut. He reared back, gathering in for a cross to the nose.

At the last second the giant threw up his hand, blocking the punch. He curled his fingers, swallowing up Gary's fist in his own massive hand.

Snarling the giant jerked his arm, pulling Gary in. His other hand shot out and closed around Gary's throat. Rising up he squeezed his mammoth hands, cutting off the flow of air. Gary struggled in vain as the giant lifted him off his feet.

"No," Malachi gasped as he watched their last hope fade.

Gary dangled from the arm of the giant. Helpless as a child he grabbed and pulled at hands that were as unyielding as stone. His face suffused in red as the cruel hands cut off the flow of air and blood.

Malachi stumbled to his feet. He swayed as the dark wind continued to howl and buffet him. It roared like the fury of a hurricane. The night around them had almost turned pitch black. On the wall Sid's light faded to a small glow surrounded by black clouds churning and roiling around him, a living darkness that sought to devour the lone power that resisted.

Gary clutched and pulled at the hands of the titan. His mouth gaped open, searching desperately for air. Feet scrambled for purchase that could find none.

The giant lifted Gary higher in the air, squeezing harder around his throat. Blood streamed from his face where Gary had wounded him, but neither the fight nor the wounds had seemed to weaken him in the slightest. The darkness had fed and fueled him, just as the light powered and encouraged Malachi and the others. And the darkness was winning.

Malachi felt the irresistible pull of despair as he struggled forward. It was all hopeless, the darkness told him. You have lost. All is lost. Gary will be dead soon. Then the giant will kill the others. Last, he will kill you. Just lay down and die. Accept your fate. You gave it a good try, but you have lost. Don't fight anymore. Rest. Rest. Rest. Just lay down and rest.

A cry escaped his lips as Malachi resisted that impulse. His body wanted nothing more than the lay down on the ground and let the dark wind consume him. His limbs weighed a thousand pounds. With each step he had to drag his leg forward and he pushed with all his might to just swing his arms. And with every step his heart cried out within him.

"I will believe," Malachi said, defying the darkness.

"I will believe!"

Gathering his strength he ran at the giant. Gary's face had gone from red to purple. He had but moments before he would lose consciousness altogether.

Nearing the giant Malachi pulled out his knife. He didn't have to kill the giant, he thought, just distract it long enough for Gary to get free. Lifting the weapon, he leaned in.

The giant turned and his free hand shot out. The back hand caught Malachi under his chin.

All of his momentum was stopped with the almost casual blow. Malachi felt his teeth rattle together as the knuckles rocked his jaw. His feet lifted off the ground as he was thrown back, soaring through the dark wind. He hit the ground with a thud, his entire body jarring as it made contact with the earth.

The hand around Gary's throat weakened as the giant delivered the blow. He gasped, breathing in a lungful of fresh air before the grip closed tight again. Beneath him his feet found ground for an instant before he was lifted up again. His fingers worked inside the vice around his neck, barely able to hold off their crushing power.

Malachi felt the world go dark as he hit the ground. His brain rattled inside his skull, sending a shock of pain through his head. Consciousness drifted from him as he struggled to hold on.

Why hold on, the darkness asked him. Just let go, Swordsmen. Let go.

Rolling to his side Malachi shook the darkness and dizziness from his head. I'll let go when there's nothing left within me, he answered the dark.

Determined, he tried push himself up. The weight of despair and the dark, roaring wind pushed him down again onto his back. The wound in his side screamed out in new pain as he felt blood trickle out of it again.

Gary had renewed the struggle but was losing again. The giant sneered as he squeezed the devouring hands, crushing and consuming. Gary's face had gone red again, his mouth open and searching for air.

Glancing up at the top of the wall he saw Sid was faring the same. He could barely make out the light around him now, almost totally obscured by the roar of dark clouds. How it managed to hang on was beyond Malachi, but it held on, defying the dark with its meager light.

Seeing the light, small but defiant, gave Malachi a new surge of strength. That's all it takes, he realized. Just one flicker of light. Just one glow, defiant, stubborn, that does nothing but shine, and it can resist the dark.

Malachi reached his hand out to push himself up. Something hard and cold touched his fingers. He turned and looked down at what his hand had found.

The sword.

Sid had him carry it into the battle as a symbol. Ripped from his back when the giant threw him the first time, it lay here forgotten. Malachi picked it up and regarded the ancient weapon. One last chance, he thought.

Pushing himself to his feet, Malachi knew the sword could do little against the giant. It was old and rusted, bitten from use. There were cracks in the blade and he wasn't even sure it had survived the fall. Likely as not it would shatter as soon as he struck with it.

Then again, Sid had told him the sword had slain dragons. Perhaps, there was something more left in it.

"Let's see if you can slay giants," he said, pulling the sword from the sheath.

A burst of golden, white light exploded from the blade.

Malachi stepped back, his hands trembling in awe. The sword was perfect and unbroken. The blade, gleaming silver was free of rust and cracks and all the chips that had been battered into it. It was a pure and flawless weapon.

And all along the blade danced the golden light of white fire. Amazed,

Malachi watched the fire dancing along the edge. It wreathed down the hilt and over his arm, surrounding him in its power and glow.

Strength surged back into Malachi as the white fire surrounded him. His pain receded, and the wound in his side faded to a dull ache. Power filled his bones as hope soared again in his heart.

"The light shines out in the darkness," he said in admiration, holding the sword aloft.

Striding masterfully across the courtyard Malachi carried the sword of bright, burning fire. Gary, struggling with his last gasp of consciousness saw the light coming towards him. It reflected glory in his eyes, and salvation in its aura. The dizziness and weakness disappeared. Gripping the fingers that clutched his throat he began to peel them away.

Malachi stepped near, drawing the sword back. The giant shot out with another backhand, aiming to knock the annoyance away.

As the massive arm came towards him Malachi swung the sword. The glowing blade sliced through the flesh without slowing down. The arm cleaved in two, just below the elbow. The severed piece flew end over and out into the howling wind.

The giant opened his mouth in a wordless scream. He dropped Gary to the ground who gasped in a grateful burst of air. He gaped at the stump of his arm. The flesh bubbled from the searing heat and blackened as the giant watched helplessly. He stumbled back, shock and pain mixing in his grotesque features.

"He said to leave our friends alone," Malachi said, stepping up to the giant.

Pulling back the sword he thrust up, aiming at the giant's chest. The sword penetrated flesh without resistance, slicing all the way up to the hilt. The blade burst out of the giant's back, still wreathed in golden, white fire.

Flames crawled all over the giant's body. Writhing and pulsing they snaked over his form, covering him in their living light. The hulking figure tried to step back; his eyes wide in panic as he watched the fire dance over him.

The flames relentlessly spilled over the towering figure, covering his body. The skin bubbled beneath the heat. It shriveled up and darkened, pulling tighter over the giant's frame. Hollows in the face sunk and opened up, exposing teeth and bone.

The giant finally found his voice. An unearthly scream tore from his throat as the fire continued to burn him away. The skin cooked and blackened on the living form.

Malachi pulled out the sword that still glowed with the power of white fire. The eyes of the giant glared at him in hate and disbelief. He reached out a trembling and charred hand, relying one last time on his massive strength. The hand dropped as the giant convulsed and fell over, his skin burning away into a hard and shriveled husk.

Chapter 39 - The Redemption of Sid Bickley

The sword trembled as Malachi watched the charred figure of the giant stiffen and go still. Power trembled up the blade and hilt, into his hands. He could feel the strength fueled by the white fire dancing over the steel, blazing in the dark and howling wind.

Gary groaned and tried to get up. His arm collapsed beneath him and he fell back to the ground. Red welts from the giant's fingers rose up over the flesh of his neck and his wounds began to bleed again.

Malachi looked at the blade in his hand, full of white fire and down at the struggling figure of his friend. He was sure the white fire didn't heal completely. The gunshot wound in his side was open and hurting and he could still feel the bruises and pains across the rest of his body. But all of these had faded to a dull ache, hurts he was only distantly aware of. His exhaustion had been replaced with a surge of energy, and all of his skills and reflexes were sharpened to a razor's edge of alertness.

Dipping the tip of the sword down he extended it towards Gary who was taking quick and painful breaths. Golden flames danced over the edge of the blade and wreathed towards the prone figure. The fire wrapped itself around him, covering him in the glow of its light.

Looking up in surprise, Gary watched as the fire moved over his body. Every place it touched the flames entered into him. Every corner of weary flesh was renewed with the strange powers of the fire.

Malachi could see the effect was immediate upon his friend. His eyes widened at the surge of strength that entered him. Pale flesh suffused with new color. A smile even crossed his face as Gary watched the fire move over him.

Still, the red welts on the neck didn't go away. The nose was still crushed, almost flat against his face. But the blood had stopped pouring and Malachi could tell Gary didn't feel the pain anymore.

"How did you do that?" Gary asked as he stood up beside him.

Malachi looked down at the sword in his hands and shrugged. The writhing flames looked alive, sentient. This was not some inert force, something he could command around at will. This was a living thing, something with will and desire. If he would use it, he would have to work with it, obey as much as use.

"Not sure I did anything," he answered.

Gary nodded and placed a hand on Malachi's shoulder. He understood, as well as any human mind could understand. In this new world they lived in, some things you just had to accept. And in accepting, you understood.

"Let's see if it can help Sid out," Gary said, gesturing to the beleaguered figure atop the wall.

Malachi lifted his eyes and felt a cry of despair bubble up inside him. The cloud that covered Sid was almost pitch black. It swirled around him and buffeted the lone figure who was only spared by the dim light from within.

Malachi raced across the courtyard. This time, with no giant to stop him and no weariness in his bones he ran unhindered to the wall. Taking the steps two at a time he bounded up until he reached the top.

On top of the wall the storm raged its most violent. Malachi had to brace himself as he was pushed back by the dark wind, almost hurled from the wall. Visibility fell away as the black, howling clouds buffeted and stung his eyes.

Holding the sword out in front of him Malachi stepped forward. The dark wind parted at the fire of blade. The pitch of the wind screamed out, almost in pain, cut in two by the sword.

All around him Malachi could feel the cold despair of the wind, the hopelessness, the fear and apathy. But in his hands, he carried the fire of hope. The two forces contended and warred with one another on the edge of the blade. The darkness tried to shroud the light, but the light overcame, carving a path in the gathering clouds of deception.

"Sid!" Malachi cried out when he reached the Keeper.

A dark glaze had fallen over Sid's eyes. Like a black cataract, the film obscured the light from within. The Keeper looked like a dead man on his feet, an animated corpse that moved and breathed but was no more alive than a stone.

A mocking laugh carried on the howl of the wind. Malachi turned but could barely see through the swirl of dark clouds. A shadowed figure loomed in the midst of the cloud; his arms outstretched in malicious glory. Violet streaks of lightning flashed, illuminating the cruel face.

"Sid!" Malachi turned back and yelled again, shaking the cold and stiff body.

Leaning in Malachi saw the black veins that had crept over the Keeper's forehead. The vines of darkness snaked into the corners of his eyes, pulsing with evil intent. They invaded Sid like some kind of contagion, a parasite, that held him in its grasp.

A swell of admiration rose in Malachi towards the Keeper. He couldn't begin to imagine what terrible, dark torture they were inflicting on Sid. He couldn't fathom how terrible the pressure would be in him now to submit to this power, to just give up and let go, releasing at last the great struggle. How Sid managed to hold on was beyond him. The darkness had all but consumed him, but he managed to hold on. Somehow, by some unbreakable power, he kept the dim light shining all alone.

A vision came alive in Malachi's mind without warning. As he looked at the Keeper, standing alone with his light barely glowing in the howl of the dark, he could see he had been doing just that for decades. All alone Sid had been standing, all of the other Keepers dead, the swordsmen gone. It was Sid alone. Against fear, despair, the encroaching darkness of the evil Fae, Sid continued to stand. He didn't advance or enjoy any victory, but he stood firm. All alone he stood, and refused to give up. And though he couldn't boast any great triumphs in those decades, Malachi could see that the stand alone was more tremendous and epic than a thousand battles won.

"You're not alone anymore!" Malachi yelled out. The light shined just a little bit brighter.

He tipped the sword towards the Keeper. White fire danced from the blade towards his forehead. As the fire touched, the black veins recoiled and drew away. Malachi even thought he could hear a scream of pain pierce the howl of the wind.

The dark cloud over Sid's eyes vanished with the retreat of the vines. He blinked and looked around him in surprise, as if waking from a dream. His eyes searched, confused, then fell on Malachi.

"Mr. Green, you made it," Sid looked up and said. A tear streamed down his face. "And you come bringing white fire."

Malachi looked down at the sword again, showing Sid better the flames along its blade.

"It seems you have a gift after all," Sid told him through a dry and cracked voice.

"Will it be enough?" he asked.

"Trust the gift and the giver," Sid answered. "Believe, and they will always be enough."

439

Nodding, Malachi turned and faced the source of the dark storm. Lightning flashed again in purple streaks. He could feel the electricity charge the cold wind around him.

Holding the sword out in front of him, Malachi advanced towards Sautorus. The blade cut through the dark. The impact shook his hand, sending a vibration up his arm that threatened to throw the sword out of his grip. Holding the hilt tightly with both hands he continued forward through the miasma of black clouds.

He moved slow at first. Stepping tentatively with one foot and dragging the other behind him. Inch by painful he inch he moved across the wall, closer to the Fae and the bloom of his power.

"A swordsmen approaches," he heard the dark and terrible voice of the Fae call out. "Like a brave soldier he advances to his death."

Malachi could make out the features of the Fae as he neared. The darkness of the cloud had shifted to a grey fog again, changed by the white fire he wielded. He could see the hatred staring out at him, the almost maniacal animosity that contorted the angry face.

"Do you know how many men Sid Bickley had led to their deaths?" he asked Malachi. "Do you know how many corpses lie at his feet? Do you? He is a mad man this Keeper. Bodies follow everywhere he goes."

Malachi inched forward, holding the sword tighter as it shook in his grip. His palms sweated with the effort and he could feel his fingers ache.

"And failure," the Fae continued with arms outstretched. "Sid is a failure. Did he not tell you that? His whole life is one broken experiment. And here you come to me, dare approach me, eager to be his latest defeat in a life littered with defeats."

Malachi moved forward. He squinted his eyes against the dark clouds. He could feel its hunger, its desire to consume him. He could almost hear it crying out to feed on his soul.

"You wish to die, swordsmen?" the Fae yelled. His face had gone crimson with the effort of his screaming.

"It will be more than death!" he continued. "I will do more than kill you! I will consume your soul! I will feed off of your essence until there is nothing left of you at all! There will be nothing to save! Do you hear me!? I will devour your soul!"

Sautorus' eyes were wide in the terrible madness of dark power. Violet streaks of lightning forked through the black clouds. He smiled as Malachi approached with the naked blade of the sword held in front of him.

Sautorus gestured to Malachi, sending torrents of the clouds towards him.

Malachi rocked back, hit full with the force of the hungry mist. He could feel the power of all the malice and hate bound up inside. A cold chill passed through him.

Sautorus screamed.

"I will crush every hope of your heart and I will dim every light in your soul!" he cried out with the howling wind. "I am fear and I am the darkness! Behold my despair and tremble!"

The cold tried to settle over Malachi and for a moment he felt the fire slipping from him. He gripped the hilt of the blade and pushed back with all of his faith, refusing to give in to the doubt that pulled at him.

Words formed in his mind. In an instant they were there, complete and familiar. He held fast to them and felt a deeper power well up inside.

"The Lord is my strength and my shield!" he screamed back at the dark Fae. "Whom shall I fear?!"

For the first time he sensed fear in Sautorus. His mouth pulled back in a rictus grin, visibly pained by the words.

"The Lord is the stronghold of my life!" Malachi yelled. He took a step forward and dropped the sword down at his side, ready to swing it around.

"Of whom!"

The sword whipped up in an arc, all of his strength behind it.

"Shall I!"

He brought it down with all the force he could muster, white fire sparking from its edges.

"Be afraid!"

Sautorus stepped back just as the blade came down. The fiery tip made contact, ripping down the Fae's chest. It trailed a searing path as it tore through immortal flesh unaccustomed to the touch of pain. Dark clouds billowed from the open wound.

The Fae's mouth opened in a soundless scream. His eyes wide and bulging, broadcast shock and horror. His mind struggled to grasp this strange turn of events. The impossible was happening.

Golden light surrounded Malachi as the darkness fled. Twisting bars of white fire erupted from Sid and twirled into a pillar of light. They passed through him and towards the crippled Fae.

Sautorus fell to his knees, his arms outstretched. Golden light reflected in eyes that watched in horror as the white fire approached.

A scream erupted from the Fae as the first flame touched his cheek. Skin erupted into bubbling fire as the light scorched him. Sautorus threw his arms up to his face and rolled away, disappearing over the edge of the wall.

Malachi hurried after him, ready to finish the threat for good. His blood pumped with the heat of the fight. Hands trembled to strike again. Even the sword was eager, its hunger hummed along the blade and into his fingers.

Raising the sword he peered over the edge. The night had grown suddenly quiet and still. Off to the horizon the edge of the sea began to lighten with the rise of the approaching dawn. A cool wind blew in from the north, spreading a balm of comfort over the land.

The ground below showed no signs of the Fae.

Chapter 40 - Rescue

"He is gone," Malachi heard Sid say from behind him.

He didn't turn at the sound. The surge of energy still coursed through him, sharpening his senses. His eyes darted all over the empty ground, not believing what they saw.

"Where is he?" Malachi asked, still aching for the fight. "He can't be far."

"He's just gone, Malachi," Sid insisted.

Malachi gestured with the sword in frustration.

"How can he just be gone?"

"But he is hurt," Sid continued, still not answering Malachi's question. "I don't think he will be bothering us anytime soon."

Malachi shook his head. He should feel elated at the win, he knew he should. But all he could feel was a sense of thwarted justice. This being, this creature, had caused an unknown amount of pain and suffering in the world. He required justice. He required a reckoning. And he had escaped.

"How can someone just disappear like that?" he asked, growing increasingly frustrated.

"Malachi" Sid told him softly as he approached. A comforting hand fell on his shoulder. "You have to let it go."

"I don't want to let it go," Malachi snapped as he tried to shrug the hand away. "I want to get this bastard. I want . . ."

He let the words trail off, not knowing where they wanted to take him. It felt all wrong. It wasn't supposed to end like this. All the work they had put into it and the bad guy escapes at the end.

"We won, Malachi," Sid told him. "And we're all alive. We can thank God for that."

"All alive," Malachi repeated.

Any sense of disappointment evaporated as those words sunk in. They were alive. All of them.

Turning he ran to the stairs and bounded down. In the courtyard below the other men were gathered around Gary. Some were bruised and covered in dried blood. They had cuts and gashes and they all looked to be in some pain. But everyone was standing up. They were all alive.

443

"Is everyone ok?" Malachi asked.

Vic laughed and had to stop and grab his ribs.

"No," he answered. "We're not ok. But I guess we fared better than those other guys. So, you know, there is that."

"What's with the sword?" Danny asked, pointing to the weapon in Malachi's hand.

Looking down he noticed the sword had gone dim again. The white fire was gone. The shine of power was gone. The energy that had pulsed through its surface had silenced. It had returned, once again, to an old medieval relic, chipped and eaten by rust.

Malachi looked at it and marveled. He didn't even know how to begin to tell them what had happened.

"We're Swordsmen," he answered with a shrug.

Malachi retrieved the scabbard and returned the sword to its place. Knotting the broken cord, he slung it over his shoulder again. He looked up at Tres who was staring at the wall.

"What if he's not there?" he asked, his voice barely a whisper.

"What are you talking about?" Malachi asked. "This is what we came here for."

"But what if we did all this and we were wrong? What if Sid was wrong? What if after all this he's still . . ."

His voice broke as he tried to finish that thought. Tears that had been building up for weeks now struggled through, glazing his eyes. He turned away, unsure and ashamed all at once.

"Let's go get your boy," Malachi said, mustering all the faith he could manage.

Together the men made their way to the stairs and the top of the wall. They paused only for a moment to admire the stillness of the new morning as the horizon continued to brighten. After the chaos of the battle, the quiet came as a welcome relief.

Movement stirred in the yard below. From out of the dormitory a woman stepped out, holding a child. She guided another by the hand. More stepped out the door behind, dozens of children, spilling out into the yard. A few grown women walked among them, shepherding them outside.

"Owen," Tres breathed. He sprinted down the stairs to the yard below.

"Owen!" he yelled as he raced across the yard.

The other Swordsmen jogged behind. Malachi felt his body shake with every step as the white fire began to wear off. But beneath his weariness a joy bloomed that gave him new strength. He felt it rise as more children poured out of the building. There were so many. More and more came out into the yard. Kids of all ages, all races, girls and boys streamed out of the dorm.

"Owen!" Tres yelled as he darted among the crowd of children, frantically searching for his son.

Any sense that they had failed completely evaporated as Malachi watched the children continue to arrive into the yard. They had saved so many. There must have been close to a hundred of them. What did it matter if one bad guy had gotten away? They had saved so many more.

"Owen," he heard Tres cry out, this time with joy.

Tresmond fell to his knees as he wrapped the child up in his arms. His body shook uncontrollably as sobs wracked him. All of the bottled-up grief came pouring out at once.

"Owen, my boy," he wept, embracing the boy close to him. "Owen. Owen. My boy. My boy."

Malachi's heart warmed as he watched the reunion of father and son. So much pain and grief, so much agony, and finally it was over. It was a greater joy, he decided, to see sadness defeated than to never see sadness at all. This was redemption. And it would be a beautiful thing indeed to see this same scene played out over and over again as the children were restored to their parents.

The smile from Malachi's face faded.

Something was wrong. He looked around at the crowd of children, horror descending upon him as he noticed.

None of the children were smiling.

It wasn't just the smiles that were missing. All emotion was gone from their faces. They stood in the rising sun, passive and unreacting. There was no laughing, no playing, none of the irrepressible energy that children are prone to. They all stood with expressionless faces, hands at their sides and eyes staring vacantly ahead.

Owen stood as passively as the other kids. His father hugged him and shook with tears, but the boy made no reaction. His arms hung limply at his sides and he looked ahead at nothing over his father's shoulder.

Tres leaned back to look at his son. He laughed through a burst of tears, taking joy just to look at him. Wiping away the tears his grew concerned.

445

"Owen?" he said his name again, this time a question hung in the air.

"Owen," he repeated with more concern.

He shook the boy gently and passed his hands in front of the boy's eyes. Owen made no reaction that he had seen or heard.

"Owen! Owen!" Tres continued to press. "Can you hear me? Owen!"

"My name is Agrippa," Owen answered in a flat voice.

Tres rocked back, struggling to his feet. He looked down at his son again, wondering if he had been wrong, that he may have had the wrong child. He shook his head and knelt by the boy again.

"No, your name is Owen," he insisted, grabbing the boy by the arms. "Do you hear me? You're Owen."

"My name is Agrippa," Owen repeated, but not as powerfully as before.

"No, it's Owen. Your name is Owen. You're my boy. My main man. Remember? My main man."

"My name is . . ." Owen trailed off as conflict began to show on his face, the first display of any real life.

"My name is . . . My name is . . ." The words faded as Owen's face went slack ad passive again.

"Owen, listen to me," Tres pressed. "Your name is Owen. And I am your father."

He picked his son up and whirled to find Sid. The Keeper was standing amid a sea of the lifeless children. His brow creased in worry as he looked over them.

"Sid, what's wrong with my boy?" Tres asked, shaking the inert figure in his hands. "What's wrong with him, Sid?"

"I don't know," Sid answered with concern. He felt the boy's forehead and looked into his eyes then shook his head.

"Sid, tell me what's wrong with my boy," Tres asked as he began to panic. "What the hell did they do to him?"

Tres let his boy down and looked around at the gathered children. With the sun rising upon their faces, they all looked as lost and distant as his own son.

"They did it to all of them," he said with his voice shaking. "What did they do to them?"

Malachi's concern turned to fear watching Sid. He could see confusion on his features as well as his own dose of worry. This was something he had not expected to see nor did it seem he was equipped to deal with.

"Do something," Tres insisted, getting in Sid's face. "Hit them with that white fire or something. You can't leave them like this."

Sid pressed Tres with the top of his cane, pushing the other man back.

"I don't know what has been done to them," he said. "Therefore, I don't know how to help them."

"Tell me you can do something," Tres said, backing away. Fresh tears began to stream down his face.

"You have to," he insisted. "You have to be able to do something. It can't end like this, Sid. It can't. Tell me you can do something."

"I'd like to know the same thing," Gary chimed in. "After all we went through. After all they went through." He gestured to the kids.

"This can't be it for them," Danny echoed.

Sid waved them off with an irritated flick of the hand. "This is beyond my power," he admitted. "But there are others who know more than me. I never was much of a healer. Especially when it came to healing the mind."

"Yeah, well maybe she knows something," Tres said, pointing to the young woman who held one of the children in her arms.

"What do they do to my boy?!" Tres asked, approaching the woman.

The woman, who couldn't have been much older than twenty-five shook her head and tried to step away. Tres reached out and grabbed her roughly and shook her towards his son.

"What did you do to him?" he demanded. "Are you listening to me? What did they do to my boy?!"

Malachi could see the woman was in sheer terror. Tears streamed down her face as she watched Tres loom over her and shake her. The wrath on his face was unmistakable. She held on tight to the girl in her arms. Her mouth opened and closed in a failed attempt to speak.

"Are you listening to me?!" Tres demanded. He pulled out his sidearm and put the muzzle to the woman's head.

"You better answer me!" he yelled. "Answer me! What did you do to my boy?!"

The other men jumped into action at the sight of the gun. Danny interposed himself between Tres and the girl. Gary grabbed his hand and pushed the gun up into the air.

"Tres, come on," Danny insisted. "She's trying to talk. You're scaring the Hell out of her."

447

"Tell me!" Tres yelled as Gary pushed him back. "What did you do to my boy?!"

The woman's lips trembled as she tried to speak. Pulling the child closer to her she finally managed to get some words out.

"I answer the internet," she said in a thick accent, something eastern European. "For nanny job. We all answer nanny job. Just nanny kids."

She gestured to three other girls who looked to be about the same age. Any attempt to engage them found out they spoke less English than the first girl.

"What happened to the children?" Sid asked her, his voice gentle but insistent.

The girl shrugged her shoulders and fell into another lapse of tears.

"They take them over wall," she said, indicating the far wall that separated the field they were in from the courtyard.

"We never allowed over there," she said. "We take care of kids. They tell us they are special needs."

"You never knew what they were doing to the kids over there?"

"Governess will know," she told them. "She take the kids over there and work with other men. Only governess will know."

The governess ended up being no help at all. They found her in her office on the third floor of the dormitory. The portly woman in a wool suit was splayed back, her mouth open and tongue hanging out. Ligature marks on her throat stood out red and angry against her pale skin.

"I guess they didn't want her talking," Vic observed wryly as they picked through the office.

"Nothing here," Gary remarked, holding up an empty file folder.

"Wonder why they didn't kill the other girls?" Danny asked as he looked over the trashed office.

"Because they don't know anything," Sid told them. "Come, there is nothing to find here. We have to get the children off the island."

Once outside again the conversation turned to how they would get the children to safety from there. Vic did a quick count and came up with ninety-four kids.

"That's more than came down with Sleeping Sickness," Danny pointed out.

"There may have been early cases that went unreported in the news," Sid theorized. "Or this may have been going on in other ways in other places. There's no way to know for sure."

448

"So how are we getting them on the boat?" Gary asked.

"What's the matter with using the beach?" Zach suggested.

"For one, there's probably another twenty guards between here and there," Vic pointed out. "And I assume some are headed this way now. Probably at the gate trying to figure out how to get in. I don't know about you, but I'm not ready for another fight just yet."

This was met with eager acclamation from all the other men. Malachi himself was beginning to feel a weariness that he knew would floor him once it took over. He was in no mood to fight anymore.

"I don't want to put these kids anywhere near the line of fire," Danny offered. "We've worked too hard to get this far. I don't want to risk losing any now."

"So, what do we do gentleman?" Sid asked. "How do we get these kids out of here safely?"

"Could you get the boat to pick us up on the north end?" Giovanni asked. "I think I can get us all out of here without having to fire a shot."

"Well, let's hear it," Vic prompted.

"Beneath the dormitory," he said. "There's a pump room, and then some stairs that lead to the water."

"Is there a place we can land the boat?" Gary asked.

Giovanni nodded. "There's a little spit of land sticking out. Big enough to hold us all, for sure."

"I remember," Danny said. "Looked like a sand bar from the satellite images."

"That's the one. And there are no guards that way as far as I have seen."

"Wow, that would have been nice to know *before* we planned our attack," Vic said as he threw his hands up. "To think we could have snuck in here without firing a shot."

Sid shook his head.

"It may seem that way, but things worked out like they were supposed to. Either way, we would have run into some difficulty."

"Maybe so," Vic agreed. "Let's get these kids down to the beach."

The nannies proved especially helpful with the children. The one who knew a little English, named Antanasia, spoke quickly to the others once Vic was able to explain what they were doing.

"*Sich anstellen!*" Antanasia yelled out.

The children moved at the sudden command. They formed a perfect

449

line, two by two. Owen pulled his hand from his father's and went to stand mechanically with the others. They waited silent and unmoving, ready for their next orders. The only child who didn't join the others was the little girl held in Antanasia's arms.

"That's at least a little weird," Vic said as he observed the line of children in perfect discipline.

"These are the words they teach us," Antanasia explained. "To control children."

"I've never seen kids controlled like this," Gary marveled in horror. "What the hell did they do to them?"

"We will figure that out later," Sid told them. "For now, we will use it to our advantage. Giovanni, lead the way."

Giovanni moved to the front of the line while Antanasia conveyed instructions to the other girls.

"Folgen!" Antanasia instructed, causing the kids to move as one, following Giovanni's lead.

As a line, they marched into the dormitory and down the stairs to the pump room. The line turned and filed into the little closet and to the stairs that descended to the beach.

By the time they had gotten to the shore the sun had risen fully over the horizon and bathed the world in light. Malachi's spirit soared as he watched the light reflect off the waves, glinting like a precious gem on the surface of the water. The whole world felt reborn. Whatever evil that had infested the night was gone. Perhaps not destroyed, but defeated. For now, that would have to be enough.

With this joy also came a deep exhaustion that was beginning to creep up his bones. He could tell his body would give out pretty soon. He needed rest in a bad way, probably worse than he realized.

As the group filed out to the spit of beach that stuck out over the ocean Malachi could see the yacht bobbing in the distance. The skiff was already on the way to pick them up. They filled the little boat as much as they could and began the process of loading the children up. It took three trips before Malachi himself was picked up, and by the time he reached the yacht it was everything he could do to keep his eyes open and his head from bobbing forward.

Inside the yacht, he crowded in with the others in the state room and collapsed on one of the couches. As soon as he landed, sleep fell over him.

When he was jostled awake Malachi felt even more tired than when he fell asleep. His body ached in a thousand places, and the wound in his side screamed out in pain with every step he took.

He followed their now large group and was only dimly aware that they had arrived at another island. A private one, he heard Sid tell them. He had arranged it for the safe return of the children.

Malachi stumbled down to the dock, wishing with every fiber of his being for a bed. Antanasia was talking to Giovanni as he made his way to the shore. She still held the little girl in her arms as she explained to him how they had arrived at the island. From what he could hear the girls were all Romanian, and had answered ads looking for nannies at an elite academy for gifted children. It was only after they arrived that they discovered the more sinister purpose of this supposed school. By then, they were trapped, and fear and intimidation were used heavy-handedly to ensure their compliance.

Something's not right, Malachi said to himself as he listened to her explain. He couldn't say what, but he knew something was wrong with Antanasia and her story. There was some connection his mind was trying to make, but his tired brain wouldn't allow it to.

Malachi let these thoughts drift away as he followed the others up the beach and towards a large, if very old mansion in the trees ahead. It was made of stucco, and painted in a blue that had faded and was peeling away. The building looked like it had been abandoned long ago, but the only thing Malachi could think of was that it probably had a lot of beds.

He paid no attention and had no concern where he was being lead as they stepped into the old mansion. Malachi moved his legs mechanically, barely able to keep his feet moving. The only sensation he became aware of was a soft bed that finally and gratefully enfolded him in its arms.

Chapter 41 - Explanations

Malachi fell in and out of sleep. Periods of dreamless slumber were punctuated by intense and disturbing dreams. He saw himself in the courtyard again, struggling to get to the other side while some nameless force kept hurling him back. Other times he dreamt he was in a thick, grey fog, wading through and trying to find something he couldn't name.

Dream and sleep were interrupted by a groggy wakefulness. In these moments he could feel the presence of others looming nearby. Voices spoke over him and of him. Sid was there once. Another time it was Danny. Still another time it was the Fae Doctor Canta.

"The wound is healing," he heard the Fae tell someone else in the room. "But wielding the white fire has taken its toll. Right now, the only thing he needs is rest."

The doctor chanted something over him and darkness fell once again. This time, there were no dreams. Malachi slumbered in a timeless journey through night and dark.

When the light did return Malachi found himself in a small and sparsely furnished room. He rolled over, hearing the squeal of old springs beneath him. Beside the bed was a rickety looking night stand with a pitcher of water and a glass sitting on it. Looking at the water he became aware of an intense and insistent thirst.

He downed the first glass without taking a breath. At the second he took in more of the room. It was small and filled with a musty smell. Chunks of plaster had fallen off the walls leaving holes in the faded, blue paint. He looked down at the stained and dirty mattress he had been sleeping on and couldn't help thinking that maybe they were squatting in an abandoned building.

With a third glass of water Malachi felt his strength return and decided to find the others. He had no idea where he was and let his feet take him through a warren of empty halls and abandoned rooms. Most of the place was painted in the same fading, blue paint, as ubiquitous as the smell of dust and mildew. Old furniture rotted in the feeble light cast through threadbare curtains. What looked like a ballroom was littered was littered with a collapsed ceiling. Birds perched in the rim of the broken dome.

It was several minutes before Malachi found another person. He made his way to a grand foyer that was fairly intact. The marble floor even looked to have been recently cleaned. He walked down a staircase from one side and saw a man in a dark suit cleaning the banister from the opposite stairs that joined his in the middle.

"Sir, excuse me," Malachi asked as he hurried across. "Can you tell me where I am?"

"Sir, you should not go in that wing," he told him in a thick, Portuguese accent. "It is not safe there."

"Yeah, I kind of noticed that," Malachi agreed. "But where am I exactly? Where can I find Sid and the others?"

"Master Sid is with the Swordsmen," the servant told him. "They are in the library."

Malachi followed the instructions through a much better part of the mansion to a faded, wooden door that stood partly open. Familiar voices spilled out and Malachi stepped in to find the Swordsmen gathered with Sid.

"Malachi!" Gary exclaimed, the first to see him.

The men all jumped up and surrounded him, covering him with well wishes and pats on the back. The only one who didn't approach was Tresmond. He sat apart from the others with his son beside him. Owen still held that distant and vacant look, but appeared to have just a little bit more awareness in his eyes.

"Welcome back to the world of the living," Victor said with a grin.

"Didn't think I could ever be that tired," Malachi remarked to the sympathetic laugh of the other men.

"Well, killing a giant can't be easy," Victor joked. "I guess that earned you a few extra days rest."

Malachi blushed under the praise, feeling immediately uncomfortable with it. He could see the men regarding him with awe in their eyes, as if he had done something epic. As he remembered it, he had done very little, certainly nothing to deserve this kind of regard. It was a deeper, stronger power that had worked in him. He was just the agent through which that power worked.

"So, what's next?" Malachi asked, eager to change the subject. "I guess we have to find a way to get all these kids back home."

An uneasy silence descended at that suggestion. The men exchanged uncomfortable and knowing looks with one another. It made Malachi wonder what they had determined since he slept.

"Malachi, we were just finishing our discussion about this when you came in," Sid began.

"Okay, and what did you decide?" Malachi asked.

"We're not returning the children to their parents. At least not yet."

A stunned Malachi looked at the faces of the other Swordsmen. Some looked away, confirming what Sid had just told him. Others just pursed their lips and nodded. Danny even turned and looked at the shelves of dusty books behind him.

"How can you even suggest this?" Malachi asked, still not believing. "These are kids. Why wouldn't we give them back to their parents?"

"It's a complicated situation," Sid argued. "And we did not come to it lightly."

"We've been arguing about it for three days," Gary echoed.

"There's nothing complicated about it," Malachi said in protest. "They're kids. They belong with their parents. How did you get to this point? Danny? You have kids. So do you Gary. Why would you agree to this?"

Danny turned to him and shrugged. "I don't like it, but it is for the best."

Malachi threw up his hands in disbelief. He crossed the room to where Tresmond sat with his son.

"What about you, Tres?" he asked. "You more than anyone else should see the insanity of this. These kids need to be taken back to their families."

"It's like he said," Tres answered, gesturing to Sid. "It's complicated."

"No, not complicated," Malachi protested. "It's very simple. It's why we did this. Why we went through all this trouble, even risked our lives, we . . . we killed other people. We did it to save these kids and bring them back to their families."

"They're still saved," Victor pointed out. "That hasn't changed."

"They're still kidnaped," Malachi charged. "And until they're back with their families, that's what they'll be; kidnaped children. All we've accomplished is changing their captors."

He could tell these words stung. Eyes that had been avoiding his turned back to him in protest.

"That's not fair," Gary insisted, the hurt evident in his voice. "We've been agonizing over this for three days while you've been sleeping, and it hasn't been easy."

"Oh, it's my fault because I've been asleep," Malachi shot back defensively. "I'm sorry I'm not as strong as the rest of you and took longer to recover."

"That's not what I meant."

"Yeah, well, what did you mean?"

"Malachi, walk with me," Sid offered as he stood up and crossed the room. He beckoned for Malachi to follow.

Reluctantly, he fell in behind the Keeper as they stepped into the hallway. Sid didn't offer any explanation, and Malachi was too busy fuming to ask questions. They walked in silence down to the foyer and out into the bright day.

The sounds of crashing waves met them as they stepped outside. A cool, ocean breeze mixed in with the sounds of the surf. Together, they had an immediate calming effect on Malachi. He could feel the tension unwind in him.

The pair continued out to the edge of the shore. Sid turned and began walking down the beach, water on one side of them and the thick tree line on the other. He didn't say anything for a while, just letting the silence stretch out. Malachi felt the anger in him give way to the insistent pounding of the surf and ocean breeze.

"It wasn't an easy decision to come to," Sid finally spoke up.

"That still doesn't change that it's the wrong decision," Malachi argued. "Those kids belong with their parents."

"I agree," Sid said. "And normally they would be returned without question. But this is hardly a normal situation we find ourselves in."

"I don't see how that matters."

"Let me try to explain."

Sid took a moment to compose his thoughts. In the silence Malachi noticed the Keeper leaned a little bit more on his cane than he had before. It punched into the sand as they walked, leaving dimples in the ground beside his footprints.

"As best as we can piece together," the Keeper began. "With what the nannies told us and what Danny could figure out looking at the programs, the Sleeping Sickness was a neurological disorder induced by whatever code they had put into that kid's show. We don't know exactly how it worked. But what it managed to do was wipe the brains of the affected children. I think Danny's term was a hard reset. Personality, memory, everything but language and motor skills wiped clean from their minds.

"I say 'wiped clean' but that isn't really what happened either." Sid corrected himself. "All those memories and personality are still in there somewhere; they've just been pushed away or pushed down somehow.

"It seems as if the Fae were trying to take away all that old information and insert new information, to reshape the children if you will. They managed to make these children forget who they were and were trying to make them someone different. They gave them new names. They were all old Roman names like Aurelius and Graccus and Agrippa, names like that. They were partly successful when we interrupted their operation, and have done significant damage to these children."

"Can't we just put that information back?" Malachi asked.

"I call it information, but it's really much more complicated than that," Sid explained. "A lot of that is Danny speaking in computer language. The human mind is not a computer, despite any similarities it may have. If Danny's analogy about the soul and brain is correct, and I believe it is, then what we are dealing with here is that the interface the children had with the outside world, their brains, have been wiped and reprogrammed. Their souls are still intact, but every way they interact with the world, and even what they remember, has been damaged. Their essence, and the heart of their true being and selves has been pushed down and even distorted by these interferences."

"How is that even possible?" Malachi asked. "I thought our spirits were, I don't know, a little tougher than that. Our souls aren't even supposed to be physical things. How can a physical thing damage it?"

"We're also creatures of flesh and blood," Sid reminded him. "All sorts of material things hurt our spirits. Words wound us, injury to our bodies can have an impact on our souls. Pictures can move us; images can make us yearn for or desire something. We may have immaterial souls, but they are intimately tied into these bodies that we walk around in. They influence each other all the time.

"But the mechanics of all this isn't important. What matters is that these are not the same children taken from their parents. They have been changed in a fundamental way. And there is nothing our current medical system can do to treat them. If we gave these children back to their parents as they are then they would likely be this way for the rest of their lives - vacant, without any affect, and answering only to some Roman name."

"You don't know that," Malachi tried to argue, but he was beginning to lose his conviction. It was, as they said, more complicated than he had previously thought.

"Maybe being with their families will bring that other part of them back out," Malachi suggested. "Maybe that's all they need is the love of their families."

"Would that were true," Sid sighed. "But love does not cure all wounds. And there is also another angle to consider. It may be that these families would not even want their children back."

Malachi jerked his head up at the suggestion. "How can you say that?" he asked. "There's isn't a parent out there who isn't dreaming of getting their kid back."

Sid spread out his hands and shrugged in a non-committed gesture.

"I'm not sure that is true. One would think. But consider that these families are beginning to move on now, to adjust to a new way of life. Then, we show up with their child whom they believed to be dead. I'm sure they would all be very happy at first, but then they quickly discover this is not the same child they buried. They are different. They are changed. They are even answering to a new name. A lot of families would accuse us of bringing back someone different, something they used to call a changeling. This isn't our son, they would say.

"Then there is all the extra care these children would require. And we don't even know what treatment they need. Will there be a mother or father out there who won't wonder that maybe it would have been better if the child remained gone?

"And none of this even answers the bigger issue: what kind of upheaval would this cause in the world if ninety children who were declared dead and buried, even had funerals, showed up alive again? Can you imagine how the world would react? The questions people would ask? The stories that would get circulated?"

"All the more reason to do it," Malachi insisted. "Don't you think it's high time we expose these people, this conspiracy, that's been going on for so long? People need to know what's going on right under their noses. They need to know who's been pulling the strings in this world. They need the truth. And we have the proof right here."

Sid stopped at a boulder sticking out from the forest's edge. He sat down and looked out over the ocean, his cane propping up his hands in front of him. He motioned for Malachi to sit next to him.

"Malachi, for thousands of years now the Keepers and their knights have protected mankind from the Fae," he said as Malachi sat down. "The Fae have tried to feed off of mankind in various ways, and we have been there to stop them. They would set themselves up as gods, or haunt some forest, or steal children, things like that. We would find out about it and put an end to it and they would set up somewhere else. Sometimes, we were better at it, and sometimes they were. People knew to fear certain places and be on the look out for these creatures. They gave them different names and spun tales about succubi and elves and even creatures like Baba Yaga and werewolves. People were afraid of the dark, and for good reason, and we were there to protect them the best we could. And we thought this is the way things would go until God ordained the next stage of history.

"But a few hundred years ago the Fae started to change. They began to act different. They became more secretive, more prone to working in the shadows. At first, it was wonderful for mankind. He encountered these creatures less and less and no longer feared the dark or the old forests, or the strange places their own dreams would takes them. Civilization flourished like it never had before. And we thought that perhaps the power of the Fae had been broken. Maybe we had won. Superstition died and technology and science flourished. All the shadows and ghosts had gone from the world and it was replaced by the light of knowledge. Or so we thought.

"What had really happened is that the Fae had changed their strategy. They began a plot that we have yet to fully grasp. Whereas before, they usually operated independently, or perhaps a few together at a time. Now, we noticed that they were mostly united. And while they always had human allies, they now began to recruit on a level never before seen. This is when they began to call themselves The Family. And though they seemed less active at first, they were only working deeper in the shadows. Their reach stretched out to touch everything. They began to control governments, corporations, universities, even churches. In the process, they became more powerful than they have ever been. With the exception of when the old gods walked the earth, these spirits are now more in charge of the world than ever before. And whatever this plan of theirs is, an important part is their secrecy."

"All the more reason to expose them," Malachi asserted. "If they want to remain secret, if their power is secrecy, then we expose them. Show people what's really going. Wouldn't that be the best way to protect them? To stop the plans of The Family?"

"That's what we thought at first," Sid agreed. "And we did try to expose them, or at least we started to. Those first efforts were met with ridicule."

"But we've got proof now," Malachi insisted. "We've got ninety kids back from the dead."

"But it was then that we realized something else," Sid told him. "We realized the danger in exposing them."

Sid paused and looked out over the waves. Malachi poked at an old conch shell with his feet. The sun had bleached it white as the sand and the tide had etched rivulets and holes over its surface, creating a natural work of art.

"We realized, or rather we discovered, how powerful The Family actually was. We discovered that they ruled this world in all but name. That if they so desired, they could rule in name also. Or nearly so. For some reason they didn't take that step, they preferred and still prefer to rule from the shadows. Right now, that is part of their plan, but that is also their only weakness."

"I don't get it," Malachi said, shaking his head. "If secrecy is their strength, how can it also be their weakness?"

"It all depends on what they're trying to do," Sid pointed out. "What we believe is that one day they will expose themselves, reveal themselves to the world as gods once again. So, the worship they steal from men in secret can one day be taken in the open and given to them willingly; that is what I believe they are ultimately after. And when that happens, they will be more powerful than ever. It will be the dawn of a new world order. They will truly be the masters of the earth and over all who inhabit it."

Malachi felt the words sink into him with dread. He could almost see it in his mind, this new world that Sid spoke of. The Fae would be the masters, cruel and darkly despotic. Mankind would be reduced to mere cattle, raised only as food for the self-proclaimed gods, or to entertain their dark lusts.

"Won't there be anyone to stand against them?" Malachi asked. "Will people just roll over and submit to them without a fight?"

"Oh yes, there will be some, maybe many," Sid answered with a shrug. "But how many and how well we can resist is the question. How successful will our fight be? Will we be able to secure whole areas and enclaves that stand against the Fae, or will we be reduced to resistance in the shadows, a secret organization fighting a secret war? I don't know if I can answer that question. Mankind has become so weak now, his spirit so small and dependent. He has been reduced to some fat and effeminate suburban creature, glutted on pornography and cheap entertainment. He wheezes to decrepitude. Everyday becomes more and more . . ."

He broke off his rant with a shake of his head.

"I'm sorry," he said. "I tend to get carried away with my cynicism and I don't think it's good for me.

"The point is that the Fae want to see a weakened and dependent mankind, one that is unable, or even unwilling, to defend itself. What they want, and what they are dangerously close to getting, is a mankind that will welcome their new gods with open arms. They will count themselves blessed to be part of such a brave new world. It will be, perhaps, the only revolution where a people welcome their own overthrow."

As he spoke Malachi thought he could see Sid age before his eyes. With every word the silent burden he had carried weighed heavier and heavier upon him. He looked fragile in that moment, propped up only by the cane, and Malachi had to wonder how the years of carrying that burden alone must have worn him down. And he couldn't help but admire the strength it took to persevere.

"Is there anything we can do to stop that from happening?" Malachi asked.

Sid turned to him and smiled.

"What we have done here already," he answered. "We keep resisting, keep foiling their plots, one at a time. Slow them down. Work so that men can be free and their spirits strong again. As long as the Fae keep to the shadows we can work and prepare for the day when they step out into the sun again.

"And that is why we prefer not to expose them. For now, they work in secret, and that need for secrecy ties their hands, binds them in a way that we cannot. It's a hidden war, and that works in our favor too. That secrecy protects that oblivious world you and I discussed back at the hospital. If this were to spill out in the open, I fear what the result would be. Until that happens, we have a chance to resist, to prepare. And who knows, with the help of God, we may be able to prevent that day from ever happening at all."

Despite his misgivings Malachi could see the sense in everything that Sid was saying. It wasn't going to be the storybook ending he had hoped for. There would be no joyful reunions of mother and child. Instead, it would have to be . . . He didn't know what it would be.

"So, what do we do with the kids then?" Malachi asked. "Don't tell me they're all going to live with you at the mansion?"

Sid chuckled at the suggestion and shook his head.

"No, not the mansion," he said. "They will be taken to a place where I hope they can heal. To Annwyn, to some of the sacred places there. Doctor Canta and some of the other Good Folk will watch over their healing. If anyone can heal them it is him. If anyplace can heal them it is there."

"Will they be safe there?" Malachi asked. "You made it sound like a dangerous place."

"It is," Sid agreed. "But there are also consecrated places there, places where the evil Fae dare not tread. They will be safer there than anywhere in our realm."

Malachi nodded but was still far from satisfied. It felt all wrong to him. That mothers would be grieving while their children lived, and children raised without their parents in some strange land between heaven and earth; it didn't feel like the right conclusion to their story.

"We will look into reuniting the children with their parents," Sid assured him as if reading his mind. "If the children make progress we will approach their parents at the right time, and in the right way. We will have to be careful, can't just come outright and tell them their children still live. We will try to gauge their ability to cope with this strange turn of events."

"What about exposing the secret?" Malachi asked. "Won't somebody notice if even one dead child returns alive to their parents?"

"There will have to be conditions for the child's return. The parents will have to move away, assume another identity in a new place. We can give them a new life and a way to start over."

Malachi prodded at the ground with his feet, making dimples in the soft, white sand. His conflicted feelings wouldn't leave him alone, no matter how much Sid assured him. Everything he said made perfect sense and he couldn't argue with the Keeper's logic.

At the same time, he hated it. Every fiber of his being loathed the very suggestion. He even hated himself for being swayed by the idea.

"It's like we did all this and still haven't won," he said aloud, letting his frustration be voiced.

Sid reached out and put a comforting arm around him. It was a fatherly gesture, full of empathy and understanding. Only Malachi didn't want to be comforted. He wanted to be sullen and angry.

"We have won," Sid told him. "You may not realize how great this victory is. It may seem small, or incomplete, but it is a big win for us. It's huge.

"There were eight of us, just eight. Look what we accomplished. We stood up to the most powerful organization in the whole earth, a literal global empire. They have millions of people on their side, not to mention supernatural powers that have been operating since the dawn of time. They have some form of control over every major government and institution in the world. They command trillions of dollars. There is no resource that exists that they cannot bring to bear upon their enterprises. All of that, and there was only eight of us. Just eight, Malachi, and we strolled into one of their strongholds and plucked out something they dearly desired and took it with us. And they couldn't stop us.

"No, Malachi, you are wrong. It was not a loss, not by a longshot. It was a great victory we won on that island. Believe me, it was a long time coming."

"I guess so," Malachi conceded

It wasn't going to turn out like he wanted to. It wasn't going to end like he thought it should. But it was a good ending. And that would have to be enough.

"I guess that will have to do," Sid echoed. "Come, Malachi, let's return to the others."

"One other thing," Malachi said as he stood up and the two made their way down the beach. "I notice you have been calling us by our first names now. No more, 'Mr. This' and 'Mr. That.' What's changed?"

Sid smiled and pointed at Malachi with the top of his cane.

"You have changed," he said. "I called you by your formal names because a squire doesn't become a knight until he completes his first quest. All of you, though fully raised to your powers, were just squires. More like servants at that point.

"But now you have completed your first quest. You have proved your valor and your faithfulness. You are servants no longer. You are knights. You are friends. And as friends we use first names, yes?"

Malachi put his arm around Sid's shoulder as they made their way down the surf. It was an uncertain world he had been thrown into, and the future held even graver uncertainty ahead. But he realized there is no future so uncertain or danger so grave that it can't be confronted with a little bit of faith and good friends by your side.

"Yes," Malachi agreed. "That's what friends do."

Epilogue - In a Dark Cave

The cave was dark and musty. Water trickled down the side, the sound echoing through the rough cavern. A torch sputtered on the wall, casting a weak, orange light that flickered in the cold breeze.

Sautorus lay on a rough, stone table in the middle of the cave. It looked more like an altar, hewn from the same rock as the walls around it, rising from the ground in one solid piece.

Three figures with vaguely female forms worked over the Fae as he writhed on the table. They wore long dresses of sheer, grey material that covered them completely. Even their heads and faces were wrapped in the light cloth, obscuring mouth, nose and eyes. Only their pale hands were free of any dressing. Long, insect-like fingers moved across the naked body of Sautorus who grimaced and twitched in the throes of pain.

Sautorus groaned as he felt the wounds still burn. He could feel the white fire tear away at his flesh, eat at him like acid. He tried for the hundredth time to wipe the sensation away from his face. For the hundredth time it only made it worse. The women shushed him and pushed his hands away as they applied balms to his body and chanted arcane words of healing magic.

Ignoring the women Sautorus touched his face again, feeling the burned flesh that covered the entire left side of his head. Another wound, long and thin, ran down his chest and torso. Both of them were wounds of white fire. And as talented as the Medelina were, he knew they would never heal completely. He would carry these scars for eternity.

Groaning in pain and impotent rage Sautorus could see it play out all over again in his mind. He saw the arrogant face of that swordsman, wielding the blade that shined in that hideous light. He saw the look of triumph on Sid Bickley's face as he poured the awful fire over him. In a flash of golden flame, it was all over.

Oh, he was so close, the Fae thought as he shuddered. Sid was all but defeated, finally gone once and for all. The Keepers were a hair away from being obliterated. And once gone, there would be nothing else in the world to stop The Family.

But then that damned fire. Always the fire. Sautorus cursed the white fire and all who wielded it. He even cursed the God from whom the fire came.

If it wasn't for the fire they would have conquered long ago. This, Sautorus knew for sure. Years ago, they would have won. It wouldn't have even been a battle. These sons of men were so weak, so pitiful. The whole race was hardly better than insects.

Except for the fire. Why did they have to be given the white fire? It wasn't fair. It wasn't right. It was the very reason why his race raged and fought against the will of heaven. He had given this fire to them, these ugly, misshapen, stupid creatures of dust. They were animals. But the Father had given them white fire.

Seething as the handmaidens of Isis tried to ease his wounds, Sautorus vowed revenge on heaven for the hundredth time in his long and immortal life. If he could not have the fire then he would devour it in those who did. If he could not be a part of that divine plan then he would see it ruined. That terrible vision, that prophecy of old; he would see that it never came to pass. Not as long as Sautorus and The Family lived and breathed.

The light from the torch flickered again, only this time it wasn't the breeze that made it move. Distracted from his vows of vengeance, Sautorus lifted his head to see what caused the stir. A woman ducked through the low doorway carrying a child in her arms.

The nanny, the one whom the Swordsmen knew as Antanasia, stepped into the cavern. She held onto the little girl who nestled in her arms, showing only the back of her head. A look of contempt was leveled at the Fae as the women continued to work on him.

"You know the scars will not go away," the woman said in a thick, Eastern European accent. "You will wear them as a sign of your failure."

Sautorus growled at the woman and waved her away.

"If you've come to taunt me then at least have the guts to look at me with your own face," he said.

The woman shrugged and the little girl slid down from her grasp. As soon as their touch was broken the features of the nanny went slack. Her mouth dropped open and her eyes went vacant as the skin of her face sagged.

The little girl turned, clad in a little, black dress that flared out with ruffles beneath the skirt. Shiny, black shoes clicked on the rock floor as she came to stand beside Sautorus, barely tall enough to see he writhing figure on the stone table. She opened her mouth and spoke with the voice of an old woman.

"You let yourself get defeated by an old man," she croaked at the Fae.

"He had swordsmen too," Sautorus said defensively.

"My mistake," she added with spite. "You got defeated by an old man and a group of barely trained squires."

Sautorus cried out in pain as he turned on his side. His face was contorted in rage and shame.

"Next time I'll let you stand up against the white fire," he growled.

The little girl smiled, coy and mocking. She shook her head and wagged a finger at him.

"Our brother Danileoth is not happy with you," she said.

"To the pit with our brother," Sautorus answered, rolling onto his back again.

"The Professor is not happy either," she followed up.

At that name Sautorus went still. He felt a wariness seep into him that he didn't like at all. One did not want to fall into the bad graces of the Professor.

"We discovered all we needed to," Sautorus said, hoping the Professor would see it the same way.

"Indeed," the little girl agreed. "Our experiment was a success. That is your one saving grace. The Professor is not pleased that his plan for the children has been thwarted, but he is quite happy with the results of our trials. He may find a use for you yet."

"What about the second site?" Sautorus asked, for a moment forgetting his pain.

"The second site is up and running," the little girl told him. She turned and walked back to the older woman who waited silent and inert.

"We have corrected the mistakes and scaled back the intensity," she continued. "And with adults the effect will be much more subtle. They will be able to go about their day, and no one, not even the person themselves, will be able to notice a difference."

Reaching out, the little girl took the older woman's hand. As soon as their fingers made contact the nanny came alive again. The light entered her eyes and her features reanimated.

"This is just minor problem," the nanny said in her thick accent. "Your failure will not hurt us."

The pair turned and walked towards the carved doorway. Sautorus forced himself up on his side, leaning on his elbow.

"And the swordsmen?" he asked. "What about Sid and his new

Swordsmen?"

Both girl and woman stopped. They turned and regarded Sautorus. A wicked smile played across the little girl's face.

"The Professor has plans for them," the nanny said. "Soon there will be no more Swordsmen—ever again."

www.ingramcontent.com/pod-product-compliance
Lightning Source LLC
Chambersburg PA
CBHW011737010726
47496CB00010B/2969